The vacuum shimmered, and the Osori homeworld came into view, approximately seventy thousand kilometers from the trio of spacecraft. Saavik checked her own readings to confirm that the *Enterprise*'s current location was safely outside the planet's gravity well. She was grateful that the Osori's navigational directions had been precise enough to eliminate any chance of the ship (or either of the other two vessels) colliding with the cloaked planet by mischance.

"Well, I'll be a mugato's uncle," McCoy said. "That's quite the magic trick."

"Indeed," Spock concurred. "To cloak an entire world—and on a permanent basis—is an astounding feat. The energy demands beggar the imagination, at least by any technology presently known to us."

Not that the Osori homeworld was completely exposed. An opaque white energy field still surrounded the planet, making it impossible to visually discern any of its physical features, not even the color of its seas, landmasses, or atmosphere, let alone any cities or continents. Osor Prime presented as nothing but a smooth white globe. Even its rate of rotation was hidden.

"What are your sensors telling you, Spock?" Kirk squinted at the screen as though he could somehow penetrate the barrier if he stared hard enough. "You seeing anything we can't?"

"Negative, Captain. The energy shell is impervious to our sensors, and based on my readings, any sort of conventional weapons fire. Osor Prime may have decloaked, but it remains very much masked . . . and invulnerable."

Possibly just as well, Saavik thought, *with both Klingons and Romulans at their doorstep.*

Granted, the Osori currently had insufficient experience with the Federation to trust it as well, a situation this mission was intended to remedy, even if it meant Starfleet having to trust their own longtime adversaries for the duration.

And vice versa.

"We are being scanned by the planet," Spock reported.

"Even though we can't scan them?" Kirk asked.

"Affirmative. Apparently the energy shell only obstructs observation from without. Not unlike a one-way window."

STAR TREK™

THE ORIGINAL SERIES

LOST TO ETERNITY

Greg Cox

Based on *Star Trek*
created by Gene Roddenberry

GALLERY BOOKS

New York   London   Toronto   Sydney   New Delhi

G

Gallery Books
An Imprint of Simon & Schuster, LLC
1230 Avenue of the Americas
New York, NY 10020

This book is published by Gallery Books, a division of Simon & Schuster, LLC, under exclusive license from CBS Studios Inc.

First Gallery Books trade paperback edition July 2024

GALLERY BOOKS and colophon are registered trademarks of Simon & Schuster, LLC

Simon & Schuster: Celebrating 100 Years of Publishing in 2024

For information about special discounts for bulk purchases, please contact Simon & Schuster Special Sales at 1-866-506-1949 or business@simonandschuster.com.

The Simon & Schuster Speakers Bureau can bring authors to your live event. For more information or to book an event, contact the Simon & Schuster Speakers Bureau at 1-866-248-3049 or visit our website at www.simonspeakers.com.

Interior design by Kathryn A. Kenney-Peterson

Printed and bound by CPI Group (UK) Ltd, Croydon CR0 4YY

10 9 8 7 6 5 4 3 2 1

Library of Congress Cataloging-in-Publication Data is available.

ISBN 978-1-6680-5005-7
ISBN 978-1-6680-5006-4 (ebook)

Dedicated, with love,
to Karen

Historian's Note

This story takes place in 2268 (CE) in the third year of the *U.S.S. Enterprise* mission, after the starship's response to a distress call from a colony on Beta XII-A ("Day of the Dove").

And in 2292 after the collapse of the Klingon Empire and the Romulan Star Empire alliance, and just prior to the explosion of the Klingon moon, Praxis (*Star Trek VI: The Undiscovered Country*).

And in 2024.

All because of a missing woman.

Chapter One

2024

"Almost forty years ago, in May of 1986, Doctor Gillian Taylor, a prominent marine biologist specializing in the care and study of whales, stormed away from her dream job at the Maritime Cetacean Institute in Sausalito, California . . . and was never seen or heard from again. What became of Gillian Taylor? Did she meet with foul play or is she still alive somewhere? Where did she go? Who did she become, after seemingly vanishing off the face of the Earth? And can we all, working together, answer these questions at last?

"Welcome to Cetacean, *a new investigative podcast series. I'm your host, Melinda Silver, and for the next several weeks we'll be digging into a baffling missing-persons case that has been as cold as the ocean depths for decades. We'll be reviewing the evidence, conducting new interviews, and, with any luck, getting fresh tips from our listeners so that we can crowd-source this investigation . . . and finally discover whatever happened to Gillian Taylor."*

Melinda clicked off the audio file on her phone, which she had recorded back at her apartment in the Mission District. *Getting there,* she thought, although she still wasn't one hundred percent happy with the intro. Was the "cold as the ocean depths" bit evocative or trying too hard? She had a lot riding on this new series, following the phenomenal success of her previous podcast, so she wanted to get every detail just right; there was a lot of competition out there on the true-crime front. Maybe she should tweak the script some more, tighten it up a bit, perhaps have Dennis blend in some poignant whale song in the background? That could be a nice touch.

The Cetacean Institute was a multilevel complex stretching along the shore of San Francisco Bay. A salt breeze rustled Melinda's bobbed, bubble-gum-pink hair, and she brushed a few stray bangs away from her eyes. She sat at a patio table near the snack bar, in an outdoor plaza overlooking an enormous saltwater tank used for the rehabilitation of beached and injured whales. Currently unoccupied by any large aquatic mammals, it housed a colorful assortment of sea life for the benefit of visitors. The institute was closed on Mondays, so the snack bar was shuttered; she and Dennis pretty much had the plaza to themselves. Sunlight glinted off the wavelets rippling across the surface of the tank. Gulls squawked overhead. From what Melinda could tell, based on her research, things hadn't changed much since Gillian had worked at the institute way back in the eighties, decades before Melinda was even born. Had Gillian once sat here as well, enjoying the breeze, listening to the gulls?

She replayed the intro again, trying to hear it with fresh ears.

"What do you think?" she asked Dennis, who was setting up for today's interview, fiddling with the settings on their pricy portable recorder. "Too long? Too short? Not grabby enough?"

"Works for me," he said distractedly. Tall and lanky, with messy blond hair and a scruffy almost-beard, Dennis Berry was more intent on making sure they got a high-quality recording despite the outdoor setting. The pockets of his rumpled army-surplus jacket were stuffed with everything they might need, from batteries to cables, and plenty of stuff they wouldn't. "Anyway, the creative stuff is your department."

"True," she conceded. He was the techie and research guy; she was the storyteller who had to craft the messiness of a real-life investigation into a serialized narrative compelling enough to get listeners to hit the Subscribe button. "But I can always use a sounding board."

Their last podcast, *Cascade*, had concerned a 1990s newlywed bride who had disappeared mysteriously while honeymooning in Niagara Falls. (How retro was that?) In searching for a suitable topic for their next series, Melinda had been looking for something closer to home, that wouldn't involve too much traveling but still had a distinctive hook—like maybe an environmental angle concerning whales? She had vague memories of visiting the Cetacean Institute as a kid, on some long-ago summer vacation, so she'd been thrilled to discover that there was a genuine missing-persons mystery in its past. It had felt like fate.

"Don't mention sounds bouncing off things while I'm setting up. You'll jinx us." He looked up from the hardware, gazing past her. "Anyway, looks like our eyewitness is here."

She turned to see an old white guy in a business suit approaching them. A rush of anticipation quickened her pulse as she cleared her brain to go into interview mode. Smiling, she waved at Doctor Robert Briggs, former director of the institute.

And the last person to lay eyes on Gillian before she vanished.

"Ms. Silver?" Briggs was in his seventies now, with a receding hairline. An ID badge accessorized his neatly pressed suit and tie. "Sorry to keep you waiting. I'm afraid I'm not as spry as I used to be."

"No problem," she said, assuming her most ingratiating tone. A long-sleeved concert T-shirt and jeans made her feel underdressed compared to him. Her petite frame conveyed an unintimidating presence, which was often an asset in putting interviewees at ease. "We appreciate you taking the time to meet with us, Doctor Briggs."

"Please, call me Bob. No need to stand on ceremony. So nice to finally meet you in person; at my age, one doesn't often receive an invitation from such a lovely young woman."

Ick, she thought, but kept her eyes unrolled. "Bob it is, then."

He sat down across from her. "You have any trouble getting in?"

"Not at all. The guy at the gate understood that we were expected. Thanks again for arranging that in advance."

She could have conducted the interview remotely, of course, but in her experience nothing topped the immediacy of an actual face-to-face interview. And to do so at the very location where Gillian worked and was last seen? The goose bumps that gave Melinda were more than worth the extra effort required to meet him on-site.

"My pleasure. I may have retired several years ago, but I like to think I still have some pull around here."

"Obviously."

She'd already gotten a self-important vibe from Briggs in the calls and emails setting up this interview, but she could work with that. Older dudes who liked the sound of their own voice usually required little prompting to get talking. She could always edit out any hot air or excess mansplaining later.

"Oh, this is my coproducer, Dennis Berry," she said. "He'll be looking after the technical side of things so I can give your story my undivided attention."

Dennis, who was not exactly outgoing, mumbled a greeting as he clipped a wireless mic to Briggs's lapel and ran a few sound checks. Melinda's own mic, a quality dynamic model on a stand, was already set up on the table. Matching bottles of water were on hand as antidotes to dry mouth. Melinda took a deep gulp in preparation.

"Looks like we're all set. Shall we get down to it?"

"Might as well." Briggs braced himself. "You want to know about Gillian."

"That's why we're here." She eased in gently, conscious that this might be a painful subject. "Tell me about her."

"She was a remarkable person, extremely committed to our work here. Dedicated, motivated, knowledgeable, with a genuine passion for marine biology in general and whales in particular. She cared deeply about educating the public, as well as for looking after the whales in her care."

"George and Gracie. A pair of rescued humpback whales."

Briggs nodded. "You've done your homework, young lady."

Imagine that, she thought. According to her research, Gillian had gone missing the very same day that George and Gracie were released from the institute and returned to the sea. That peculiar coincidence, if it was a coincidence, was one of the things that had leaped out at Melinda when she'd first started looking into Gillian's disappearance as a possible subject for her next true-crime podcast. The ecological angle would add an extra subtext to the mystery, making it more than just another missing-persons case. Melinda liked the idea of working an environmental message into the series; no reason she couldn't do a little good while also chasing listeners and ad revenue.

"I gather she was quite attached to those particular whales?"

"Very. Perhaps too much so."

"How so?"

"As I mentioned, Gillian was nothing if not passionate when it came to *her* whales. If we're being honest, this could sometimes compromise her professional detachment. She could be quite opinionated, emotional even." He smiled ruefully. "Let's just say she was not afraid to speak her mind."

Good for her, Melinda thought. But had that come at a cost, maybe even played a factor in her eventual disappearance? Speaking up too loudly and too often could get a person branded as "difficult"—and perhaps even as a problem to be disposed of? *Or am I getting ahead of myself?*

"About the whales, they were released the same day Gillian vanished, correct?"

"That's right." A pained expression came over his face. "We lost them both on the same day."

"Tell me about it, the last time you saw Gillian."

He paused to take a sip of water, apparently needing a moment before going there. "You have to understand, this part is difficult to talk about."

"I can imagine. I just want to understand what happened, in your own words." She treaded lightly, not wanting him to have second thoughts about doing the interview. "I understand there was some . . . drama . . . surrounding the whales' departure?"

News coverage at the time, along with the initial police reports, which she had carefully reviewed in preparation, had alluded to a heated argument between Briggs and Gillian right before she stormed off, witnessed by a few coworkers and passersby.

"We did not part on the best of terms," he admitted. "She was already heartbroken about her beloved whales being released, putting them at risk from whalers, so I made the executive decision to quietly have the whales removed the night before they were officially scheduled to be released, after Gillian had already left for the day. I did this partly to avoid a media circus, but also because I honestly thought it would be easier on her if she wasn't there when they left. Or maybe I just wanted to spare myself an awkward emotional scene." He sighed, looking downcast. "In hindsight, that might not have been the right call."

You think? Melinda thought. "And Gillian's reaction, when she discovered the whales were gone?"

"She was furious at not being allowed to say goodbye to George and Gracie. She railed at me, even slapped me hard across the face." His hand went to his cheek, as though reliving the sting of that slap. "But I swear, when she stormed off in a huff, it never occurred to me for a moment that I'd never see her again. Even when she didn't show up for work the next day, I figured she just needed some time to get over it. At worst, I feared that she might tender her resignation." He shook his head sadly. "But then days went by, my calls went unanswered . . . and the police found her truck abandoned by the park."

Melinda nodded. She would be looking into that ominous discovery soon.

"What do you think happened to her?"

"No idea! Even if she was fed up with me, this place . . . why abandon her entire life and career? It baffled me then. Baffles me now."

It didn't make sense to Melinda either, which was what made the mystery so intriguing. "Did she have any enemies?"

"Not that I knew of," Briggs said. "Police asked me the same thing back in '86."

"No jealous ex? Obsessed stalker? Disgruntled coworker?"

"Honestly, I never got the impression she had much of a social life. She was all about her work . . . and her whales."

A crazy idea occurred to Melinda. "You don't think she took off looking for George and Gracie, do you?"

"Unlikely. They were airlifted to Alaska in a 747, then dropped off in the Bering Sea, a long way from here. And even if she somehow made her way there, what could she expect to do if she found them? These weren't homeless cats or dogs she could adopt. They were massive aquatic mammals weighing more than forty tons. She couldn't rescue them even if she had been able to track them down via the transmitters."

"Transmitters?" That hadn't been mentioned in the reports on Gillian's disappearance.

"Both whales were tagged with radio transmitters so we could track their movements. Or at least that was the plan. As it happened, we lost their signals within hours of them being returned to the sea."

"The same day you last saw Gillian?"

Briggs nodded. "An ironic coincidence."

Was it? Melinda wondered. "How come you lost the signals?"

"Who knows? Possibly the tracking devices failed. Or, sadly, George and Gracie could have quickly fallen victim to whalers. Or possibly killed by a random boat strike. Believe it or not, more whales are actually killed by boat strikes these days than by whaling, although that wasn't necessarily the case back in the eighties."

Melinda made a mental note to read up on the subject. That Gillian's whales had not just been released but had also dropped off the radar the same day she had was a tantalizing new revelation. *I can make hay with that, maybe.*

The rest of the interview offered little she didn't already know. Briggs sang Gillian's praises while expressing total confusion as to what happened to her. She couldn't help feeling sorry for him; he was obviously still troubled by what went down between him and Gillian decades ago.

"Well, thanks again for speaking with us," she said, wrapping things up. "Please let me know if you think of anything else that might be relevant to our investigation."

"Certainly. And I'd appreciate knowing if you come up with anything concerning Gillian's disappearance. I've spent almost four decades now wondering what happened to her, whether there was something I could have said or done differently that might have changed things. I could use some answers after all this time."

You and me both, Melinda thought.

Chapter Two

"One of the passengers insists on speaking with you, Skipper."

Captain Jerry Yamada was at the helm of the *S.S. Chinook*, a commercial transport three solar days out from Planet G, when his chief purser, Violet Achebe, visited the bridge to deliver a request from one of the forty or so travelers who had booked passage on the ship. The compact, utilitarian bridge was manned only by Yamada and his first mate. A viewscreen depicted a clear stretch of interstellar space.

"Their accommodations not to their liking? Or the meal service?" Yamada asked with a sigh, wondering what kind of deluxe treatment this particular passenger was demanding. "Can't you handle this?"

It wasn't that he couldn't spare a moment to step away from the helm. This was a routine five-day run ferrying an assortment of civilians of various species to Cibonor Prime, out near the border of Federation space. Nothing his copilot or even the autonav systems couldn't manage. *Chinook* had made this run countless times before, following a well-established route known to be free of any lurking singularities, plasma storms, or Orion pirates. Yamada simply wasn't in a hurry to be groused at by some dissatisfied customer who didn't find the modest transport up to their exalted standards. What had they expected, a *Constitution*-class starship?

"I tried, Skipper, but he insists on speaking with you directly. Claims it's a matter of vital importance that must be dealt with at once. His words, not mine."

"Understood." He knew that Achebe had surely done her best to placate the unhappy passenger; as head of the cabin crew, she had always excelled at customer relations. He rose reluctantly from his seat, girding himself for the onerous chore ahead. He straightened his custom white uniform with braided gold epaulets, slicked back his thinning brown hair, and put on his captain's hat. "So which of our current guests is giving you trouble?"

"Pierre Fortier, the traveling salesman."

The captain nodded. He prided himself on familiarizing himself with the passenger list on each run. Fortier was a nondescript humanoid of terrestrial descent traveling alone on business. As Yamada recalled, the man was a merchant or sales rep peddling a variety of exotic tonics and elixirs of questionable provenance; in short, a modern-day snake-oil salesman plying his trade on frontier colonies and settlements on the fringes of the Federation. Harmless enough, by all appearances, but apparently making a pain of himself at the moment.

"Very well. Let's see what's bothering him." He turned to his first mate. "Miguel, you have the helm."

"Aye, sir."

Yamada found Fortier waiting in the starview lounge, where the salesman was sharing a table with a few other passengers. Surveying the scene as a matter of course, the captain saw nothing amiss, just a cross section of ordinary people socializing with their fellow travelers: having cocktails, munching on snacks from the food dispensers, playing cards or chess or *kal-toh*, or maybe even chatting up an attractive stranger. Midvoyage, *Chinook* was still a few days away from Cibonor Prime, so folks were looking to pass the time as painlessly as possible. Picture viewports offered a panoramic view of distant stars and nebulae streaking past at warp speed. Caitian torch songs purred in the background. Artificial translators facilitated conversation. Everyone appeared in good spirits, except perhaps Fortier.

"You asked to see me, Mister Fortier?" Yamada addressed the man in a polite and professional manner; it was possible after all that Fortier had a legitimate grievance of some sort, although why it might require the captain's personal attention remained a mystery. His crew were perfectly capable of sorting out most difficulties on their own.

"Ah, Captain, thanks so much for joining us." Fortier didn't seem particularly cranky; if anything, he seemed inordinately pleased by Yamada's prompt arrival. He was a slight, unprepossessing fellow with limp black hair, somewhat protuberant blue eyes, a cheap suit, white gloves, and a rather oily demeanor. He smiled ingratiatingly at the captain and gestured at an empty seat across from him. "Please make yourself comfortable."

"I'm a busy man, Mister Fortier," Yamada said, not entirely accurately. He remained standing to avoid giving the impression that he was at any passenger's beck and call. "Perhaps you can tell me what this is all about? Unless you'd rather discuss this privately?"

"No, no, I prefer an audience." He nodded at the vacant chair, then shrugged as the captain declined the invitation once more. "No? Very well then. Tell me, Captain, what do you know of Horta acid?"

"Excuse me?"

The seeming non sequitur perplexed Yamada, who'd been anticipating some mundane complaint about the man's luggage, fees, cabin, or a perceived slight from an insufficiently attentive crew member.

"Horta acid," Fortier repeated. "The remarkably corrosive chemical secreted by the Hortas, which allows them to tunnel through solid rock as easily as we pass through empty air. You are familiar with the species?"

"To a degree." Yamada recognized the name as belonging to an exotic new sentient life-form that had recently been discovered on a remote mining planet; after some initial misunderstandings and conflict, the Hortas had formed a working relationship with the humans prospecting beneath the planet's surface for precious ores, to the benefit of both. "But I fail to see what relevance that might have to your stay on this ship."

"Patience, Captain. Believe me, you want to hear what I have to say."

Yamada frowned. "If this is a sales pitch—"

"Nothing of the sort," Fortier said, all innocence. "Anyway, Horta acid is quite fascinating, with a variety of potential applications, as I was just explaining to the esteemed professor here."

He indicated the woman on his left: a middle-aged woman, perhaps pushing fifty, whose bluish complexion and snow-white hair suggested that she was part Andorian, as did her two small, stubby antennae. She was neatly but sensibly attired. Searching his memory, Yamada placed her as Doctor Taya Hamparian, a scientist on her way to an academic conference on Cibonor Prime. He hadn't spent much time getting to know her, leaving that to Achebe and her crew, but he'd gathered that she was fairly celebrated in her field, whatever that was.

"From what I've heard," she said, "the Hortas are indeed a unique species, given that their body chemistry is based on silicon rather than iron. Their discovery caused quite a stir in xenobiology circles, I can tell you that. Federation science is just beginning to scratch the surface of what we might learn from them about the myriad forms life can take throughout the galaxy."

"I have no doubt," Yamada said, "but unless there's reason for me to be here, I'll leave you two to discuss this topic on your own. I have ship's business to attend to." He smiled courteously at Hamparian, who bore no responsibility for dragging him from the bridge. "If you'll forgive me, Doctor."

"But this *is* ship's business, Captain," Fortier insisted, "as I'll now demonstrate."

To Yamada's surprise, the other man peeled off the glove on his right hand to reveal a gleaming metal prosthetic of fairly sophisticated design, complete with a small, blinking control panel embedded in the underside of its wrist. The captain couldn't remember if the man's artificial hand was listed on his travel visas, not that this would have affected his passenger status in any way. Over the years, *Chinook* had transported any number of travelers with various special needs or conditions; this was hardly the first prosthetic limb or implant Yamada had encountered in his voyages.

"Alas," Fortier explained, "I lost the hand I was born with due to an unfortunate misunderstanding with an Orion gambler who accused me of cheating him, but its replacement is ever so versatile."

He twisted off the tip of a metallic index finger to reveal a small nozzle hidden beneath it. He pointed the finger at the tabletop, rather like a child playing at shooting a phaser pistol, and squirted a short stream of orangish fluid onto the table.

"Ye gods!" the captain exclaimed, alarmed given Fortier's talk of Horta acid; to his relief, however, the minuscule spurt of fluid merely puddled atop the spill-proof plastene tablecloth, forming a small pool about the size of a quarter. (The *Chinook* had once hosted a long-winded Venusian numismatist who had bent the captain's ear at length about archaic American currency.) "What the tox is that?"

"Horta acid, of course, but in its inactive form. A Horta does not always burn through everything it touches; it can control its corrosiveness at will. A natural catalyst, rather like a hormone, is required to activate the acid . . . like this."

Before anyone could stop him, he pressed a control on his wrist. A few drops of a different solution spurted from his finger, joining the puddle on the table, which immediately sizzled and steamed as the fluid burned through the table and rained down on the carpeted floor below. A harsh, acidic odor assailed Yamada's nostrils. Hamparian gasped out loud.

"Blast it, Fortier!" The captain hastily peeked beneath the table, where he saw, through a hole in the carpet, a badly scorched ceramic tile. "That's willful vandalism. The repair costs will be added to your fare, along with the appropriate fines for knowingly bringing hazardous materials aboard this ship. Any such cargo needed to be reported upon boarding!"

The destructive chemistry experiment, as well as Yamada's indignant tone, caught the attention of Fortier's other companions at the table, a somewhat tipsy couple who had been preoccupied with chatting each other up until then. They gaped in surprise at the aftermath of the demonstration, even as the acrid white fumes dissipated into the filtered atmosphere of the lounge, where the remainder of those present appeared largely oblivious to the increasing tension at the table. The lounge's piped-in music interfered with eavesdropping.

"Ah, but that's precisely the point I was trying to make, Captain. These two substances are not hazardous in themselves, only when combined. They are also quite new to modern science, which is doubtless why they evaded the fairly rudimentary security scanners all passengers and their possessions were subjected to before boarding." Fortier grinned slyly. "That and the fact that, being as the Horta are uniquely silicon based, their secretions won't even register as biological materials, contraband or otherwise, on any standard scans."

Yamada felt a sinking feeling, his earlier annoyance and indignation giving way to a genuine sense of foreboding. Fortier was practically bragging about smuggling a dangerous organic substance past *Chinook*'s security procedures. Why would he do that—unless this was the prelude to some darker purpose?

"But how in the cosmos did you even get your hands on a sample of Horta acid?" Hamparian asked. "I've only read about it in scientific journals."

"A trade secret, Professor." Fortier waved away her query. "What matters are its applications." He once again indicated the empty chair. "You really should sit down for this next part, Captain. I strongly advise it."

"Hey there, what's this all about?" the other man at the table asked, rather late to the party. He was a travel writer touring the sector, name of Nestrom; extravagantly lobed ears betrayed Tiburonian roots. "Is there a problem here?"

"What's a Horta?" his companion asked. Kybra Larrol was a youngish widow from Argelius II, apparently getting on with her life.

"Sit tight and all will be made clear, my friends." Fortier waited until the captain grudgingly sat down at the table, just to hasten things along. "Where were we? Oh yes, applications. Imagine, for example, if a bulb containing sufficient amounts of both chemicals, separated by only a thin barrier, was discreetly and inconspicuously placed in proximity to a baffle plate in this ship's energy pile, perhaps late at night during the graveyard shift when most crew and passengers are abed and only a skeleton crew is minding the store?"

A chill ran down Yamada's spine. "That's a disturbingly specific example."

"But very apropos." Fortier indicated the control panel blinking on his mechanical wrist. "Now imagine if that barrier is on a timer, programmed to self-destruct after a certain interval, unless the timer is reset remotely via a signal from my hand, causing the two chemicals to combine, thereby activating the acid . . . need I elaborate?"

Yamada stared at the hole in the table, which was still sizzling around its edges. If enough Horta acid dissolved one of the plates regulating the matter-antimatter reaction, the entire warp core could explode in an instant, taking *Chinook* with it, along with every living soul aboard, reduced to atoms by a white-hot blast.

"Heaven help us," Hamparian whispered, getting it as well. The previously distracted couple appeared equally alarmed. They peered anxiously at the captain, looking to him for reassurance. Nestrom gripped Larrol's hand.

"But . . . you would be destroyed as well," Yamada pointed out.

"Theoretically, yes, but I can't imagine you would risk your ship, your crew, and all the innocent travelers in your care just to test my resolve. And just so you know, Captain, that would *not* end well for any of us." Fortier paused to let that ominous advice sink in before continuing. "Let me spell it out before you waste any precious time trying to think your way out of this dilemma. The acid bulb is real, it is in place, and any attempt to tamper with it will trigger its activation. Nor would I advise attempting to shut down the warp engine." He indicated the stars streaking past the viewing windows. "I'm quite capable of triggering the bulb remotely at the first indication that you are trying to ingeniously circumvent my plans. Do you understand me, Captain?"

Loud and clear, Yamada thought. "This is a spacejacking."

Nestrom started to get up from the table. He tugged on his companion's arm. "C'mon, Kybra, we're getting out of here."

"Please stay where you are," Fortier said, his eyes and tone at odds with his affable smile. A flesh-and-blood finger hovered over the control pad at his wrist. "I insist."

Swallowing hard, Nestrom sat back down. He and Larrol grasped each other's hands as though clinging to a tether during a spacewalk. She drank deeply from a full glass of wine.

"Relax," Fortier assured them. "You have nothing to worry about. The good captain is not going to allow any harm to come to you. Are you, Captain?"

He has me there. Yamada was acutely aware of all the passengers in his charge; not just those present in the lounge, a few of whom were perhaps starting to pick up on some sort of issue at the table, sending curious and/or worried looks in his direction, but also the ones currently in their cabins or enjoying *Chinook*'s other recreational facilities. Their faces, names, and stories flooded his mind: the elderly couple on the way to meet their first grandchild, a high-school swim team traveling to compete in a sector tournament, a few other scientists and academics heading for the same conference Doctor Hamparian was attending, a quartet of Andorian newlyweds who had barely emerged from the ship's honeymoon suite, and so many other unsuspecting souls, all counting on him to convey them safely to their destinations.

"What are your demands?"

Fortier beamed at him. "I knew you would be reasonable about this." His organic hand reached inside his jacket and extracted a microtape, which he handed to Yamada. "This tape contains the coordinates for a specific location outside Federation space. I'm afraid you need to make a slight detour from our planned course." He shrugged. "My apologies for the inconvenience."

Inconvenience was the understatement of the century; this was terrorism pure and simple. Yamada kept his voice and anger tightly under control to avoid panicking his passengers.

"Why are you doing this? What's going to happen to us once we reach that location?"

That sector of space bordered the Neutral Zone of Klingon space. In theory, both the Federation and the Empire did not encroach on that buffer zone, but could they count on the Klingons to abide by those terms once *Chinook* was beyond the Federation's borders? Trusting Klingons to restrain themselves was seldom a safe bet.

"Nothing untoward will befall you," Fortier promised. "You'll drop me off and continue on your way, having fallen only a day or so behind schedule." He glanced around the lounge at the other passengers, more and more of whom were starting to watch and whisper about whatever drama was playing out at the table. "In the meantime, Captain, I don't presume to tell you how to do your job, but perhaps it would be best to confine the rest of the passengers to their cabins for the time being?"

Yamada would have preferred to clap Fortier in irons, or, better yet, beam him out into the void, but his hands were tied. His jaw was clenched so tight he had to spit out his response.

"Anything else?"

"That's all for now. I'll have more instructions once we arrive at the designated coordinates. Do as I say and this ship will arrive safely at Cibonor Prime, albeit somewhat tardily."

Yamada wished he could trust him.

"Can we go now?" Larrol asked anxiously. "Back to our cabins, like you said?"

"Be my guest." Fortier waved bye-bye at them as they scurried from the table, taking an open bottle of Château Picard with them. "Thanks for being so obliging."

Hamparian started to rise as well. "I guess I'll be leaving too."

"Not you, Professor."

She froze, her face turning a paler shade of blue. "I don't understand. I'm just a bystander here. This is between you and the captain."

"I'd rather you stay to keep me company, as well as to discourage any ill-advised heroics. Please remain seated."

"Blast it, Fortier!" the captain said, seething. "You don't need a hostage. You already have this entire ship at your mercy."

"Indulge me, Captain. By my estimate, our new destination is roughly thirteen hours away. Time enough for you and your crew to hatch some reckless scheme to take back your ship. I like to think I've anticipated every countermeasure you might employ, but I'm not going to make the mistake of underestimating you . . . or believing myself infallible. Hence, an auxiliary plan to ensure your cooperation." He pointed the nozzle on his index finger at the frightened scientist, who gripped the edge of the table with both hands as though to keep herself from bolting in panic. "My hand still holds an adequate supply of Horta juices. I doubt anyone wants me to dissolve all or part of the professor, particularly when I'm offering you a much less messy alternative in which no one gets harmed."

Hamparian gasped once more. "You wouldn't . . . not really!"

"That's entirely up to the captain." He smirked at Yamada. "Well, what do you say?"

Yamada kept his voice down to a low growl, even as he tried not to imagine what the powerful acid could to do to flesh and bone. Hadn't he heard something about a Horta burning some human miners alive before the Hortas and humans found a way to coexist?

"What kind of fiend are you?"

"Irrelevant. The question is: What kind of man are you? And are you willing to risk all our lives to obstruct me?" He kept his finger pointed at Hamparian like a phaser set on kill. "I thank you for your time,

Captain, but I believe you have business on the bridge? Some urgent course corrections, perhaps?"

"All right, Fortier. We've taken your blasted detour. What now?"

Thirteen point four hours at warp six had brought them to the outskirts of an unclaimed system smack-dab between Federation and Klingon space, as laid down by the latest round of border negotiations. Yamada, who was feeling every one of those thirteen hours, was more than ready to get on with whatever Fortier had planned and get the slimy spacejacker off *Chinook* as soon as possible, at which point he intended to race back to the Federation at top speed—assuming Fortier didn't have any more unpleasant surprises in store.

"Excellent, Captain. We've made good time."

Fortier remained camped out in the now-emptied lounge alongside his unwilling companion, Doctor Hamparian. He appeared in good spirits, albeit in need of a shave and a shower, while she appeared understandably wan. Cups of black coffee, frequently refilled, resided on the table before them, along with the residue of assorted meals from the ship's galley. Fortier had eaten heartily throughout the crisis; to her credit, Hamparian had managed to down some food as well, if only to maintain her strength. Yamada admired her courage and grace under severe pressure. She was holding up better than might be expected. He couldn't imagine that the middle-aged scientist had ever been taken hostage by a spacejacker before.

"Is that it then?" she asked, the strain of her ordeal audible in her voice. Her stubby, rudimentary antennae drooped like wilting flowers. "Is this finally over?"

Violet Achebe lingered nearby, having spent the last several hours attending to Hamparian and her smarmy captor. She had bravely volunteered to take the endangered passenger's place, but Fortier had declined her offer, quipping that he had no desire to switch hostages in midwarp. Yamada assumed he judged an innocent civilian to be a better and safer bargaining chip than a crew member who might feel obliged to somehow turn the tables on him. He had allowed Achebe to sub in only briefly to permit Hamparian a few bathroom breaks.

"Over?" he echoed. "That remains to be seen, I suppose."

Yamada braced himself for more treachery, already indignant in anticipation.

"What do you mean by that?" He wanted to tear Fortier's blinking steel hand from its moorings and cram it down the other man's throat. "We've done our part, per your demands. You had better not have been lying to us before about letting us go."

Long-range scans had detected no waiting vessels in the vicinity, Klingon or otherwise, but Yamada wouldn't rest until *Chinook* was fully out of harm's way.

"Have no fear, Captain. Your fine ship will soon be on its way, and in one piece no less." Fortier took one last gulp of coffee before rising and stretching his legs. "If you'll please escort us to the nearest convenient escape pod."

"Us?" Hamparian's antennae shot upward in alarm. "But—"

"I'm afraid that conference on Cibonor Prime will have to do without you, my dear professor. I need you to accompany me on the last leg of our journey."

She recoiled in shock. "You can't mean that, not after you promised to let us go!"

"This is unconscionable!" Yamada raged. "It's bad enough that you've held this woman hostage all this time, but—"

"Spare me the dramatics, please." Fortier held up his organic hand to fend off their protests. "Don't forget, Captain, this ship and everyone aboard are at my mercy. Your righteous posturing is merely delaying the inevitable."

Yamada wished he could refute that. "But why do this? What do you gain?"

"A clean escape. *Chinook* has phasers to defend against bandits and other hostiles, does it not? And a working tractor beam? What's to stop you from targeting my escape pod once I've disabled the acid bulb threatening your warp engine? Or pursuing me in the name of justice? Or perhaps you've had the foresight to already sabotage all the escape pods in anticipation of me departing in one? Or even have, unknown to me, deviated from the prescribed coordinates in order to strand me in deep space, far from my intended destination?"

"We've done nothing of the sort!"

"I'm pleased to hear that, Captain, sincerely, but I still think it best to give you a compelling reason to not come after me, one way or another, once we part ways. Namely, the professor's well-being."

"I swear on my life, we won't do anything to pursue you or impede your escape. Believe me, I want nothing more than to see the back of you . . . forever!"

"Of that I have no doubt, but you'll forgive me if I don't have the luxury of taking your word for it. Doctor Hamparian comes with me, for my own peace of mind."

Yamada shook his head. "I can't allow that. Not in good conscience."

"You have no choice, Captain. It's her or the lives of all your other passengers and crew."

"Would you both stop talking about me as though I'm not here!"

Taya Hamparian rose slowly to her feet. Taking a deep breath to compose herself, she looked Fortier squarely in the eye. "Tell me the truth. Would you truly destroy this ship if you have to?"

"I have little to lose otherwise." He aimed his lethal prosthetic at her face. "And make no mistake: although I'm loath to do so, I will melt you with Horta acid if forced."

She flinched at the threat but did not retreat.

Yamada clenched his fists at his sides, feeling this nightmarish situation slip further and further out of his control. "Listen to me, Doctor Hamparian. You don't have to do this."

"We both know that's not true, Captain." She shook her head sadly. "I've no desire to play human sacrifice, but if it means that everyone else survives . . . what else can I do?"

Yamada was again impressed by her poise and presence of mind under these most hellish of circumstances, as well as her sheer, straightforward heroism. He glared furiously at Fortier.

"How do I know you won't just let *Chinook* blow up once you're free and clear, just to cover your tracks?"

"That's where the professor comes in. I'm where I want to be. Get us into a working escape pod, and I'll disable the acid bulb there and then. At which point, I'll be relying on your legitimate concern for the professor's safety to bring this matter to a satisfactory conclusion . . . without any needless death or destruction."

Yamada remained skeptical. "And that matters to you because?"

"There are degrees of criminality, Captain. Is it that hard to conceive that I would just as soon *not* commit mass murder if I don't have to?"

Was he speaking honestly? Yamada had no way of knowing, and the hell of it was that trusting Fortier to keep his word was pretty much their best shot at living another day.

"It's all right, Captain," Hamparian said. "I understand the position you're in. Don't blame yourself for what we both have to do now."

Yamada's throat tightened. "You're a remarkable woman, Doctor. I hope we meet again someday."

"That strikes me as unlikely, Captain, but I appreciate the sentiment."

"Yes, yes, this is all very touching, but can we get a move on?" Fortier took Hamparian by the arm, the deadly nozzle directed at her side. "Our lifeboat awaits, Professor."

She maintained her dignity, her chin held high.

"Just one question: Why me?"

"Luck of the draw, I'm afraid. There just happened to be a vacant seat at your table." He let Yamada escort them out of the lounge. "Nothing personal, I assure you."

Chapter Three

"We have arrived at the rendezvous point," Lieutenant Saavik announced from the helm of the *Enterprise*-A. "Obviously."

As anticipated, two other vessels could be seen on the viewscreen, maintaining a judicious distance from the *Enterprise* and each other: a Klingon bird-of-prey and a Romulan warbird. Saavik, serving as helmsman now that Hikaru Sulu was captain of his own ship, easily suppressed any distaste or trepidation she might have regarding either vessel, despite her negative association with both empires. Duty and logic superseded any matters of personal history.

"Yellow alert," Captain Kirk said from his chair. "Defensive systems only."

"Aye, sir." Commander Chekov was stationed to Saavik's right at the nav station, where he also served as the ship's tactical officer. "Shields raised, but weapons systems offline."

A prudent response, Saavik judged. Although this was intended to be a peaceful encounter, it would be illogical not to factor in the frequently adversarial relationships involved and take all reasonable precautions. Shifting down from impulse to thrusters, she maintained a stationary position relative to the two other vessels, which were also staying in place in a seemingly empty portion of the Osor system, a remote location that was home to the Osori, a very old and reclusive alien species who had long resisted any overtures, peaceful or otherwise, from the Federation and its rivals. Recently, however, the Osori had declared themselves possibly open to establishing diplomatic relations with their galactic neighbors, under specific terms and conditions; chief among them, they wished to make contact with the Federation, the Klingons, and the Romulans simultaneously, to avoid showing favoritism toward any one faction over another. That the Osori were believed to possess technology far in advance of all three civilizations, as demonstrated by the fact that they had kept their world cloaked and shielded for centuries, was inducement enough to make all three parties agree to their terms. If nothing else, no government wanted to risk the others allying with the Osori before them.

"The Klingon and Romulan vessels have their shields in place as well." Captain Spock occupied his customary place at the science station. "No indications of their weapon systems powering up."

"Thank heaven for small favors?" Doctor McCoy loitered within the command well, leaning on a railing. "How dicey is this whole get-together if it's notable that nobody is shooting each other yet? Talk about a low bar."

Saavik had noted that the doctor seldom felt obliged to confine himself to his sickbay if more intriguing happenings were transpiring on the bridge.

Kirk took McCoy's typically astringent remark in stride. "Let's get this party started. Open hailing frequencies."

"Aye, sir," Commander Uhura responded; it was a measure of Kirk's superior leadership abilities and the loyalty he inspired in others, Saavik deduced, that so many of his longtime crew members had chosen to serve under him, often in their original posts, for almost as long as Saavik had been alive. "Both vessels answering our hails."

Kirk nodded. "On-screen."

Two separate communications windows divided the screen in half. On the right, an older Romulan male of dignified mien and bearing faced the bridge; on the left, a Klingon woman who looked fierce even by the aggressive standards of her famously warlike species. Uncertainty over who was to speak first produced a momentary pause. Kirk characteristically took the initiative, rising to his feet to address the screen.

"This is Captain James T. Kirk of the *Starship Enterprise*, representing the United Federation of Planets on this historic occasion. We look forward to a fruitful joint operation benefiting all involved, including the Osori."

"*Captain B'Eleste of the* Lukara," the Klingon growled, speaking over the Romulan, who politely deferred to the warrior woman. She seemed younger than both Kirk and the Romulan and, clad in layered black body armor, presented a deliberately intimidating appearance. A voluminous mane of wild black hair haloed her striking features like the corona of an angry star, radiating several centimeters above and to the sides of her face. As was the fashion among modern Klingons, said hair was swept away from her brow to display prominent cranial ridges. Her teeth had been filed to points. The murky red glow of the bird-of-prey's bridge framed her menacing visage. *"Honor demands we adhere to the terms agreed upon. We demand nothing less from you and the Romulans."*

Her gravelly voice imbued the latter term with contempt. Saavik recalled that the uneasy alliance between the Klingon and Romulan Empires had recently collapsed into bitter acrimony.

"Commander Plavius of the Harrier," the Romulan said. Graying hair conveyed age and experience, while a monocle over his left eye was either an affectation or evidence of a visual disability resistant to conventional treatment, not unlike, perhaps, Captain Kirk's occasional need for reading glasses. An opaque screen behind his head and shoulders offered no glimpse of the warbird's bridge, no doubt by design; Romulans guarded their secrets zealously. *"I assure you, Captains, that the Romulan Star Empire also desires this conclave to proceed without any unnecessary strife. If hostilities do break out, we shall not have initiated them."*

With his tapered ears and sober expression, Plavius could easily be mistaken for a Vulcan, aside from his quilted metallic uniform. A carmine shoulder drape denoted his status. This resemblance was deceptive, Saavik knew. Although they shared a common ancestry, mingled in her own bloodstream, Vulcans and Romulans had very different values.

"Nor will we," Kirk said.

"Nor we," B'Eleste echoed, *"without provocation."*

"Sounds as though we're all on the same page," Kirk said, evidently choosing to overlook the Klingon's qualifier in the interests of diplomacy, "which bodes well for the journey ahead . . . and first contact with the Osori."

"Let us hope they do not test our patience by keeping us waiting," B'Eleste said. *"We are here. Where are they?"*

"We're still within the designated time frame," Kirk observed. "No reason yet to expect we've been stood up."

"That would be most regrettable," Plavius said. *"We have all gone to considerable effort to accommodate the Osori by arriving at the appointed time and coordinates. It would be a pity if those efforts proved a waste."*

Negotiations for the meeting had been conducted by long-range subspace transmissions, initiated by the Osori after years of silence. The distances involved meant that weeks passed between queries and responses.

"Such fears appear premature," Spock said, entering the discussion, "judging from certain energy fluctuations in our immediate vicinity." He looked away from the swirling bandwidth monitor above his console. "With your permission, Captain, switching main screen to external view."

Kirk nodded. "Maintain audio link to other vessels, Uhura."

"Aye, sir."

B'Eleste and Plavius vanished from the screen, replaced by a view of seemingly empty space just beyond the rendezvous point. At first glance, and to all but the most sophisticated sensors, the Osor system consisted of just a few uninhabitable gas giants, dwarf planets, comets, and asteroids. No Class-M planets seemed to occupy the "Goldilocks zone" conducive to carbon-based life-forms. Only the gleam of far-distant stars relieved the airless darkness before them.

Then the planet decloaked, more or less.

The vacuum shimmered, and the Osori homeworld came into view, approximately seventy thousand kilometers from the trio of spacecraft. Saavik checked her own readings to confirm that the *Enterprise*'s current location was safely outside the planet's gravity well. She was grateful that the Osori's navigational directions had been precise enough to eliminate any chance of the ship (or either of the other two vessels) colliding with the cloaked planet by mischance.

"Well, I'll be a mugato's uncle," McCoy said. "That's quite the magic trick."

"Indeed," Spock concurred. "To cloak an entire world—and on a permanent basis—is an astounding feat. The energy demands beggar the imagination, at least by any technology presently known to us."

Not that the Osori homeworld was completely exposed. An opaque white energy field still surrounded the planet, making it impossible to visually discern any of its physical features, not even the color of its seas, landmasses, or atmosphere, let alone any cities or continents. Osor Prime presented as nothing but a smooth white globe. Even its rate of rotation was hidden.

"What are your sensors telling you, Spock?" Kirk squinted at the screen as though he could somehow penetrate the barrier if he stared hard enough. "You seeing anything we can't?"

"Negative, Captain. The energy shell is impervious to our sensors, and based on my readings, any sort of conventional weapons fire. Osor Prime may have decloaked, but it remains very much masked . . . and invulnerable."

Possibly just as well, Saavik thought, *with both Klingons and Romulans at their doorstep.*

Granted, the Osori currently had insufficient experience with the Federation to trust it as well, a situation this mission was intended to remedy, even if it meant Starfleet having to trust their own longtime adversaries for the duration.

And vice versa.

"We are being scanned by the planet," Spock reported.

"Even though we can't scan them?" Kirk asked.

"Affirmative. Apparently the energy shell only obstructs observation from without. Not unlike a one-way window."

"That hardly seems fair," Chekov grumbled.

"Their party, their rules," Kirk said. "Let them take a good look. See we mean them no harm."

"I doubt we could harm them if we wanted to," Spock stated, "as long as they remain behind their protective shell."

Saavik reviewed what little was known of the Osori, most of which consisted of myth and speculation. Cryptic references to them in the records of long-lost civilizations, such as the Kalandans and the Fabrini, suggested that they were regarded as ancient even by those bygone peoples, but their origins had been lost to history, and it was not until recent years that it was confirmed that they actually existed and were not merely an enduring legend like El Dorado, Atlantis, or the Lost

Colony of Sh'Gol. Gravitational anomalies, detected by long-range sensors and probes, had hinted at a phantom planet hidden in what was eventually found to be the Osor system, although all attempts to communicate with its inhabitants had been rebuffed until their subspace summons was received months ago. Legend had it that the Osori were effectively immortal, but Saavik was reluctant to take that literally; that was likely just a myth.

Then again, the Osori were once believed to be imaginary.

"Captain!" Uhura's voice rang with excitement. "We're being hailed by the planet, as are the Klingons and Romulans."

"Let's see them," Kirk said.

"No visual, sir. Audio only, but piping it through."

Saavik listened with interest, her curiosity understandably aroused. A pleasant tenor voice, less stentorian than she had anticipated, issued from the speakers:

"Greetings, Young Ones. We thank you for answering our call and journeying to meet us. Long have we held ourselves apart from fledging civilizations such as yourselves, for our sake and yours, but the galaxy grows smaller every cycle, and your continuing expansion, along with your propensity for exploration and conquest, makes it evident that concealment alone is no longer a viable strategy for us; it was only a matter of time before you ventured into our space in greater frequency and numbers. For this reason, we have chosen to explore the possibility of future dealings between our respective peoples . . . even though our final decision is yet to be determined."

"So we understand," Kirk said, the plural pronoun no doubt meant to encompass the Klingons and Romulans, "but I'm curious. You refer to us as 'young ones.' May I ask how old your civilization is, compared to ours?"

"Not so ancient as, say, the Organians or the Metrons, who we understand you have encountered in the past. Unlike those ascended entities, we retain corporeal form and possess no semidivine powers over time and space. We deem ourselves a 'middle' species, not so transcendent as those who came before us, yet far older than the youthful races of your generation."

Saavik would have preferred a more precise description than "far older," specifying an exact quantity of time in numerical units, but allowed that there would be time enough for a more exhaustive recounting of the Osori's history once diplomatic relations were well and truly established. This was an introduction, not an investigation.

"*You call us children?*" B'Eleste bristled. "*I would caution you not to treat us as such. The old and complacent should often think twice before dismissing younger challengers.*"

"*We mean no disrespect,*" the Osori replied. "*The gap in ages between our species is simply a reality, not an occasion for judgment. Whether that gap poses an insurmountable barrier to understanding remains to be seen.*"

Plavius entered the conversation. "*Are the myths true? Are you actually immortal?*"

"*Not absolutely,*" the Osori answered, "*but, barring extreme accidents or violence, our life-spans are indeed measured in millennia, which we know to be exceptionally long compared to most other organic beings. Before you ask, there is no secret technique or substance involved; it is simply a happy accident of evolution, dating back to the dawn of our species. It has always been thus with us.*"

"My God," McCoy murmured in a hushed voice. "A whole race of Flints."

Saavik, whose acute hearing easily registered the whispered remark, caught the reference. Although that particular incident had occurred well before she enrolled in Starfleet, she had familiarized herself with the *Enterprise*'s earlier missions, including the time, twenty-three years ago, when Captain Kirk and his original crew had encountered a seemingly immortal earthman who proved to be more than six thousand years old. Flint, as he was then known, believed himself to be unique: a mutant whose remarkable regenerative abilities were not passed on to his offspring, rendering him an evolutionary dead end, but Saavik imagined a scenario where natural selection played out differently, with immortals like Flint becoming the dominant species on Osor, outlasting and outbreeding their more short-lived cousins to the extent that any nonimmortal Osori succumbed to extinction eons ago. Had just such a scenario occurred in Osor's prehistory?

"Fascinating," Spock intoned, and she was inclined to agree.

"I'm sure you must have many questions about us," Kirk said graciously. "Is there anything you would like to know?"

"All in good time. For now, we require only that you arrange yourselves as agreed. We will be monitoring the procedure. Once it is complete, you may expect our envoys to join you. We anticipate meeting you face-to-face at last."

"Likewise," Kirk said.

No reply was forthcoming.

"The Osori have ended the transmission on their end," Uhura confirmed. "Shall I reestablish visual communication with the other ships, Captain?"

"By all means, Lieutenant." Kirk reclaimed his chair as B'Eleste and Plavius returned to the screen. "That seemed to go well enough. I trust both of you were also satisfied with the Osori's welcome."

"It was suitable for the occasion," Plavius agreed. *"I cannot fault them for their caution and discretion at this early juncture."*

"Then let us waste no more time on pleasantries," B'Eleste said, *"and proceed with the exchange of hostages, the sooner to comply with the Osori's requests."*

"Observers," Plavius corrected her. *"Not hostages."*

B'Eleste snorted. *"Spare me your devious euphemisms, Romulan. We all know what is meant."*

Saavik saw her point. At the Osori's insistence, the conclave was to be held on neutral territory, specifically Nimbus III, the so-called Planet of Galactic Peace, where top diplomats and intellectuals from all three superpowers awaited the arrival of the Osori's representatives. In addition, each of the three Osori envoys was to be transported to the conference site on a different ship: one from the Federation, one from the Klingons, one from the Romulans. To further ensure amity and cooperation, each of the three ships would also host "observers" from the other two ships. In short, the *Enterprise* would take on an Osori envoy *and* high-ranking officers from the Klingon and Romulan vessels, with similar arrangements on the other two ships. Subtleties of universal translation notwithstanding, to describe the exchanged crew members as "hostages" to each side's good behavior was blunt, but not inaccurate.

"*Plavius*," the Romulan corrected B'Eleste again. "Commander *Plavius*, not 'Romulan.' *Please extend me the courtesy of addressing me by my name and rank, Captain B'Eleste, and I will do the same.*"

The Klingon rolled her eyes. "*I hope your 'observer' is not so thin-skinned,* Commander."

"Regardless," Kirk interjected, "it's true that the Osori are expecting us to swap personnel before they proceed any further, so we should probably indeed get on with it."

"*Did I not already say that, Kirk?*" B'Eleste huffed.

"So you did." Kirk settled back into his chair. If he had any reservations about sending two of his crew into the hands of his longtime foes, his expression did not betray them. Saavik admired his "poker face," as he called it. It was impressive . . . for a human.

She would do well to emulate it in the days to come.

"Spock, Saavik," he ordered. "Report with me to the transporter room."

Chapter Four

"Every single product whales are used for can be duplicated, naturally or synthetically, and usually more economically than by hunting whales. A hundred years ago, using hand-thrown harpoons, humanity did plenty of damage, but that was nothing compared to what we've achieved in this century."

"Dinner's almost ready," Dennis called out from the kitchenette of their modest two-bedroom apartment. Street noises filtered in from outside.

"Great," Melinda said absently, her gaze fixed on the vintage video playing on the flatscreen TV in their living room, where Gillian spoke out against whaling in footage recorded back in the eighties, not long before she vanished. Seated on a thrift-store couch facing the screen, Melinda paused the video to contemplate the attractive, earnest woman on the screen. Gillian had wavy blond hair, lively blue eyes, and obviously believed deeply in what she was saying. Melinda wished she could have known her, despite the decades between them. Gillian was thirty-four when she disappeared; she would be seventy now if she was still alive.

What happened to you, Gillian? Where, if anywhere, are you today?

She closed the video, reducing it to a thumbnail on her virtual case board, which resembled the boards seen on TV detective shows, but with the advantage of being entirely digital. With a swipe, she could easily move photos, files, and virtual index cards around the screen without having to fumble with actual yarn and thumbtacks. At the moment, the board was notably sparse, but she expected it to fill up as she got deeper into the investigation and, hopefully, listeners started coming forward with new tips and leads.

Here's hoping, she thought.

A lot depended on this podcast taking off. *Cascade* had gone viral, allowing her and Dennis to quit their day jobs to focus on podcasting full-time, which meant the pressure was on to prove she wasn't just a one-hit wonder. And she had to get *Cetacean* up and running quickly, so they didn't lose the momentum generated by *Cascade* or run out of funds. The last thing she wanted to do was go back to her old nine-to-five gig scripting corporate training videos. *Cetacean* had to be a hit.

"Chow time."

Dennis strolled out of the kitchen and handed her a big bowl of one of his signature dishes: paprika chicken on pasta. The mouthwatering aroma reminded her that she hadn't eaten anything substantial for hours, briefly distracting her from obsessing over the case.

"Thanks, roomie. Smells great as usual."

Dennis was definitely the master chef in this partnership. Left to her own devices, Melinda would rely on food carts, DoorDash, and microwave dinners to keep from starving, if she remembered to eat at all while immersed in a new project. Not for the first time, she thanked her lucky stars that their paths had intersected a few years back. She'd actually been dating his previous roommate when they first met; ultimately, she'd ditched the boyfriend and poached the roommate, which was working out well for both of them. They made a good team; he was an indefatigable researcher who didn't mind letting her be the public face (or, more accurately, voice) of the podcast. If anything, he preferred to stay out of the spotlight.

That he also knew his way around a kitchen was also a bonus.

"No problem. I played around with the recipe a little this time around: added a bit more garlic and oregano." He helped himself to a bowl, then plopped down beside her on the couch. He peered up at the screen. "Solved the mystery yet?"

"As if." Her own gaze shifted to a thumbnail portrait of Bob Briggs, linking to the interview they'd conducted at the Cetacean Institute. "What was your take on Briggs?"

"I don't know. Kinda felt sorry for the old guy. Gotta suck never knowing what happened to somebody you used to see every day, especially considering how they left things right before she went poof." He paused to consume a bite of pasta. "What did you think?"

"A bit old-school sexist and condescending, but sincere. What he told us matches what was already reported back in the day." The sudden disappearance of a local scientist—and a pretty blond one at that—had been all over the news in the spring of 1986, until the media finally moved on, having no new developments or answers to report. "I didn't get the impression that he was holding anything back."

"So you think it *was* all about the whales being released early?" Dennis asked. "That she quit her job and ghosted him because she was that pissed off about not getting to say goodbye to George and Gracie?"

Melinda shook her head. "Has to be more to it than that. Even if she never wanted to work with Briggs again, why would she abandon her whole life, seemingly overnight?"

"Such as it was," Dennis said. "Not as though she had a whole lot to ditch, at least as far as I can tell."

He had a point. So far their probing into Gillian's personal life seemed to confirm Briggs's assessment that she hadn't had much of one. Gillian Catherine Taylor was an only child, born late in life to an older couple who had, perhaps mercifully, passed away before she went missing, leaving Gillian only a few out-of-town relatives she didn't see very often. News reports at the time stated that she was not known to be seeing anyone, casually or seriously, just as Briggs had suggested. Granted, given that this had all gone down pre–social media, what info was readily available was mostly about her education and professional life, gleaned from high school yearbooks, college alumni magazines, academic articles, and such. Nowadays, it would be easy enough to find out her hobbies, favorite TV shows, vacation spots, political inclinations, and friends lists, but people didn't live online back in Gillian's day, making getting to know her much more challenging. To date, everything they could turn up about her, circa 1986, was that she was indeed all about her work with whales.

Not that I'm one to talk, Melinda thought. Dennis at least was in a long-distance relationship with a girlfriend in Oslo, but she'd put dating on hold in order to focus on *Cetacean.* Indeed, at times it felt like she was in a long-distance relationship of her own—with Gillian.

"Even still, why would she walk away from her career, her apartment, her truck, and all her worldly possessions, just like that? It's almost as though she went into the Witness Protection Program on a moment's notice."

Dennis froze, his fork suspended before his mouth. A noodle dangled precariously.

"You think?" A worried look came over his face. "Maybe she found out something she wasn't supposed to, making her a target for, I dunno, Big Whaling or whoever. Or maybe the CIA or the Pentagon stole the whales to train them for underwater sabotage missions."

Uh-oh, Melinda thought. *Here we go again.*

She kicked herself mentally for even joking about Melinda going into hiding. Dennis was a bright guy, but he was a sucker for conspiracy theories, the more sinister the better. She'd had to pull him out of more than a few online rabbit holes, playing Scully to his Mulder, except that, in the real world, the level-headed skeptic wasn't always wrong.

"So let's get this straight," she said patiently. "The government rushed her into Witness Protection to hide her from . . . the government?"

"Could be. The FBI versus the CIA, one faction of the military-industrial complex pitted against another for their own Machiavellian reasons." He put down his dinner, the better to gesticulate with his hands. "But fine, forget the FBI. Maybe she had to go on the run, drop off the grid, to hide from . . . somebody. Or maybe she was simply eliminated, or shanghaied into working for some black-budget marine lab overseas, or—"

"Whoa!" Melinda held up a hand to halt this runaway train of thought before it jumped the rails entirely. "Let's not get carried away here."

But he was already on a roll.

"What? You don't think *they* are capable of disposing of Gillian, or her whales, one way or another? Or any number of other nefarious options? History is full of spooky conspiracies and cover-ups. What about that orbital weapons platform that mysteriously self-destructed back in '68? Or those rumors of top-secret eugenics programs back in the day? Or Roswell or Area 51?"

"Not saying fishy stuff doesn't go on." She carefully maintained a neutral expression, not wanting to rehash every conspiracy theory from the twentieth century up to the present. "Just saying we ought to consider less . . . exotic . . . possibilities before jumping to conclusions. Occam's razor and all that."

He scowled.

"Okay, razorgirl, what's your explanation."

She had nothing.

"You got me there," she admitted, surrendering for the time being. Xing out the screen, she exited the case board for the night and turned her attention to the paprika chicken instead. "Wowsers, this is really good. I can definitely taste the extra garlic."

As hoped, the rave review appeased him somewhat, turning his mood around.

"Really? I was hoping that would add some zest to the recipe, but I wasn't sure. It was kinda an experiment."

"Consider it a success, dude. Please tell me there's enough for seconds."

"And leftovers," he assured her, beaming.

Conflict averted, they dug into their dinners, even as Melinda's mind remained squarely focused on more pressing matters.

Maybe that ex-cop can throw some light on Gillian's case, she mused, thinking ahead. *Or at least give us some juicy soundbites for Episode Two.*

Chapter Five

2268

"... to my relief, and surprise, Fortier disabled the acid bulb as promised, so my engineering crew were able to—gingerly—remove the device from the energy pile without incident. To my dismay, however, we were unable to stop Fortier from fleeing in an escape pod while he still held Doctor Hamparian's life in his hands. The last I saw of the pod, it was moving away from us, heading deeper into the system, after which we had no choice but to make tracks back to Federation space to deliver the rest of our passengers to safety. What became of Hamparian afterwards? I wish I knew..."

"End recording," Kirk said.

The testimony of Jerry Yamada, skipper of the *S.S. Chinook,* vanished from the viewscreen in the *Enterprise's* main briefing room, where Captain James T. Kirk was conferring with his senior officers regarding the particulars of their current orders from Starfleet. Kirk's heart went out to Yamada, who had clearly been placed in an untenable position. The man was a civilian captain, not a Starfleet officer, but the loss of his passenger surely weighed heavily on him. Kirk hoped it wasn't too late to safely recover Taya Hamparian.

"And there you have it, gentlemen," Kirk said. "A firsthand account of what transpired aboard the *Chinook* several days ago. And the impetus for our present assignment."

"A spacejacking of all things!" Doctor Leonard McCoy vented, understandably offended by the brazen crime. A scowl deepened the lines on his careworn face. "In this day and age! What century is this again?"

"Aye," Chief Engineer Montgomery Scott agreed, equally incensed. "And by wreaking mischief on the ship's very engine no less. I'd like to get my hands on that sabotaging blackguard, and I'm not ashamed to say it. Gets my dander up thinking about how he put that poor vessel and all aboard in jeopardy just for his own devilish purposes."

First Officer Spock's reaction was characteristically less emotional. "Alas, Doctor, no era is entirely immune to lawlessness, and all the more so out on the more distant frontiers of the Federation. And in this instance, the operation appears to have been planned and executed with admirable precision."

"Admirable?" McCoy bristled. "Don't tell me you're giving this outrage a good review?"

"Hardly, Doctor. I merely note that this was neither a crime of passion nor opportunity; considerable thought and preparation went into its implementation. We would do well to take that into account when calculating our response."

Kirk agreed. "Your point is well-taken, Mister Spock. This was a sophisticated crime committed by a bold and meticulous felon. We should not underestimate him . . . and whoever else might be involved."

Along with the other three officers, Kirk sat at the conference table facing the viewscreen. Yeoman Martha Landon was also on hand to record the proceedings and manage the viewer via a control panel embedded in the table. Kirk had left Lieutenant Sulu in charge of the bridge with directions to make good time to the last reported location of the spacejacker and his hostage. Meanwhile, Lieutenant Uhura was monitoring subspace transmissions for any new developments or clues concerning Doctor Hamparian's whereabouts.

"The motive behind the crime also remains obscure," Spock observed, "assuming that the abduction of Doctor Hamparian was indeed simply a matter of chance."

"That's what has Starfleet worried," Kirk said. "Beyond a natural concern for the well-being of a Federation citizen, which we cannot take lightly, there are also larger issues at stake. It seems that the noted Doctor Hamparian was involved in some top-secret, highly classified biomedical research. More specifically, she was well on her way to developing treatments that, conceivably, could lead to regenerating damaged or lost humanoid tissues, maybe even allowing patients to regrow organs lost to disease or injury."

"Fascinating." Spock raised an eyebrow in appreciation. "If successful, that would be a significant breakthrough in modern medicine, bringing relief to many."

Kirk wondered if, like him, Spock was also thinking of poor Christopher Pike, whose irradiated nervous system had been ravaged beyond even the Federation's most advanced medical treatments. Pike had ultimately found a balm of sorts on Talos IV, but perhaps someday Hamparian's work could provide less illusory hope to countless others stricken by equally debilitating catastrophes.

"Good God," McCoy exclaimed. "I recognized Hamparian's name from assorted medical journals, and knew she was well-respected in her field, but I had no idea she was working on anything so groundbreaking!"

"That was deliberate, Bones. Although her work is benign in intent, there are concerns that her techniques, if perfected, could be misused if they fell into the wrong hands, such as the Klingons or the Romulans. Imagine the military advantages of creating soldiers who can regrow lost limbs or organs, or who possess superhumanoid healing factors. Certainly, it wouldn't be the first time that a well-intended scientific breakthrough was weaponized in ways its creators never intended."

Spock nodded. "Your own world's devastating Eugenics Wars come immediately to mind."

"Not just 'our' world, Spock," McCoy said. "Need I remind you that half your genes come from Earth as well?"

Spock stiffened. "That is hardly necessary, Doctor, nor appreciated."

"In any event," Kirk said, "growing new livers or kidneys is one thing. Crossing over into Khan Noonien Singh territory is another, which is why Hamparian's work has been closely monitored and classified by the authorities up until now, and why they are so distressed by her abduction. Put bluntly, rescuing her is not *just* an errand of mercy; it's a vital matter of Federation security."

"Just as her disappearance is a potential loss to science and medicine as well," Spock observed.

McCoy shook his head somberly. "Of all people for that bandit to take hostage."

"Exactly, gentlemen," Kirk said. "The powers that be want her back, top priority."

"So are we thinking then that the lady was not merely at the wrong place at the wrong time," Scott asked, "but that perhaps the villain knew exactly who he was snatching?"

"Impossible to determine at this time," Spock said, "but in light of what we now know about the potential value of her work, we cannot rule out the possibility that the abduction of Doctor Hamparian was indeed the very motive behind the crime."

"Or, alternatively, her kidnapping *was* just a matter of chance," Kirk said. "Coincidence or conspiracy? That's the question."

As Spock had noted, no definitive answer could be determined just yet, but the fact that the sector in question, where Fortier had insisted on being taken, bordered Klingon space was cause for concern. Kirk didn't want to think about the Klingons getting hold of Hamparian and forcing her to weaponize her work on their behalf. He assumed that the kidnapped scientist would never do so voluntarily, but Klingons seldom took "no" for an answer—and could be brutally persuasive when it suited them.

"What do we know about the culprit himself?" McCoy asked. "This Fortier scoundrel, if that's his real name?"

"Very little." Kirk had already reviewed whatever biographical materials Starfleet, and the *Enterprise*'s computerized database, had managed to dig up on the man. "He's kept a fairly low profile, staying on the right side of the law, mostly, with only a few minor infractions and run-ins with local authorities over the years. Peripatetic in his habits, never staying put at one planet or system long enough to set down serious roots. Prior to the *Chinook* incident, he was barely on anybody's sensors."

He nodded at Landon, who put a recent image of Fortier, taken from his travel visa, onto the viewscreen. There was nothing about the man's appearance to trigger any red alerts. Kirk didn't recognize him and had no reason to expect that anybody in the room would. Fortier's record, meager as it was, was hardly suspicious. Harry Mudd he was not, at least not on paper.

"I have to wonder if Fortier is truly the brains behind this operation," Kirk said. "Nothing in his file suggests that he's anything but a small-time hustler, drifting from world to world. I'm finding it hard to see him as a criminal mastermind apt to pull off such an audacious crime."

"Appearances can be deceiving," McCoy said. "Hard to get the full measure of a man from a skimpy résumé. Who knows what anyone's truly capable of if they're desperate or motivated enough? Look at Ben Finney, or Laurence Marvick."

Kirk took McCoy's meaning. He would have never guessed that Finney's frustration and bitterness over his stalled career in Starfleet would have led him to fake his own death to get back at Kirk, whom he blamed for his blighted prospects, or that an accomplished starship engineer like Marvick, who'd had a spotless record before, would be driven to attempted murder by jealousy over a woman who rejected him. Had some similar obsession, gnawing away at Fortier, compelled him to his actions?

"True," Kirk said. "Fortier was motivated enough that he was willing to blow himself up, along with everyone else, to get where he wanted, but what could be more important than his own life?"

"The devil if I know," Scott said. "Perhaps he had a circuit loose in his wiring?"

"Unless," Spock said, "he felt certain that the *Chinook*'s captain would accede to his demands, in which case his life was never actually at risk."

"A hell of a gamble," McCoy said, frowning. "Playing the odds with life."

"Maybe, maybe not." Kirk gamed out the scenario. "We have no way of knowing what Fortier would have actually done if Yamada had called his bluff. He might have folded and accepted prosecution over death. As it was, however, his gamble paid off, as he had every reason to expect it would. Few responsible captains would *not* capitulate to save the lives of their passengers, at least where ordinary civilians are concerned."

Kirk had on occasion risked the lives of his ship and his crew, sometimes even tempting death rather than surrender, but that was different. His crew knew the risks when they enlisted in Starfleet and accepted their postings aboard the *Enterprise*, just as they understood that sometimes their missions took priority over their personal safety.

The captain of a civilian transport, whose primary duty *was* to see his passengers safely across the void, would necessarily have a different perspective. Fortier could have indeed felt confident that Yamada would not risk calling his bluff.

"But to what end?" Scott asked. "To be dropped off in an escape pod in the middle of nowhere?"

"Not quite nowhere," Kirk said. "Mister Spock, if you could fill us in on the relevant geography?"

"Certainly, Captain."

Spock inserted a microtape into the tri-screen viewer on the table, and Fortier's image on the main viewscreen was replaced by a computer-generated graphic depicting the sector where Fortier had abducted Doctor Hamparian. A glowing red dot indicated the precise coordinates the spacejacker had directed *Chinook* to. Kirk grimaced at the dot's relative nearness to the Klingon border, only a few star systems away. That was far too close for comfort.

"As noted by Captain Yamada in his testimony, the coordinates of the drop-off spot lie within a negotiated buffer zone between the Federation and Klingon space." Spock zoomed in on the red dot, revealing it to be within a system labeled VXY-8P33. "In accordance with Federation regulations, the *Chinook*'s escape pods were equipped with rudimentary ion drives to allow them to reach the nearest safe harbor, assuming one was at hand. As it happens, this system contains only one Class-M planet within range of the pod: a world known to its pre-warp inhabitants as Atraz. Given that Fortier expressly selected the coordinates for his escape, we may safely assume he had studied the region and knew that Atraz was attainable by pod. I suggest we begin our search for Doctor Hamparian there."

The planet appeared on the viewer, in shades of blue, green, and brown. Kirk noted with relief the absence of any moons, habitable or otherwise. Fewer locations to search or for Fortier to hide out at. *Thank fortune for small favors,* he thought.

"A logical assumption, Mister Spock, but how can we be sure that, instead of making its way to Atraz, the pod didn't rendezvous with a ship that swung by to pick it up after *Chinook* fled the system?"

"We cannot," Spock admitted, "but *Chinook*'s sensors detected no other vessels in the vicinity at the time of their departure. Furthermore, the presence of a Class-M planet conveniently within range of the pod is . . . suggestive."

"Some would say suspicious," Landon commented.

"That it is," Kirk agreed. "If nothing else, it gives us a place to start looking."

He hoped Spock was correct, and that Fortier and his hostage had ended up on Atraz, at least temporarily. If they had instead been intercepted by a ship piloted by unknown parties, they could be anywhere by now, including well into Klingon space. In which case their odds of recovering Hamparian became vanishingly small.

"There may be additional data to be found once we arrive at the system," Spock said. "An extant ion trail leading from the drop-off point to Atraz perhaps, particulate antimatter residue, or energy signatures indicating the recent passage of another starship besides *Chinook*."

"Aye, maybe." Scott looked dubious. "But time is not on our side. Days have passed already since that blackhearted vandal absconded with the doctor, and any ion trails or other clues are dissipating as we speak. The trail is going cold."

"Quite right, Mister Scott," Spock replied. "All the more reason to reach the scene of the crime, as it were, before all evidence is lost. Working to our advantage, however, is that Atraz is a pre-spacefaring world and its system far away from any established space routes, meaning that whatever tracks remain will not have been muddied by any subsequent vessels traversing the region, in theory."

McCoy eyed Spock skeptically. "And if we don't find any lingering ion trails or some such? Then what?"

"We proceed to Atraz regardless," Kirk stated. *For lack of any better options,* he amended silently.

"And then what?" McCoy asked. "We search the entire planet for two missing individuals? Need I remind you that planets are big places with plenty of places to hide? Why, I hear that some of them even have multiple continents and oceans to explore."

"Four continents and nine oceans, Doctor," Spock said, "but there may be ways to narrow our search when the time comes, depending on what we discover on our arrival."

"Glad to hear it," McCoy said without sarcasm. "For Hamparian's sake."

For once, he didn't seem inclined to debate Spock. Like everyone, he was doubtless hoping that their famously brilliant science officer could point them in the right direction. Hamparian's life—and the security of her classified scientific expertise—depended on it.

"What can you tell us about Atraz, Mister Spock?"

"Only what is in Starfleet's databases. According to various long-range probes and scans, most of them conducted many years ago, Atraz is home to a preindustrial humanoid population predicted to be centuries away from developing spaceflight. There are a few major city-states, but most of the planet is still an untamed wilderness inhabited by various barbarian tribes, some more peaceful than others. Gravity and atmosphere are within conventional Class-M standards; the climate, naturally, varies from biome to biome. Significantly, Atraz is also off-limits to both the Federation and the Klingon Empire, per the Organian Peace Treaty."

Kirk was acutely aware of that fact. "Which means any search party we dispatch to Atraz will need to be *very* discreet to avoid attracting undue attention."

"Precisely," Spock said. "Along with the treaty, the Prime Directive also applies here."

None of which was going to make finding and rescuing Hamparian any easier if she was indeed being held prisoner somewhere on Atraz. Nor could they necessarily count on the Klingons to abide by the terms of the treaty if they had conspired to get their hands on the kidnapped scientist. They'd been pushing the limits of the treaty, meddling and scheming to bring other planets and resources under their influence, since before it was even signed.

"I'd like to volunteer for any search party, sir," Landon said, speaking up. "From what I gather, she sacrificed herself for the sake of everyone else on *Chinook*. I can't say I like the idea of her being on her own now, wherever she is."

"Request duly noted and appreciated, Yeoman." Kirk knew Landon could handle herself in a tight spot and deal with harsh, even savage circumstances; she'd proven that on Gamma Trianguli VI and subsequently. "I'll take it under consideration."

"Thank you, Captain."

"Just so long as the bloody Prime Directive doesn't apply to Fortier getting what's coming to him," Scott muttered balefully. "Threatening to dissolve a baffle plate in a warp engine, what kind of monster even contemplates such a thing?"

"You'll get no argument from me, Scotty." Kirk had not forgotten what had become of the *Antares* after Charlie Evans had telekinetically deleted a baffle plate from the cargo ship's engines; there had been nothing left of the *Antares* and its crew except a few scraps of debris. "But let's be clear on one thing: Recovering Hamparian, both for her sake and for the sake of Federation security, is our top priority. Apprehending Fortier and bringing him to justice is a secondary concern."

"Amen to that," McCoy said. "The sooner we rescue her, the better."

Spoken from the heart, Kirk thought; he knew he could count on McCoy to keep the human element of this mission in focus, despite any other issues involved. "My thoughts exactly."

Leaning forward, Kirk activated the intercom at the control panel before him.

"Kirk to Bridge. Mister Sulu, increase speed to warp eight."

Chapter Six

Kirk paused the turbolift. "A word, Lieutenant, before we go any further."

"Captain?" Saavik asked, puzzled.

She, Kirk, Spock, and McCoy were en route to the transporter room to begin the process of exchanging crew members with the Romulan and Klingon vessels, per the Osori's instructions. Saavik had volunteered to serve as an observer-slash-hostage aboard the Klingon bird-of-prey for the duration of the voyage to Nimbus III. This was her first major diplomatic mission, and she was determined to excel.

"I just want to make certain you aren't having any second thoughts regarding this assignment," the captain said. "No one would think any less of you if you were, considering"—his voice faltered almost imperceptibly—"what you went through that other time you were surrounded by Klingons."

She understood what he alluded to. Only seven years had passed since she'd been literally taken hostage by Klingons on the Genesis Planet. During that ordeal, she had found herself moments away from death before being forced to watch as Kirk's only son, David Marcus, was brutally slain before her eyes. David, for all his very-human faults, had become a friend. She still regretted his death.

"We have already discussed this," she said stiffly, uncomfortable with this line of inquiry. "I am fully prepared to carry out my duty."

"No one doubts that," McCoy said gently, deploying his bedside manner as though she was in need of it; she found this vexing. "But why put yourself through this if you don't have to? It's not too late to find somebody else to take a road trip with the Klingons."

"I believe there is a human saying about 'getting back on the horse,'" she observed. "Starfleet officers expect to face mortal peril at times. I can hardly expect one negative experience, no matter how harrowing," she added, not wishing to minimize David's murder, "to limit my ability to conduct future assignments."

She challenged McCoy calmly, betraying no trace of discomfort or embarrassment. "Unless, Doctor, you consider me psychologically unfit for this mission. In your professional opinion, that is."

"No, no, nothing like that," he backtracked. "You're fit as a fiddle, mentally and physically, and as ridiculously level-headed as the next Vulcan. We just thought this particular task might be rough on you, for perfectly understandable reasons."

"Your concern is not necessary, Doctor. In any event, I am the logical choice. Commanders Chekov and Uhura are needed aboard the *Enterprise* to assist with the Osori and our other guests, while Lieutenant Logovik is perfectly capable of manning the helm in my absence. Furthermore, as noted, I *do* have firsthand experience in dealing with Klingons."

"That's what we're worried about," McCoy grumbled.

Saavik repressed a very un-Vulcan-like flash of irritation. She appreciated that the captain and the doctor had her best interests at heart, and she could only imagine how difficult this discussion must be for Kirk, considering the tragic loss of his son. She did not envy him having to play the gracious host to a Klingon observer for the length of the voyage to Osor.

"What about you, sir?" she asked Spock. "Do you also share these worries?"

"Your abilities are not in dispute," her mentor stated, to her private relief; she would not want to think that he considered her emotionally compromised by her trials years ago. As first officer, Spock was beaming over to the Romulan ship as part of the crew exchange. "Only you can judge whether you are prepared to endure the company of Klingons for a prolonged interval."

In truth, the prospect held little appeal, but that was scarce reason to warrant special treatment in this instance. The mission was what mattered, not her personal comfort level or lack of same.

"I do not require a pleasure cruise, only an opportunity to further our goals to the best of my abilities." She gazed squarely at Kirk. "I will not disappoint you, Captain."

He smiled wryly. "That's all I needed to hear, Lieutenant."

The turbolift resumed its course, and they soon arrived at the main transporter room, where they found Chief Engineer Scott already in attendance, assisted by two transporter technicians. The procedure ahead, which involved simultaneous beam-ins and departures between three ships, was complex enough to require three operators at the transporter controls, which were located behind a clear protective screen. Scott had naturally insisted on overseeing the exchanges himself, while an honor guard of four security officers were also on hand to "greet" the new arrivals and ensure their good behavior. Saavik suspected that Chekov would have also preferred to be on hand to supervise the security arrangements, but he was presently in command of the bridge.

Kirk strode into the transporter room. "Everything in order, Mister Scott?"

"Aye, Captain. Transporter controls and coordinates are synchronized with their equivalents on those two ugly birds across from us, although I don't mind saying that took some doing, and not just because Romulans and Klingons are hardly the most agreeable souls to work with." Exasperation showed on his rotund, mustached countenance. "Between you and me, I'd rather share a pint with a Gorn than haggle with those high-handed, obdurate schemers and ruffians."

His fretful attitude would have troubled Saavik had she not become accustomed to Scott's mannerisms. The engineer typically fussed over the ship and its systems like an Arcturian eagle tending its nestlings. She felt confident that Scott and his team had matters well in hand, and had no choice but to assume that the Klingon and Romulan technicians were equally adept and prepared.

"Your forbearance is duly noted, Scotty." Kirk positioned himself near a wall intercom unit. "Are we ready to make the swap?"

Scott nodded. "As soon as we lower our shields, Captain, while hoping to heaven our friends out there lower theirs as well, instead of using us for target practice as soon as we drop our guard."

"It would be illogical for either the *Harrier* or the *Lukara* to attack at this critical juncture," Saavik pointed out. "Why would they wreck this entire operation, destroying their chance to ally themselves with the

Osori, simply to fire on a single Federation starship? The cost of such an action would far outweigh the reward."

"There is that," Scott conceded. "In for a penny, in for a pound, I suppose."

"Just so," Kirk said. "We've all come this far already, the Klingons and the Romulans included." He gestured toward the waiting transporter platform. "Spock, Saavik, please take your places."

"Gladly, Captain."

She stepped confidently onto the platform, and Spock did the same, occupying circular transporter pads at opposite ends of the platform. The plan was for them to beam to separate locations at the same time, even as a Klingon and Romulan beamed aboard the *Enterprise* from their respective ships.

"Kirk to bridge," the captain said into the wall unit. "Inform the *Harrier* and the *Lukara* that we are standing by for the exchange."

"*Acknowledged,*" Uhura replied. "*They are ready to initiate the countdown.*"

"Signal to start the timer. Chekov, lower shields at mark zero."

"*Aye, Captain. You may expect Russian-quality precision on our end.*"

Chuckling, Kirk turned toward the departing crew members. "*Bon voyage,* my friends. Enjoy your cultural exchange with our distinguished fellow travelers—and try not to start any wars. I'll see you both on Nimbus III, two weeks from now."

"Vulcans do not start wars," Spock reminded him.

"Without reason," Saavik added, by way of a witticism. Humans, she had learned, often employed humor to defuse tense situations, such as after awkward conversations.

Kirk rewarded her effort with a faint smile. "Don't forget to write."

She was mentally composing a suitable rejoinder when the staticky tingle of the transporter beam enveloped her.

Instants later, she found herself in the murky confines of the *Lukara's* transporter room, facing a most unwelcoming welcome party. A complement of armed Klingon soldiers, their expressions ranging from sullen to surly, glowered at her, looking far too indistinguishable from the Klingons who had once held her captive. A dim incarnadine glow suffused the scene, while the air seemed marginally thicker and hazier than aboard the *Enterprise*. A notable stench, redolent of Klingon, caused Saavik to regret that the Klingons had never seen the need to master olfactory cloaking. Conspicuously absent was Captain B'Eleste, who had apparently not deemed it necessary to greet either of the observers on their arrival.

Klingon hospitality leaves much to be desired so far.

A sideways glance confirmed that she was not alone on the transporter platform. As expected, a Romulan occupied a pad less than a meter away from her. A junior officer, she estimated, roughly the same age as her. He was tall, poised, and well-groomed, his hands clasped behind his back as he coolly maintained a formal posture. He met her regard with a distinctly disdainful expression. Regrettably, this came as no surprise to Saavik; despite their common ancestry, Romulans and Vulcans had been at odds for much of their recorded history, and that ancient enmity persisted to the present, something she knew too well from her harsh childhood on Hellguard, a failed Romulan mining colony. She declined to acknowledge his scorn.

"Clear the platform!" a nameless Klingon sergeant barked at them. "Submit to inspection!"

She and the Romulan stepped down from the platform and were immediately subjected to a scan by two more Klingons, wielding sensor wands.

"We are unarmed," Saavik informed them, "as stipulated."

Nor had she brought along a tricorder or communicator as an agreed-upon precaution against espionage; there was to be no covert scanning of vital systems or technology while they were aboard. Only a few personal effects and changes of clothing had been allowed; a travel case carrying these items was to be separately beamed over to the *Lukara* via the cargo transporters. She expected to be reunited with her luggage after it had been thoroughly inspected by the Klingons. Accordingly, she had packed nothing of a classified or confidential nature.

"So you say!" the sergeant snarled. "Security demands we see for ourselves!"

Their word alone deemed insufficient, she and the Romulan were both scanned and patted down for weapons or contraband. The

Romulan endured the process with only a sour expression indicating his displeasure. "By all means, take your time," he said archly, a patrician tone indicating aristocratic roots. "I wouldn't want to rush you."

"Clean!" an inspector finally pronounced them, stepping back from the visitors.

The Romulan sniffed the air, wrinkling his nose. "Would that I could say the same." He yawned theatrically, covering his mouth as he did so. "Are we done yet?"

"No!" the sergeant growled. "Medical! Confirm these aliens are free of disease!"

"Of course. That's why I'm here."

A middle-aged Klingon stepped forward, bearing what Saavik assumed to be a medical tricorder of Klingon design. Short and bald, with bushy gray eyebrows, he wore a leathery gray lab coat over his military uniform. His bearing and body language struck Saavik as less ostentatiously aggressive than the other warriors, perhaps because he was a healer as well. She wasn't sure she'd ever met a Klingon doctor or medic before.

"Is this necessary?" she asked. "Our transporters' biofilters are programmed to detect and eliminate any infectious agents, and I assume your own transporters are similarly equipped."

"Just a formality," the doctor said, his voice deeper than even the average Klingon's. Age had furrowed his brow, making his ridges stand out even more prominently. "Unless you'd rather remain in quarantine for the duration of your stay aboard our ship?"

"That would not be my preference," Saavik admitted. "Please proceed, Doctor."

"Kesh, son of Khull," he said as he scanned her with the tricorder, which emitted a grating buzz in place of the subdued hum of a Starfleet model. "Chief medical officer."

She appreciated his attempt at hospitality. "Lieutenant Saavik."

"Ah, yes, the half blood," the Romulan said. "Who takes refuge among humans no less."

Clearly, her reputation preceded her. She did not find this remarkable; Romulan intelligence was nothing if not thorough. It stood to reason that they would have compiled dossiers on the *Enterprise*'s bridge crew prior to this mission. Her intimate involvement in the Genesis crisis might have also placed her on their sensors.

"Half blood?" Kesh raised a shaggy eyebrow.

"I am half Romulan, although raised as a Vulcan." She turned toward the Romulan. "And you are?"

"Subcommander Taleb." He lifted his chin as though he was accustomed to his name conveying privilege. Having deigned to answer her query, he now addressed Kesh instead of her. "Why is your captain not here to welcome us?"

Kesh concluded his scan of Saavik and moved on to Taleb.

"Captain B'Eleste is not one for socializing while on duty. She remains on the bridge to monitor our communications with the Osori." He lowered the tricorder as he finished scanning the Romulan. "No bacteria, viruses, or biotoxins detected. You're both cleared to board, although we must schedule a visit to the medbay in the immediate future so I can conduct a more thorough health examination, per protocol."

Taleb scoffed. "So you can study our weaknesses for military gain?"

"That's hardly necessary," Kesh said. "Generations of conflict have provided us with no shortage of enemy combatants to examine, living and dead. There is little about Romulan, Vulcan, or human physiology that we don't already know." He eyed Saavik quizzically. "Although I confess I've never had the opportunity to examine a Romulan-Vulcan hybrid. Simply as a matter of scientific curiosity."

"Indeed," Saavik said diplomatically.

With the inspections complete, she expected that they would be escorted to the bridge or perhaps shown their temporary quarters aboard the *Lukara*. Instead they were kept under guard in the transporter room while the bird-of-prey went into orbit around Osor after receiving word from the Osori that the exchange had been completed to their satisfaction and they were ready to dispatch their envoys to all three orbiting vessels. Captain B'Eleste finally made an appearance in the transporter room, indicating that the arrival of the Osori envoy ranked higher in the captain's priorities than greeting her earlier visitors.

"It would seem the Osori is the guest of honor," Saavik commented.

"And this surprises you?" Taleb mocked her. "We are inconveniences, tolerated only out of necessity."

"Merely an observation, nothing more."

"A blindingly obvious one if you ask me."

"Then it is good that I did not. Ask you, that is."

Saavik was starting to think that keeping company with a shipload of Klingons was going to be preferable to spending time with this insufferably arrogant Romulan.

"Prepare to receive the envoy." B'Eleste ignored both Saavik and Taleb as she focused on the task at hand. Seen in person, the Klingon captain was even more imposing than she'd appeared on the viewscreen, at least a head taller than Saavik. She flaunted her authority by brandishing an abbreviated painstik as a baton or swagger stick. "Without delay."

The sergeant consulted the transporter controls. "The Osori have not lowered their planetary defenses, Captain."

"I suspect that will not be necessary," Saavik said, recalling Spock's discovery that the Osori energy shell was only a one-way barrier. Her predication earned her an appraising glance from B'Eleste and was vindicated as, within moments, the Osori took control of the Klingon transporter control remotely. A shimmering column of scarlet energy manifested upon the transporter, then coalesced back into matter.

"Sorry to keep you waiting," the Osori said. "My elders can be quite fussy sometimes."

The figure on the pad bore some resemblance to the Osori as depicted in ancient Arretian pictographs and illuminated manuscripts. She appeared reptilian or possibly amphibian in nature, her face, arms, and legs covered by scintillating orange scales that gleamed even in the subdued, ruddy lighting of the Klingon ship. She was triocular, with one spherical, amphibian-like orb nestled in her forehead and one each at her temples. She was slight and slender, appearing almost childish in contrast to the looming Klingons. Her attire consisted of a metallic mesh poncho, slippers, and elbow-length gloves that seemed to glisten like liquid mercury. A lilting soprano voice had a musical quality to it.

"You may call me Cyloo."

"Welcome to the Klingon *Bird-of-Prey Lukara*. I am B'Eleste, daughter of Glukra. Captain of this vessel."

Gruffly delivered, the greeting seemed positively effusive for the Klingon leader. Or so Saavik thought.

"And such a ship!" Cyloo glanced around excitedly, as though even three eyes were not enough to take it all in. "I can't wait to explore every corner of it!"

Despite the Osori's reputed immortality, she practically radiated youthful high spirits and curiosity. Saavik wondered how old she actually was.

Cyloo's central eye lighted on Taleb and Saavik. Her face lit up even more than it already had. "And you must be my fellow passengers!"

Saavik found "passengers" more appealing than "hostages." She came forward to greet the Osori, being careful not to appear to intrude too much on Captain B'Eleste's moment.

"I am Lieutenant Saavik of the *Starship Enterprise*, on behalf of the United Federation of Planets."

"And I am Subcommander Taleb of the Romulan Star Empire." He smiled and bowed at the waist, displaying more charm than Saavik would have thought him capable of. "It is a privilege to make your acquaintance, Madame Envoy."

"Cyloo, please!" she insisted. "I'm sure we are all going to be the best of friends!"

Saavik feared her expectations were overly optimistic.

Chapter Seven

"Thanks for meeting with me, Detective Fulton."

"Retired detective, Ms. Silver, and I have to say you were pretty damn persistent. Could tell right away that you weren't going to take no for an answer."

It was a gorgeous fall day in Golden Gate Park. Bill Fulton, formerly of the San Francisco Police Department, sat across from her at a picnic table offering a view of a grassy green meadow beside beautifully culti-vated trees and gardens. Dennis hovered nearby, listening attentively as he monitored the sound levels, while avoiding eye contact with Fulton. Cops made him nervous.

"I'll take that as a compliment." Melinda waited for Dennis to give her a go-ahead signal before launching into the interview proper. The recorder rested on the table between her and Fulton. "You were the officer in charge of the initial investigation into Gillian Taylor's disappearance?"

"That's correct. Spring of '86." Fulton was a stocky black man in his sixties or seventies, with just a fringe of snowy-white hair frosting the back of his head. Unlike Bob Briggs, he was dressed casually, in a neatly pressed polo shirt and khakis. He fished a small spiral notepad from a battered file folder he'd brought with him and consulted the notes to refresh his memory. "Initial report was filed by her coworkers a few days after her last known appearance."

"At the Cetacean Institute in Sausalito?"

"Correct. A wellness check on her apartment found no signs of struggle, nor any evidence of a hasty departure. Her suitcases were still in the closet. No clothing or personal effects appeared missing. There were dirty dishes in the sink, leftovers in the fridge, clothes in the dryer, and an upcoming dentist appointment jotted down on a calen-dar. We even found her passport tucked away in a drawer." He looked up from the pad. "On the bright side, there was no indication that she had harmed herself or intended to."

"No suicide note?" Melinda prompted.

"And no body," he said bluntly. "Judging from the state of the dirty dishes, she hadn't been home for a few days. Mind you, she was a grown woman, so there was no real reason to be alarmed at first; it was entirely possible that she was simply staying with someone while blowing off work. We found her address book and worked our way through it, calling every listed contact and acquaintance, but . . . no luck. Nobody had heard from her since Tuesday, May 6, when she stormed away from the institute after her whales were let loose."

Melinda's ears perked up. "I don't suppose you still have that address book?"

"Afraid not. That was a long time ago. It's probably gathering dust in a police warehouse by now, if it wasn't chucked out altogether sometime in the last thirty-eight years."

"Figured it couldn't hurt to ask." Melinda made a mental note to possibly try to get her hands on that address book down the road, in hopes of getting in touch with any surviving members of Gillian's social circle. "So, you checked out her apartment and . . . ?"

"No real leads, until her vehicle turned up abandoned." He swiveled to point out a nearby drive running past the field. "Right over there."

Melinda scoped it out, visualizing a 1976 light-blue Chevy pickup sitting empty along the side of the road. "Tell me about that."

"Not much to tell. An apparently abandoned vehicle got called in, somebody ran the plates and matched it to our missing-persons case. Again, no signs of violence; the door was unlocked and her purse was found under a seat, undisturbed. We found a few prints that didn't match up to Gillian's, but none of them were on file. There were no matches to any known perpetrators." He looked away from the road. "You have to remember, young lady, it's not as though we had computerized databases back then; it wasn't as easy to do a nationwide search on fingerprints like they can do these days. Then again, even today there are still plenty of individuals whose prints aren't on file with law enforcement. It's possible that we couldn't have made a match in '86, even with today's integrated computer searches."

"But there was somebody in the truck with her at some point."

"A couple of somebodies, but that's no proof of foul play. She could have just picked up a couple of hitchhikers at some point or given some friends a lift."

Melinda's spirits sagged. So far this interview was turning out to be something of a bust. Sure, she could probably get some mileage out of the way Gillian's apartment seemed to have been abandoned so abruptly, but that wasn't enough of a twist to power an entire episode. Fulton was mostly just telling her what she already knew, while, at most, the discovery of the truck just hinted at a depressingly bleak conclusion to Gillian's story. She hoped to God that Gillian hadn't just fallen victim to some random mugging or assault in the park. That would be anticlimactic as well as tragic.

No body, she reminded herself. *Let's not automatically assume the worst.*

"Nothing overtly suspicious? No smoking gun?"

"Nope, for better or for worse. Always mixed feelings there; you never *want* to find evidence of a violent crime, but you do need clues to get to the bottom of a case." He paused to collect his thoughts. "There was one odd thing, though, that never made it into the press or the official reports, mostly because nobody knew what, if anything, it meant."

He eyed the recorder between them. "Can we step away from the table, just for a few yards?"

Melinda looked at Dennis, who scrutinized their mics' wireless connections. "Not too far," he cautioned. "Don't want to strain the transmission."

"Not far at all," Fulton promised. "Just want to show you something."

He got up from the bench and led them over to an empty stretch of grass some yards away from where Gillian's pickup had been found decades ago. He squinted at the lawn, as though comparing it against an old memory.

"Right here," he said. "There was this deep depression in the lawn, like something extremely large and heavy had been sitting there, pressing down so hard that it left this big dent in the field, at least four to six inches deep. And get this, there was a flattened metal trash can lying in the middle of the depression, and when I say flattened, I mean *flattened* . . . like a pancake. As though it had been crushed beneath a hydraulic press."

Melinda didn't get where he was going with this. "What are you saying, that there was another vehicle parked here around the time Gillian vanished? Like a van or mobile home?"

"More like a jumbo-sized tank, except there were no tracks or tread marks leading to or from the depression, just this big sunken spot in the ground." He swept his gaze over the now-level green swath. "Looks like the grounds have been restored since then, no surprise."

"A helicopter?" Melinda speculated. "Going straight up and down?"

"Doubt it. I've seen police copters set down in all sorts of locations. Never seen one leave a footprint like that. If it was a copter, it was bigger and heavier than any I've ever run across."

"Some kind of stealth aircraft?" Dennis blurted, overcoming his usual reticence around strangers. "Landing long enough to abduct Gillian and carry her up into the sky?"

That was *an* explanation, Melinda supposed, although it raised more questions than it answered. How would the pilot and passengers know where Gillian was? Did they track her to the park? And why the heck would anybody want to abduct her by air anyway? Unless she flew off with them voluntarily, leaving her life behind?

Watch it, she warned herself. *You're starting to think like Dennis.*

"I don't know. That seems like a stretch, no offense." She got back to questioning Fulton. "So, if not a copter, what *do* you think left that impression?"

"Hell if I know. Assuming it had to anything to do with our missing woman at all."

Melinda added this bewildering new tidbit of information to her mental case file. Perhaps an aeronautics expert could shed some light on this latest puzzle, or would that be just an extraneous detour at this point, given the somewhat circumstantial connection to Gillian's disappearance? A few red herrings and false trails could add some twists to a narrative, but she didn't want *Cetacean* to wander too far down what was likely a blind alley for fearing of losing focus and testing her audience's patience. This early on in the investigation it was hard to tell what was truly relevant.

Something to consider, though.

At Dennis's insistence, they returned to the picnic table to avoid any sound-quality issues. "Moving on," she continued, "where did your investigation go after you found the truck? Any suspects? Person of interests?"

"No actual names surfaced, although we had a few vague leads that looked, if not promising, at least like they *might* be promising."

"Such as?" she asked, praying for something juicy.

"You heard about the kook who went for a swim with Gillian's whales the day before she went AWOL? Much to her distress, reportedly."

"No!" This was news to her; she shot a look at Dennis to make sure they were getting this. "What happened?"

Fulton grinned, pleased by her reaction. He clearly enjoyed having surprised her.

"Seems there was a disturbance at the institute that day. Gillian was conducting a tour when one of the visitors decided to take a dip with the whales in that big outdoor tank of theirs." He flipped through his notepad. "According to an eyewitness who came forward after Gillian's disappearance hit the news, she was quite upset about what happened."

"I'll bet, given how protective she was of George and Gracie."

Melinda wondered why Briggs hadn't mentioned this to her. Perhaps his big blow-up with Gillian the next day, which was the last time he saw her, had eclipsed that previous incident in his memory. She resolved to send Briggs a follow-up query about it.

"You talk to the guy who jumped into the tank, after Gillian went missing?"

Fulton shook his head. "We never ID'd him. From the description, he sounded like some hippy-dippy freak, wearing a white bathrobe and headband. Maybe a cult member of some kind? Apparently no harm was done, however, except possibly to Gillian's state of mind, and no charges were pressed at the time. The soggy perp was shown the door and, as far as we know, never returned. No way of knowing whether this incident had anything to do with Gillian vanishing the following day. Could be he was just a flake or pothead wanting to 'commune' with the whales."

"The timing is provocative, though," Melinda observed. "You said something about an eyewitness?"

"Just one. A nun, believe it or not." He double-checked his notes. "Sister Mary Michelle, of the Sisters of Saint Francis in Monterey."

Interesting, Melinda thought. *Here's hoping she's still around and hasn't taken a vow of silence or whatever.*

"Anything else?"

He nodded. "A waiter at a local pizza place wasn't one hundred percent sure, but thought he remembered serving Gillian the night before she disappeared. She was a regular, of sorts, so he recognized her photo when it showed up on the nightly news. He said she was having dinner with some guy, but they left abruptly at one point, taking their pizzas with them. He got the impression that something urgent had come up."

"Like what?"

"No idea. Just our luck, he wasn't a particularly nosy waiter. Hadn't really been eavesdropping on them."

Melinda took a moment to place this hitherto-unknown pizza date in the timeline, predisappearance. This would have been after the nameless "flake" took an unauthorized swim with George and Gracie, and the evening before Gillian discovered that her whales were gone and she fought with Briggs. So whatever had happened that night had not kept her from showing up at work the next morning to say good-bye to the whales.

"Who was the guy she was having dinner with?" A crazy notion crossed her mind. "*Not* the same dude who jumped into the tank, I presume?"

"Nah. Completely different description." Fulton's meticulous notes proved their worth again. "According to the waiter, Gillian's date was a, quote, 'good-looking' Caucasian male, roughly forty to fifty years in age, with short, curly brown hair and wearing a red, possibly maroon, jacket." Fulton looked at her. "No white robe or headband."

The description of Gillian's dinner date didn't ring any bells with Melinda, based on their preliminary survey of Gillian's social circle. He certainly didn't sound like Briggs, who would have surely mentioned going out to dinner with Gillian the night before he last saw her. What's more, he would have been busy orchestrating the whales' after-hours relocation that night.

"Since you haven't volunteered a name yet, I'm guessing you never ID'd Gillian's mystery date either?"

"Correct. He never came forward after the story hit the news. Mind you, that could just mean he didn't want to be involved, or was married and didn't want his missus to know he was stepping out on her, or that he left town before she went missing and never found out about it, or any number of other explanations for not contacting us." He let out a weary sigh. "You'd be surprised how many people simply don't want to talk to the police."

Imagine that, Melinda thought. "So, another dead end?"

"Pretty much." A sly smile lifted his lips. "But would you possibly be interested in seeing an artist's sketch of Gillian's dinner companion?"

"Are you kidding? Hand it over, you big tease!"

Grinning a bit like Santa Claus pulling a surprise gift from his bag, Fulton fished the item from his file folder. Protected by a clear plastic sleeve, the Xeroxed sketch depicted a handsome, clean-shaven guy who certainly looked dateable enough. The anonymous sketch artist had captured a certain wry intelligence and charm in the man's eyes and expression. He didn't look like a potential kidnapper or serial killer, but who could tell really? Then again, Gillian had shown up at the institute the next morning, alive and well, expecting to say goodbye to her whales, so maybe the date was just a date?

"How come I've never seen this sketch before, in any of the news reports or SFPD press releases at the time? Wouldn't you have wanted to make this public to see if anybody recognized him?"

Fulton's smiled faded. He squirmed uncomfortably on the picnic bench.

"Well, the thing is, we had nothing on him besides the fact that he'd gone out for pizza with Gillian. Not really enough to suggest that he might have something to do with her disappearance. Not to the press, at least."

Melinda didn't buy it. "Then why bother having a sketch done? This guy was hanging out with Gillian the night before she vanished. He might be the only person to know where her head was at that evening, or where she went to after she lost her whales. And you didn't go all out to find him?"

"I wanted to, but—" He caught himself before finishing the sentence.

"But what? What aren't you telling me?"

A guilty vibe radiated from the ex-cop. Sensing that he wanted to tell her, she pressed harder. "Why are we even talking if you're going to hold out on me?"

He gestured at the recorder. "Off the record."

"I need audio for the show," she protested. "The whole idea is to—"

"Off the record." He unclipped his lapel mic.

She weighed her options. She hated the idea of not getting any new revelations on audio, but whatever Fulton wanted to tell her might point her in the right direction down the road. She nodded at Dennis, who grudgingly switched off the recorder. He lingered beside her, looking just as curious as she was to find out what Fulton had to say that was so hush-hush, although Dennis seemed more than a little apprehensive as well. Melinda hoped this wasn't triggering his paranoia, but she'd deal with that later if she had to, after she got the scoop from Fulton.

"Okay." She took off her own mic as a gesture of good faith. "Shoot."

Fulton took a deep breath. "Truth is, we were ordered to drop the case. Word came down from the Feds that we were to stop investigating Gillian's disappearance—in the interests of national security."

Melinda's jaw dropped. She hadn't seen that coming at all.

"What the heck?" She'd trained herself to avoid profanity to avoid dropping an F-bomb on audio. "I don't get it. What's a missing marine biologist have to do with national security?"

"You tell me," Fulton said. "Trust me, I wasn't happy about it, raised a real fuss with my superiors, but it was no use. Folks way above my pay grade made that call and I had to live with it." He nodded at the drawing of the Pizza Date guy. "Which is why we never went public with that sketch. The Powers That Be wanted the whole investigation shut down, period."

"Oh crap." Dennis went pale. Predictably, he looked more alarmed than intrigued by this bombshell. "That's not good."

Melinda felt exactly the opposite.

"So why are you telling me this now?" she asked Fulton.

"Guilty conscience, I suppose. I never felt good about how that all went down back then. Probably why I held on to this file all these years, even after I retired from the force." He took a deep breath and released it. "Feels good to finally get it off my chest."

"Even off the record?"

He nodded. "You'll forgive me for not wanting to endanger my pension . . . or worse."

"Worse?" Dennis's voice went up an octave. "What do you mean by that?"

She shushed him. "Later," she promised before turning back to Fulton. "I appreciate you trusting us with this."

"Not sure I'm doing you a favor, to be honest." He eyed her soberly, coming off as slightly guilty once more. "Look, you two seem like nice young people. Maybe you'd be better off leaving this alone?"

"No way." If anything, she was more excited than ever about digging deeper into the case. "Sounds to me like we're on to something big."

"That's what I'm afraid of," Dennis said.

Chapter Eight

2268

Captain's Log, Stardate 4730.2: *Upon arriving at the spacejacker's last known coordinates, Spock was able to detect, with difficulty, the faint remains of an ion trail leading from the escape pod's drop-off point to the planet Atraz. As that world remains off-limits to the Federation and Starfleet, the* Enterprise *is maintaining a discreet distance from the planet rather than entering a standard orbit around it. Leaving Spock in command of the ship, I am leading a search party to Atraz via a shuttle-craft since the* Enterprise *is not within transporter range of planet, and also in the hope that a single shuttle will be somewhat less conspicuous than parking a* Constitution-*class starship above this forbidden world . . .*

They found the pod abandoned in a gully in a grassy savanna in the planet's southern hemisphere, just where *Galileo's* sensors had indicated. Locating the pod had required considerable time and effort, conducting sensor sweeps of the planet in search of certain advanced alloys and energy cells that were unlikely to be found anywhere else on Atraz, given the planet's current level of technology. Sulu had brought *Galileo* down in the same broad gully, which was hidden from view by the gently sloping rises defining it. Kirk had wasted no time exiting the shuttle once they confirmed that the environment was indeed hospitable to human life. It felt good to stretch his legs after having been confined to the shuttle for hours, and to make some progress in their search for Doctor Hamparian.

"Looks like they made a safe landing at least," McCoy said, emerging from the interior of the pod. The emergency escape vehicle, which was roughly the size of an industrial cargo container, rested atop its landing gear, which was fully deployed. Its impulse and altitude thrusters were cold to the touch. "No bodies, no blood, no smoke or ash or charred seating, nor any other evidence of casualties, thank goodness."

The doctor had insisted on joining the landing party, leaving his sickbay in the able hands of Doctor M'Benga and Nurse Chapel, in case Hamparian required medical attention beyond Atraz's capabilities. Besides Kirk and McCoy, the party also included Sulu, Martha Landon, and two additional security officers, Lieutenant Peter Levine and Ensign Shirin Akbari, who were currently on watch for any locals, hostile or otherwise.

"No obvious damage to the pod either." Sulu circled the pod, scanning its exterior with a tricorder. "Its fuel cells are pretty much exhausted, and there's some scorch marks on the casing from its entry into the atmosphere." He took a deep breath of the latter. "Which seems nice and fresh to me. There are definitely worse places they could've ended up."

"Probably not an accident," Kirk guessed. McCoy had already confirmed that they wouldn't need tri-ox or any other specialized medications to cope with conditions on the planet. That the pod had landed in a temperate zone, as opposed to any barren deserts, polar wastes, or far out to sea, was also almost certainly by design; Fortier had known exactly where he was going, both in the sector and on the planet. What remained unclear was why he'd gone to such lengths to reach Atraz, and whether Hamparian had simply been taken hostage to cover his escape as he had claimed or if he'd had some ulterior motive for abducting her specifically.

"So we know they made it to Atraz in one piece." Kirk paced restlessly around the landing site. Because Starfleet's records were fairly skimpy, inconsistent, and most likely out of date regarding clothing styles across the planet, with its varied cultures and climates, Kirk had opted for the search party to wear their usual duty uniforms down to Atraz, minus any identifying Starfleet insignia or stripes. With luck, a basic tunic, trousers, boots, or, in Landon's and Akbari's cases, skirts, would not attract too much attention—or at least not brand them as visitors from another world. Type-1 phasers had been issued because they were less noticeable than type-2 sidearms. "But where did they go from here?"

It was late afternoon, local time, with the sun sinking rather disorientingly toward the east; Kirk made a mental note not to let the planet's reversed rotation, compared to Earth, confuse his sense of direction. By their calculations, it was early summer in this hemisphere, the weather comfortably warm but not too humid or oppressive. A light breeze rustled the tawny, knee-high grasses carpeting the slopes and floor of the gully. There was little in the way of wildlife visible, but Kirk kept on the lookout for any lurking predators, parasites, or aggressive plant life. The last thing they needed was to be taken unawares by a venomous insect, serpent, or creeping vine.

Scanning for Hamparian had not been an option. Even with her being one-quarter Andorian, the Atrazians were too close to baseline humanoid biology for the scanners to pick her out from the planet's native population. Had that also factored into Fortier's choice of destination, the better for him to blend in with the locals?

"The nearest large population center is approximately sixty kilometers northwest of here," Landon reported, consulting her own tricorder, "according to the surveys we conducted while orbiting the planet, which more or less matches up with the data from the old unmanned probes. There are also some smaller communities and agricultural regions between here and the city." She looked up from the tricorder's display. "Possibly they headed for the closest thing to civilization in the vicinity?"

"Could be," Kirk said. "I only wish we had a better idea of what Fortier's actual motive is. It would be easier to predict his movements if we had some clue as to what he's up to in the long run."

"Isn't that the truth." McCoy slung his medical tricorder back over his shoulder. "Do you think he abandoned Hamparian once he made it to Atraz, or is he still forcing her to accompany him? I'm honestly not sure which scenario might be better for her, being deserted on a strange planet or remaining the hostage of a ruthless fugitive?"

"I'd take the former any day," Landon said. "Rather take my own chances than be anyone's prisoner."

Kirk was inclined to agree with her.

"Captain!" Levine called out from farther down the gully. "We found something!"

Kirk hurried over to join Levine, accompanied by McCoy and the rest of the landing party. "What is it?"

"Take a look, sir."

A trim, dark-haired young man with a muscular build, Levine pointed down at a shaded stretch of soil before him, where Kirk saw what appeared to be parallel ruts, possibly made by wagon wheels, as well as paired sets of hoofprints leading out of the gully. The tracks looked relatively fresh; Kirk thanked providence that apparently it hadn't rained recently.

"Good eye," he praised Levine. "Seems as though our quarry caught a ride upon arrival, from a confederate waiting for Fortier . . . and his hostage?"

"But to where?" Landon asked. "That city I spoke of?"

"I wonder," Kirk said.

He scrambled up the northern (southern?) slope to check out the lay of the land. Above and beyond the gully, great swaths of grasslands, broken up by sporadic trees and scrub, stretched out in all directions. Rolling hills obscured the horizon, hiding the distant city. No other habitations presented themselves; wherever the wagon bearing Fortier and Hamparian had been heading, it was nowhere in sight.

The rest of the party followed him onto the rise. Landon handed Kirk a pair of compact Starfleet binoculars before he could even ask for them. "Thank you, Yeoman."

"Nice view." McCoy shaded his eyes with his hand as he scoped out the sprawling savanna. "How far away is that city again?"

"A substantial march." Kirk glanced back at *Galileo* resting within the gully. "Perhaps we can fly in closer to the city, under the cover of dark?"

At least they wouldn't have to worry about being exposed by moonlight.

"That could be tricky, sir," Landon said. "The nearer we get to the city, the more populated the surrounding farmlands and hamlets."

"And thus the greater chance of *Galileo* being spotted by the locals," Kirk inferred, "and fewer places to land undetected."

"And to hide the shuttlecraft once we've touched down," Sulu added. "As I understand it, this planet doesn't have flying machines yet."

"All very good, if inconvenient, concerns," Kirk said with a sigh; times like this, he envied the Romulans their cloaking devices. "Too bad there's no welcome wagon waiting to give us a lift."

"Don't tell me we're going to have to hike all the way to this so-called city," McCoy groused, glumly contemplating the vast spread before them. "Never thought I'd hear myself say this, but I'm missing the *Enterprise*'s transporters all of a sudden."

"You and me both, Bones."

Kirk weighed the pros and cons of contacting the *Enterprise* via *Galileo*'s long-range communications array and bringing the ship close enough to Atraz to make its transporters available to them, even if that meant trespassing on the Prime Directive even more than they were already doing. Using the binoculars, he surveyed the landscape as he considered their options. The terrain didn't appear too difficult or dangerous to traverse, the distance daunting but doable. If they left immediately, leaving Akbari behind to guard *Galileo*, they could conceivably make it to the city in a day or two.

And then what? Ask around to see if any other obvious foreigners had arrived in the city lately? Hope that Fortier felt safe enough on Atraz, far from the Federation's jurisdiction, that he wasn't lying low?

A cloud of dust off to the east (west?) caught Kirk's eye. Increasing the magnification on the binoculars, he discerned a caravan of some sort making its way across the savanna—in the direction of the nameless city. He made out a string of wagons drawn by Atrazian livestock as well as mounted guards or escorts riding similar if slenderer animals. *If we hustle,* Kirk realized, *we can intercept the caravan before it passes us by.*

"Never mind any transporters, Bones. I believe we may have a more homegrown alternative."

He passed the binoculars over to McCoy, while alerting the rest of the party to the approach of the caravan. With no time to lose, he made his decision.

"Everyone except Akbari, secure your gear and get ready to head out, pronto. Let me do the talking and remember the Prime Directive: volunteer as little information as possible about our origins, and avoid using your phasers and communicators in view of the Atrazians." He turned toward Akbari, a young Iranian officer who had recently transferred over from the *Yorktown*. "Ensign, stay with *Galileo* and await further instructions. We'll check in regularly, but if the shuttlecraft is in danger of discovery or worse, lift off and find a more secure location to wait for us. Keep in touch with the *Enterprise*, and if you haven't heard from any of us in twelve hours, inform Commander Spock and do whatever he deems best."

"Aye, Captain," she replied. She was a stocky young woman with a good track record as a security officer. She'd proven herself reliably cool and level-headed on past missions. "I just wish I was going with you and the others."

"Somebody has to look after our ride." Kirk kept one eye on the approaching cloud of dust, which was now visible to the naked eye if you knew where to look. "We wouldn't want to leave it unattended."

"Understood, sir, and good luck. *Galileo* will be waiting for you, count on me."

"I expect nothing less, Ensign."

Kirk turned toward the caravan, tucking his phaser and communicator beneath the hem of his mustard-colored tunic. The planet's Earth-normal gravity worked in their favor here; it would not slow them down unduly.

McCoy sidled up to him, characteristically worried. "You sure about this, Jim?"

"You'd rather walk all the way to the nearest population center?"

"Well, when you put it that way."

A brisk trot through the tall grass, which left Kirk grateful for his regular workouts in the ship's gymnasium, brought them to a well-traveled dirt road across the savanna. They arrived just in time to see the caravan coming toward them, led by three riders mounted on hooved beasts that resembled a cross between a moose, a goat, and a pachyderm. Their general shape and build suggested an ungulate akin to an elk or wapiti, but instead of antlers they sported curved, ram-like horns, while their snout extended into a flexible trunk like an elephant's or a Denevan coral rooter's. Looking past the lead riders, Kirk saw that the caravan's tented wagons were drawn by comparable ungulates, albeit somewhat larger and more ponderous. Draft animals rather than steeds, he assumed, but of the same basic breed.

In contrast to the chimerical nature of their livestock, the Atrazians themselves confirmed Starfleet's assessment that they, like so many

other humanoids throughout the galaxy, were largely indistinguishable from *Homo sapiens* of terrestrial descent, lacking even the telltale
tapered ears of Vulcans and Romulans or the porcine attributes of
Tellarites. Kirk hoped that would smooth relations during the landing
party's stay on the planet, since they could hardly avoid *any* interaction
with the Atrazians while searching for Doctor Hamparian. The Prime
Directive required only that they refrain from interfering in Atrazian
affairs and that they make every effort not to reveal that they were
from other worlds, or at least that was how Kirk interpreted it in this
context. He'd always thought of the Prime Directive as a crucial moral
compass, not a cage.

Time to introduce ourselves, he thought. *Here's hoping it goes well.*

As ever, and despite the pressing demands of this particular mission, he felt the same thrill he always felt when encountering a new
sentient species for the first time. Such meetings were often fraught
with danger, but always held great potential as well. Indeed, seeking
out new life and new civilizations was what Starfleet was all about.

"Hang back, stay alert," he instructed the others, "but make no sudden, aggressive moves. We don't know how these travelers will react
to strangers on the road, so follow my lead and keep your hands away
from your phasers."

That last command was hopefully superfluous since none of the others, right down to Landon and Levine, were known for being trigger-
happy, but Kirk wasn't taking any chances. He'd seen first contacts go
south because of a single rash or unguarded reaction, like that time on
Capella IV when the late Lieutenant Grant took a razor-sharp *kleegat*
to the chest because he reached instinctively for his phaser at the first
sign of trouble. Kirk didn't want a replay of that tragedy.

"Give them the famous Jim Kirk charm," McCoy quipped. "Hardly
the first time our hides may depend on it."

Sulu chuckled. "Wouldn't have it any other way."

"Thank you, gentlemen. I'll try not to disappoint."

Holding out open palms to show he was unarmed, Kirk stepped
out in front of the procession while the rest of the party lingered at the
edge of the road. He placed himself directly in the path of the lead riders, who were now only a few meters away and proceeding at a steady,

measured pace well suited to a long ride, which meant that he was in no immediate danger of being trampled by galloping ungulates stampeding down the road.

For the moment at least.

"Hello there!" he called out, relying on a smile, a friendly tone, and his communicator's built-in universal translator to convey his peaceful intentions. "Excuse me."

A pair of wooden crossbows immediately targeted him.

The weapons belonged to the two riders flanking the central rider, whom Kirk judged to be the leader. Like the other Atrazians, she wore loose, comfortable linen garments of mixed colors, but also boasted various adornments suggesting an elevated status, most notably a hooded cloak festooned with a brilliantly hued feather collar, as well as a vest and boots seemingly made from the scaly hide of a large reptile, of a sort Kirk had yet to encounter in the windswept savanna. A luxury item from distant parts?

"Out of our way," she said, the translator failing to entirely compensate for some exotic regional accent. Freckles adorned golden skin, slightly creased with age. A scowl marred her handsome features. "At once."

Kirk pushed his luck, fully aware of the potentially lethal weapons aimed at him. He flashed what he hoped was a winning smile.

"Please forgive me for interrupting your journey, but my companions and I"—he indicated McCoy and the others, who smiled and waved in an attempt to look harmless—"find ourselves sorely in need of assistance."

One of the leader's escorts, brandishing a surly expression along with his crossbow, muttered sourly to the cloaked woman. A bristling red beard failed to conceal his displeasure. "What do you say, Pujal? Shall I shoot to wound or kill?"

Kirk wondered if "Pujal" was her name or title, while hoping that McCoy's services would not be necessary.

"There's no need for bloodshed," he insisted. "We mean you no harm, and would not delay you if we had any better choices."

"Stay your hand, Wutlo." The woman brought her steed to a halt and signaled her escorts to do the same. She peered down at Kirk from atop the horned ungulate, which differed from the others in that its horns were larger and more elaborately curved, while its shiny coat of cerise fur was brighter and glossier than the other beasts, whose fur was more of a russet hue. Pujal threw back her hood, exposing braided silver hair. "Who are you, and what do you seek?"

Encouraging, he thought. Better questions than a crossbow bolt or two.

"My name is Kirk. My friends and I have come a long way, searching for a stolen countrywoman, but . . . well, fortune has not been kind to us. We find ourselves adrift in unfamiliar territory and without any transportation other than our own two legs. At the risk of imposing, perhaps we can hitch a ride and accompany you to your destination?"

He stuck to the truth, mostly, in the interests of sincerity.

"We're prepared to pay our way," he added.

She arched a silvered eyebrow. "How?"

Kirk had come prepared for that question. Assuming that Federation credits would be worthless on Atraz, he'd had Scotty synthesize a quantity of once-precious gemstones to barter with; they lacked the practical utility and rarity of dilithium crystals, but would probably still be valuable on a planet that had not yet developed the technology to readily manufacture diamonds, rubies, emeralds, sapphires, and the like. Moving deliberately, keeping his hands always in sight, he retrieved a pouch affixed to his belt and poured a small handful of gems into his palm; every other member of the landing party had also been supplied with a pouch of artificial gemstones to bargain with as needed. He held the polished jewels up for Pujal's inspection, letting them catch the fading sunshine as the day edged toward twilight. A spectrum of vibrant colors—from red to purple—gleamed enticingly, or so Kirk hoped.

"Will this be sufficient to compensate you for your hospitality?"

The surly fellow, Wutlo, snorted. "What's to stop us from simply taking your treasure from you and your fellow stragglers?"

"I'd like to see you try," Kirk said, the Prime Directive precluding any demonstrations of what his phaser could do. He returned the gems to the pouch, which he placed back on his hip. "And not from behind the safety of your crossbow."

Wutlo gave him an offended look. "What do you mean by that?"

"Just that it's one thing to threaten an unarmed wayfarer. Let's see how fearsome you are, one on one, without a peaceful stranger already in your weapon's sights."

"Jim!" McCoy called anxiously from the sidelines. "What do you think you're doing?"

"Not now, Bones."

Kirk's gut told him this was no time to show weakness. Trusting his intuition, he looked Wutlo squarely in eyes, knowing that he was liable to get perforated if he'd misjudged this situation. Displaying the gems had been a calculated risk.

"Well?" he challenged Wutlo in front of the other riders. "Prove to me you're not just a bandit who hides behind his weapon."

Wutlo's bewhiskered face flushed with anger. He looked to his leader. "Pujal?"

She shrugged, as though she had no strong opinion either way. "As the stranger said, you are welcome to try him."

Not kill me on the spot, Kirk noted. He recalled Khan Noonien Singh's observation, at a notably tense formal dinner a couple years back, regarding the tactical advantages of letting one's lieutenant confront a possible adversary while you sit back and observe, gauging their strengths and weaknesses. Was Pujal employing a similar strategy here?

"Very well," Wutlo growled, possibly feeling put on the spot by Kirk's challenge. "Allow me to clear this impudent roadblock from our path."

Lowering his crossbow, he hung it from his saddle, dismounted, and stalked belligerently toward Kirk, his fists clenched and ready. No longer astride his ungulate, he proved to be both taller and heavier than Kirk. A crooked nose and a few missing teeth hinted that he'd been in his fair share of brawls. Maybe even won more than a few to earn his place at the front of the procession, flanking Pujal.

"Last chance, vagrant. Hand over your treasure, to pay for wasting our time, and maybe you and your pathetic companions can crawl away with your spines intact. If you actually possess any backbone, that is."

"Captain," Sulu asked, "do you require assistance?"

"Stand down," Kirk replied for Landon and Levine's benefit as well.

Given his training and duty as a security officer, Levine was surely primed to come to his captain's defense. "This is between me and Mister Wutlo here."

For better or for worse.

He risked a quick glance at Pujal, long enough to see that she was indeed studying the scene, her intent expression betraying only concentration and curiosity. Kirk admired her poker face; he couldn't even tell whom she was rooting for in this encounter.

"My spine, and my treasure, are staying right where they are." Kirk raised his voice, playing to the audience as well as his opponent. He adopted a defensive stance, raising his hands to attack or defend while adjusting his footing to more evenly distribute his weight. "I'm willing to pay a fair price, but if you'd rather roughhouse instead . . . well, what was that you were saying about wasting time?"

Wutlo responded with a roar, charging at Kirk like an enraged bull or ungulate. The captain greeted the attack with a textbook hip throw: turning Wutlo's momentum against him by grabbing onto him with both hands and rotating at the waist so that Kirk could steer Wutlo across his hip and onto the ground, where Wutlo landed hard on his back. Kirk sprang forward, aiming to quickly end the fight with a well-placed karate chop; he wasn't entirely sure what constituted fair play here, if there were any rules at all, but he wanted to avoid any move that might be construed as underhanded. A swift and decisive victory was called for.

Just to demonstrate that we can defend ourselves.

Unfortunately, Wutlo had other ideas. Recovering from his crash landing faster than Kirk liked or expected, he rolled over onto his hands and knees and propelled himself into Kirk, ramming his head into the captain's gut and tackling him at the waist. Gasping, Kirk staggered backward but managed to stay on his feet. He dropped an elbow into the back of Wutlo's neck, forcing the other man to release him. Kirk bounced back a few steps to give himself some breathing room, then delivered a doubled-fist wallop to Wutlo's solar plexus just as the hostile Atrazian straightened up, then floored him with a good old-fashioned roundhouse punch to the chin. Wutlo dropped like a deflector shield that had run out of juice.

This time he didn't jump right back up again. Down for the count.

Massaging his bruised knuckles, Kirk turned his back on the unconscious man and addressed Pujal directly.

"Seen enough?"

"You handle yourself well," she granted. "Come closer."

His gut still sore from Wutlo's headbutt, Kirk approached the woman on her steed, only to be taken slightly aback when the ungulate's trunk reached for him. He tried hard not to flinch as the prehensile proboscis snuffled him, running its damp, bristly tipped nostrils over his face and neck, blowing its hot, pungent breath over him, before finally withdrawing. Kirk thought the unpleasantness was over—until the beast stepped closer and licked his face with its sandpapery tongue.

Pujal laughed, smiling for the first time.

"Nesefess approves of you." She stroked the ungulate's furry head between its great, curved horns. "That speaks in your favor." She leaned forward in her saddle. "You say you seek a stolen countrywoman?"

"That's right. A noted scholar and healer among my people."

"This individual, they were taken unwillingly?"

"Very much so."

"A chivalrous quest," she pronounced after a moment's thought. "Very well. You may share our company and journey . . . for a fair price."

Kirk reached again for his pouch.

With the sun setting, the landing party joined the caravanners in camping out overnight on the side of the road. Glowing glass orbs, filled with a bioluminous fungus, hung from poles and the upright masts of the wagons, combating the moonless dark. Sharing a meal of meat jerky, nuts, and fermented vegetable juices (all of which were covertly scanned by McCoy to confirm they were suitable for human consumption), Kirk politely evaded queries about where precisely they hailed from to avoid being caught in a lie; better cryptic than provably dishonest, he judged. Pujal, which turned out to be her actual name, surely noted the vagueness of his replies, but seemed to have chosen to grant Kirk and his compatriots the benefit of the doubt, even though he noticed that at least one of her people had eyes on them at all times, which made checking in with Akbari challenging but not impossible; Kirk or one of the others simply contacted *Galileo* while stepping briefly away from the camp, ostensibly to answer a call of nature. As for Wutlo, he occasionally cast sour looks at Kirk, but didn't seem too eager for a rematch or revenge; Kirk gathered that Pujal had told her bellicose lieutenant to drop the matter. Just the same, the landing party planned to sleep in shifts, taking turns standing guard over the others. Accepting the caravanners' hospitality was one thing. Leaving themselves vulnerable to a double cross was another.

Extend trust, Kirk thought, *but don't take anything for granted.*

In the meantime, cautiously mingling with Pujal and her people proved highly informative. Their destination, Kirk discovered, was a city called Reliux, a major trading center profitably located at the hub of several established land and water routes. The caravanners were transporting wares from foreign realms, including the luminous fungus, which apparently came from an extensive cave system far beyond the other end of the savanna, as well as the hides, bones, and eggs of certain oversized birds and reptiles found in a distant marshland, in order to trade them for valuable delicacies, spices, perfumes, and other rarities from myriad far-flung corners of Atraz. By way of advertising, the prows of the many of the wagons sported the colorfully decorated skulls of various large avian life-forms. *Fascinating,* Kirk imagined Spock saying. He looked forward to updating Starfleet's scanty datafiles on Atraz—after they recovered Doctor Hamparian.

"Thank you again for letting us join you," Kirk told Pujal as they sat together beneath the glow of the orbs, sharing a meal. "We appreciate the meal and the good company."

"A profitable arrangement for all," she observed, "and lucky for you in particular. You faced an arduous, even hazardous trek to Reliux without our aid." She eyed him curiously. "I don't suppose you care to elaborate on how you came to such a sorry state?"

"I would prefer not to," Kirk admitted. "Nothing personal, believe me, but let's just say that we're breaking certain taboos by visiting these realms at all, even in a good cause. That being the case, it's probably best that we conduct this rescue mission quietly, without advertising where we came from or how we got here. Ideally, we will recover our stolen countrywoman and return home without anyone being the wiser." He smiled slyly. "Officially, we were never here."

"I see." Pujal nodded in understanding. "So you *are* renegades after all."

"Only in a manner of speaking."

An ungulate, grazing in a field nearby, trumpeted in the night. Kirk had learned that Atrazians called these animals *vusecos*. Pujal looked to the field, then back at Kirk.

"Tell me, Kirk. Can you ride?"

Chapter Nine

2292

"Unlike my fellow envoys, I am old enough to remember when last we Osori met with sentients from other worlds. It seldom ended well."

Gledii, the eldest of the three envoys, was being honored with a reception in the *Enterprise*'s forward observation lounge. Located at the leading edge of the saucer section, the spacious chamber boasted panoramic viewports, a polished hardwood floor, comfortably upholstered chairs, and generally sumptuous surroundings. A decorative ship's wheel, from the golden age of sail, evoked a proud maritime tradition, as did the inlaid compass design in the center of the deck and the antique brass astrolabe facing the vast stellar distance before them. A buffet, featuring a selection of human, Klingon, and Romulan specialties, had been prepared by hand in the ship's galley, as opposed to being synthesized by food processors. An amateur string quartet played softly in a corner. Whether the ship's three new guests appreciated classical music from Earth, Andoria, and Alpha Centauri was anybody's guess.

"How so?" Kirk asked. Like the rest of his command crew, he sported his dress uniform for the occasion. "We have only vague and contradictory records of your encounters with various extinct civilizations."

Gledii held court from a plush easy chair, surrounded by milling crew members, as well as by the Klingon and Romulan observers who'd preceded him in boarding the *Enterprise.* The Osori elder's scales were larger, thicker, and more weathered than those of his younger colleagues, judging from the images transmitted from the other two vessels: more like crocodilian plates than delicate, iridescent scales. He carried himself slowly but confidently; Kirk imagined that practical immortality lent itself to patience. Gledii's strong tenor voice, similar to that heard on the bridge earlier, issued with careful deliberation.

"Understand that my people are not driven to expansion, as more fertile, shorter-lived species are. A few daring souls dabbled in space exploration long ago, but by and large we are bound to our native world by tradition, inclination, and biology. Indeed, we cannot long survive away from the environment that produced us. Only a few decades at most."

Not unlike Flint, Kirk thought. Flint's immortality had turned out to be inextricably tied to Earth's ecosystem, so that it eventually expired when he ventured out into space. *Seems the Osori share that limitation.*

"Most of our encounters with alien races came from spacefaring cultures visiting us, too often in search of the 'secret' of our extreme longevity. They refused to believe that we were not hiding an answer from them, so they sought to wrest it from us by conquest, extortion, abduction, even vivisection." Gledii shuddered at ancient memories. "In time, we elected to recuse ourselves, abstaining from contact with other species."

"You chose to hide, rather than fight?"

The Klingon observer did not hide his disapproval. Motox, first officer of the *Lukara*, was a grizzled veteran who was built like a gym rat. Bare arms and a low neckline showed off a prodigiously muscled physique, possibly to overcompensate for the notably subdued ridges on his brow. Cropped gray hair and a drooping horseshoe mustache accompanied a prickly attitude.

"We chose to keep to ourselves," Gledii clarified.

"So what, if I might ask, inspired you to change your mind?"

Varis, the Romulan observer, was a slight, almost petite woman who seemed as at home at a cocktail party as aboard the bridge of a warbird. Tapered ears and upswept eyebrows gave her a Vulcan profile, but there was nothing stoic about her. She laughed and smiled readily, her eyes sparkling with mischief even as they also seemed to carefully study everything and everyone, missing nothing. In lieu of a uniform, she wore an elegant and highly flattering evening gown, somewhat reminiscent of the one worn by a certain Romulan commander who had been briefly forced to enjoy the *Enterprise*'s hospitality many years ago. Lustrous auburn hair fell to her shoulders. Slender fingers held a champagne flute, but Kirk noted that she sipped rarely from it. Clearly, she intended to keep her wits about her.

"We have yet to reach a final decision on the matter," Gledii reminded her. "In truth, I have profound reservations about the wisdom of ending the isolation that has protected us for so long. Still, with the passing of ages, and the gradual rise of younger generations of Osori, I have been persuaded that it may be worth revisiting that venerable policy after all this time, if only to confirm that we made the correct choice before."

Kirk saw that he had his work cut out for him when it came to persuading Gledii to pursue further contact with the Federation and its allies.

"Never a bad idea to reexamine old assumptions from time to time," he said congenially. "From what you tell us of your history, I can certainly appreciate why your people chose seclusion after such negative experiences with past alien visitors. On the other hand, the Federation believes that the potential rewards of reaching out to other civilizations and life-forms, in the spirit of peaceful coexistence and cooperation, ultimately outweigh the risks involved. Perhaps we can convince you and your fellow Osori to give the rest of the galaxy a second chance."

"We shall see," Gledii said skeptically, "but let me ask you, Captain, have your hopeful encounters with other peoples always ended peacefully?"

"No," Kirk admitted. "I'm not going to lie to you. Peace can be challenging, and first contacts don't always end well." Too much bloodshed stained galactic history, and the *Enterprise*'s own logs, to maintain otherwise. "But the very existence of the Federation, which now comprises hundreds of diverse worlds and species, proves that mutual cooperation is possible . . . and worth striving for."

Motox snorted. "Says James Tiberius Kirk, lifelong soldier and warrior, currently commanding a fully armed Federation starship." He dipped his head in respect. "Do not mistake that for an insult, Kirk. For a human, you have an honorable number of battles and victories to your name, but let us not pretend that Starfleet does not carry a sword as well as an olive branch."

"Only in self-defense," Kirk said, "and as a last resort."

Unlike some other empires he could name, but Kirk refrained from pointing that out. This was a diplomatic function; coming to blows, verbal or otherwise, would not make a good impression on the Osori, endangering the mission's chances of success.

I'm not just a soldier, he thought. *Not tonight.*

"In any event," Varis cooed to Gledii, "how brave of you to come among us, Envoy, considering your people's history. And unarmed no less, with no thought for your own personal safety." She poured on the charm, beaming at him. "I am most impressed by your courage."

"Your flattery is duly noted," the Osori said, "although not entirely warranted. I am unarmed, true, but not defenseless."

That caught Motox's interest. The Klingon scrutinized Gledii, who appeared to be distinctly lacking in weapons or armor; the Osori's mesh poncho did not look substantial enough to deflect a serious attack. "Explain."

"Allow me to demonstrate." Gledii rose leisurely to his feet. His eyes briefly closed in concentration and his shimmering liquid-metal gloves produced a luminous rose-colored aura that flowed over the Osori's entire form, clinging closely to his flesh and clothing.

A personal force field? Kirk wondered. Starfleet had experimented with such devices over the years, with mixed results. The energy demands, coupled with the long-term health effects on its users, had rendered the technology problematic at best. Had the Osori managed to overcome these obstacles?

"Commander Motox." Gledii gestured at a Klingon *d'k tahg* sheathed at the warrior's hip. "I assume that weapon is not simply decorative?"

The weapon in question had been a bone of contention when Motox had beamed aboard the *Enterprise* since the foreign observers were supposed to arrive unarmed. Motox had indeed left his disruptor pistol behind on the *Lukara*, but had insisted that keeping the *d'k tahg* was a matter of honor; for a Klingon to represent the Empire without so much as a blade on his person would be a disgrace, as well as an insult to the Osori, implying that they were not even worth defending against. After some tense, last-minute negotiations in the transporter room, Kirk had grudgingly agreed to let Motox retain the weapon for ceremonial purposes, reasoning that Chekov and his security officers were up to handling a knife-wielding Klingon if worse came to worst; the grisly Klingon proverb about a running man cutting four thousand throats in one night notwithstanding, a single *d'k tahg* was no match for multiple phasers wielded by well-trained Starfleet personnel. Even Varis had waived her objections eventually, after Kirk personally vouched for her safety.

"Of course!" Motox bristled at the suggestion that his dagger might be only for show. "No true warrior would carry a counterfeit weapon."

"Excellent," Gledii said. "In that case, Commander, will you do me the courtesy of attempting to strike me?"

Kirk instantly went into red-alert mode. "Now just one minute—!"

"Envoy!" Varis entreated. "You must not joke about such things! Not to a Klingon!"

Even Motox seemed taken aback by the Osori's request. "What?"

"It's quite all right, everyone." Gledii raised his voice and held up a hand to quiet the spate of shocked gasps and protests. "'Attempt' is the operative word here, I assure you." He stepped toward Motox, clasping his hands behind his back to fully bare his torso to the Klingon. "You may strike when ready, Commander."

"Jim!" McCoy pressed forward to the front of the crowd. "You can't allow this!"

"Captain?" Chekov looked to Kirk as he and his officers closed in to shut down any potential altercation, while unarmed partygoers backed away cautiously. The musicians stopped playing, picking up on the suddenly anxious atmosphere. Chekov's hand went to the relatively inconspicuous type-1 phaser fastened to his belt. "Say the word, sir."

Varis retreated, but looked on keenly. "It's your party, Kirk. I leave this up to you."

"You needn't worry, Captain," Gledii stated, no doubt appreciating Kirk's predicament. "I am not at risk."

Kirk appraised the Osori. The last thing Kirk wanted was for the senior envoy to be stabbed to death on his watch, but Gledii did not appear at all concerned about that prospect. The Osori's confidence in his own safety was convincing.

"Stand down, Chekov, everyone. That's an order." He nodded at McCoy. "That means you too, Bones."

Motox remained hesitant, his hand on the hilt of the sheathed *d'k tahg*. "I was not sent to kill you. I do not require your death."

"Nor shall you cause it," Gledii said. "As I said, I merely seek to demonstrate what measures we envoys have taken to ensure our own protection." A roseate glow still wrapped around him like a second skin. "Surely you must be curious? Believe me, Commander, you cannot harm me with that blade, even if you wield it with all your might."

The challenge, along with the opportunity to test the Osori's defenses, proved too much for Motox to resist. Drawing his weapon, he lunged forward and thrust it at Gledii's chest. Kirk held his breath, hoping and expecting the *d'k tahg* to be blocked by a force field. He anticipated sparks or a flash of energy when the knife collided with the barrier.

Instead it *passed through* Gledii as though he was immaterial.

Motox let out a growl. Frustrated, he slashed viciously at the Osori, but his second attack was no more efficacious than his first. The lack of resistance threw the Klingon off-balance so that he stumbled forward, passing through the intangible envoy altogether.

"Oh, this is priceless!"

Varis laughed in delight, earning her a volcanic glare from Motox. Concerned, Kirk hoped it wouldn't be necessary to defend the amused Romulan from the embarrassed Klingon, which, it occurred to him, might well be playing into Varis's slender hands. The Romulans were fond of playing their enemies against each other; pitting Starfleet against a Klingon right in front of the Osori's senior envoy could only benefit the Romulans.

Clever, he thought, *if deliberate.*

Perhaps to Varis's disappointment, however, Motox showed more restraint than might be expected. Jamming his unbloodied *d'k tahg* back into its sheath, he confronted Gledii instead.

"What trickery is this?"

"Each of our envoys," the Osori explained, "is equipped with apparatus that can temporarily move us out of phase with our surroundings, effectively rendering us intangible and therefore impervious to harm or captivity. Not an offensive weapon, but sufficient to protect us from any immediate threat."

Kirk flashed quickly on that time he had been briefly trapped between universes, existing only as an untouchable apparition slightly out of phase with conventional reality. He had found it a most unnerving experience.

"How long can one exist in such a state?" he asked.

"Not indefinitely," Gledii said. "One can only stay out of phase for a limited interval before dissipating entirely, but at least long enough for us to remove ourselves from peril."

"How remarkable," Varis enthused. "You Osori never cease to amaze."

Motox eyed the Osori with interest. "What about energy weapons?" he asked, sounding more intrigued than frustrated now. Keeping his eyes on the prize, as it were.

"Energy weapons too." Gledii turned toward Chekov. "If you would oblige us with your phaser, Commander?"

Chekov swallowed hard, his uncertain expression reminding Kirk of the green young ensign the Russian had once been. "Captain?"

"On stun, Chekov, and be conscious of where you're aiming."

"Absolutely, sir!"

Chekov carefully positioned himself so that nothing and nobody was behind Gledii except a solid bulkhead. Sweating nervously, he fired at the Osori, but the crimson beam passed just as harmlessly through its target as the Klingon *d'k tahg* had. Lacking a nervous system, the bulkhead was unscathed by the beam.

"Satisfied?" Gledii lowered himself back into the easy chair. The aura flowed off him, retreating back into his gloves. "We Osori are not so foolhardy as to venture out into the wild without taking reasonable precautions."

"Which is precisely why the *Enterprise*, although built for exploration, is prepared to defend itself if necessary," Kirk said. "Although I admit our defenses now seem primitive compared to yours."

"To put it mildly," Varis said. "This is far beyond anything our sciences are capable of, at least for now."

Her eyes gleamed avidly, while Motox stroked his chin, no doubt pondering the military applications of such technology. Kirk felt certain that the astounding level of technology displayed by Gledii's demonstrations was not lost on anyone in the vicinity; getting to know the Osori better had just become even more enticing than ever.

"I don't suppose," Varis asked, smiling, "you would be willing to share your phasing technology with certain chosen allies?"

Motox sneered at her. "Not wasting any time, are you, Romulan?"

"Please," she retorted, "we were all thinking it."

She's not wrong, Kirk thought.

"Such considerations are premature," Gledii said. "We have not yet decided to pursue relations with outsiders, let alone share our technology with them."

"Of course," Varis replied. "We wouldn't want to get ahead of ourselves . . . although it may be worth noting that you're not obliged to embrace *every* outsider, all or nothing, as opposed to being more selective about who you choose to partner with. Indeed, you may well discover that some of us might make better allies than others."

"Such as who? The Romulans?" Motox laughed harshly. "You green-blooded snakes would betray your own mothers if it served your own ends, as we Klingons know better than most. Allying ourselves with you was a costly mistake!"

Varis shrugged. "Or was it perhaps you Klingons who proved a disappointing and unreliable ally." She blithely sipped her champagne. "Present company excluded, naturally."

"Don't hide behind your smug condescension, Romulan. I know your kind. You're no soldier. You're a politician at best, a spy at worst!"

"Or all of the above, depending," Varis said. "I pride myself on my versatility on behalf of the praetor. But please don't take any of my remarks about your own empire personally, Commander. That you're still only a first officer, not a captain, after so many years means that you can't be held responsible for the folly of your superiors, and that you are clearly no politician yourself. Indeed, I have to wonder who you offended to be shipped off to the *Enterprise* as a hostage and forced to rub shoulders with the likes of us? Is this a punishment or were you simply considered expendable?"

"Watch your tongue, Romulan!" Motox snarled, clenching his fists. Angry veins pulsed along his arms, neck, and barely ridged brow. "Before I feed it to a trash disintegrator!"

"Now, now!" Kirk attempted to dampen the fireworks. "Let's not argue politics in front of our distinguished guest."

"To the contrary," Gledii said, "I am finding this . . . contretemps . . . most illuminating."

"I'll bet," McCoy muttered.

"Look," Kirk addressed the envoy, "it's no secret that our civilizations haven't always gotten along. As I said earlier, peace and understanding take time and effort, but the very fact that we're all gathered here together, trading words instead of phaser blasts and photon torpedoes, speaks volumes about how far we've come in just my lifetime alone. If you had told me decades ago that one day I'd be entertaining a Klingon and a Romulan on the deck of a Starfleet vessel, and at the same time no less . . . well, let's just say that the universe is still capable of surprising me."

And testing me, he added silently. Making nice with Motox in particular was difficult after what had happened to David, who had been killed by a Klingon *d'k tahg* just like the one Motox flaunted so proudly. In the years since his son's murder, duty and circumstances had sometimes forced Kirk to be civil with other Klingons, even join forces with them on rare occasions, but he'd be lying if he claimed that ever came easily. Part of him would never forgive the Klingons for killing his son.

But tonight is not about me.

"Eloquently said, Captain." Varis raised her glass to him. "Your reputation for stirring oratory is well deserved. Small wonder Starfleet trusted you with this crucial mission, along with command of this magnificent vessel." She paused to admire the lounge's well-appointed interior before adding slyly, "But this is not the first *Starship Enterprise* you've captained, correct? Refresh my memory. What happened to your previous vessel?"

An indelible image erupted in Kirk's memory: his first *Enterprise* going down in flames over the Genesis Planet, the same day David died. Both victims of the Klingons, one way or another.

Which Varis absolutely knew, of course.

There she goes again, Kirk thought, *oh-so-politely pushing buttons and stirring up trouble, trying to play us and the Klingons against each other while she cozies up to the Osori. How very Romulan.*

"Lost," he said simply, declining to take the bait. "We all have losses and hardships in our pasts, but tonight is about the future and the promise it holds for all of us, if we're brave enough to seize the opportunity."

"Hear, hear," McCoy said. A smattering of light applause from the crew also supported their captain. "I couldn't have put it better myself."

"Don't sell yourself short, Doctor," Kirk quipped. "And speaking of promises and rewards, our own Commander Uhura has generously offered to treat us to a song or two, and I don't wish to deprive you all of that enchantment for any longer." He nodded at Uhura, who headed over toward the musicians. "Never mind politics and science for the moment. Consider this just a sample of the artistic and cultural gifts we can share with each other if we so choose."

Gledii sat back in his chair, making himself comfortable. "By all means, Captain. I look forward to enjoying the performance."

"You won't be disappointed, Envoy. I say that with all confidence."

But would even Uhura's undisputed talents be enough to calm the stormy waters they were sailing through? Kirk contemplated the antique ship's wheel facing a vast ocean of space. If tonight's fractious reception was any indication, they had a turbulent voyage ahead of them. Would the cause of coaxing the Osori out of hiding be scuttled and lost at sea before the ship even reached the conclave on Nimbus III? Kirk knew he had a tricky course to chart.

Here's hoping Spock and Saavik aren't in similar straits.

Chapter Ten

Melinda had never interviewed a nun before.

It had taken some digging, but it turned out that Sister Mary Michelle, late of Monterey, was now residing in a convent in Pescadoro, only about an hour north of San Francisco. Melinda and Dennis had rented a car and driven up to the convent to meet her face-to-face. Still on edge after what they'd heard from ex-detective Fulton about how his missing-persons investigation had been quashed back in the day, Dennis had spent much of the drive speculating about how the Catholic Church could fit into a nefarious government conspiracy against Gillian, forcing Melinda to remind him that there was absolutely no reason to imagine that the then-twentysomething nun had been anything more than just another visitor touring the Cetacean Institute, enjoying an afternoon outing, back in 1986.

"Naturally I remember that day," Sister Mary Michelle said, now in her early sixties. "Especially after what became of that nice Doctor Taylor afterwards." She shook her head mournfully. "That poor woman. I've always wondered what happened to her."

The interview was being conducted in a cozy outdoor garden behind the main convent building. Secular to her bones, Melinda felt a bit out of place, but she got a good vibe from the older woman, who seemed quite hale and hearty and easy to talk to. She was a far cry from the stereotypical stern, intimidating disciplinarian. Rosy cheeks warmed a round, open face. Melinda could easily visualize a younger Sister Mary Michelle oohing and aahing over George and Gracie one sunny afternoon long ago.

"Why don't you take us through what you remember in your own words?"

"Gladly. Sister Mary Christine and I were part of a large group of visitors—maybe a dozen people or so—being given a guided tour of the institute by Doctor Taylor. She started out with a brief lecture about whales and how they were endangered, then took us outside to see George and Gracie in their tank. After that, she led us downstairs, where we could view the interior of the tank through a large under-water window. We were watching the whales through the window when this one fellow swam down and joined the whales, who didn't seem all that alarmed by his presence. He even swam up to one of the whales—Gracie, I believe—and placed his hands against her head. At first, I thought maybe it was part of the exhibition, but then Doctor Taylor, who'd had her back to the window as she spoke to us, noticed the man in the tank . . . and she was *not* amused, to say the least. She dashed upstairs to deal with the situation, leaving us behind, and that was the end of the tour." The nun paused to reflect on her memories. "Imagine my dismay when poor Doctor Taylor was reported missing later that week."

Melinda nodded. So far this gibed with what she'd heard second-hand from Fulton. She'd also reached out, via email, to Bob Briggs, who confirmed that Gillian had discussed the incident with him afterward but that she had assured him it was no big deal. According to Briggs, she had been much more concerned about the imminent departure of George and Gracie; the business with the swimmer had been men-tioned only in passing, which is why it had slipped his mind, compared to the more dramatic events of subsequent days.

"What can you recall about the man who swam with the whales?"

"Oh, I noticed him right away, even before he slipped away from the tour to dive into the tank. He was quite distinctive, with his long white robe and all. There was something very dignified and rather other-worldly about him. I remember wondering if he was a Buddhist monk of some sort." She smiled impishly. "Call it professional curiosity."

Melinda was grateful for the nun's sharp memory. "Did you get the impression that Gillian knew or recognized him? Like possibly she'd had problems with him before?"

"No, but he spoke up when she was telling us about the dangers posed to whales by whaling. He seemed troubled that they were being hunted to extinction."

"Can't blame him there."

Melinda had been pleased to discover that the humpback population had made a remarkable comeback since the eighties, thanks in large part to a ban on commercial whaling back in 1986; according to one report, humpback whales had rebounded to more than ninety percent of their numbers prior to the advent of modern whaling, even if other forms of marine life still struggled with the effects of pollution and climate change. Melinda liked to think that Gillian would be pleased by the humpbacks' recovery, wherever she was.

"Nor I," Sister Mary Michelle said. "You should have seen the gruesome footage of whales being butchered Doctor Taylor showed us at the beginning of the tour. Most disturbing."

It sounded to Melinda like the nameless swimmer had good reason to be troubled by what he heard on the tour, despite Fulton dismissing him as a flake or pothead.

"About the man in the white robe, did he seem like he was mentally disturbed or possibly on drugs?"

"Not at all." Sister Mary Michelle appeared surprised by the question. "To the contrary, he struck me as very thoughtful and composed. I was totally bewildered when he suddenly appeared in the tank with the whales. And so was his companion, from the looks of him."

"Companion?"

Melinda's pulse sped up. This had somehow escaped Fulton's notepad.

"Oh, yes. There was another gentleman with him during the early part of the tour. I recall wondering how they knew each other, since the other man did not appear at all monkish."

"No white robes? Unworldly air?"

"Far from it. As I recall, he was a handsome fellow with a confident manner. Blessed with movie-star good looks."

"Good-looking?" Melinda had heard that description before, very recently.

Sister Mary Michelle grinned. "I'm a nun, not blind. Although truth to tell, I found the other man—the swimmer—even more compelling somehow. He had a certain . . . magnetism . . . to him that certainly drew my attention."

"Uh-huh." A wild idea distracted Melinda from the nun's musings. Taking out her phone, she called up the sketch of Gillian's mystery pizza date, which Fulton had been persuaded to let her take a photo of. She showed the portrait to Sister Mary Michelle. "Any resemblance?"

The nun squinted at the phone. "Why, yes. I'm almost certain that's the gentleman who was with the swimmer that afternoon. How is it you have a drawing of him?"

"A confidential source."

Ohmigosh, Melinda thought, her mind racing to connect the dots. Why had Gillian been dining out with an associate of the robed interloper who had messed with her whales just hours before, the night before she was last seen?

She and Dennis had tried to track down the waiter who had served Gillian and her date at the pizza place nearly forty years ago, only to discover that he'd died in a motorcycle crash several years later. Dennis, of course, had found this suspicious, despite her assurances that people were killed in traffic accidents every day, so it was hardly beyond probability that someone from 1986 might not have survived to the present. Heck, Melinda considered themselves lucky that so many principals from back then were still around to be interviewed.

"Does this help you?" Sister Mary Michelle asked. "If you don't mind me asking."

"No problem. To be honest, I have no idea what this means yet, but the plot is definitely thickening."

"Well, I do hope you find out what became of Doctor Taylor. I only met her briefly, but she seemed to have a good heart, especially where her whales were concerned. I do hope nothing dreadful happened to her."

Me too, Michelle thought. "Who knows?" she said to lighten the mood. "Maybe she ended up taking holy vows?"

"Stranger things can happen." Sister Mary Michelle blessed Melinda with a smile. "Would you believe I used to be a runway model? Did beer commercials too."

Chapter Eleven

2268

"These steeds are somewhat different than I'm used to," Kirk admitted, riding alongside Pujal atop one of the sleeker *vuseco*s, "but I like to think I'm getting the hang of it."

The caravan had resumed its journey to Reliux at first light. To better blend in on Atraz, Kirk and the rest of the landing party had traded for native clothing to wear over their Starfleet uniforms, while politely refusing any offers for their tricorders, communicators, phasers, and other equipment. Not that Pujal and her people knew what those exotic-looking accouterments were or what they could do; they'd just regarded them as potentially tradeable ornaments or curiosities. While Kirk rode an ungulate, McCoy and the others made do with safer if somewhat less exciting transportation, finding seats aboard the wagons immediately following Kirk, Pujal, and her mounted escorts. Landon had expressed disappointment at not getting to ride a *vuseco* as well. McCoy had just grumbled about how bumpy the road was.

"Fortier couldn't have fled to someplace less rustic?"

Kirk was simply impatient to get to Reliux and continue their search for Doctor Hamparian. He was about to ask Pujal for more details about the city and its layout when he heard someone shouting frantically farther up the road, where a large, leafy tree could be spied rising amidst the high grass.

"Keep back, you feathered devils! Stay away! I'm not carrion yet, curse you!"

Reacting instinctively, Kirk urged his steed to greater speed, holding on for dear life as the long-legged ungulate broken into a run. Pounding hooves swiftly brought him nearer to the solitary tree, where he was shocked to see that an Atrazian man, stripped to the skin, had been hung by his wrists from a thick branch, his feet dangling several centimeters above the ground. A flock of seemingly flightless, apparently carnivorous birds, somewhere in size between a turkey and an emu, were attacking the man, squawking and pecking and clawing at him. Feathered in shades of green and brown, the birds boasted long legs and necks but short wings. Three-toed feet sported nasty-looking claws. The hanging man shouted and kicked at the voracious fowls, fighting what looked like a losing battle to keep the meat on his bones. A viscid, greenish sap or syrup had been spilled over him, perhaps to attract predators? Blood, as red as any human's, trickled down his bare legs from several vicious cuts and scratches. Hope flared in the man's eyes as he spotted Kirk riding toward him pell-mell.

"Help me, please!" His voice was hoarse and ragged. "They're going to eat me alive!"

Kirk had no idea how the man had ended up in this fix, but he wasn't about to let him be picked apart by the hungry birds. Kirk's mount balked momentarily at riding into the avian feeding frenzy, but he prodded the recalcitrant ungulate onward. Trumpeting loudly, in protest or defiance, the *vuseco* charged into the midst of the feast, scattering the birds, who squawked and screeched indignantly, loath to abandon such easy pickings.

"Shoo! Scram!" Kirk hollered, reluctant to resort to his phaser in front of the endangered Atrazian, as well as within view of Pujal and the caravan coming up behind him. Kirk waved an arm wildly while gripping the reins with the other. "Get out of here! Go!"

One of the larger birds, not quite the size of a Klingon *targ*, tried to stand its ground, scratching at the ground, angrily flapping vestigial wings, and snapping its beak. Kirk snatched a canteen from his saddle and hurled it at the contrary fowl with pinpoint accuracy, bouncing it off the bird's plumed head. Screeching unhappily but getting the message, the bird abandoned its prey to scurry off into the tall grass beyond the tree's verdant canopy. Meat that could fight back was less tempting, it seemed, than a meal hung up for the taking.

"Praise the stars!" the rescued man said, his throat sounding parched. Scrawny and sunburnt with curly auburn hair, he had lean, haggard features and a cracked front tooth. Purple bruises indicated rough handling even before he had been strung up for the birds. "Cut me down, please, before something even worse comes along!"

Kirk wondered what other predators the man might be afraid of, beside whoever had strung him up like this. Calming the agitated *vuseco* and bringing it to a halt, Kirk dismounted and headed toward the man, pausing only to retrieve the leather canteen. Glancing back over his shoulder, he saw Pujal and her escorts catching up with him, with the rest of the caravan close behind her. *Good*, he thought. *That should discourage those bloodthirsty birds from coming back for seconds.*

"Don't worry," he assured the hanging man. "You're safe now."

"Many thanks, merciful one! You are truly a prince among men!"

"It was the least I could do," Kirk said, deflecting the man's effusions. "I'm just glad we found you before those creatures could do too much damage." From what he could tell, the man's injuries were not life-threatening. "I'll have you down from there in no time."

"Hold!" Pujal called out sharply from atop her steed, displeasure evident in her tone. "Do nothing rash, Kirk, beyond what you have already done."

Uh-oh. Kirk hoped he hadn't put his foot in it by rescuing the endangered Atrazian, but he had no real regrets. "I couldn't just stand by and let him be ripped to shreds by those feathered carnivores."

"Couldn't you?" Pujal asked. "Did you not wonder what this stranger might have done to warrant such a punishment?"

"Not in the moment," Kirk said. "I simply saw a fellow being in jeopardy, facing a cruel and torturous fate."

And likely to meet the same end if left as he was.

"You do not know our ways, Kirk. Think twice before judging them."

Wagons pulled up behind her. McCoy and the others, along with any number of curious Atrazians, jumped from the wagons and rushed to see what was happening. Levine was the first to reach Kirk's side.

"Are you all right, sir? We got here as quickly as we could!"

Kirk noted with approval that the security officer had not drawn his phaser prematurely. "I'm safe and sound, Lieutenant, although we seem to find ourselves in a sticky situation here."

"Sticky?" McCoy gazed in dismay at the injured man hanging from the tree, understandably appalled. "Barbaric is more like it!"

McCoy was already reaching for his medkit.

"Hold off just a moment, Bones," Kirk said in a low voice. "Let's see how this plays out before rushing in."

"Look who's talking," McCoy said, but contented himself to merely scrutinize the man's seemingly minor injuries from a distance. Blood streamed from the wounds, rather than spurted, which suggested that no major arteries had been severed, but the man was obviously weak and in need of care. Probably starved and thirsty as well.

Kirk stepped aside to let Pujal take the lead here, at least for the present. He had no intention of leaving the vulnerable man hanging helplessly from the tree, but he wanted to avoid a direct confrontation with their hosts if possible.

"You there!" She rode up to the tree, looking over its captive warily. "What are you called, who hung you here, and, mostly importantly, why?"

"My name is Jaheed, Lady, and I'm innocent as a newborn calf, I swear to you on my life!"

"A rather precarious asset at the moment," she observed. "Innocent of what, precisely?"

Jaheed swallowed and licked his lips, as though trying to muster enough saliva to explain himself. Kirk was tempted to offer his canteen, but didn't want to antagonize Pujal by interrupting her interrogation. The sticky green syrup oozed slowly down Jaheed's defenseless form as he spoke:

"A prize *vuseco*, the pride of our band's commander, sickened and died, through no fault of mine. If anything, it was the fault of the commander's worthless son and heir, who neglected the beast when it was in his care, letting vermin nest in its feed, but *someone* had to be blamed, other than that feckless youth, and as I lacked status and powerful friends, I was made the scapegoat, accused of everything from incompetence to witchcraft to simply being a carrier of bad luck." Bitterness contorted his haggard features. "That I was hardly in the commander's good graces to begin with didn't help."

"A likely story." Wutlo sneered at Jaheed from atop his own *vuseco*. "No doubt your people had good reason to feed you to the hunting wings."

"No!" Jaheed cried out. "It is as I said! I am blameless!"

"So you claim," Pujal said skeptically, "but we have only your word for it. In truth, we have no way of knowing what offense you might have committed."

"Does it matter?" McCoy protested. "This is savage and inhumane. We can't in good conscience leave him like this!" He glanced over at Kirk. "Sorry, Jim. I can't keep quiet another moment. That man needs medical attention."

Kirk couldn't blame him for speaking up. Where the doctor was concerned, his Hippocratic oath took priority, even over his Starfleet one. What's more, Kirk fully understood how impossible it could be to just stand by and let an atrocity be committed even when that might be the safer and more politic thing to do, as when he had instinctively taken action to keep a pregnant woman from being put to death for no good reason, even though that had severely compromised his mission at the time—and nearly gotten him, Spock, and McCoy killed.

And he would do it all again if necessary.

"No need to apologize, Bones. I get it."

Pujal observed their exchange. "And you, Kirk, will you take responsibility for this man? And for whatever harm or treachery may come of this?"

Kirk looked at Jaheed, who was almost certainly doomed to a horrific death if he wasn't cut down from the tree. Terrified of being left to die, he pleaded with Kirk.

"I beseech you, my deliverer, do not desert me now! Spare me, please! You will not regret it! I will be forever in your debt!"

Kirk saw no way out of it. *In for a penny, in for pound.*

"All right. I accept the responsibility."

"Then do what you must." Pujal drew a knife from a sheath at her side and lobbed it to Kirk, who plucked it from the ground where it landed. "I pray, for your sake, this is not a mistake."

Me too, Kirk thought.

Then again, perhaps they could use a local guide once they got to the city?

Chapter Twelve

"More ale!" the Klingon demanded. "More ale for all!"

Dinner took place in the officers' mess aboard the Romulan warbird. Plavius, commander of the *Harrier*, played host from the end of the table, while Spock sat across from his fellow observer, a boisterous young Klingon lieutenant named Chorn, who was taking advantage of his current posting to enjoy generous quantities of Romulan ale, which had contributed to his rather exhausting good spirits and sloppy table manners. Blue ale dribbled from his lips, staining his luxuriant black beard. A large personality matched his physical dimensions, the latter of which put Spock in mind of a human sumo wrestler. Chorn belched heartily, and not for the first time.

"Drink up, fellow travelers! Tonight is a good night to dine!"

Spock exchanged a bemused look with Plavius. If nothing else, the Klingon's obstreperous presence and behavior had provided them with a common irritant to bond over. Spock was less certain what impression Chorn was making on Nawee, the Osori envoy seated at the opposite end of the table. The Klingon was taking up so much space, conversationally as well as physically, Nawee could barely get a word in.

"An intriguing libation to be sure," the Osori managed to insert. "A credit to your culture, Commander Plavius."

The famously potent beverage appeared to have minimal effect on Nawee, who professed to be middle-aged by Osori standards. Thickening scales retained an opalescent sheen, and his lilting voice fell into the alto range. He accepted a refill from a helmeted centurion while enjoying a plate of steamed Romulan mussels in a coppery green cream sauce. Spock, for his part, appreciated the vegetarian soup and salad Plavius had courteously provided for him. He nursed his own glass of ale deliberately.

"Romulan civilization is exceptional in all respects," boasted Hepna, a junior officer seated at Plavius's right hand. Her burnished helmet had been set aside, revealing short brown hair and bangs, cut with military precision. A severe expression crossed into naked distaste as she cast a pointed glance at Chorn. "As are our manners."

"Ha! A shot from starboard!" The Klingon laughed off her barb. He slapped her back in appreciation, earning him a venomous look from Hepna, which bounced harmlessly off Chorn's ebullience. "Tell me, Subcommander, is it true what they say about Romulan women?"

"I'm certain I don't know what you mean, Klingon."

"Sure you don't," he said, grinning. He raised an empty cup. "More ale!"

Spock speculated, somewhat uncharitably, as to whether Chorn had been dispatched to the *Harrier* because even his fellow Klingons desired a break from him. Spock attempted to steer the focus of the table talk back toward their guest of honor.

"May I inquire, Envoy, as to your views regarding the possibility of the Osori developing closer ties with other species?"

"I prefer to keep an open mind," Nawee said. "Perhaps more so than my esteemed colleagues. Gledii is highly skeptical, while Cyloo is quite excited by the prospect. My own feelings are mixed. On one side, why change a policy that has kept us safe for millennia? On the other, there may be danger in not adapting to a changing universe. Who knows which approach promises the most security in the long term?"

"Why think only of safety?" Chorn challenged him. "Klingons do not base our decisions on fear, but on what we can wrest from life with our might and courage." He brandished a cup of ale in one meaty hand and a jumbo-sized mollusk in the other. "Why hide behind your shields when a galaxy of undiscovered prizes and pleasures are just waiting to be seized if you have the will. Klingon bloodwine! Orion women! Caitian wrestling! Whole new worlds of treasure and adventure ready to be claimed by the bold!"

Interesting, Spock thought. In his own unabashedly hedonistic way, Chorn was framing the Osori's dilemma in terms of rewards rather than risks, and making a case for seeking out new experiences and knowledge in the greater galaxy. *Perhaps Chorn has been assigned this mission for better reasons than I first thought.*

"A singular perspective," Nawee said. "Certainly, I mean to study all facets of the question before arriving at a conclusion. That is, after all, the purpose of this exploratory expedition."

"To that end," Plavius asked, "are there any questions you wish to ask us? To help you achieve a better understanding of those facets?"

Nawee looked around the table, pondering the commander's offer.

"Maybe you *can* illuminate me on one matter. While Lieutenant Chorn is manifestly of different stock than you and your crew, Captain Spock appears to be very much of the same breed, with only his Starfleet uniform to distinguish him from the other faces aboard. What then is the difference between a Romulan and a Vulcan?"

"Much," Hepna said forcefully.

Plavius turned toward Spock. "Would you care to enlighten the envoy, Captain? Being the source of his confusion?"

"By all means."

Spock wondered at the commander's motives in passing the question over to him. Simple courtesy—or a desire to avoid weighing in on such a potentially contentious topic? Spock suspected the latter; he knew enough of Romulans to appreciate that even the commander of an imperial warbird had to watch his words carefully, for political reasons.

"Our peoples indeed share a common ancestry," he explained, "but we diverged many generations ago due to . . . philosophical differences. For better or for worse, we have charted very different paths since then."

"Worse for you perhaps," Hepna said. "We have stayed true to the proud martial history of our ancestors, instead of rejecting power and cunning in favor of placid, bloodless intellectualism. Small wonder you have allowed the humans to eclipse you; at least they still have some spirit and ambition. We are *nothing* alike, not anymore."

Spock was unperturbed by her words. "With all due respect, that is not how I would characterize the status quo. I would rather think there remains common ground between us, from which deeper bonds might still grow and prosper in time."

"To what common ground do you refer?" Nawee asked.

Plavius entered the discussion, perhaps to mitigate his underling's combative attitude. "I suppose it can be argued that our philosophies are not *so* far apart. Romulans are devoted to duty, Vulcans to logic, but duty and logic can be seen as cousins of a sort. Both involve mastering one's personal ego and desires, cultivating the virtues of self-restraint and discipline in the service of a higher ideal."

"Vulcans also have a keen sense of duty," Spock agreed. "As do Starfleet officers."

"To duty!" Chorn raised his cup in a toast. "And honor and glory!"

Hepna winced at the Klingon's vociferous volume. She edged her seat farther away from him, while making a point of putting her own cup down lest she appear to be joining him in his toast. She toyed with her table knife instead.

"But if you are so alike," Nawee pressed, "why do you remain divided and at odds?"

"Family feuds are often slow to heal," Spock said, speaking from personal experience. "There can be much history to overcome, sometimes of a painful nature."

"Is there no hope of reconciliation?" the Osori asked.

"There are still some on Vulcan who hold out hope for reunification, if not in our lifetimes, then perhaps generations from now. I cannot say whether such aspirations are ever entertained on Romulus as well."

Nawee turned a curious gaze on Plavius. "Commander?"

"Careful, sir," Hepna cautioned, her eyes narrowing. "These are treacherous waters. You would not want to give our guests the *wrong* impression."

"I am aware of that, Subcommander."

Plavius took a moment to wipe clean his monocle, buying time to craft his response with care. Spock inferred that the subject of reunification was not something he could speak freely about, or at least not in such a public venue. He wondered what the commander might say were he less constrained.

"As my subordinate so helpfully reminds me, this is a somewhat controversial topic that is probably beyond the scope of this discussion. Certainly, I would not presume to speak for the praetor or the senate, let alone the Romulan people, on such a sensitive matter."

Chorn chuckled. "Could you dance any more carefully, Commander, while saying nothing at all? No surprise you Romulans invented the cloaking device. You're the masters of concealment!"

"We owe no answers to you, Klingon," Hepna said icily.

Nawee frowned. "I find this enmity between Vulcans and Romulans somewhat discouraging. How can we Osori hope to establish ties with your peoples if you cannot even make peace with your own kin?"

"Your situation is quite different," Spock said. "Whereas we have an unfortunate legacy of past conflicts to overcome, the Osori have no history, negative or otherwise, with our respective peoples. The future is a clean slate on which we can write whatever we choose, unhobbled by past grievances."

"Maybe." Nawee did not sound entirely convinced. "And what of the humans? Where do they fit into this fraught history of yours?" Nawee glanced at a viewport, through which the *Enterprise* could be seen cruising alongside the *Harrier*, just out of weapons range. "Nothing personal, Captain Spock, but I regret that I will not have an opportunity to spend time with a human before we arrive at the conclave on Nimbus III."

"For what it is worth, Envoy, I *am* half human."

There was a time, indeed for much of his life, when Spock would have been hesitant to admit this so readily, but he had since come to terms with both sides of his nature. Although he still adhered to Vulcan teachings, he was no longer ashamed or embarrassed by his human heritage. He now appreciated that his mixed background could be a strength, not a weakness, lending him a unique perspective.

"It can be said, in fact, that my presence here is living proof that beings from very different worlds and cultures can unite to create something new, and live together in harmony, as my parents do to this very day."

"I have met your father," Plavius volunteered. "He is a statesman of considerable skill and wisdom. Alas, I have never had the pleasure of encountering your mother, but I am certain she must be a woman of distinction."

Spock heard no judgment in his voice.

"That she is, Commander, and very human . . . in the best way."

"A Vulcan wed to a human," Hepna said incredulously. "I confess I'm unclear who has married up in that scenario. Or down, as the case may be."

"That will be enough, Subcommander," Plavius rebuked her. "Our guest's family is above reproach, do you understand me?"

"Yes, sir." A sour look belied her compliance. "I did not mean to speak out of turn."

Spock judged her contrition insincere but chose, in the interests of diplomacy, to accept it at face value. "You are hardly the first, Subcommander, to find my parents' union puzzling. I cannot say I always understand it myself."

"Just so!" Chorn said, chortling. "Who can understand the mysteries of mating? Red blood, green blood . . . the heart is a wild beast that cannot be tamed!" He raised his cup again, slopping blue ale on the tablecloth. "To fighting our friends and bedding our foes . . . and drinking too much to tell the difference!"

He emptied the cup in a single gulp, then broke wind ferociously.

"More ale! The night is young!"

Hepna's face curdled. Nawee politely lifted his cup in response. Spock and Plavius shared another moment of silent endurance.

They had a long journey before them.

Chapter Thirteen

"I'm really enjoying your new series, by the way," Javier Valdez said. "Excited to help out if I can."

"Glad to hear it." Melinda never got tired of hearing from enthusiastic listeners. "And I'm eager to hear your story."

Cetacean had finally launched, and they were already getting feedback and tips from their audience. Sifting through them, trying to mine actual leads from a slurry of wild guesses and random commentary, was a challenge, but Valdez's message had caught Dennis's attention. Something about spying a UFO in Golden Gate Park the day before Gillian disappeared? Frankly, it sounded a bit out-there to Melinda, who wasn't keen on steering *Cetacean* into paranormal territory, but Dennis had insisted and she'd given in, especially when it turned out Valdez lived in the Lower Haight, not far from their own digs in the Mission District. The convenience made it easy to indulge Dennis, who was her partner in this enterprise after all. And who knew? Maybe Valdez *had* seen something unusual—and usable—back in '86.

The three of them—Melinda, Dennis, and Valdez—were seated around a table in a funky neighborhood bookstore/coffee shop furnished with easy chairs, crowded bookshelves, and displays by local artists. It was roughly ten in the morning, post–rush hour and before the lunch crowd, so the place was relatively quiet without much ambient chatter to contend with. Light jazz played softly in the background; Melinda hadn't decided yet on whether to filter it out in the editing.

"Thanks for coming down my way," Valdez said, his cane leaning against the table. An older man wearing a mustache and a sweater, he had taken off his reading glasses earlier. "I don't get around as well as I used to."

"No problem, Mister Valdez," she said. Her first impression was that he didn't seem like a nut.

"Call me Javy." He surveyed the recording equipment between them. "We good to go?"

"Anytime you're ready."

"All right then." He settled back into his chair and took a sip of water before diving into his story. "I was working as a trash collector for the Parks Department back then, just to pay the bills while I worked on my novel, you see. It was early morning and me and this other guy, Ben Mc-Intyre, were driving around the park, emptying the garbage cans into the compactor at the rear of our truck, same as usual, when out of nowhere this crazy wind whipped up, blowing everything around, knocking over trash cans, causing dust and leaves and litter to whirl wildly all around us."

"Just a wind?" She tried to convey reasonable skepticism rather than ridicule.

"Nothing 'just' about it. I've lived in the Bay Area my whole life, had been working that early-morning shift for months at that point, and I had *never* experienced anything like that before. We're not talking some gusty breeze blowing in with the tide. We had to grab on to the truck to keep from being blown off our feet. And then, just like that, it was over . . . as suddenly as it had started. Like lightning out of a clear blue sky." He shook his head, remembering. "It was damned freaky, is what I'm saying."

"Got it," she said, but not really. She wasn't exactly blown over by his story so far. "But there was more to it than that, right?"

"Just wait." He didn't appear offended by her skepticism, which he had possibly encountered before when telling this story to others. "That was only the beginning. We were still standing there, trying to make sense of that freak windstorm, when we heard this weird, high-pitched whine drilling into our ears, and then . . ."

He paused to milk the moment.

"Yes?" she prompted.

"A doorway or a portal or something opened in the air several yards above a nearby field. This brilliant white light shone through the doorway and a ramp descended from . . . nothingness. Just empty air. And that's not all. Figures appeared in the doorway and started down the ramp toward us."

"Whoa!" Dennis blurted. "For real?"

"Swear to God," Valdez said. "Saw it with my own eyes, and so did Ben."

She leaned forward, caught up despite herself. "And?"

"We got the hell out of there, that's what. Ben panicked, dragged me back into the truck with him, and hit the gas before we could get abducted or probed or worse. I glanced back quickly as we were speeding away, but the glowing doorway had already vanished back into thin air." He sighed. "In hindsight, I kinda wish I had stuck around to meet whoever or whatever came down that ramp, but in the moment . . . well, I'd be lying if I said I put up any sort of fight when Ben decided we should hightail it out of there."

"Probably a good call, man." Dennis looked equal parts spooked and captivated. "No telling what they might have done to you."

Melinda was less eager to entertain alien-abduction scenarios, even if UFO reports were back in the news and might have some audience appeal. She was into true crime, not sci-fi.

"What are you saying, exactly? That you saw a UFO? An honest-to-goodness Unidentified Flying Object?"

"Don't know about the flying part, but it was definitely unknown and not of this world. Possibly a gateway to another dimension?"

"Let's put a pin in that and just try to nail down the more terrestrial details for now. You say your coworker witnessed this as well? Ben somebody?"

"Ben McIntyre. Passed away a few years back, I'm afraid. Heart attack. Anyway, at the time we opted not to tell anybody about what we saw, mostly because we didn't want our supervisors to think we'd been drinking or doping on the job. Plus, we knew how crazy it would sound. Didn't want folks to think we'd lost our minds."

Can't have that, she thought. To be fair, though, she still wasn't getting a psycho vibe from Valdez. Maybe he did see *something* that night and had simply let his imagination get the better of him. She recalled that deep indentation in the ground Detective Fulton had found at the park, prompting the wild notion that Gillian had been carried off by some manner of stealth aircraft after she left the institute.

Is it possible . . . ?

She opened her purse and took out a folded map of Golden Gate Park she'd brought with her just in case Valdez's story turned out to be worth taking a closer look at. She spread the map out on the table, facing him.

"Can you show me where this all happened back then? If you remember."

"As if I could ever forget." He pointed, without hesitation, at a spot on the map. "Right there, exactly."

"Oh my God," Dennis said, beating her to the punch. She got goose bumps.

It was the very same spot where Gillian's truck had been found abandoned days later, where Fulton had discovered the inexplicable imprint of something large and heavy that had apparently come and gone without leaving any tracks, and where once, it seemed, Javy Valdez had witnessed . . . what?

Ohmigosh.

She and Dennis exchanged glances. She thanked her lucky stars that she'd let Dennis talk her into following up on this lead *and* that she'd latched on to Gillian's case in the first place. This sure as heck wasn't some random mugging after all. They'd stumbled onto something sensational here. Way bigger than *Cascade* . . .

"You see," Valdez said, sounding vindicated. "Right where Gillian's truck was found, just like you said on your series. Gotta admit I never made the connection before I heard your podcast. Maybe I should have talked to the police back then, but I didn't even know what we'd seen that morning. It never even occurred to me that it might be related to some sad missing-persons case in the news, which, if I'm being honest, I wasn't paying much attention to at the time. I was too busy rewriting my book."

He rummaged in a tote bag at his feet and produced a paperback novel, which he proudly presented for their inspection. *The Door from Nowhere* by J. V. Valdez. The cover painting depicted a humanoid figure, clad in skintight silver attire, emerging from a glowing rift in space. A printed blurb read: "Had he come to save Earth—or destroy it?"

"Book One of a trilogy," Valdez said. "And still available as an e-book. Turns out that amazing morning in the park was just the inspiration I needed to kick-start my creativity to a whole other level. I may never know what exactly I saw, but it got me published at last." He beamed at them. "Would you like me to autograph it for you?"

Chapter Fourteen

2268

Captain's Log, supplemental. Commander Spock in temporary command: *The Enterprise is circling Atraz at a distance exceeding the usual standard orbit while remaining in communication with the Galileo shuttlecraft currently located on the planet's surface. While we await news from the landing party regarding the search for Doctor Hamparian, I am taking the opportunity to more closely review her work, including various classified materials transmitted to the Enterprise via an encrypted signal from Starfleet Command.*

"Curious," Spock murmured to himself as he studied a series of top-secret proposals and progress reports via a portable data slate, while also overseeing the bridge from the captain's chair. He would have preferred to work at his customary post at the science station, but appreciated the symbolic importance of not leaving the captain's post unoccupied; Ensign Chekov was ably manning the science station in his place, ceding navigation to Lieutenant John Farrell. Adjacent to him, Lieutenant Naomi Rahda had the helm in Sulu's absence.

"What's that, Mister Spock?" Scott asked. With the ship cruising on impulse, the engineer had remained on the bridge to better monitor the situation. He entered the sunken command well to converse with Spock. "You come across something of interest?"

"Perhaps." Spock lowered the data slate, taking the opportunity to share his concerns with Scott. "A careful review of Doctor Hamparian's recent communications suggests that she had been increasingly chafing at the restrictions imposed on her by the Federation's ban on human genetic engineering. Although I am not personally afflicted by such emotions, I can readily discern an impatient and even occasionally indignant tone to her protests at such restrictions. Reading between the lines, as it were."

Despite his Vulcan heritage and training, Spock prided himself on having a better grasp of human emotions than the average Vulcan, thanks to many years in Starfleet, serving under and alongside any number of more emotional beings. He often found such responses an impediment to efficiency, but he liked to think that he had learned to recognize and predict them—to a degree.

"I can believe it," Scott said. "She wouldn't be the first daring scientist or inventor to feel she was being held back by faint-hearted skeptics and supervisors. I'd be lying if I said I haven't thrown out the rule book on occasion . . . when there was no way around it, of course."

"Striking the proper balance between boldness and caution can often be challenging," Spock agreed, "but Hamparian's evident dissatisfaction and frustration raise the disturbing possibility that she might have staged her own 'abduction' to escape the constraints imposed on her by the Federation."

Scott's eyebrows shot upward. "You think she was in league with the spacejacker to fake her own kidnapping?"

"I do not think or know that this is the case, but we cannot rule out the possibility that she seeks greater freedom to pursue her work as she sees fit, beyond the borders of the Federation."

"Aye, and doesn't that muddy the waters." Scott glanced at the astrogator installed between the helm and nav stations, which was used for long-range course plotting. "And none too far from the Klingon border at that. You don't suppose she's defecting to those blackhearted scoundrels."

That troubling scenario had already crossed Spock's mind. "Her work, militarized, might indeed be of great value to the Klingons. Furthermore—"

"Mister Spock!" Chekov called out from the science station. He was peering into the viewing scope, which cast a blue glow on his youthful features. "I'm picking up something on the midrange sensors. Another ship, it looks like!"

"Klingon?" Scott asked.

Spock shared the other man's concern but avoided jumping to conclusions. "Can you identify the vessel?"

"I think so, sir. Give me just a moment."

Spock rose from the captain's seat. He and Scott quickly crossed the bridge to the science station, where they looked over Chekov's shoulders as he worked the sensor controls to refine its readings. Spock resisted the urge to take over the station. Chekov was well trained; he knew what he was doing.

"Almost have it." A tactical display appeared on the primary monitor above the station's control panel. A blinking dot, flashing against a blue schematic, indicated the movement of another ship relative to the *Enterprise*'s position. Swirling patterns on the bandwidth display monitor fluctuated as Chekov homed in on the other vessel while the entire bridge crew watched and listened intently; Spock noted an increase in the ambient tension level among the humans under his command. Chekov appeared to be handling the pressure well, given his youth and emotional tendencies. "It's just on the edge of our sensor range, but coming closer. We should be able to determine its configuration . . . now!"

The blinking icon was supplanted by a graphic representation of a large vessel, comparable in size to the *Enterprise*, whose winged primary hull was preceded by a bulbous command pod at the end of a long neck. Twin nacelles rested beneath its wings. Sharp intakes of breath could be heard across the bridge. All present recognized that distinctive outline.

"A Klingon battle cruiser!" Scott said. "Speak of the devil."

"D7 type, to be precise." Spock perceived that their mission to Atraz had just become significantly more hazardous. "Condition yellow."

Striding back to the captain's chair, he triggered a ship-wide alert via a switch on the left-hand armrest. Amber annunciator lights flashed across the bridge and, theoretically, the rest of the ship.

"Aye, sir," Rahda reported from the helm. A *bindi* dot adorned her furrowed brow. "Deflectors to full power."

Scott gave Spock a quizzical look. "Not battle stations?"

"That would seem premature, Mister Scott." Spock settled into the chair. "Mister Chekov, any indication that the Klingon vessel is about to take immediate action against us?"

"*Nyet*, sir. They are staying out of weapons range . . . for now."

"Their course and velocity?"

"Slowing as they approach Atraz—from the opposite end of the system, naturally—but they don't appear to be entering a standard orbit. They're keeping their distance from the planet." Chekov looked over at Spock. "Just like us, sir."

"Intriguing." Spock steepled his fingers before him as he considered the variables of the evolving situation. "On main viewer."

"Aye, sir," Chekov said. "One Klingon battle cruiser, coming right up."

The D7 cruiser appeared on the screen. An inset graphic indicated that the Klingon vessel was circling Atraz at a right angle to the *Enterprise*'s own course, in a long-distance orbit along the planet's axis while the *Enterprise* circled Atraz's equator. Keeping the enemy ship in view would require effort, but the cruiser's commander would face the same difficulty. For the moment they were evenly matched, the D7's defenses and firepower roughly equivalent to the *Enterprise*'s. Both ships remained out of transporter range of the planet.

"It would appear that the Klingons are also taking a measured approach to infringing on the treaty," Spock observed. "Going no farther than we have as yet."

"And how likely is that to last?" Scott rejoined Spock in the command well, leaning against one of the curved red railings as he grimly contemplated the intimidating vessel on the viewscreen. "That blasted eyesore is not called a *battle* cruiser for nothing."

"Your point is well taken, Mister Scott. Still, the Organian Peace Treaty *has* obliged the Klingons to be more circumspect in their rapacity in recent years, and in this instance it can be argued that we committed the original provocation by entering the neutral sector in the first place. This vessel may simply be responding to our presence here . . . and is in no hurry to escalate the situation."

"Or they're here to get their hands on Doctor Hamparian and all that classified biomedical know-how in her head, with or without her consent."

"Possibly." Spock factored the cruiser's arrival into his unconfirmed theory that the missing scientist might be seeking to defect to the Klingons. "Which begs the question, however, of why we arrived on the scene first. If the plan was indeed for Hamparian to be delivered into the Klingons' grasp, voluntarily or otherwise, why is this vessel just now arriving in the system?"

"You got me there, Mister Spock." Scott scratched his head. "It's a puzzle to be sure."

"Which may require additional data to solve." Spock swiveled the chair toward the communications station behind him. "Lieutenant Uhura, hail the Klingon vessel and ask their intentions." He assumed that the commander of the battle cruiser was fully aware of the *Enterprise*'s presence, but whether the Klingons already knew the nature of their mission to Atraz remained undetermined. "In addition, alert *Galileo* to the Klingon vessel's arrival at your first opportunity."

"Yes, Mister Spock." Her fingers danced expertly over the controls at her post, pausing only to adjust her specialized earpiece. "On a secure channel, I assume."

"Correct, Lieutenant. Maximum encryption."

Spock reviewed the parameters of the present crisis. Although he deemed it imperative that Captain Kirk and the rest of the landing party be informed of the Klingon ship as expeditiously as possible, he was also aware that, even if the *Enterprise* were to come within transporter range of Atraz, they would not be able to beam the landing party aboard without lowering the ship's shields, which could be problematic if the Klingon ship followed them into the planet's orbit. Nor, for that matter, could Spock dispatch reinforcements to assist Kirk on the planet if the *Enterprise* needed to keep its shields in place. Nor could the shuttle return to the ship without possibly coming under fire.

The permutations rivaled a challenging game of three-dimensional chess. Depending on the Klingons' next moves, the landing party could well find themselves cut off from the *Enterprise*.

Chapter Fifteen

The medical bay aboard the *Lukara* was significantly smaller and less well equipped than its equivalent on the *Enterprise*. Still, Doctor Kesh appeared quite proud of it as he gave Saavik and the ship's other guests a tour of the facilities. Captain B'Eleste was not in attendance; it had swiftly become obvious that she had little interest in mingling with her passengers, preferring to spend the majority of her time on the bridge, overseeing the voyage to Nimbus III, while delegating hosting duties to Kesh, her somewhat more gregarious medical officer. The visitors were also accompanied at all times by one or more armed Klingon escorts, who were not about to give the guests free rein aboard the ship. In this instance, the tour of the medbay was overseen by a glowering warrior named Kulton, who watched them like a Therbian merchant on guard against shoplifters. Saavik found his relentless surveillance . . . irksome.

"I'm rather surprised to discover that Klingon warships even have medical facilities." Taleb surveyed the meager array of biobeds. "Don't you all prefer fighting to the death?"

"That is an oversimplification, my Romulan friend," Kesh said. "In the words of Kahless, it is better to win a war than lose gloriously. Medicine has its place in combat, to get wounded warriors back in fighting form as soon as possible."

"The better to battle another day," Saavik said. "Quite logical."

Taleb sighed. "I believe that is what the doctor just said."

Nearly two days had elapsed since they had arrived on the *Lukara*, yet the arrogant young Romulan still seemed to find Saavik's presence no less distasteful, even as he remained cordial to the Osori envoy. If he intended his attitude to nettle or provoke Saavik, he greatly underestimated the degree to which she was inured to such treatment, and not just from Romulans. Her mixed ancestry sullied her in the eyes of a significant percentage of Vulcans as well, subjecting her to varying quantities of condescension and pity. Like her mentor, Spock, she had sought a more accepting environment in Starfleet.

"Be nice, Taleb," Cyloo chided him gently. "I for one welcome Saavik's perspective."

Unlike the aloof Romulan, the young Osori, who was apparently no more than three hundred years old, had proved quite personable. She strolled through the medbay, taking it in with three wide eyes.

"So much equipment and technology . . . just to keep people alive and well? Who could have imagined it? Our people heal quickly from all but the most devastating accidents, and illness is practically unknown to us."

"How fortunate for you," Kesh said dryly.

"Oh dear!" A stricken look came over her scaly face. "I hope that didn't sound as though I was bragging. I don't mean to be insensitive."

"No harm was done," Saavik assured her. "Every species has its own distinctive traits and life cycles, as defined by their biology. It would be illogical to begrudge the Osori the benefits of their evolution. We must each of us accept the fundamentals of our nature, including our respective life-spans."

"Must we?" Kesh asked. "I like to think that medical science also plays a part there."

"To a degree," she agreed. "I certainly did not intend to disparage your chosen profession, Doctor."

"Understood." He looked her over, not for the first time. "And speaking of medical science, I still hope to examine you more thoroughly sometime soon, to study how your hybrid nature varies from baseline Vulcans and Romulans along a range of parameters: genetic, metabolic, neurological, glandular, and so on. Even the most subtle variance could prove most illuminating . . . and possibly open up promising new avenues of inquiry."

"We shall see," she replied in an expressly noncommittal fashion. She detected nothing particularly unsavory in Kesh's scrutiny, but was uncomfortable being regarded as a medical curiosity. "Perhaps later."

Or not.

"I look forward to it." He crossed the bay to a computer terminal at his desk. "It may interest you all to know that we waste few resources on cosmetic reconstruction; Klingons bear their battle scars as badges of honor, but we *are* making substantial progress in the area of practical, combat-ready prosthetics." He tapped away at a control panel. "Let me call up some nonclassified schematics—"

A strident, atonal klaxon blared abruptly. An artificially guttural voice issued from concealed speakers:

"Defense condition one! We are experiencing a warp-core emergency situation! General quarters!"

"By Morath's Shame!" Kesh exclaimed. "If the core should rupture . . ." Dismay contorted his visage as he turned toward his guests. "We must get you to an escape pod immediately. There's no time to lose!"

Taleb glared at Kesh, looking personally offended by the emergency. "What is the meaning of this?"

"I don't understand," Cyloo said, bewildered. "Are we in danger?"

Saavik kept a cool head, relying on both her Vulcan and Starfleet training, despite the distressing nature of the alert. She was puzzled by what could have possibly caused such a dire malfunction; there had been no sudden jolts or turbulence prior to the announcement, no indication of an attack or collision. Moreover, it was her understanding that Klingon warp engines were very solidly constructed, due to the expectation that their ships would regularly engage in combat. What could have produced such a sudden engineering crisis?

"Halt!" Kulton ordered. "No one is going anywhere!" The Klingon peered at Saavik and her fellow interlopers suspiciously, and drew his disruptor pistol from its holster. "Stay where I can see you . . . and don't try anything!"

"But there's no time!" Kesh protested over the din of the klaxons. "We must—"

"Not until I hear from the captain!" Kulton kept a close watch on his charges as he marched over to a wall-mounted intercom unit. He jabbed the activation button and barked into the microphone grille. "Kulton to bridge! I have the aliens. What are your orders?"

Static erupted from the grille, along with a spray of white-hot sparks. Kulton yanked back singed fingers. He growled like an angry *le-matya* repelled by fire.

Curious, Saavik thought. Why would a warp-core malfunction cause the intercoms to short-circuit? Were both symptoms of a ship-wide systemic breakdown?

"Kulton!" Kesh spoke sharply. "We are losing precious moments. The lives of these visitors are our responsibility. Honor demands—"

"Quiet, bone-stitcher!" Kulton said, visibly frustrated and flustered. "Let me think!"

Saavik sympathized. Events were occurring very swiftly, providing insufficient opportunity to analyze them with precision. It was a most dynamic situation, complicated by the inconveniently volatile personalities involved.

"I demand answers!" Taleb said. "What treachery is afoot?"

"You dare speak of treachery, Romulan?" Kulton advanced on Taleb, pistol in hand. "I know sabotage when I smell it. You expect me to believe this but a coincidence, with our sworn enemies aboard?"

"It is premature to suspect foul play." Saavik too wondered whether Taleb might have had a hand in this emergency, but she was uncertain when he would have had the opportunity to commit sabotage; Captain B'Eleste ran a tight ship. "We lack sufficient data to accurately determine the cause of this crisis."

"We can assess blame later," Kesh said forcefully. "Right now we must save our—"

"Save them? These point-eared spies may have doomed us all!" Kulton menaced Taleb with his pistol. "I've half a mind to—"

"Correct." Taleb executed a spinning high kick that sent Kulton's sidearm flying across the medbay. "It's obvious you have only half a mind."

"Son of a *targ!*" Kulton drew a *d'k tahg* from his belt. "I'll paint this butcher shop green with your blood!"

Taleb adopted a defensive stance, perhaps already rethinking his impetuous move. Kesh scrambled to claim the fallen disruptor. Saavik, seeing the situation spiraling out of control, took swift and efficient action, slipping quietly behind Kulton while he was focused on Taleb. A nerve pinch dropped the irate Klingon to the deck, where his blade clattered harmlessly against the deck, even as the nonstop klaxons, flashing alarms, and computerized voice reminded Saavik that the larger emergency was ongoing.

"Condition one! Repeat: Condition one! Warp core in jeopardy!"

She noted, even in the midst of more pressing concerns, that the Klingon computer's voice was gruffly masculine, as opposed to the familiarly feminine voice of the *Enterprise*. A cultural difference worth pondering perhaps, if and when she survived the immediate crisis, which continued to perplex her. Sabotage? A cascading system failure? An undetected spatial anomaly? None of these hypotheses struck her as probable.

"Hurry!" Kesh, now in possession of Kulton's disruptor, began herding them toward an emergency exit. "There are escape pods just a few short corridors away. We can still reach them if we make haste!"

Saavik nodded. She was familiar with the basic layout of a bird-of-prey, having escaped the Genesis Planet in a captured Klingon vessel, which then-Admiral Kirk had commandeered to convey them to Vulcan. There was indeed a complement of escape pods located on this deck, a short distance from the medbay.

"What about him?" She indicated Kulton, who was sprawled limply on the deck. She did not relish the prospect of having to carry him when speed was of the essence, but saw no other alternative. Perhaps Taleb could assist her in the interests of expediency?

"Leave him!" Kesh snapped. "There's no time, and no room in the pod anyway."

His brusque response was unexpected coming from a physician, and there would be more than one pod available to them. Why was Kesh so quick to abandon a member of his crew while the ship was in peril?

"Stop," Saavik said. "Something is not right here." She hastily reviewed the various incongruities puzzling her and concluded that the equation was incomplete. "What are you not telling us, Doctor?"

"Damn it." His concerned expression slipped, along with his Klingon accent. He reached beneath his leathery gray lab coat and produced a *second* disruptor pistol. He aimed both weapons at the visiting trio. "I should've known better than to try to trick even a half Vulcan."

She surmised the truth. "There is no imminent warp-core breach. You staged a counterfeit alert for our ears alone, and sabotaged the medbay intercom as well."

"Guilty as charged. I'd hoped to avoid any crude gangster tactics if possible, but . . . no more games." He nodded toward the exit. "That way, and step on it."

"No," Cyloo said. "I don't think I want to do that."

A roseate glow enveloped her, rendering her untouchable. She'd previously demonstrated her gloves' defensive capabilities shortly after her arrival on the *Lukara*, so Saavik derived some relief from knowing that the envoy was not in danger from Kesh's weapons *or* the fictitious warp-core malfunction. Only the two observers needed to be concerned about the disruptor pistols arrayed against them.

"Up to you." Kesh aimed one weapon each at Saavik and Taleb. "But your new friends will pay the price if you refuse to cooperate."

Saavik realized she had just become a hostage in a much less theoretical sense. *Crude gangster tactics, indeed.*

"Save yourself," she told Cyloo. "Your safety is paramount to the success of our mission. Do not allow yourself to be extorted in this manner."

Taleb glanced at her, raising an eyebrow. "I am also prepared to sacrifice myself."

"How very noble, but I'm not talking to either of you," Kesh said before addressing Cyloo directly. "My apologies for putting you in this difficult position. Again, I had hoped to get you into the pod by subterfuge instead, but their lives, as brief and ephemeral as they are, are in your hands now, Osori. Will you truly deprive of them of their fleeting futures simply to protect yourself?"

"Do not listen to him," Saavik said. "Our deaths, should they happen, will be on his hands, not yours. You will not be to blame."

"But you'll still be killed regardless." Cyloo looked anxiously at Saavik and Taleb. "I cannot allow that."

"A creature of conscience." Kesh smiled triumphantly. "Your choice does you credit. Now, hurry. Our chariot awaits."

Saavik feared there was no dissuading Cyloo. "At least remain out of phase for now," she counseled. "As a precaution against possible weapons fire."

"Yes." Cyloo looked nervously at the twin disruptor pistols. "That does seem wise."

"Do as you please," Kesh said impatiently. "Just get moving, now!"

As anticipated, the exit led to a short service corridor adjacent to the medbay. Klingon signage pointed toward pod access points directly ahead. Contrary to uninformed stereotypes, Saavik knew, Klingons were not militantly opposed to abandoning ship provided there was no hoping of saving it—and no risk of being taken prisoner. As with the medbay, escape pods offered a chance to fight another day. In this case, however, the alert status did not extend beyond the medical facilities; no klaxons or flashing warnings accompanied the party down the hall. The rest of the ship and crew were apparently unaware of the faked catastrophe.

Naturally, Saavik thought. *Kesh would not want competition at the pods.*

His devious plan was nevertheless complicated by a random Klingon crewman crossing their paths at an intersection. The warrior reacted with surprise to the unexpected sight of the ship's doctor escorting the visiting aliens at gunpoint. The man reached for his own sidearm.

"What goes on here?" he demanded. "Do you require assistance?"

"Far from it."

Kesh fired *through* the intangible Osori, the sizzling veridian beam knocking the startled warrior off his feet. Smoke rose from a charred wound on the warrior's chest. Clearly, the pistol was not set on stun.

"Did you . . . kill him?" Cyloo stared at the body, aghast. "Just like that?"

It was likely, Saavik guessed, that she had never witnessed a death before, let alone a killing.

"Regrettable." Kesh shook his head sadly. "But now you know not to underestimate the lengths I'm willing to go to achieve my aims. Nothing less than eternity is at stake."

What does he mean by that? Saavik wondered.

They hurried past the murdered Klingon, arriving at a thickly shielded entry hatch that resembled the armored door of a Zaranite treasure vault. A polarized inset window offered a glimpse of the pod's compact interior. Kesh instructed Saavik to open the hatch. Lights and controls panels activated inside the pod as the hatch swung open. She wondered where Kesh intended to escape to—and how far he expected to get.

"Get in," he commanded. "Going to be a tight squeeze, I'm afraid, but we'll have to make do."

"You do not need *two* hostages to coerce Cyloo," Saavik observed. "Leave Taleb behind."

The Romulan scowled at her. "Do not martyr yourself on my behalf, half blood. I do not require your beneficence."

"You are receiving it anyway."

It is the logical choice, she thought. Taleb's testimony incriminating Kesh would carry more weight with his Romulan superiors, possibly averting conflict between the various parties. *And beyond that, I can no sooner abandon Cyloo than she did me.*

Kesh frowned, losing patience. "Save your breath, both of you. The Romulan is coming with us, period." Saavik opened her mouth to reason with him further, but he did not grant her the chance. "I have my reasons."

She made a last attempt to persuade Cyloo to save herself.

"You must not do this. Future relations between our peoples are at stake."

"And let him end your life, as he did that Klingon's?" Cyloo retracted her aura, coming back into phase with the rest of them. "No, I could not bear to witness that again."

She entered the pod.

Chapter Sixteen

2024

The case board was filling out.

Melinda peered at the screen, shifting a few links around to try to suss out how they all connected: George and Gracie, the pizza date, the Zen dude who went swimming with the whales, the abandoned pickup at the park, a high-level government cover-up, and now . . . an alleged UFO sighting?

That last puzzle piece still had Dennis stressed out. He paced back and forth across their apartment, too worked up to sit still. Javy Valdez's sci-fi novel rested on the kitchen counter; Melinda hadn't read it yet, but Dennis was studying it assiduously. Post-its bookmarked selected pages and passages.

"Seriously?" he said. "You're just plowing ahead, damn the torpedoes, even after what Valdez told us about that glowing doorway in the air? And after that cop warned us to back off earlier?"

She held back a sigh. She'd hoped he'd get over this latest bout of paranoia once he'd had a chance to chill out and get a little perspective, maybe soothe his frayed nerves by cooking something delicious for both of them, but apparently there was no avoiding this conversation. She put aside the tablet.

"All right, let's talk about this. What are you suggesting, that we drop *Cetacean* altogether, just when this story is taking off in ways we never imagined?"

"I don't know." He ran a hand through his hair, as though trying to smooth his unruly thoughts. "But we're not talking about just another bygone missing-persons case anymore. This isn't about a reluctant newlywed who faked her death at Niagara and ended up living happily ever after as a sideshow performer on Coney Island. You heard what Valdez said about what he saw in the park years ago. No wonder the authorities don't want that getting out."

"Okay, about that freaky 'sighting' in the park," she replied. "I won't lie. I got all caught up in that story too. I got chills when he pinpointed the exact spot where Gillian's truck had been found, but now that I've had a chance to think it over it dawns on me that we really only have his word for it. There's no corroborating evidence or testimony, and we'd already mentioned where the truck had been found *and* that mysterious depression in the field on the show; he was just giving us a location we'd already cited on *Cetacean*. And the only other witness, his fellow trash collector? Conveniently deceased. I hate to say it, but maybe Valdez was just trying to piggyback on our podcast to hype his book?"

"Not a chance," Dennis insisted. "I did some poking around and verified that he worked as a sanitation worker for the Parks Department right when he said he did. Spring of '86."

"Doesn't mean he and his late buddy had an actual Close Encounter. Just that he didn't make up the part about his job back then."

"Come on! You don't really believe he was conning us, do you? Tell me the truth, when you were listening to him, did you sense for a moment that he wasn't being straight with us?"

"No," she admitted, "but we have to consider the possibility, if only because it's way more plausible than believing that an unearthly 'door from nowhere' actually appeared above Golden Gate Park one night. That's a lot to swallow on just one guy's say-so."

"What about the dent in the ground and the flattened trash can? Valdez didn't make those up. Or the Feds shutting down the investigation into Gillian's disappearance? It was the cop, Fulton, who told us about that. He was the one who warned us to back off, not Valdez. Are we just ignoring that?"

"Darn right we are!" Melinda said, bristling. "We're investigative journalists, for Pete's sake. We're *supposed* to turn over rocks looking for new or buried clues, then go where they lead us even if it means asking unwelcome questions and prying into the past. What's the point of probing a mystery if we're going to retreat the minute somebody tells us a spooky story or urges us to let things lie?" She dialed down her righteous indignation to avoid an argument. "This is nothing new. When we were doing *Cascade*, there were folks who didn't want us reopening that can of worms. Remember that sheriff's office that wouldn't return our calls at first, and the suspicious in-laws who tried to get a restraining order against us? But we stuck to our guns, found out what happened to Eleanor, and, with all due modesty, generated twelve episodes of addictive content."

Dennis remained unconvinced. "That was small potatoes by comparison. Just some embarrassed cops and family members who didn't want their dirty laundry aired. Now we're not just poking folks in very high places, we're messing with . . . I don't know, extraterrestrials, alternate realities, top-secret conspiracies, and so on. Heavy-duty Area 51, Philadelphia Experiment shit."

"Can we please stick to reality?" She threw up her hands in exasperation. "This case is already tangled enough; I don't need to hear any more crazy theories about how Amelia Earhart got abducted by aliens, or Mark Twain ran into time travelers right here in San Francisco. You don't seriously expect me to believe that Gillian was abducted by aliens? And her whales, too, I suppose?"

"At this point, I'm more worried about us getting disappeared by, you know, *them*."

"Whoever 'they' are."

"Exactly," he said, her sarcasm eluding him completely. "We don't even know who is behind this or how far up it goes."

"All the more reason to keep digging. Look at it this way: If Valdez *is* telling the truth, we've hit the jackpot here. It's just like you said, *Cascade* was peanuts by comparison. We're on to a story that could rocket us into the big time."

"But is it really worth the risk to both of us? What good is a hit podcast if we're not around to enjoy it?"

"What risk? Let's take a deep breath, step back, and put things in perspective. Has anybody actually threatened us yet, really? Or even objected to our investigation?"

"Fulton—"

"Told us about a cover-up *nearly forty years ago*, and Valdez claims to have seen something weird in the park, again nearly four decades ago. Which is all very intriguing and, sure, it certainly sounds as though *something* fishy was going back in 1986, but has there been *any* indication that we're in jeopardy, here and now? Heck, we haven't had so much as a door slammed in our face yet. And that mysterious 'UFO' or 'doorway,' whatever it might have been, is surely long gone by now."

"You'd think," he began, "but—"

The doorbell buzzed, cutting him off. Melinda welcomed the distraction. "You expecting anybody? Or order something?"

He shook his head. "You?"

"Nope." She got up from the couch and headed for the door.

"Wait!" His eyes widened in alarm. His gaze darted from the TV screen to Melinda's phone, which was resting on a coffee table in front of her. "What if they were just listening to us? And decided we were getting too close to the truth?"

If only, she thought. "Pretty sure the Men in Black don't buzz politely before entering."

Slipping out of the apartment, she traipsed down the stairs to the foyer and checked out the front steps of the building. Sure enough, a taped cardboard box bearing her name and address waited on the stoop. A quick inspection revealed no return address or corporate logo on the package. She hefted the lightweight package and sniffed it. No delicious aromas indicated a surprise meal delivery.

Curiouser and curiouser, she thought.

Intrigued, she brought the box upstairs and, rescuing a knife from the silverware drawer, got to work opening it. Dennis peered anxiously over her shoulder. "You certain this is a good idea?" he asked.

"You'd rather I call the bomb squad? Chances are, this is just a care package from an avid fan who somehow got hold of our home address."

"And that doesn't worry you?"

"A little." She'd taken pains to keep that info private. "But only for fear of obsessed fans and stalkers, not lizard people from the ninth dimension."

"Eighth," he corrected her, "with regards to the Reptilians, that is."

She honestly wasn't sure if he was joking or not.

"Whatever." She sawed through the last piece of masking tape; whatever was inside the box had been packed to survive a nuclear war. "But feel free to back up a few yards if it will make you feel better."

"I'm good," he said, sounding anything but.

Packing popcorn spilled onto the kitchen counter as she opened the box, revealing a sealed paper envelope resting atop the packing material. Letters printed on the envelop read:

DO NOT READ ALOUD

"Okay, that's not ominous at all," she said, "but they've got my attention."

Unable to contain her curiosity about the box's actual contents, she handed the envelope over to Dennis as she plunged her hands into the pink foam popcorn and extracted what appeared to be a cheap mobile phone swaddled in bubble wrap.

A burner phone? Really?

Tearing open the wrapping, she turned to Dennis, who was already reading the letter inside the envelope.

"What's it—?" she began before catching herself. *Don't read aloud.*

He held a finger to his lips, shushing her, and handed her the note, which she scanned rapidly:

Do you want to know where Gillian went after she lost her whales? Call me on this phone to arrange a meeting. Do not call anywhere near your other devices. See number below.

"Ohmigosh," she whispered, figuring that didn't give anything away. She was half-surprised to see that the note was simply printed out on a white sheet of Xerox paper and not composed of letters cut from a newspaper like in some vintage movie thriller. Then again, who read actual newsprint anymore?

Still pretty enticing, she thought. *Give the sender points for drama.*

She and Dennis traded looks: hers excited, his not so much. She nodded at the apartment door, and they stepped out into the hallway, which was typically empty. She briefly contemplated resorting to American Sign Language, which they'd taken a course in a few years ago, but decided that was overkill. She simply lowered her voice instead.

"What do you think?"

He glanced up and down the hall, then made sure the door was fully closed behind them.

"I don't like this."

"But it's encouraging, too, right? Like it means we're on the right track, unless"—a depressing thought struck her—"it's just a prank."

Please, don't let this be somebody's idea of a joke.

"I wish." He sounded like that would be preferable. "Pretty elaborate for just a gag. What was that you were just saying about the cover-ups being old news?"

"I stand corrected, possibly, but don't you see? That just makes our cold case fresher and more relevant. This could be big news today, not just a fascinating puzzle from long ago."

He fished a small bottle of Tums from his pocket and gulped down a handful to settle his stomach. "I think I liked it better when the mysteries were safely stowed in the past, not buzzing at our front door." He regarded her glumly. "Should I bother asking what you're going to do?"

"Call them right back, of course."

His shoulders slumped in defeat. "That's what I figured."

The roof seemed far enough away from their phones, laptops, television, and other devices to satisfy the note's instructions. Melinda had considered trekking over to Dolores Park, a brisk hike away, but it was getting dark and she wasn't quite sure how safe that park was at night; the roof was a better option, not to mention being closer at hand. The flat, tar-paper roof offered a nice view of the neighborhood, along with Sutro Tower rising above the skyline to the west, but she barely registered it. The burner phone demanded her attention.

"Let's not keep them waiting," she said, phone in hand.

Dennis started to say something, then thought better of it. Because, deep down, he was as curious as she was—or simply because he knew her too well to try to stop her?

She dialed the number printed at the bottom of the note. Someone picked up the call on the second ring.

"That was quick. You wasted no time, I see."

The voice was electronically distorted. *Great,* she thought, *more cloak-and-dagger hijinks.* She hoped this proved worth it. She was going to be seriously irked if whoever this was was just jerking them around.

"Who is this?" She put the phone on speaker so Dennis could listen in.

"*Not so fast. Where are you?*"

"Up on the roof of our apartment building. Chilling in the breeze instead of staying warm and snug indoors."

"*No phones, tablets, or recording devices nearby?*"

"Just me and the view." She glanced over at Dennis, who was pacing again. "And my partner on *Cetacean*, Dennis Berry. We're a package deal. Take it or leave it."

He winced at the mention of his name. She'd figured he'd appreciate being acknowledged, but maybe he would have preferred to keep his name out of this conversation? It was too late for that, though; not only was he credited as coproducer on the podcast, but anybody who could deliver a phone to their doorstep presumably already knew they were cohabitating as well.

"*Very well,*" the voice said, after a brief but worrisome pause. "*But nobody else. We need to keep our communications private.*"

"Cut to the chase." She wanted to take charge of the conversation and get past any further haggling. "Who are you, what do know about Gillian Taylor, and why all the 'Deep Throat' shenanigans?"

A distorted chuckle sounded like static.

"*I'm impressed a person your age would even recognize a Watergate reference, let alone make one.*"

The condescending tone pegged the speaker as a Boomer.

"Well, I'm definitely not citing the porno," she said. "One more time: Who am I talking to?"

"*No names for now, but you can call me 'Halley,' as in the comet.*"

"Because it last came along in 1986, the same year Gillian vanished?"

"*Very good, Ms. Silver, and, yes, I've been following your podcast with interest, because I know something of those events, including some context that's never been officially provided to the press or public. In fact, I'm fairly certain it's still classified, hence the 'shenanigans,' as you termed them.*"

"Classified?" Dennis whispered under his breath. He hastily tugged his hoodie over his head—to hide from drones or spy satellites. It briefly occurred to her that maybe the roof was a less secure location than she'd initially assumed, then she shoved those concerns away. She had to be careful; paranoia could be contagious.

"And you're privy to this top-secret dirt because . . . ?"

"*Not over the phone. We need to have that talk in person.*"

"Please tell me we're not talking an underlit parking garage at midnight, 'cause I've had about as much of these spy-movie theatrics as I can handle."

"*Choose a location. Someplace safe and public, where we can simply blend in with a crowd.*"

"That works." A few suitable locations came to mind. "In theory, that is. How do I know this is legit? Give me a reason to make the effort. Not the full scoop, if that's too much to ask, but just a taste to whet my appetite?"

"*A reasonable request. Suppose I told you Gillian Taylor is suspected of aiding and abetting a Russian spy and saboteur?*"

Gillian blinked in surprise. Whatever she'd thought "Halley" was going to tell her, that wasn't it. Had she heard him right?

"Come again? Gillian and . . . a Russian spy?"

Static chuckled at her confusion.

"*You want to know more? Let's set up a meeting.*"

Chapter Seventeen

"Follow me, O Captain! Have no fear, I shall find our party lodgings for the night!"

Jaheed, now much recovered from his ordeal, thanks to McCoy's expert ministrations, not to mention fully clothed, guided Kirk and the rest of the landing party through the bustling streets and back alleys of Reliux. Grasslands had given way to fields and villages, bumpy dirt roads to a paved highway, before they'd arrived at one of the walled city's looming gates, where they'd parted on good terms with Pujal and her caravan. Jaheed had since proved a handy guide to the city, as Kirk had hoped after rescuing him from the tree. Trusting the fulsomely grateful Atrazian to lead the way, Kirk took stock of their surroundings. The sooner they got settled in and properly oriented, the sooner they could get down to the business of locating Doctor Hamparian and her kidnapper.

High walls of quarried blue stone enclosed Reliux, which was dominated by a formidable-looking fortress on a steep hillside overlooking the city; according to Jaheed, the city was ruled by a hereditary monarch named Varkat, the latest in a long dynasty stretching back generations. Reliux also boasted spacious plazas, thriving marketplaces, and a wide variety of shops, taverns, temples, baths, residences, and neighborhoods, some obviously more affluent and elegant than others. Crowds gathered outside the entrances of a large public amphitheater. An admirably diverse population, sporting a range of complexions, hairstyles, and attire, revealed a cosmopolitan environment befitting Reliux's status as a major trading hub, attracting travelers, merchants, riverboat captains, runaways, and immigrants from across the planet. *All the better to blend in with,* Kirk noted, *for both us and Fortier.*

"Nobody seems to be paying much attention to us," McCoy confirmed as they traversed the city, occasionally jostling their way through packed streets and sidewalks; Kirk had already reminded the others to be wary of pickpockets. Ungulate-drawn vehicles shared the streets with pedestrians, so that one sometimes had to step carefully to avoid manure. A raucous medley of discordant noises and odors contrasted sharply with the clean, controlled environment aboard the *Enterprise*. The general hubbub meant that McCoy's voice was just one of many. "Guess they're accustomed to strangers in these parts."

"Can't complain about that," Kirk said. The anonymity of a large city had its advantages, particularly where the Prime Directive was concerned. They were less conspicuous than they might be in a smaller, more homogenous community.

Sulu grinned as he took in the sights and the sounds. "Kind of reminds me of the Bedlam District on Neo-Luna, minus the microgravity."

"My aching feet wouldn't mind a little less gravity at the moment." McCoy shot an impatient look at Jaheed. "How much longer to those promised lodgings?"

"Just a trifle longer, healer beyond compare. Come, I know a shortcut."

Veering away from a busy thoroughfare, Jaheed led them through a maze of alleys to a broader avenue running along the inward side of the city's high stone walls. Kirk noted a high concentration of cafes, taverns, warehouses, stables, and such, as well as even more conspicuously varied passersby than elsewhere in Reliux. His general impression was of a relatively presentable section of town, neither a slum nor overly ritzy.

"Let me guess," he commented, "this neighborhood caters to out-of-towners visiting the city on business?"

"Quite right, O Captain!" Jaheed had enthusiastically adopted addressing Kirk by his rank after overhearing Sulu and the others do so. "Here one can find affordable accommodations for traders from abroad. I have patronized this district often, on many past visits."

He did seem to know his way around. In short order, the landing party had secured lodgings on the third floor of a modest public house, where their arrival had elicited only commercial interest from the innkeeper. For propriety's sake, they were obliged to hire a separate room for Landon, but a connecting door (and a wink from the innkeeper) implied that any actual segregation was purely voluntary. The furnishings were spartan, but clean and in decent condition; Kirk had roughed it in harsher locations on far less developed worlds.

"About time." McCoy plopped down on a sturdy cot. "I'm not averse to house calls, but Starfleet's going to need to issue me a new pair of boots if this keeps up."

"Tell me about it," Sulu agreed. "I'm a pilot, not a hitchhiker."

Levine double-checked the locks on the doors, including the connecting one. "Crude, but serviceable. I'd still recommend sleeping in shifts, Captain."

"Definitely." Kirk didn't anticipate any trouble, but it never hurt to be on guard while visiting an unfamiliar city or world. "Why take chances?"

The day was already ebbing outside. Kirk was glad to have found shelter before night fell. With any luck, the meals served in the tavern below were just as acceptable as their rooms.

"So now what, Captain?" Landon asked. "How are we going to find Doctor Hamparian in a city this size, assuming she's even here?"

"Good question, Yeoman." Kirk refrained from pointing out that she had advised checking out Reliux in the first place; her reasoning had been sound then and remained so, even if the task before them was undeniably daunting. "We put our ears to the ground and start asking around, I suppose." He glanced over at Jaheed. "Any suggestions as to where to best catch up on any local news or gossip?"

They had already brought Jaheed up to speed on their rescue mission, without mentioning their extraplanetary origins. He understood only what Kirk had already told Pujal: that they were searching for a kidnapped countrywoman whom they'd tracked to this general region.

"A few such locations occur to me, O Captain, but allow me to make inquiries on your behalf. Rest here and restore yourselves while I call on various establishments and individuals well known to me. I shall return shortly with whatever news I can glean from new and old acquaintances." He held out an open palm. "I will, of course, need to buy drinks enough to engender convivial conversation . . . and loosen tongues."

Kirk held on to his remaining gems. "We'll go with you. Lead the way."

"More pavement to pound?" McCoy sighed wearily. "Oh joy."

"Forgive me, O Captain, but I fear that some hereabouts may speak less freely in the presence of too many strange faces. I will travel more swiftly, and hear much more, on my own."

Kirk assessed the situation. Would they ever see Jaheed again if they sent him off alone to forage for information? The man had given Kirk no reason to doubt him so far, but what did they really know of him or why he'd been hung out to die? One thing was for certain, though: Jaheed surely had more contacts and connections in Reliux than Kirk and the others did.

"Very well. I supposed we don't *all* need to accompany you on your rounds, but . . . Mister Sulu, why don't you tag along with our new friend, just in case he requires assistance?"

"Aye, sir."

Jaheed looked wounded. "That's hardly necessary, O Captain. Do you not trust me?"

Kirk tactfully ducked the question. "There's a saying among my people: two heads are better than one. You know this city and its people, Sulu knows our mission. Combined, you stand a better chance of success. Beyond that, I didn't cut you down from that tree just to risk you running into trouble again, with no one to help you out next time. I'd rather have one of my own people watching your back, just in case."

"As you wish, O Captain," Jaheed said with a shrug. "Come, friend Sulu. The night will be upon us soon and we have many doorways to call upon, some more inviting than others."

"Oh boy," Sulu said. "This should be interesting."

"Watch yourself, Sulu," McCoy said, frowning.

"Bet on it." Sulu patted the phaser discreetly affixed to his belt, then indicated his communicator as well. "You'll hear from me soon enough, if not sooner."

"See that we do, Lieutenant." Kirk considered joining them, or at least dispatching Levine to provide additional security, but remembered what Jaheed had said about too many unfamiliar faces discouraging folks from speaking openly. He also doubted that Levine would want to leave his captain and the rest of the party unguarded in an alien locale. "Keep your ears *and* your eyes open."

The two men departed into the gathering dusk. Kirk waited until

Levine locked the door again, then flipped open his communicator, taking advantage of their privacy to check in with the shuttlecraft. Before he could contact *Galileo*, however, the communicator chirped to alert him of an incoming transmission from Akbari, beating him to the punch by moments. Kirk tensed in response; to avoid an ill-timed message blowing their cover, he had instructed Ensign Akbari to avoid initiating communications except in case of an emergency.

"Kirk here. What is it?"

Akbari responded immediately. *"Sorry to interrupt you, Captain, but I have urgent news from Commander Spock and the* Enterprise."

"Report, Ensign." Kirk immediately gave her his full attention. McCoy and the others gathered around, listening in.

"We have a Klingon sighting, Captain."

The word "Klingon" sent an almost palpable shock wave through the room. Kirk locked eyes with McCoy, who looked as though he'd just received a worrisome diagnosis. Levine reached instinctively for his phaser. Landon's eyes widened.

Damn it, Kirk thought, *as if we didn't already have enough on our hands.* He listened intently as Akbari reported that a Klingon battle cruiser was currently circling Atraz, keeping pace with the *Enterprise*. Both ships, he gathered, were waiting and watching for the other's next move, a standoff that struck Kirk as far too volatile for his liking. Peace treaty or not, any encounter with the Klingons was bound to turn hot at the slightest provocation by either side.

"Acknowledged."

He hated the idea of being stuck down on the planet while his ship was playing cat and mouse with some Klingons, but what else could he do? Taking the shuttlecraft back to the ship was a dicey proposition that would require the *Enterprise* to lower its shields—and possibly put *Galileo* in the crosshairs of the Klingons' targeting sensors.

Plus, he still had a mission to complete here on Atraz.

Spock can handle this, he reminded himself, *and Scotty and Uhura and the others too.* He couldn't ask for a more capable first officer and crew to look after his ship, even with Klingons on the viewscreen. None of which kept him from wishing the hell that he was there on the bridge.

"Keep us informed," he instructed Akbari, before updating her on the status of the landing party and its mission so she could relay that information to the *Enterprise* with all deliberate speed. Doing so was a deliberate risk since the Klingons were sure to detect the transmission from the shuttlecraft, if they hadn't already, alerting them to *Galileo's* presence on the planet, but neither he nor Spock could afford to be operating in the dark; they needed to stay in touch with each other. "Stay on your toes, Ensign. If the Klingons start getting too close for comfort, or paying too much attention to you, contact *Enterprise* immediately and take whatever evasive measures are necessary."

"Evasive?" Akbari's reluctance to abandon the search party came through the communicator. *"What about you and the others, Captain?"*

"Protect yourself and the shuttlecraft, Ensign. *Galileo* can't help us if it's destroyed or captured by the Klingons. Do you read me?"

"Aye, sir. Loud and clear."

"Very good. Kirk out."

He put away his communicator and turned toward his companions, who regarded him with understandably grave expressions.

"So . . . Klingons." McCoy released a heavy sigh. "Just what we *didn't* need."

"Always a possibility, Bones, once we crossed the border into this sector. At least they don't seem to have charged in, disruptors blazing. From the sound of it, they're just monitoring the *Enterprise* . . . for now."

"Perhaps they're waiting for reinforcements, sir?" Levine suggested. "Holding their fire until they outnumber the *Enterprise*?"

"No doubt Mister Spock has taken that possibility into account and is making plans for that eventuality," Kirk said. "How exactly we factor into those plans remains to be seen."

"Why don't I find that reassuring?" McCoy said wryly.

"I trust Spock to make the right call, if and when more Klingons show up. In the meantime, we need to find out what's become of Hamparian sooner rather than later. I'm not inclined to test the Klingons' patience any longer than we have to."

"Klingon patience." McCoy snorted. "Pretty sure that's an oxymoron."

"Let's hope not, Bones. We're here for Hamparian, not to butt heads with the Empire and its soldiers."

"From your lips to Providence's ears, Jim."

Landon checked her own phaser. "Do you think we can expect company, Captain? Down here on the planet?"

"I wouldn't be surprised, Yeoman. We should operate on the assumption that the Klingons know about *Galileo*. They may come calling in response."

"To beat us to Doctor Hamparian?" she asked.

"Unknown, unfortunately."

Restless, Kirk strode over to a window, which offered an elevated view of the city. Streetlamps were being lit as the sun departed for the night. He peered up at the darkening sky as though searching for the reported battle cruiser, which, in theory, was both too far away to be seen and much too close by. Lowering his gaze, he contemplated the fortress looming over the city, which looked solid enough to withstand any assault not involving heavy artillery or modern energy weapons. Forbidding battlements, ramparts, gates, and watchtowers discouraged unwanted visitors. One particular tower, at the right rear corner of the castle, caught his eye as night came on fully. What were those lights flaring to life on the upper floors of the tower? They didn't glow like flickering torches or candles, or even the luminous fungus peddled by Pujal and her caravanners. Was it just his imagination, or did those lights look more like the kind of artificial white illumination one would expect to find on more modern, technologically advanced planets?

"Bones, Landon, Levine, come over here and take a look at something." He pointed out the tower's peculiar lights, which appeared unique among the lights emanating from the fortress's other windows as well as in the surrounding city. Their own rooms, he noted, were illuminated by hanging bowls of glowing fungus, with additional lamps and lanterns placed here and there, waiting to be lit as needed. "What do you think?"

"Does stand out, doesn't it?" McCoy agreed. "Don't really seem to be trying to hide it either."

"No, they don't." Kirk wondered what the story was there. "Perhaps Jaheed can shed some light on this, no pun intended, when he and Sulu get back. It may be that tower warrants a closer look."

"Speaking of which." Landon once again supplied binoculars on her own initiative.

"Thank you, Yeoman."

Not for the first time Kirk wondered how Chekov had let Landon get away from him. Then again, he knew how hard it could be to maintain a lasting relationship *and* a career in Starfleet, even when serving aboard the same ship. Or maybe especially when serving aboard the same ship?

Accepting the binoculars, he zeroed in on the tower, which grew even more interesting as he spied solar panels and a highly anachronistic sensor dish attached to the tower's conical roof, as opposed to the slate and ceramic tiles evident elsewhere in Reliux. Whoever occupied that tower clearly had access to technology far beyond Atraz's current stage of development. Not exactly a smoking gun as far as Hamparian's abduction was concerned, but as Spock might say, the discovery was . . . intriguing.

Kirk handed the binoculars over to McCoy. "Take a gander, Bones. Give me a second opinion."

The doctor needed only a moment to complete his exam.

"Well, I'll be damned."

A knock at the door announced the return of Sulu and Jaheed, who rejoined the party in the wee hours of the morning. Kirk was sitting up with Levine, while McCoy and Landon got whatever sleep they could before resuming their duties. It was Levine's turn to stand watch, but Kirk had known that he wasn't going to be able to rest easy until the two men got back in one piece. To his relief, both Sulu and Jaheed appeared safe and sound, although Jaheed seemed a trifle inebriated. Sulu just looked fatigued, but also pleased with himself. Kirk found that encouraging.

"Any luck?" he asked.

Sulu grinned. "And then some."

"Report, mister," Kirk said, energized by the positive tidings. McCoy stirred nearby, roused by the activity. Landon hurried in from the adjacent room, drawn by the noise of same, while Jaheed helped himself to an available cot. Sulu plopped down in a chair before cutting directly to the chase.

"I can give you a full account of our outing later, but the gist of it is that there *is* some very relevant gossip circulating through the local bars, dance halls, gambling dens, and such. Seems that, for some years now, the city's ruler, Varkat, has employed a personal alchemist by the name of Siroth, who is reputed to possess extraordinary skills and know-how. It's said that he's personally responsible for preserving Varkat's health and vitality, and that he can even transform base materials into precious jewels."

Not unlike the gems we synthesized back on the ship. Kirk observed that Sulu's pouch of artificial jewels appeared somewhat depleted after his expedition into the city's nightlife. "This Siroth doesn't by chance occupy a tower in the fortress?"

Sulu nodded. "You called it. People report seeing strange lights coming from his tower, often late into the night."

"So we've noticed," Kirk said. "What else?"

Sulu's grin widened. "Just this—rumor has it that Siroth has, in the last few days, acquired a mysterious new companion: a bluish-skinned lady who, so the stories go, sports two small blue 'horns' on her brow."

Kirk's eyes widened. *Horns—or antennae?*

"Doctor Hamparian," McCoy presumed.

"I'd stake my rank on it," Sulu said, beaming. "Who else could it be?"

"No one," Kirk stated. The odds of another part-Andorian showing up in Reliux in the last few days were vanishingly small. "Good work, Sulu, and you too, Jaheed."

"You are very welcome, O Captain," the latter called from the cot, where he was comfortably stretched out. His sunburned features were flushed from heavy drinking as well. "Did I not promise to find the clues you sought? And that you would not regret delivering me from my undeserved ordeal?"

"So you did, on both counts." Kirk returned to questioning Sulu. "What about Fortier?"

"No luck there, I'm afraid. Nobody we encountered recognized his name or description." Sulu shrugged. "Guess he's keeping a low profile, or maybe he just isn't memorable enough to inspire any idle chatter among the populace."

"Could be." Kirk recalled that, unlike Hamparian, the spacejacker wasn't terribly distinctive in appearance. Most Reliuxites wouldn't give him a second glance.

"Could this Siroth be Fortier in disguise?" Landon asked. Her blond tresses needed combing after jumping straight out of bed to take part in the discussion.

Sulu shook his head. "Unlikely. From what I gather, Siroth has been advising Varkat for at least four or five years now, so unless he somehow slipped off Atraz long enough to go spacejack *Chinook* as Fortier, the timing doesn't work."

"Agreed," Kirk said. "Fortier's record, patchy as it is, has him plying his trade out on the frontier up until he seized control of *Chinook*. There's no chance he could have also been living a double life on Atraz the past few years."

"Right, right." Landon yawned and rubbed her eyes. "Guess I'm not fully awake yet."

Kirk sympathized. He could also use a cup of whatever the Atrazian equivalent of black coffee was.

"Never mind Fortier for the moment. The takeaway here is that we now know for certain that Hamparian is in Reliux, and where to look for her." He strode back to the window and peered up at the sleeping castle, which looked no less impregnable than it had hours ago, even if the lights had finally been extinguished in Siroth's tower. "The question is: How do we get to her?"

"Not easily." McCoy frowned at the looming citadel, with its rock-solid ramparts and towers. "Pretty sure we're not going to be able to just stroll in the front gate and start poking around."

"Maybe a surgical raid on the tower?" Levine suggested. "Let me go do some covert recon now, try to scout out a workable incursion route." He scrutinized the fortress from afar as though searching for chinks in its armor. "Perhaps via the sewers?"

McCoy grimaced. "Be still, my beating heart."

"Don't look so glum, Bones," Kirk ribbed him. "You were planning to get some new boots anyway, remember?"

He tried to figure out the best way to infiltrate the tower that didn't involve disintegrating the fortress's defenses with their phasers. Part of him wanted to charge up to the citadel right that very minute, but Levine was right that they needed to survey the site and work out a plan before taking any drastic actions, while still racing to get to Hamparian before the Klingons did.

"One way or another, we need to gain access to that tower."

"Perhaps not, O Captain." Jaheed grinned slyly. "I may have a better idea."

Chapter Eighteen

Commander Pavel Chekov found the captain's chair more uncomfortable than usual.

At this point in his career, he was accustomed to taking the conn on occasions such as this, when Captain Kirk was charming their VIP guests in the *Enterprise*'s lush botanical gardens, but not when the ship was warping through space alongside a Klingon bird-of-prey *and* a Romulan warbird.

And with their shields lowered, no less.

Granted, the three vessels were, by mutual agreement, staying safely out of weapons range of each other, and certainly maintaining yellow alert status during a joint diplomatic mission would send a distinctly mixed message. Just the same, as the *Enterprise*'s security chief and tactical officer, Chekov couldn't help squirming inside. This felt unnervingly like that recurring anxiety dream in which he forgot to don his trousers before reporting to the bridge. He was far too exposed.

"Commander Chekov," Ensign Dupic, a bright young Deltan officer, called out from the science station. "The *Lukara* has just released an escape pod."

Chekov sat up straight, experiencing an instant rush of adrenaline. He did not know what this meant, but it couldn't be good. He resisted the temptation to immediately sound an alert.

"The *Lukara* has slowed to impulse," Dupic continued. "And the Romulans as well."

So as not to leave the pod light-years behind in a matter of seconds. "Do the same," Chekov ordered the helmsman. "Uhura, notify the captain at once. Dupic, scan pod for life signs."

Perhaps an empty pod had simply been ejected by accident? Chekov wanted to think so, but his instincts, along with his Russian sensibility, led him to doubt they could be so lucky. He braced himself for trouble.

"The pod's shielded against easy scanning," Dupic said. "I'm increasing power to the sensors, but can barely make out three . . . no, four life signs aboard: an Osori, two Vulcanoids, and . . . a Klingon, I think? It's hard to tell."

Vulcanoids, Chekov registered. In other words, a Romulan observer— and Saavik.

"Can we lock onto them with our transporters?"

"Negative, sir. Not unless they lower their shields."

Typical, he thought morosely. *Stubborn Klingons won't even be rescued except on their terms.*

"Chekov," Uhura said. "The *Lukara* is hailing the pod, demanding it return to the ship." She swiveled toward him. "The pod is not responding."

"On-screen," he ordered.

The bird-of-prey appeared on the main viewer, dwarfing the small pod rocketing away from it. Chekov needed a moment to spot the pod relative to the larger battle cruiser. Thrusters flared as the pod sped toward the Oort cloud at the outermost edges of a nearby solar system. He recalled that, as with most Federation escape pods, Klingon pods were equipped with small, rudimentary impulse engines.

"Increase magnification on the pod."

An inset window zeroed in on the pod, which was blockier and more heavily armored than its Starfleet equivalents. Chekov didn't *believe* Klingon pods were equipped with weaponry, but couldn't discount the possibility that the design had been upgraded since Kirk had captured that older bird-of-prey years ago. They would have to approach it with care if it came to that.

"Keep an eye on it," he ordered. "Don't let it out of our sight."

Turbolift doors whished open and Kirk rushed onto the bridge, followed closely by his guests. Chekov winced inwardly at the presence of a Klingon and Romulan on the bridge, but gratefully surrendered the chair to Kirk as he quickly briefed the captain on the developing situation.

"I thought you would want to see this, Captain."

"You thought right, Chekov." He looked to Uhura. "Hail the *Lukara.* Find out what's happening."

"I'm trying, sir. They're not answering." She glanced over at the viewer. "I think they have their hands full, Captain."

On-screen, the *Lukara* had changed course to pursue the pod. "Match speed and course," Kirk ordered.

"Aye, sir," Lieutenant Logovik replied from the helm.

"*Harrier* also flanking the *Lukara*," Dupic reported, "but maintaining a safe distance."

The pod had just reached the outer fringes of the cloud, which was composed of myriad small planetesimal bodies, when the *Lukara* latched onto it with a tractor beam and began drawing it back toward the ship. Chekov could not fault Captain B'Eleste's swift response. The pod's thrusters fought against the beam, but it appeared to be a losing battle.

"What is this all about?" Gledii asked anxiously. He and the other guests crowded into the command well, keeping close to Kirk. Chekov lingered just outside the railing in case he needed to clear the space around Kirk of any overly agitated civilians. The Osori's central eye was riveted to the screen. "Is Cyloo in danger?"

"You know as much as I do, Envoy." Kirk turned to the Klingon observer. "Can you shed any light here, Lieutenant Motox?"

"Only that no Klingon with any honor would desert his vessel against his captain's orders." He looked past Kirk at his Romulan counterpart, who had staked out a spot on the opposite side of the captain's chair. Contempt colored his voice. "I cannot speak to the motives of any of the *Lukara*'s less trustworthy passengers."

"Be thankful, Lieutenant, that Subcommander Taleb cannot hear you impugn his integrity so," Varis said coolly. "He's much less tolerant of Klingon boorishness than I." She adopted a more concerned tone for Kirk and Gledii. "I promise you, Captain, Envoy, I'm as baffled as anyone regarding this peculiar complication . . . although it should be noted that there are no such issues where the *Harrier* is concerned. All this drama and uncertainty is coming from the Klingon side of our awkward triangle."

Gledii nodded solemnly. "That is not lost on me."

"Beware, Envoy," Motox growled. "This smooth-tongued Romulan twists everything to her advantage."

"Only because you blustering Klingons make it so easy—"

Uhura interrupted the wrangling. "I can confirm that the *Harrier* is also hailing the *Lukara*, demanding an explanation . . . without notable results. The *Lukara* is now warning us all to keep our distance and let them deal with this situation their way. Our assistance is very much *not* requested."

Chekov wondered what the Klingons were up to. Were they simply out to clean up their own mess, to keep their dirty laundry private, or was this all being staged as part of some larger deception? Or was Motox right and the Romulan observer aboard the *Lukara* had hijacked the escape pod for some insidious purpose? And where did Saavik fit in? Had she needed to flee the bird-of-prey, taking the other Osori envoy with her? Chekov couldn't rule out that possibility. He could all too easily imagine having to escape from a Klingon vessel for good reason.

"Isn't there something you can do, Captain?" Gledii asked. "Cyloo is scarcely more than a child. She has a vast future before her."

"I have a crew member aboard that pod too," Kirk reminded him, no doubt acutely aware that Saavik's life might also be in danger. "But Captain B'Eleste seems to have matters in hand. We need to give her a chance to recover the pod, *then* provide us with a much-needed explanation."

"And if she refuses to provide one?" Varis asked. "What then?"

"We cross that bridge *if* we come to it. For now, let's see what happens before—"

A blinding white flash lit up the viewscreen as the pod *exploded* before their eyes. Chekov shaded his eyes, unable to look away, as a miniature starburst flared up brightly before being extinguished by the void, leaving only an empty tractor beam behind. The beam itself blinked out a moment later as somebody aboard the *Lukara* realized there was no longer any purpose to it. A stunned hush fell over the bridge.

The pod was gone, annihilated in an instant.

"Saavik," Uhura whispered, giving voice to what they were all thinking. "Please, no . . ."

Gledii's three eyes blinked in confusion. Chekov's own eyes watered, not from the glare.

"How did this happen?" the elder Osori moaned. "How can this be so?"

Chekov had a pretty good idea, but Motox spoke up first.

"Our escape pods are equipped with antimatter charges, to be detonated if the pod is at risk of falling into enemy hands. Escape is one thing; allowing oneself to be captured is another. Self-destruction is then the only honorable course of action."

"But why would they fear being recovered by their own ship?" Kirk demanded, his voice throbbing with emotion. He lurched from his chair, unable to sit still after what had just occurred. "That makes no sense, damn it!"

Motox had the decency to look uncomfortable. "I have no answers for you."

"That's not good enough," Kirk said. "Not by a long shot."

Varis backed away from the captain, shrewd enough to refrain from any more pointed barbs under the circumstances. Chekov wondered how well she'd known the Romulan aboard the pod. Had they been close? Was she grieving now, too?

Chekov didn't have to imagine how anguished and angry Kirk had to be after suddenly losing Saavik so horribly.

Because he felt exactly the same.

Chapter Nineteen

2024

Left over from the 1915 World's Fair, the Palace of Fine Arts remained a popular attraction for tourists and locals alike. On any given day, you could find folks ambling beneath the domed roof of the imposing Greco-Roman rotunda or along the titanic colonnades flanking the rotunda, which looked out over an artificial lagoon. Eucalyptus trees adorned the landscaping. Picnickers occupied inviting green lawns. Swans cruised the lagoon. It was an overcast weekday afternoon, so it wasn't as crowded as it might be on a sunnier weekend, but there were still plenty of people about as Melinda and Dennis strolled the grounds, discreetly scoping out the other pedestrians. She judged the locale safely public, although she still had a small canister of Mace tucked in a jacket pocket just in case "Halley" proved threatening. At his insistence, they had left their phones and podcast gear back at their apartment.

"So how are we supposed to find this comet dude again?" Dennis asked.

"He said he'd find us," she reminded him.

"Because of course he knows what we look like, because why wouldn't he? He already knows where we live, he knows how to lure us in, and we don't know anything about him." He nervously opened a fresh roll of Tums. "Not exactly an even playing field."

"The price of semicelebrity," she observed. "Can't build an audience without becoming a public figure to some degree." She reached out and gave his hand a comforting squeeze. "For what it's worth, thanks for providing backup, despite your reservations."

"Only because I don't want to end up like Briggs, spending the rest of my life wondering what happened to somebody who just up and vanished on me." He shrugged in resignation. "At least this way we'll get abducted together."

"I'm going to take that in the spirit in which it's intended, although I wouldn't be so quick to assume that—"

"Good afternoon, Ms. Silver, Mister Berry." A random passerby strolled up to them: an older white guy with a ruddy complexion, lugging a picnic basket. "A pleasant fall day, wouldn't you say? I approve of your choice of locale."

Melinda felt a rush of adrenaline. "Halley's Comet?"

"A few decades ahead of schedule, but yes."

To her relief, he wasn't sporting a trench coat with an upraised collar to conceal his face. Instead he wore a baseball cap, sunglasses, a faded red windbreaker, and slacks. A neat black mustache carpeted his upper lip. Possibly glued on by spirit gum? She wouldn't be surprised.

Here we go, she thought. "We came alone, as promised."

"I know." His voice, no longer distorted, bore no readily identifiable accent. "I've been tailing you for a few minutes, simply to ensure that no one else was shadowing you."

"Taking no chances?"

"Old habits are hard to break." He gestured toward one of the looming Corinthian columns lining the walk. "This way, please."

He guided them back behind the large concrete column, out of view of any passing visitors, where she and Dennis grudgingly consented to being patted down for a wire. To Halley's credit, he didn't take advantage of the opportunity to cop a feel or grope either of them. Nor did he object to the Mace he found in her pocket.

"A sensible precaution, times being what they are."

"Satisfied?" she asked. "We're not trying to pull one over on you. We just want to hear what you have to say."

"So it seems."

They relocated to a stretch of lawn out of earshot of any other seeming picnickers, where they could speak more comfortably. Halley produced a blanket and sandwiches in the interests of camouflage, but Melinda wanted answers, not lunch.

"No more delays," she said. "What the heck did you mean about Gillian being mixed up with a Russian spy?"

"Fair enough." Halley selected a sandwich for the benefit of any observers. "Let me start by telling you something else that transpired the night before Gillian Taylor vanished. How familiar are you with the former U.S. naval base at Alameda?"

The query caught Melinda by surprise.

"Vaguely. Didn't it close down decades ago?" She dimly recalled the occasional news story about various disputes and controversies over how best to develop the site. Hadn't there even been a ballot measure or two on the issue? Frankly, she'd never paid much attention to the subject, which seemed to involve planning commissions, zoning waivers, and other equally thrilling topics. Not anything she was particularly interested in.

"In 1997, to be exact, but back in '86, the base was still very much a going concern, and among the ships docked at the base that spring was the *U.S.S. Enterprise*, a nuclear-powered aircraft carrier. On the night of May twelfth, an apparent Russian spy was apprehended in close proximity to the ship's nuclear reactor, having somehow snuck aboard undetected. While being interrogated aboard the ship that night, he identified himself as one Pavel Andreievich Chekov, a lieutenant commander in, get this, 'Starfleet,' representing the 'United Federation of Planets,' if you can believe it."

"Star Fleet?" Dennis blurted, despite keeping quiet up to now. "As in outer space? And 'planets,' plural, as in multiple worlds other than our own?"

Melinda cringed, hoping her partner wasn't blowing their credibility with Halley. On the other hand, she couldn't help recalling Valdez's account of seeing something unearthly manifest in Golden Gate Park earlier that same day. Why did this investigation keep heading into the Twilight Zone?

"That's what he said," Halley replied. "Granted, at the time, it was hard to tell if he was bullshitting us or if he just had a screw loose. But a Russkie snooping around a U.S. aircraft carrier, and its nuclear generator no less, was not something to take lightly. You have to remember the Cold War was still raging. The Soviets had invaded Afghanistan, the Berlin Wall was still standing, Reagan was pushing his 'Star Wars' initiative to defend us from the Evil Empire. Tensions were high between the U.S. and Russia."

"As opposed to nowadays," Melinda said dryly. "But what does this have to do with Gillian?"

"Patience. I'm getting there." He took a bite out of his sandwich before proceeding. "As I was saying, the intruder—'Chekov'—was being questioned aboard the *Enterprise.* Security wasn't as tight as it should have been, however, and he made a break for it, leading the guards on a chase across the ship, which ended when he fell over a ledge, landing hard a long way down. He was critically injured, with an apparent skull fracture, and rushed to Mercy General Hospital under heavy guard. Honestly, he wasn't expected to survive."

"Did he?" Melinda still didn't see a connection to Gillian, but was curious anyway.

"Just wait. This is where we get to the really interesting part, especially as far as you're concerned. While Chekov was in surgery, three intruders invaded the operating room, pulled some kind of laser weapon on the surgical team, and absconded with the patient, rolling him out on a gurney, never to be seen again. The intruders consisted of two men and a woman. The men have never been identified, not even to this day, but the woman? She was later ID'd as Gillian Taylor, a missing marine biologist."

"Come again? Gillian stole a Russian spy from a hospital? That can't be right!"

"Assorted hospital personnel—doctors, nurses, security—identified her from her photo, which was all over the newspapers and TV not long after. They remembered her blond hair, blue eyes, et cetera. Seems she posed as a patient, in extreme distress, while her accomplices posed as doctors, wheeling her into the surgical wing. She was just faking it, though, since witnesses saw her hop off the gurney and take part in the escape after they reached Chekov. By all accounts, she was a willing participant, not a hostage."

"But that's insane. That doesn't sound like her at all," Melinda said.

Not that she'd ever actually met Gillian . . .

"Maybe she was brainwashed?" Dennis said. "Or cloned? Or replaced by an alien body snatcher?"

Halley did a double take, then shot Gillian a look that all but shouted: *What's up with this guy? Is he for real?*

How to explain that Dennis wasn't a nut but merely got carried away sometimes? She laughed as though he was just clowning around.

"But seriously," she said, "let me get the timeline straight. When exactly did this business at Mercy Hospital take place?"

"Maybe an hour, tops, after she left the Cetacean Institute that morning, following her altercation with her boss. By our calculations."

So Gillian went straight from slapping Briggs to liberating an injured Russian spy from an operating room? If what Halley was saying was true, why would she do that? What had possessed her? Melinda couldn't make sense of it, unless maybe she didn't actually know Gillian Taylor at all.

Who were you, Gillian, really? And what on Earth were you mixed up with?

A thought occurred to her, and she showed Halley the artist sketch of Gillian's pizza date. "This mean anything to you?"

He nodded. "I've seen that police sketch and, yes, it does match the description of one of the men who invaded the OR with Gillian. The one who pulled the ray gun on the real doctors and nurses, in fact. Can't tell you who he is, though."

"Can't or won't?"

"Can't, I'm afraid. Like I said before, the two men have never been ID'd."

"What about the other imposter? I don't suppose he was a rather cool, Zen customer known to go swimming with whales on occasion? Gave off a kind of otherworldly vibe?"

Halley shook his head. "To the contrary, the other man was an older, rather weathered Caucasian male in scrubs who was described by some witnesses as 'grumpy,' 'argumentative,' and even 'cantankerous.' They got the impression that he had some genuine medical expertise . . . and strong opinions on the subject, particularly with regard to Chekov's treatment."

She had to admit that didn't sound like the "Buddhist monk" Sister Mary Michelle had been so intrigued by. "How come I've never read about any of this?"

"Like the navy or the FBI or anyone in charge wanted to advertise that a suspected Russian operative managed to slip aboard one of our nuclear-powered aircraft carriers . . . and then got snatched right out from under our noses. That wasn't just embarrassing; that was a matter of national security. We couldn't make our vulnerabilities public or compromise our own classified investigation into the incident."

"So you quashed the SFPD's missing-persons case," Melinda realized. At least this part of the puzzle fit together. "Because Gillian wasn't just missing; she was part of this whole Cold War espionage scandal."

"Well, not me precisely, more like my superiors, but . . . pretty much. We didn't want the police or the press sticking their noses into a major breach in military security, especially with so many questions still outstanding, such as how this Chekov got aboard the ship in the first place, what he was doing—or intending to do—with that nuclear generator, how Gillian and her accomplices spirited him out of the hospital without being caught, and what became of them afterwards. Those were our mysteries to solve, not the SFPD's."

"And did you ever find out anything? About what happened to Gillian?"

She held her breath, waiting for his response.

"Afraid not. Trust me, no stone was left unturned, but *that* was the last anyone ever heard of Doctor Gillian Taylor . . . or 'Lieutenant Commander' Pavel Chekov, for that matter. Despite our best efforts, we hit a brick wall. It was as though they had literally dropped off the face of the Earth."

"Or left Earth altogether," Dennis chimed in. "For another world, another dimension, another time."

Halley shrugged. "Might as well have, for all the luck we had finding them."

"You keep saying 'we' and 'our,'" she said. "What exactly was your role in this?"

"Sorry, you're not getting my name and position, then or now. Suffice it to say I was there that night, on the *Enterprise,* and was present at Chekov's botched interrogation, which, in hindsight, could have been handled better. I was also involved in the subsequent investigation into those events."

"And the cover-up?"

"That too."

"So why spill the beans now?" she asked, as she'd asked Fulton before. "Guilty conscience?"

"Hardly. What's to feel guilty about? Trying to defend our country and its armed forces from foreign espionage? My only regret is that we couldn't get any intel out of Chekov before he cracked his stubborn Soviet skull open, and that he slipped out of our grasp when we were trying to save his life."

"So why then? Why now?"

"Because maybe you can crack the puzzle the way we never could." He stared out over the lagoon, as though peering into the past. "It's been nearly forty years and we've gotten nowhere. Who knows? Maybe you and your listeners actually can crowd-source a solution, as you say. At this late date, where's the harm? Personally, I'd like to get this cleared up, one way or another, although you didn't hear that from me."

"Got it, I think." She wondered if, despite his denials, Halley did possibly blame himself to some degree, if not for stepping on Fulton's investigation, then for letting that captured spy get injured and then get away. Was this leak solely of his own initiative—or was it being backed by his past and present superiors, unofficially?

Assuming any of this could verified, that was.

"No offense, but I have to ask: How do we know you're not just making this up? You have any unredacted classified files or documents you're prepared to pass along?"

"No offense taken, but no, I'm not willing to stick my neck out that far. I don't know if you've heard, but the authorities take a dim view of walking off with classified files these days. But you don't need to take my word for it regarding what happened back in '86. I've already told you where to look next."

It took her a moment to figure out what he meant.

"Mercy General Hospital."

Chapter Twenty

"Mister Spock," Uhura announced, "the Klingon vessel is finally responding to our hails."

And none too soon, Spock observed. The *Enterprise* remained at yellow alert, shields up, while he speculated as to why the Klingons had delayed responding until now. Perhaps they had hoped that their mere arrival would be enough to send the *Enterprise* retreating from the sector, or, alternatively, to provoke the *Enterprise* into taking preemptive action against them, thereby casting Starfleet in an even more negative light? If the latter had been their intention, they had severely underestimated this crew's discipline and self-restraint.

"Acknowledged, Lieutenant. Put them through."

"Aye, sir."

Moments later, the typically bellicose visage of a Klingon officer appeared on the main viewer. A bifurcated beard ended in two separate points beneath his chin. Spock immediately recognized him as the Klingon who had commanded a D7 battle cruiser against the *Enterprise* during the Troyian affair months ago. On that occasion, the Klingons had been forced to retreat after a brief skirmish; that the Klingon captain still held a grudge was an almost mathematical certainty.

"*This is Captain Khod of the* Imperial Battle Cruiser BortaS. *Your presence in this sector is a flagrant violation of treaty. On behalf of the Klingon Empire, you are ordered to depart this space at once!*"

To depart, not to surrender, Spock noted. The distinction suggested that the Klingons would rather chase them away from Atraz than attempt to capture the *Enterprise*, perhaps because their primary objective was to secure Doctor Hamparian, not to engage in battle?

"This is Commander Spock of the *U.S.S. Enterprise,*" he replied. "We appreciate your concerns, but our temporary presence in this system cannot be helped. We are on a mission of mercy to rescue a Federation citizen whose escape pod found refuge on this planet after she was forced to abandon a civilian vessel during an emergency situation." This description, while not the whole truth, was nevertheless accurate. "Rest assured that neither the Federation nor Starfleet has any long-term ambitions regarding this system. We shall depart immediately upon the completion of our mission."

Diplomacy was his father's vocation, not his, but Spock judged his response suitably conciliatory and nonconfrontational. He could only hope the Klingon would also find it so.

"Not good enough!" Khod's eyes narrowed as he peered at his own viewscreen. *"Where is Kirk, Vulcan?"*

Confirmed: Khod had not forgotten the *Enterprise.*

"The captain is not available at present, but the facts as I presented them to you remain the same. You are welcome to observe our activities in this system in order to see for yourself that our rescue mission is simply that."

"We do not require your permission, Vulcan! You have no right to be here."

"Neither do you, per the terms of the same treaty. This is neither Federation nor Klingon space, so we would both be well advised to tread judiciously."

"Save your advice for yourself, Vulcan. I demand to speak to Kirk."

"That is not possible at this time."

"You mean he is already on the planet!" Khod sneered at Spock. *"It's said that Vulcans cannot lie, but we Klingons know better than that. You're far too logical not to bend the truth when necessary . . . like any other sensible species."*

"There has been no attempt to deceive you."

"Do you deny that you have landed a shuttlecraft on Atraz? And that your captain is even now violating treaty by setting foot on the planet?"

"I see no logic in denying that which you are evidently aware of, so you will understand that the *Enterprise* cannot leave this system while we still have a rescue party on Atraz, engaged in the mission of mercy I spoke of earlier. We are not in the habit of deserting our fellow crew members . . . or an endangered civilian."

"You can and will!" Khod shook his fist. *"Their personal safety was forfeit the moment they trespassed upon forbidden soil."*

"I regret I cannot oblige you in this respect. Your government is free to file a formal protest through the proper diplomatic channels."

"Klingons do not talk. We act." Khod gestured to an off-screen subordinate, raising his palm as though to deliver a vicious chop. *"Consider yourself warned!"*

He completed the chopping motion and the transmission halted abruptly, the Klingon's image replaced by a magnified view of the orbiting battle cruiser.

"He doesn't mince words." Scott scowled at the screen from his post at the engineering station. "I'll give him that."

"But what did he mean, Mister Spock?" Uhura asked. "About taking action, I mean."

"That worries me as well, Lieutenant. Maintain yellow alert status."

"He didn't mention Doctor Hamparian," Scott said. "You think that means they already have the lady in their clutches?"

"That is impossible to infer with certainty, but I would surmise not. Why go to such efforts to make us abandon our mission if they already have the doctor in their possession? Why not simply convey her to Klingon space with all deliberate speed, leaving us behind?"

"Aye, you've got a point there, Mister Spock. Maybe the captain still has a chance to find her first."

Spock wanted to think so, but had insufficient data to calculate Kirk's odds of success with any degree of accuracy. "Continue monitoring the battle cruiser's movements and energy readings. Be prepared to—"

"Mister Spock!" Chekov called out excitedly from the science station. "The Klingons have launched a shuttlecraft!"

Spock overlooked the young ensign's undue emotion, considering the urgency of his news.

"Bearing?"

"For the planet, sir! Where the captain and the others are!"

"I am quite aware of their location, Ensign."

Rahda looked anxiously at Spock from the helm. "Shall I attempt to intercept, sir? Or fire a shot across their bow?"

"On what grounds, Lieutenant? We can hardly object to the Kling-ons dispatching a shuttlecraft to Atraz when we have already done the same. To take action against the Klingon shuttle invites retaliation from the *BortaS*, against either *Enterprise* or *Galileo.*"

"But you just know they're going after the landing party," Scott protested, lurching from his seat, "or Doctor Hamparian, or both! We can't just sit by while they send a squad of bloody-minded Klingon butchers down there to stir up the devil knows what kind of mischief."

"I share your apprehensions regarding our colleagues' safety, Mister Scott, but escalating this confrontation will not increase our chances of recovering Hamparian and completing our mission." His reasoned response and measured tone belied the effort required to keep his own visceral reaction to the landing party's increased peril thoroughly under control. "Lieutenant Uhura, alert *Galileo* that they can expect Klingons on Atraz shortly. Instruct Ensign Akbari to relay that information to the captain at once."

"Aye, sir. Already on it."

Chekov looked up from the science scanner, his anxiety painfully obvious. "Do you think the captain and the landing party will be all right, sir? If we warn them in time?"

"I see no reason to assume otherwise." Spock raised his voice, conscious of the need to maintain morale while commanding humans. "I remind you all that Captain Kirk has dealt with Klingons before, and seldom on friendly terms. He has always prevailed in the past."

Except that I am usually there at his side, Spock thought. He suppressed an irrational urge to rush to Kirk's aid, leaving Scott in command of the ship. Duty required him to remain on the bridge, no matter what threat the Klingon shuttlecraft posed to the landing party. He also acknowledged, silently, that this duty was not to his liking.

Be careful, Jim.

Chapter Twenty-One

They were only days from Nimbus III, but the Planet of Galactic Peace had never felt farther away. Kirk was starting to suspect they were never going to get there.

"This is a crime against the Klingon Empire!" Captain B'Eleste railed from the viewscreen, which she shared with Commander Plavius of the *Harrier* as well as Nawee, the other surviving Osori envoy. In the immediate aftermath of the escape pod's explosive demise, annihilating everyone aboard it, emotions were running high. *"One of my officers assaulted, another murdered, and my chief medical officer killed while being abducted. Let no one dare suggest that we are responsible for this outrage!"*

The three ships faced off against one another in deep space, not far from where the pod had self-destructed. They each remained barely out of firing range of the other ships, but Kirk had already put the *Enterprise* on yellow alert in case armed hostilities broke out. Sensor scans confirmed that both the bird-of-prey and the warbird had also raised their shields and elevated their combat readiness. Kirk wished Spock was not still aboard the *Harrier*; he could use his friend's cool head and sage advice during this tense confrontation, which threatened to escalate into a full-blown interstellar incident, if not open warfare.

"And who else are we to hold responsible for the loss of one of our own?" Gledii challenged B'Eleste. "We trusted Cyloo's safety to your care!"

"Look to either the Romulan or the Starfleet 'observer' aboard our ship, or possibly the both of them conspiring together. Lieutenant Saavik was half Romulan, correct?"

"Wait just one blasted minute!" McCoy protested, having rushed to the bridge upon news of the tragedy. He glared at the screen from beside Kirk's chair. "Saavik's atoms aren't even cold yet, and you have the gall to accuse her of . . . what? Blowing herself up for no reason?"

"It is hardly unknown for Romulans to choose destruction over capture," B'Eleste said, not inaccurately. Kirk recalled his first encounter with a warbird many years ago; that ship's commander had blown up his own vessel rather than surrender. *"They could not escape our tractor beam, so they destroyed themselves, taking Doctor Kesh and the Osori with them."*

Saavik would never do that, Kirk thought. The pain of her loss struck hard, but he couldn't succumb to it now. Later, if they were lucky, there would be time to wonder if he should've let her volunteer for that mission, or if he should have responded faster after the pod exited the *Lukara*, but at the moment he didn't have the luxury of second-guessing himself. His ship, his mission, and maybe even the uneasy truce between three galactic superpowers were at risk. Damage control was his first order of business.

"Nonsense," Plavius objected. *"What motive could we have for sabotaging this joint diplomatic mission?"*

"Perhaps to drive a wedge between us Klingons and the Osori." Motox stepped forward to address the screen. He pointed an accusing finger at Varis. "This one has been trying to poison the Osori against us since the moment she beamed aboard the *Enterprise.*"

The Romulan in question smiled maliciously. "An unnecessary effort, it seems, since you Klingons have done such an exceptional job of it yourselves . . . by failing to keep that unfortunate young Osori alive and well."

"You may cease jostling for our favor," Gledii said, scowling. "As far as I'm concerned, this misconceived initiative is over. I knew this was a mistake on our part, and now Cyloo has paid for our foolishness with her life." The elder Osori turned toward Kirk. "There will be no conclave, Captain. I demand you reverse course and take us back to Osor at once. And Commander Plavius, I expect you to do the same."

"Hold, Gledii, let's not be too hasty," Nawee urged from the Romulan vessel. *"I grieve Cyloo as well, but is this what she would have wanted? More than any of us, she believed strongly in the conclave and wished for it to mark a new beginning for our people."*

"Yes," Gledii said bitterly. "And look what became of her."

"Nevertheless, it seems an insult to her memory to cancel the conclave because of her tragic end. She would have never wished to be the reason we abandoned her dream."

Kirk saw both sides of the argument. Like Gledii, he was also tempted to abort the mission before things went from bad to worse, but Nawee had a point too. Kirk did not want Saavik to have died in vain.

"And what of my own warriors?" B'Eleste said. *"In light of these foul doings, I can no longer trust their lives to the suspect hospitality of our rivals. Return both Motox and Chorn to the* Lukara *in short order."*

The "or else" was implied by her tone.

"That is not possible at this time," Plavius replied, sounding more rueful than defiant. *"The death of Subcommander Taleb cannot be brushed aside. Those responsible must be identified and made to face Romulan justice. Until that is done, I am not at liberty to release the observers currently in our custody. There must be consequences for what has transpired."*

In other words, Kirk translated, he couldn't let go of his own hostages after what happened to the Romulan hostage aboard the Klingon ship.

Which did not bode well for Spock.

"Before this goes any further," Kirk said, "I want to speak to my first officer."

"I regret I cannot allow that," Plavius said. *"Captain Spock and Lieutenant Chorn have been confined to quarters for the time being."*

"Over my strenuous protests," Nawee stated. The Osori was obviously getting preferential treatment aboard the warbird. *"This was not of my choosing."*

"A more than reasonable measure," Plavius insisted, *"under the circumstances. Be assured that both men are unharmed and will remain so. Indeed, their confinement is, at least in part, for their own protection. Subcommander Taleb's shocking extinction is still a fresh wound in my crew's heart; there is much anger and suspicion regarding it."*

Kirk didn't like the sound of that. Spock in the hands of vengeful Romulans looking for someone to blame? Or guilty Romulans seeking to shift blame elsewhere?

"With all due respect, Commander, that does not reassure me." Kirk appealed to Varis for assistance. "Can you talk reason to your commander?"

Shaking her head, she sidled closer to him and whispered in his ear: "This is about politics, not reason. Taleb's family is well connected and will demand satisfaction. For Plavius to discount that would be . . . unwise."

Kirk could believe it, but he wasn't about to sacrifice Spock's safety on the altar of Romulan politics and infighting.

"Listen to me, Commander," he addressed Plavius sternly. "I sympathize with your position. No one wants answers about what happened to our people more than I do, but don't think for a moment that I'm going to let Spock be detained indefinitely, let alone be taken back to Romulus to be punished for a tragedy he had *nothing* to do with. Do I make myself clear?"

"*Spock knew the risks when he beamed aboard my ship,*" Plavius said, "*as a hostage to the safety of our observers on the other vessels, one of whom came to harm. Taleb's death forces my hand.*"

"So an eye for an eye, regardless of who is truly responsible? You've met Spock. You know his reputation. Do you really think he's to blame for what happened to Taleb . . . and our Lieutenant Saavik for that matter? She was Spock's protégée, for heaven's sake!"

"*And what of the hostages aboard your ship, Kirk?*" B'Eleste pointed at him with her painstik, as though she could jolt him from the screen. "*Will you return my first officer to me? And your Romulan hostage to the warbird?*"

McCoy huffed. "So I guess we're not bothering to call them 'observers' anymore."

That had not been lost on Kirk.

"I wish I could." He didn't want to play that game, but he needed leverage here. He couldn't just give it away. Granted, B'Eleste was no longer holding any hostages aboard the *Lukara*, but Motox's presence aboard the *Enterprise* just might discourage B'Eleste from firing on them in retaliation for the loss of her slain warriors. And how would Plavius react if Kirk returned Motox to the *Lukara*, but not Varis to the *Harrier*? This crisis was volatile enough; he had to be careful not to throw fuel on the fire. "But that depends on how well we can all work together to resolve matters."

"What's this? You mean to hold me against my will?" Motox angrily drew his *d'k tahg*. "Think twice, Kirk, before—"

Twin phaser beams, from two different security officers, converged on the irate Klingon, stunning him into insensibility. Motox hit the deck loudly. Kirk silently commended the officers' quick reflexes, even as he braced himself for B'Eleste's reaction, which was just as ferocious as he expected.

"Have you no shame, Kirk? No honor? My first officer assaulted before my eyes, while you mouth empty platitudes about 'working together'? I will not stand for this, nor shall the Empire!"

"Motox drew a weapon on my bridge, in the presence of foreign dignitaries under my protection. My security officers acted appropriately, and with restraint. Motox will wake up in detention with nothing more than a minor headache to remind him to behave less recklessly on my ship." Kirk was not about to apologize for his crew defending their other guests from a potentially violent outburst. "Suppose a bad-tempered visitor drew a *d'k tahg* on *your* bridge?"

"Don't presume to lecture me, Kirk! My crew has been attacked, my ship's hospitality abused, Klingon lives lost!" Spittle sprayed from her lips, visible thanks to the fine resolution of the viewscreen. *"Hear me, Kirk, Plavius: I am not leaving without my officers, and justice for my fallen comrades. You have two standard hours to return Motox and Chorn . . . or face my wrath."*

"You might do well do reconsider that, Captain B'Eleste." Plavius's sorrowful tone hardened, along with his expression. *"Our Empire does not respond well to ultimatums, from the Klingons or the Federation."*

"Lovely," McCoy groused. "A three-way standoff in the middle of nowhere. Wonder whose trigger finger is itchier?"

"My money is on the Klingons," Chekov said from the nav station.

"To start the battle," Varis asked, "or to finish it? For the latter, one should never bet against Romulans with a score to settle."

Gledii's three eyes viewed all present with contempt, simultaneously. "And this is why my people have always shunned outsiders. It was madness to leave our world."

So much for Galactic Peace, Kirk thought, *thanks to one hijacked escape pod.*

Was that the whole point of that business with the pod, to scuttle the conclave on Nimbus III before it even began? But who was behind it, and why was this feeling oddly familiar? An elusive memory tickled the back of his brain, like a name on the tip of your tongue that you can't quite recall. Something about another stolen escape pod?

"Is it just me, Bones, or does it feel like we're being played?"

Chapter Twenty-Two

2024

"I'll never forget that day for as long as I live. In all my years nursing, I never experienced anything like it!"

Jane Temple (née Yoder) addressed Melinda and Dennis via Skype. Ironically, even though Mercy General Hospital was just a few blocks away from their apartment, the retired nurse now resided in Scotland, forcing Melinda to conduct the interview remotely. Dennis had fretted about discussing these matters over the internet, given all the clandestine precautions Halley had put them through, but she'd reminded him that they were in the podcast business after all; it was going to be hard to cover the story without going online sometimes.

And it wasn't as though they had any other options. Before parting company with them at the Palace of Fine Arts, Halley had slipped them a list naming the members of the surgical team that had allegedly been waylaid by Gillian and her anonymous cohorts back in the day. Of the half dozen names on the list, Jane Temple was the only witness they could track down who was also willing to talk to them about the incident. For that, they could sacrifice the immediacy of a face-to-face interview—and risk letting their devices listen in.

"Take me through it again." Melinda was still trying to wrap her head around the idea that Gillian was somehow mixed up with Russian spies and naval espionage on top of being upset over the loss of her whales. That just didn't mesh with everything they'd learned about Gillian up to now and the picture Melinda had been forming of the missing cetologist, who hardly seemed the type to invade an operating room and make off with a critically injured patient. Perhaps Temple's apparently vivid memories could paint a clearer picture of what happened on that tumultuous afternoon long ago?

"It's just as I told you before." The retired nurse, now in her sixties, had a sunny, outgoing personality. Purple hair, streaked with fluorescent green, suggested an independent soul who didn't feel obliged to act her age. "We were in the OR, prepping for surgery, when these three strangers barged in, waved a ray gun at us, and locked us in an adjoining room while they did something to the patient, then rolled him out of the OR—and apparently the hospital as well. I heard secondhand that they somehow vanished from a moving elevator without explanation. Like a locked-room mystery!"

A well-stocked bookcase could be glimpsed behind her. Dennis, who was carefully staying out of view of the camera, mimed firing a weapon to remind Melinda to ask about something.

"Tell me more about that 'ray gun' you mentioned."

"Well, it didn't look much like a gun, to be honest. More like a boxy TV remote. But the leader of the group, the good-looking fellow from that sketch you showed me, pointed it at us as though it was a weapon, and nobody wanted to call his bluff. Then, after he herded us into the other room, he zapped the door handle with a laser beam, fusing it shut. So I guess he wasn't bluffing after all!"

Dennis gave Melinda an "I told you so" look from off-camera, no doubt taking this as further evidence of extraterrestrial involvement. Melinda wanted to roll her eyes back at him, but had to admit that this oddball detail had her perplexed. Why not just use a plain old handgun if you're going to break a patient out of a hospital? Why some sort of souped-up laser pointer or whatever?

"And you're certain that was Gillian Taylor you saw that day? And the man from the police sketch?"

Temple nodded confidently. "Trust me, their faces are burned into my memory. Not every day you get taken hostage during surgery."

"And the third man? What do you recall about him?"

"He was pretty memorable too. Argued vigorously with Doctor Ellis, the surgeon leading the operation, over the best way to save the patient. He certainly sounded like an actual doctor, and was quite heated on the subject. He wasn't about to let Doctor Ellis perform cranial surgery on the patient to relieve the pressure on his brain."

"What did he look like?"

"Older, somewhat weathered features, maybe a trace of a southern accent?"

Not remotely the Buddhist monk in the whale tank then. So who was this very opinionated medic? And why was a southern doctor hijacking a Russian patient?

"At first, I thought he was simply another physician brought in to consult," Temple continued, "until the other man pulled out his ray gun and cleared us out of the OR. I didn't get a good look at what happened next, since we were all crowding around this one small window in the locked door while hollering for help, but the doctor-ish fellow placed a blinking device on the patient's forehead, which appeared to rouse him, but I can't swear to that."

"And then they took Chekov."

"If that's what you say his name was. We weren't told that at the time, nor much about the circumstances of his accident. Just that it was all very hush-hush and security was tight, although obviously not tight enough! And afterwards we were all sworn to secrecy."

Melinda asked her usual question. "So how come you're willing to talk to us now?"

"That was umpteen years ago. What can it matter now? If you must know, it feels good to finally talk about it."

"The authorities might not feel the same way."

"What are they going to do? Come after an expatriate former nurse, living abroad, over some old business dating back to the Reagan years? I like to think our glorious leaders have better things to worry about these days."

Here's hoping, Melinda thought. She liked the old lady's attitude.

"That was a crazy day, though. Not just because of the raid on the OR, but what with that weirdness with the magic kidney pill as well."

"Kidney pill?"

"You haven't heard about that?" Temple grinned. "That was a trip in itself."

Was this case about to get even more bizarre? Melinda braced herself for whatever new wrinkle might be coming her way. "Enlighten me."

Jane Temple didn't have to be asked twice. "Oh, you're going to love this. That very same afternoon, around the very same time the OR was invaded, an elderly patient, Mrs. Coates, somehow grew a brand-new kidney. Claimed a doctor gave her a pill while she was in a hallway waiting to undergo dialysis and . . . boom, suddenly she had a new kidney."

"What?" Melinda had thought nothing more could surprise her about this case, but found herself startled again. "She grew a new kidney? How is that possible?"

"It isn't, but somehow it happened anyway. They ran her through every scan possible, all of which verified the unbelievable. She had indeed grown a healthy new kidney . . . in less than thirty minutes."

"And the doctor who gave her the pill?"

"Never identified, but the talk was that he was the same rogue doctor who barged into the OR and stole our patient from us. The argumentative one."

Melinda's head was spinning. She visualized adding this latest reveal to her case board, which was starting to look less like an organizational diagram than an exercise in surrealism. Why had Halley neglected to mention that part of the story? Because he and his bosses had been more fixated on the Cold War espionage aspects?

"What happened next to the kidney lady?"

"Coates. Mildred Coates. Milly to her friends."

"I'm impressed you still remember her name after all this time."

"You don't forget a bona fide medical miracle. That was quite the medical sensation, at least for a while."

"But then?"

Temple shrugged. "Turned out there was nowhere to go, research-wise, and nothing further to study. It was a freak, irreproducible event that defied explanation. Milly soon tired of being treated like a test animal, subjected to every test and procedure you can think of, and stopped cooperating with the researchers. And that was the end of it. No revolutionary new discoveries were made, nobody got rich and famous because it, no groundbreaking studies or reports were published; I think the whole medical establishment eventually just wanted to forget about it and pretend it never happened." She snorted in derision. "Wouldn't be surprised if most folks dismiss it as a hoax these days, if they remember it all, but it happened all right, swear to God, just like I told that one really pushy guy way back when."

Melinda didn't let that slide by. "What guy? When?"

"You're not the first curious soul to come snooping around, although it's been some time since the last one. Back in the eighties, not long after all that craziness, this one young guy showed up at my door-step wanting to know all about Milly's new kidney and the anonymous doctor who supposedly fixed her with one pill."

That didn't seem too surprising to Melinda, considering. "Another eager medical researcher?"

Or perhaps Halley or one of his associates?

"Maybe, but there was something kinda shady about him. He was very intense, very persistent. He offered me serious money, like lottery money, if I helped him find out where that pill came from, never mind that we'd been sworn to secrecy about the raid on the OR. At the time, I debated whether that gag order applied to Mrs. Coates's case as well, because the money *was* tempting. The question was academic, though, since, unfortunately, I didn't have any real info to sell him. Otherwise, I would have retired a whole lot earlier!"

Melinda ran through the possible suspects in her head. Not the two men with Gillian in the OR, since Temple would have recognized them on sight, so . . . the swimming monk? Halley? Somebody else?

"Describe him to me."

"Young, like college-age young, if that. Short, maybe five foot one, tops. Bald head . . . shaved, I assume. Bushy black eyebrows. Deep voice. And like I said, *very* serious and determined to find out about that pill. Kinda reminded me of Javert in *Les Miz*, if you know what I mean, just younger and shorter."

The description didn't ring any bells with Melinda.

"He didn't, by any chance, seem Russian to you?"

"Nope. And, looking back, he wasn't all that interested in our stolen patient, your Mister Chekov. He was laser-focused on Mrs. Coates and her kidney." Her brow furrowed as she pondered that long-ago encounter. "I don't know. Maybe he was just a sick millionaire who was desperate for a miraculous new kidney of his own?"

"Do you recall his name?" Melinda had no idea how important or relevant this individual might be with regards to Gillian's disappearance, but maybe it was worth pursuing?

"Perhaps, I'm not sure. I only met him once, and the circumstances were far less exciting than what went on that day in the OR." She chuckled wryly. "Maybe if he'd pulled a laser on me, or grown a new organ, it would have stuck in my mind more. Offels? Osterman? Something like that."

Her gaze turned inward, searching her memory.

"He gave me a business card so I could contact him if I learned anything worth paying for, but I have no idea what became of it. That was at least eight addresses, six cities, five countries, and three marriages ago. Sorry."

"No problem," Melinda said, concealing her disappointment.

A miracle cure for kidney disease? Strangers sniffing around trying to discover its origins? It was possible that none of that had anything to do with Gillian's disappearance, but Melinda didn't believe it, not at this point. Too much weird, freaky stuff had taken place over the same forty-eight hours back in '86 for them not to be linked somehow.

Who was this new character, covering the same ground decades ago?

Chapter Twenty-Three

2268

The coliseum was built into a portion of the high blue wall surrounding the city. Tier after tier of long concrete benches curved along its inner circumference, offering seating enough to accommodate much of the populace, or so it appeared to Kirk as he and the rest of the landing party joined the throngs of jubilant citizens pouring through the gates and up the aisles for today's lavish spectacle. According to Jaheed, the suzerain regularly hosted public entertainments to keep his subjects happy. Chances were, Varkat and his court would be in attendance—including the "blue lady" said to be keeping company with Siroth these days?

Here's hoping, Kirk thought.

Locating Doctor Hamparian at a public arena would certainly be easier than trying to gain entry to the seemingly impregnable fortress, so Kirk and company jostled their way through the crowd, sticking closely together despite the surging press of bodies, to secure seats in an upper level of the massive amphitheater, above and across from the segregated VIP section, which was lavishly decked out with sumptuous silks and velvets and other trimmings. The deluxe seating area was currently unoccupied, awaiting the arrival of its distinguished guests.

"Just our luck." McCoy sat at Kirk's left, while Sulu and the others sat one row behind them, looking over their heads. "We would get stuck in the nosebleed seats."

"We're not here for the show, Bones," Kirk reminded him. "Just to see and *not* be seen, ideally."

Aiming to keep a low profile amidst the crowd, he scanned the packed coliseum for any lurking Klingons. Spock had alerted him, via *Galileo*, that the *BortaS* had also dispatched a shuttlecraft to Atraz, so Kirk was on yellow alert, on guard for any unwanted interference from hostile Klingons (as if there were any other kind), but would he or Sulu or any of the others even be able to spot any newly arrived Klingons in this crowded setting if the Klingons were also out of uniform and going incognito? Most of the Klingons Kirk had encountered in the past resembled your average humanoid, albeit with notably belligerent attitudes. Like the disguised Starfleet crew members, they would easily blend into Reliux's diverse, cosmopolitan population, where foreigners came and went regularly.

All the more reason to stay on our toes, Kirk thought.

He waited impatiently for the festivities to commence. Vendors worked the aisles, hawking snacks and refreshments. A clear sky provided plenty of sunshine. The concrete bench was sturdy but unforgiving; Kirk noted that more seasoned patrons had brought their own seat cushions. He was definitely missing his usual chair on the bridge by the time a fanfare of horns, rattles, drums, and cymbals heralded the arrival of the suzerain and his court. The audience rose to their feet in respect, prompting Kirk and his companions to follow suit. The captain peered over the heads of the folks in the rows below him as a regal figure, whom Kirk assumed to be Varkat himself, accepted the acclamation of his subjects before magnanimously gesturing for them to be seated once more.

The suzerain was an older male, ornately costumed and bejeweled, with craggy features and a leonine mane of snowy-white hair. Despite his apparent years, he appeared healthy and vigorous, reputedly thanks to the esoteric knowledge of his personal alchemist, the one with the suspiciously high-tech tower at the fortress. Kirk searched for Siroth amidst Varkat's sizable retinue, which boasted an impressive assortment of consorts, heirs, relations, ministers, courtiers, and miscellaneous hangers-on, along with multiple armed guards standing watch over the royal box, crossbows, truncheons, and short swords at the ready. Kirk had a clear view of the figures in the VIP section, although they were far enough away that he couldn't readily make out their faces with his naked eyes.

"Do you see Siroth?" he asked Jaheed, who was seated one row behind and a seat over from Kirk. "Or the blue lady?"

"Indeed, O Captain!" Their guide helpfully pointed at one corner of the royal box. "A few seats to the left of the suzerain, just as I predicted. He's wearing dark green, she saffron."

Now that he knew where to look, Kirk located the pair in question.

Siroth turned out to be a short, robed figure with a bald dome and bushy black eyebrows, who bore no resemblance to Louis Fortier, settling that issue once and for all. Kirk registered that discovery before swiftly turning his attention to the woman at Siroth's side. A wide-brimmed yellow headpiece, the same hue as her gown, served to conceal any vestigial antennae, but even from a distance her complexion did appear to possess a pale blue tint. To be certain, he used the mini-binoculars to zoom in on the woman's face, revealing the unmistakable features of Doctor Taya Hamparian.

"It's her," he announced. "Alive and well, so it seems."

"Thank goodness," McCoy said with feeling. "What about Fortier?"

Kirk searched the VIP section with the binoculars, but didn't spot the spacejacker anywhere. "No sign of him."

"That's damned peculiar," McCoy said, scowling. "What became of him, and how did Hamparian end up associating with this Siroth character?"

"Both good questions, Bones."

Sulu leaned forward from above. "Now what, Captain?"

Kirk assessed the situation. They had found Hamparian and determined that she appeared unharmed. What was less clear was whether she was being held against her will. Spock had shared, via Akbari, his hypothesis that Hamparian might have staged her own abduction in order to escape the Federation's stringent restrictions on her research. Would she welcome being "rescued" or not?

"We need to make contact with her while she's still in public view," he said, thinking aloud, "so we can find out how she's faring and try to work out an extraction plan. Perhaps we can somehow smuggle a communicator to her during the show? Before she disappears back inside the fortress?"

If it wasn't for the Klingon battle cruiser patrolling the space around the planet, Spock could bring the *Enterprise* within transporter range and attempt to beam Hamparian aboard the ship if and when they successfully got a communicator to her, but with the *BortaS* on the scene? Bringing the *Enterprise* closer to Atraz would provoke the Klingons further, while beaming Hamparian up would mean lowering the *Enterprise*'s shields in the presence of the enemy battle cruiser.

"Easier said than done, sir," Levine said. "Can't imagine the locals are going to allow us anywhere near their ruler and his party, let alone barge in and take custody of Hamparian on the spot. Unless we want to employ our phasers, set on stun of course."

Kirk shook his head. Firing energy weapons in full view of thousands of Atrazians, including a regional head of state, would do serious violence to the Prime Directive; it was absolutely to be avoided if it all possible.

"The doctor doesn't seem to be in immediate danger. We don't need to charge in with our phasers blazing."

"I can try to persuade someone to pass a parcel to her, containing a note and communicator," Landon volunteered. "Maybe tip a guard or attendant to do me a favor and deliver a gift to the blue lady? While doing my utmost to appear nice and harmless?"

She demonstrated a simpering smile.

"Possibly." Kirk took the suggestion under advisement. "Any other ideas?"

By now, the show in the arena below had gotten underway. Jugglers and acrobats and clowns warmed up the audience in anticipation of the main events, which Kirk understood to involve bloody gladiatorial contests of the sort that, sadly, were all too common in less-advanced civilizations throughout the known galaxy. He wasn't looking forward to enduring carnage as entertainment, but their mission did not include shutting down such practices on a planet they weren't even supposed to be visiting in the first place. Rescuing Jaheed from a gruesome death was one thing; he'd been just one lone individual out in the wilderness. Interfering with an established Atrazian institution was far beyond Kirk's purview and abilities.

That being said, Kirk winced as a thundering blast of music interrupted the landing party's whispered conference, signaling the start of the first contest. The audience cheered as one, drowning out any possible discussion for a few moments. Bracing himself for the brutality to come, Kirk was unable to look away as a half dozen or so men and women were herded out onto the sandy floor of the arena from a gated archway located at ground level, several meters below the front rows of the seating areas. The contestants were a ragtag bunch, of mixed ages and body types, most of whom already appeared somewhat worse for wear. Far from the brawny warriors of romanticized fictions, they looked just like what Jaheed had explained they were: condemned criminals sentenced to fight for their lives for the amusement and edification of honest citizens.

"Those poor souls," McCoy said, compassion and disgust warring in his voice. "How many worlds have to keep reinventing these same atrocities? What in blazes is wrong with us humanoids anyway?"

"I know, Bones, but there's nothing we can do."

Keep telling yourself that, Kirk thought as the grisly spectacle unfolded. Simple short-range weapons, incapable of endangering the audience, were thrown to the prisoners, who scrambled to claim a whip, a net, a staff, a mace, or a rope, while already fighting among themselves for whatever might give them the best chance of survival. Brutal memories of Triskelion, Magna Roma, and even life-or-death ritual combat on Vulcan stirred Kirk's sympathy for the unwilling gladiators. He'd been in their sandals more than once.

"Captain!" Landon pointed urgently at one of the unfortunates in the arena. "Isn't that Fortier?"

What? Kirk hastily turned the binoculars on the indicated contestant, who he now noticed was missing one hand. A closer look at the man's distraught, bug-eyed face cinched it; there was no mistaking Louis Fortier, whose fortunes had obviously taken a severe turn for the worse. Not only was he missing his prosthetic hand, but his mouth had been wired shut as well.

To prevent him revealing any embarrassing secrets?

"It's him," Kirk stated. "Fortier."

"Good God!" McCoy reacted in horror. "I wanted that spacejacker to get what was coming to him, but not like this!"

Down in the arena, Fortier got his remaining hand on a whip, which he snapped tentatively, perspiration streaming down his face. Instead of the Federation-contemporary attire he'd sported on the *Chinook*, he was now clad in torn and ragged Atrazian garb that had seen better days. Bulging eyes stared fearfully at a gate across the way from the one that had disgorged the prisoners. A metal portcullis rose to release . . .

Wild, feathered beasts.

"Bloodbeaks!" Jaheed went pale at the sight of a flock of long-legged, flightless birds even larger than the ones that had attacked him in the savannah. He made a protective gesture over his heart and gut. "Man-eaters!"

The avian creatures were comparable in size to an Australian cassowary or the winged leopards of Betelgeuse Prime. Their long necks and legs might lead a human biologist to classify them, along with their smaller cousins, as ratites of some variety. Orange and green plumage feathered their bodies, while the males boasted lurid red crests atop their heads. Curved beaks and talons looked far too sharp for comfort.

Squawking and screeching, the bloodbeaks charged at the hapless contestants, who, lacking any apparent plan or organization, tried to defend themselves as best they could. A bony, half-starved woman hurled a net at an oncoming bird, hoping to snarl or tangle the creature, but her throw went wild, flying over the bird's crested head and sliding uselessly off its back. Panicking, she turned and ran, but didn't get far before the ferocious ratite pounced on her, knocking her face-first into the ground. Avian screeches and all-too-humanoid screams reached a hideous crescendo as the bird's razor-sharp beak and claws tore at her, turning the sandy floor crimson, much to the excitement of the bloodthirsty audience, who again leaped to their feet, cheering and hooting exuberantly.

"Monsters!" Levine reached for his phaser, but Sulu placed a restraining hand on the other man's arm.

"Don't do it, mister. Not our world, not our mission."

Levine nodded, jaw tight. "It's just that . . . this is inhuman."

If only, Kirk thought. He lifted his gaze to see how Hamparian was reacting to the barbaric spectacle. Was she pleased to see her kidnapper facing death in the arena or was she as sickened by the proceedings as Kirk was? To her credit, she was indeed averting her eyes from the sanguinary display, unlike Varkat and the bulk of his court, who were clearly enjoying the show as much as the commoners they ruled over. Siroth was the only noticeable exception; the alchemist maintained a neutral expression, betraying neither approval nor disapproval of the grisly contest.

I wouldn't want to play poker against him, Kirk thought.

Another prisoner fell prey to the bloodbeaks, igniting a feeding frenzy among the greedy creatures. The surviving contestants were already on the defensive, frantically trying to fend off the feathered carnivores with their rudimentary and woefully inadequate weapons. Cracking his whip, Fortier struggled to hold three ratites at bay as they closed in on him from all directions. His eyes were wide with fright. Muffled cries escaped his wired jaws.

"He doesn't stand a chance, Jim," McCoy said. "Unless we do something!"

"Like what, Bones?" Kirk shared his friend's dismay and anguish. No matter what Fortier had done or threatened on the *Chinook*, the man was still a Federation citizen and a human being, but in attempting to elude Federation justice, he seemed to have run afoul of a far harsher variety, and there wasn't a damn thing Kirk could do about it. His own instructions to the landing party came back to him: Recovering Hamparian was their top priority.

Not Fortier.

For better or for worse, the end came quickly. Warding off one bloodbeak, Fortier didn't spin around swiftly enough to stop another bird from leaping at him from behind. A vicious kick sliced open his back and sent him sprawling onto the sand, where the birds converged on him. Any chance of the spacejacker ever seeing the inside of a Federation courthouse vanished within moments.

"So much for Fortier," Kirk said grimly over the roar of the crowd. The dead man had endangered the lives of an entire shipload of innocents, but that hadn't made his final moments any easier to watch. "He's escaped us for good."

"Poetic justice?" Sulu asked.

Kirk shook his head. "No poetry. Just brutality."

The carnage was apparently too much for the nameless Atrazian gentleman seated to Kirk's right, nearer to the aisle, who got up and left even as the birds were feasting on Fortier's remains. Still troubled by the spacejacker's ghastly demise, Kirk barely registered the slender, dark-haired woman who quickly claimed the empty seat beside him—until he felt the point of a blade pressing against his ribs.

"The spectacle is not to your liking, Kirk?" she said in a low voice.

"I am not surprised. You Earthers are too softhearted to see the savage beauty in such blood sports. We Klingons have stronger stomachs."

Damn it. Kirk kicked himself for letting Fortier's ugly death distract him from the woman's approach. Granted, that horrific sight would capture anyone's attention, but that was no excuse for letting his guard slip.

"Captain," Sulu whispered urgently, "don't look now, but I think I've spotted a couple of Klingons—in local garb—heading toward us. Pretty sure I recognize one of them from that crew that tried to take over the *Enterprise* a while back. They must be from the shuttlecraft we were warned about. Looks like they've found us."

You don't say, Kirk thought wryly. "Thank you, Mister Sulu, but I'm afraid I'm already quite aware of that."

He tipped his head to indicate the woman beside him, who smirked at Sulu. "No sudden moves, please," she informed Kirk's startled companions, "unless you wish to treat the crowd to the sight of your captain's blood . . . in generous quantities."

"Blast it!" McCoy reached for his medkit, just in case. "Hasn't there been enough pointless bloodshed already? Can't you Klingons go five minutes without threatening violence?"

"Steady, everyone." Kirk held up a hand to deter Sulu and the others from taking any rash actions while he had a knife to his ribs. "Let's find out what the lady has in mind."

He slowly turned his head to inspect their new acquaintance. She appeared to be roughly his age and size, with jet-black hair tidily piled in a bun above a shrewd angular face. Smooth pink skin was closer in hue to Koloth's than Kang's. Indigo eye shadow highlighted dark eyes that gleamed with icy intent. Atrazian attire provided no way to determine her rank.

"You seem to have the advantage of me," Kirk said evenly. "Captain . . . ?"

"Colonel Yorba of Imperial Intelligence. We're here for Hamparian and will brook no interference. I advise you and your officers to sit quietly while we claim our prize."

Glancing about, Kirk spied the Klingons Sulu had spotted, mere moments too late. Maybe three in all, they were closing in on Kirk and company, climbing or descending the aisles or squeezing horizontally along the rows of seating. Their brusque manners and menacing glares made it clear they now wanted to be recognized by their Starfleet counterparts.

To let us know Yorba isn't alone—and cow us into staying put?

We'll see about that.

Kirk stalled while strategizing. "I don't suppose that seat just happened to open up next to me?"

"Don't be ridiculous. I gave that inconsequential native a substantial bribe for surrendering his seat. No doubt he assumed that I wished to make the acquaintance of a handsome stranger."

"I'm flattered."

"Don't be." Her blade pressed harder, not quite drawing blood. "No offense, Kirk, but I prefer Klingons. Humans are too . . . tender . . . for my tastes."

"I'll try not to take that personally."

In the arena, a handful of contestants were still fighting for their lives against the frenzied bloodbeaks, holding the attention of the crowd. Peering across the coliseum, Kirk made out two more Klingons, identifiable by their determined tread, martial bearing, and obvious lack of interest in the featured entertainment, advancing toward the VIP section—and Doctor Hamparian.

"What exactly is your game plan here?" Kirk questioned Yorba. "If you don't mind me asking."

"Seize the scientist by force, in exchange for the life of the suzerain. Preferably without resorting to our disruptors, but . . . we'll see. What is that expression you Earthers have about needing to shatter eggs to scramble them?" Yorba kept watch over her men as they made progress toward the royal box. "Not that we're constrained by your insipid Prime Directive, of course, but the treaty regarding this sector *does* mandate that my soldiers not be too obvious about our incursion on this backwards world."

"Your discretion is commendable." Kirk digested what she'd just told him. "I take it then you don't expect Doctor Hamparian to go with you willingly?"

There went Spock's defection theory, unless it wasn't the Klingons Hamparian was defecting to?

"That is entirely up to her," Yorba said, "but we are taking her regardless. The Empire has need of her brilliance . . . and her secrets."

Just then, a desperate contestant miraculously managed to leap onto the back of an unsuspecting bloodbeak and wrap a rope around its neck. Gripping the rope with all her might while the alarmed bird frantically tried to throw her off, she succeeded in strangling the huge bird, who collapsed onto the increasingly scarlet sand. Thrilled by this unexpected upset, the entire audience surged to its feet, cheering the woman's victory.

Kirk seized the opportunity.

Just a fraction of a second behind the crowd, he leaped to his feet as well, then delivered a sideways kick to Yorba that knocked her into the startled spectators between her and the aisle. Her knife flew from her grasp, clattering onto some nearby steps.

"A fine way to treat a lady," McCoy quipped.

"That was no lady, that was a Klingon." Kirk landed nimbly back on his feet, ready to take on Yorba, who was entangled with the confused Atrazians she'd fallen among. He couldn't imagine that a single kick would slow her down for long. "And I didn't see you rushing to my rescue, Doctor."

"Never known you to need my help with a woman." McCoy also sprang to his feet. "But it looks like we're in for it now."

He wasn't wrong. Even as Yorba struggled to disengage herself from the overly solicitous Atrazians wanting to make certain she was okay, her men rushed into the fray, abandoning any pretense of stealth. They charged down the aisles and across the crowded rows to get at their Starfleet foes, shoving and elbowing their way past indignant spectators, who swore at them profanely, only to be tossed aside, tumbling into the rows below, eliciting yet more shouting and commotion. Less bellicose Atrazians scrambled to flee the uproar, vacating their seats to avoid being caught up in the sudden brouhaha. Drinks and edibles were spilled and splashed over unhappy audience members.

"Saw this coming." Sulu adopted a defensive stance. "Because . . . Klingons."

Levine raised his fists. "No kidding."

"Merciful fates!" Jaheed clambered up to a higher row to get clear of the conflict. "Fighting belongs in the arena, not in the stands! Not where the guards can see!"

Tell that to Yorba and her men, Kirk thought.

The Klingons came on in a rush, from all sides, not unlike the predators in the arena. Kirk and his crew met them in kind.

A typically bearded male Klingon slashed at Sulu with a serrated steel dagger, but the helmsman deftly dodged the attack. Snatching up an abandoned seat cushion from the row above him, he parried a second slash with the pillow, snagging the blade in the cushion before delivering a high kick to the Klingon's jaw. . . .

A meter away, Levine traded punches with a hefty Klingon who had several centimeters on him. This didn't intimidate Levine, whose combat training included plenty of sparring matches against opponents of all shapes and sizes. He dodged the Klingon's right fist and countered with a left uppercut to the other man's whiskered chin. The blow caught the Klingon off-guard, and Levine took advantage of the opening to block the Klingon's hasty counterpunch and deliver a solid left hook that staggered the burly Klingon, who should have known better than to consider a Starfleet security officer easy pickings.

A third Klingon lunged at Landon, but she executed a flawless judo flip that sent him hurling over her shoulder into the audience below. Kirk recalled her pulling a similar move on Gamma Trianguli VI just as effectively. McCoy ducked as the upended Klingon plunged past him.

"Hey, watch where you're throwing those things!"

Getting out of the line of fire, the doctor scrambled down to the row below, where he joined an unruly exodus of agitated spectators shoving their ways toward the aisles. Meanwhile, Kirk found himself confronted by a scowling Atrazian male upset over Kirk's seemingly unprovoked attack on an innocent woman. The man got between her and Kirk, much to the snarling Klingon's annoyance. "I don't need your help, you idiot."

"Don't worry, miss. He's not going to strike you again!" He threw a punch at Kirk, who easily deflected the clumsy blow.

"Hold on!" Kirk urged. "I don't want to fight you."

"Should've thought of that before you kicked a woman!"

Other Atrazians, already hyped up by the violence in the arena, joined the free-for-all erupting in the stands. A lone guard, racing to deal with the disturbance, was furtively tripped by Jaheed, causing him to somersault down an aisle into assorted spectators hurrying toward or away from the brawl, depending on their inclinations. A random citizen seized the guard's fallen truncheon and waded into the melee, whooping it up as he challenged humans, Klingons, and Atrazians alike. Pandemonium engulfed the scene.

"O Captain!" Jaheed hollered over the din. "More guards will come! We must flee before we all end up in a dungeon . . . or worse!"

The man now calling himself Siroth could hardly miss the ruckus on the opposite side of the coliseum. From his vantage point in the royal box, the court alchemist watched the fight break out among the hoi polloi drawn to Varkat's barbaric spectacles. God only knew what had ignited the brawl, which was mushrooming like a chain reaction, drawing attention from the bloody contest in the arena.

"What's happening?" Taya Hamparian asked at his side, sounding distinctly alarmed by the disturbance. He couldn't blame her; she was still getting her bearings here on Atraz and was not yet inured to its more primitive customs. "Is this normal at these . . . events?"

"Not in my experience." He feared that the festivities were not making a good first impression on his recently arrived collaborator. Unfortunately, there had been no polite way to decline attending Varkat's latest savage extravaganza, particularly with Fortier on the menu; they couldn't afford to boycott his lawful doom if they wanted to avoid any guilt by association. "Don't worry about it, though. We're perfectly safe here among Varkat's entourage."

Indeed, even now the suzerain's personal guards were tightening the security around them in response to the disturbance. Additional guards, armed with crossbows, truncheons, and short swords, joined those already standing watch over Varkat and his court. No one was going to get anywhere near the royal box while the riotous donnybrook was raging in the cheap seats across from them. Siroth wondered how far out of control the tumult had to get before Varkat's guardians decided it would be safer to whisk them all back to the fortress in an excess of caution.

"I suppose every world has its hooligans," Hamparian said, relaxing to a degree. "And sadistic 'sporting events' like this can hardly be expected to bring out the best in people."

He didn't argue the point. "The price of setting up shop on a less socially advanced world, beyond the Federation's influence and oversight."

Not that brawls and disorder were entirely unknown within the Federation's borders, especially out on the frontier, on hardscrabble mining colonies and such. Indeed, he had once narrowly avoided being caught up in a similar fracas in a nightclub on Brecillien II. Curious as to what had set off this particular free-for-all, he extracted a miniature spyglass from the interior of his robe and directed it at what appeared to be the heart of the melee. At first he spied nothing remarkable, just random men and women trading blows for no discernible reason, but then the handcrafted lenses brought him a close-up look at a face near the center of the storm, one he knew too well.

James T. Kirk. Celebrated captain of the *Starship Enterprise*.

"Here . . . on Atraz?"

For a moment, his thoughts were thrown back to another era, another name, lifetimes ago. Memories from a distant past surfaced as though waking from cryogenic sleep. Then the present demanded his attention. If Kirk was here, he had surely come for Hamparian.

Something had to be done about that.

"Guards! Guards!" he called out to the nearest sentries. "We have a dangerous intruder in our midst!"

"More guards will come! We must flee before we all end up in a dungeon . . . or worse!"

Kirk registered Jaheed's warning as he contended with the overly chivalrous fellow out to teach Kirk a bare-knuckle lesson about attacking defenseless women, regardless of whether Yorba needed or wanted protection—which she most certainly didn't. Kirk blocked the man's clumsy swings, while keeping a close eye on his real enemy, who impatiently freed herself from the other Atrazians trying to assist her, only to find her would-be defender between her and Kirk.

"Out of my way, you fool!"

An open-handed chop to the man's neck, delivered by Yorba from behind, clipped the man's strings. Before he could even hit the floor, she roughly tossed him aside, into the fleeing crowd below, to get at Kirk. She grinned wolfishly in anticipation of the battle to come.

"Not bad, Kirk . . . for a human. I'm going to enjoy returning the favor."

"I hate to spoil your fun, but I think we all need to make a strategic retreat while we still can."

Unsurprisingly, more guards were already rushing to quell the disturbance. Their crossbows would be of little use in these close, crowded quarters, but they still had their swords and truncheons and force of numbers. Kirk saw a silver lining in that the brawl had visibly resulted in an increase of security around Varkat, making it harder for Yorba's agents to get to the suzerain or Hamparian, but both landing parties being taken into custody was not in anyone's best interest.

"What's that expression *your* people have?" Kirk reminded Yorba. "Only a fool fights in a burning house?"

Yorba hesitated. Cold, cunning calculation doused her eagerness for battle, turning her grin into a frown as she surveyed the increasingly volatile situation.

"*QI'yaH!*" she cursed, the profanity defying universal translation. Producing a handheld communicator of Klingon design, she barked orders to her men. "Abort operation. We'll seize the scientist later, under more advantageous conditions. Yorba out."

"Good call." Kirk issued a similar command to his own team, while keeping a close eye on Yorba. "Scatter to avoid capture. Rendezvous at our lodgings."

With any luck, the escalating brawl would provide cover for the disguised Starfleet visitors, who would be lost amidst the general bedlam, along with their Klingon counterparts, which was possibly just as well; Klingons getting taken prisoner on Atraz, or blasting their way free with their disruptors, was a galactic incident in the making.

Putting away his communicator, he nodded at Yorba. "Until we meet again, Colonel?"

"Why wait?" She drew a disruptor pistol from beneath a colorful flap of fabric and aimed it at Kirk's chest. "You're coming with me, Kirk."

"I beg to differ," McCoy said, coming up behind her. A hypospray hissed against her throat and her eyes rolled upward until only the whites could be seen. Her disruptor slipped from her fingers, thudding onto the concrete floor. The doctor, who had circled around to come back down the row from the aisle, caught her limp body before it could collapse onto the hard concrete floor. "Mind giving me a hand here?" he asked Kirk.

"Don't mind if I do."

Kirk took a moment to confiscate the fallen disruptor before assisting McCoy. Supporting the slumping Klingon between them, her boots dragging against the floor, they let the exodus carry them down an aisle toward the amphitheater's arched exits. Kirk spotted Sulu and the rest not far ahead of them, also heading for the gates. Levine hesitated, looking like he wanted to push his way back toward Kirk and McCoy, but Kirk shook his head and waved Levine and the others to keep moving forward; he and McCoy and their tranquilized companion could catch up with the others once they were safely clear of the arena.

Not that Yorba's men were going to let them abscond with their leader without a fight. Scattered through the crowd, the Klingons not still brawling glared balefully at Kirk as they strove to keep pace with the retreating humans and their Klingon captive. Kirk braced himself for a rematch in the streets and alleys outside the coliseum—unless he could use Yorba as a bargaining chip to forestall any further combat? Assuming, of course, that the Klingons would choose recovering their commander over battling their enemies. How loyal to her were Yorba's men?

We'll find out soon enough, Kirk thought.

"Coming through!" He used Yorba's obvious incapacitation to speed their progress toward the exit. "Let us through! This woman needs air!"

Not everyone was willing or able to step aside to let them pass, but enough considerate spectators and guards made way for them that they soon reached the bottom of the seating area and came within sight of an archway leading out of the arena. Jaheed had already made it out the gate, with Sulu, Levine, Landon close behind him, just ahead of Kirk and McCoy. Also caught up in the crush of bodies: Klingons before and behind Kirk, waiting to reengage.

"Who knew Klingons were so heavy?" McCoy said, grunting with exertion. "What do they feed their troops, pulverized duranium?"

"Just a few meters more," Kirk said. *Then we'll see what happens.* "Coming through!"

Already thinking ahead, he was caught by surprise when a gruff voice called out:

"Those two, with the woman! Seize them!"

Any hope that somebody else was being singled out evaporated when Kirk saw the shouter pointing directly at him and McCoy while barking commands at the other guards manning the gate.

"Don't let them get away! By order of the royal court!"

"Oh brother," McCoy muttered. "When it rains, it pours."

"Easy, Bones. You're a doctor, not a weatherman."

With admirable, if inconvenient, promptness, guards surrounded the trio, targeting them with crossbows. "Surrender at once, strangers!"

Already at the gate, Sulu and the others stared back at them in dismay and confusion. Meeting their eyes, Kirk again shook his head. No point in them all getting arrested. He and McCoy would be better off with the rest of the landing party still free and at large.

Sulu nodded reluctantly.

Good man, Kirk thought. Glancing around, he saw unhappy Klingons hanging back as well. It appeared they were in no hurry to see Yorba perforated by crossbow bolts.

Klingons looking out for their own. Who knew?

"Please, there must be some mistake," Kirk dissembled to the guards. He and McCoy could not raise their hands without dropping Yorba, but he was careful not to make any sudden movement that might be construed as threatening. "Our friend here has just fainted from all the excitement. We're simply trying to find her some peace and quiet, away from the commotion."

"Save your lies for someone who cares, outlander." The face behind a loaded crossbow turned to the guard who had first sounded the alarm. "Are these the ones you want?"

"Aye." The latter stepped forward to scrutinize Kirk's face. "This is him, the one Siroth warned of. No question."

Siroth? Kirk tried to make sense of what was happening. From the sound of it, the court alchemist had ID'd him, but how? Had Hamparian blown their cover? He wondered how she had recognized him. As far as he knew, he'd never met the woman. It was possible, he supposed, that she knew of him by reputation; captain of the *Enterprise* wasn't exactly a low-profile position, particularly in light of some of the ship's exploits, discoveries, and first contacts in recent years, but even still . . . his face wasn't that well known, was it?

"Hamparian." McCoy's brain had obviously followed the same breadcrumbs. "It has to be. The 'blue lady' ratted us out."

"Possibly. Let's not jump to conclusions."

"But who else . . . ?"

"Silence!" a crossbow wielder barked before consulting the lead guard. "What about the woman?"

The first guard shrugged. "Take her, too."

Chapter Twenty-Four

2292

"Where are we?" Saavik asked. "What is this place?"

Her relief at not being annihilated along with the escape pod was tempered by the fact that she, Taleb, and Cyloo were apparently now being held captive at an unknown location. Only moments before the pod self-destructed, they'd been beamed to an unfamiliar transporter room, where Doctor Kesh was greeted by an accomplice.

"Welcome back, sir." A Rhaandarite, identifiable by her towering stature, high-domed brow, and yellow eyes, manned the transporter control station facing the platform. The metallic disk adorning her forehead indicated her gender. A beige coverall gave her the look of a technician, augmented by a standard wrist communicator. "Everything went as planned?"

"More or less, despite one regrettable fatality." Kesh had materialized at the rear of the platform, his twin disruptor pistols still aimed at the three abductees to coerce their cooperation. "Thank you for the expeditious beam-out, Wight. I take it you had no problem locking onto our life signs just as I deactivated the pod's shielding?"

"The split-second timing was tricky, and I had to factor in interference from the *Lukara*'s tractor beam, but I managed." She appeared both relieved and pleased with herself. "On the plus side, the tractor beam should mask any evidence of our simultaneous transporter beam."

"Well done."

Kesh herded his captives off the platform. Saavik observed that the Rhaandarite was also armed, with a phaser of unfamiliar design. Taleb glared balefully at this new antagonist. Cyloo looked understandably fearful; Saavik wondered if the young Osori was having second thoughts about leaving her world.

"I repeat," Saavik said evenly. "Where are we?"

"Hiberna Base. A nondescript planetesimal, roughly twenty kilometers in diameter, situated at the far edge of the Oort cloud of an obscure solar system along the *Lukara*'s route to Nimbus III," Kesh said. "To be more specific, we're deep beneath the frozen surface of a lifeless ball of ice, where no one will ever find us."

Taleb scoffed. "You underestimate the resources of the Romulan Star Empire."

"I doubt it," Kesh replied. "And you should not discount the efforts I have taken to hide us from any interfering parties, including your vaunted empire."

"But I don't understand." Cyloo looked about anxiously; she remained visibly shaken by both their forced abduction *and* Kesh's coldblooded murder of that Klingon crewman back on the bird-of-prey. "Why are you doing this? What is this all about?"

"I am curious about that myself," Saavik said.

"I'm sure you all have many questions, but a cramped transporter room is no place for a lengthy discussion. Let's remove ourselves to a more comfortable venue." Kesh indicated a doorway leading out into a hall. "No need to make that necessary talk any more unpleasant than it has to be."

Taleb subjected him to a withering display of scorn. "Says the duplicitous Klingon assassin holding us captive."

"*Touché.* I supposed that's an accurate enough description . . . these days." He smiled thinly, as though at a private joke. "Come along now, and all your questions will be answered."

Truthfully, Saavik hoped.

Exiting the transporter room, she caught glimpses of an adjacent laboratory and medical facility before a turbolift carried them up a level to what appeared to be the hidden base's living quarters. Kesh and Wight escorted them to a stately library or study, complete with a sofa, wingback chairs, coffee table, bookcases, wood paneling, wainscotting, and other furnishings. A pair of framed holo-paintings were mounted on walls across from each other: one depicted a view of San Francisco Bay; the other a rather forbidding stone fortress overlooking a walled city. Conspicuously absent, Saavik noted, were any notably Klingon landscapes.

A suspicion began to formulate in her mind.

"Please make yourself at home." Kesh gestured at the sofa. "I see Wight has thoughtfully laid out some refreshments. Help yourselves."

The captives occupied the couch, with Taleb and Saavik flanking Cyloo. On the low coffee table before them, a semipermeable stasis field kept a small selection of hors d'oeuvres fresh. Translucent plastic bottles of Antarian glow water were also provided. No cutlery or glassware, Saavik noted. Nothing that could be readily weaponized, like a knife or fork or broken glass.

Hospitality mitigated by mistrust, she thought. *An unappetizing combination.*

"No shackles?" Taleb asked dryly. "Agonizers? Mind-rippers?"

"Hardly necessary, I would hope." Kesh settled into an easy chair facing them from across the room. He laid one of his disruptor pistols on an end table, within easy reach, but held on to the other. Wight stood by attentively, keeping watch over their involuntary guests. "And pointless in the case of Cyloo, who could phase out of any restraints, but let me stress that, even if you did attempt to flee, there is nowhere to go. You are stuck inside a desolate chunk of frozen methane and ammonia, with no outer atmosphere to speak of, surrounded by the vacuum of space. You could not survive on the surface, let alone find a way off Hiberna—"

A high-pitched squeak interrupted his deliberately discouraging exegesis. Saavik raised an eyebrow at the unexpected sight of a small albino rodent scurrying into the study from an adjoining chamber. At first glance, it appeared to be of the Terran subspecies *Rattus norvegicus domestica*, once commonly used as laboratory test subjects before the advent of more humane and sophisticated computer models and simulations. The rat clambered up Kesh's leg to find a place on the doctor's knee; the apparent Klingon did not seem to find this distressing.

"Well, hello, Enkidu. I've missed you, too."

Taleb's face registered disgust. "So now we're keeping company with literal vermin as well? Lovely."

Saavik glanced at the stasis field protecting the hors d'oeuvres. Such measures typically produced a staticky, tingling sensation when one reached for a morsel. Apparently the field was not just intended to keep the snacks fresh, but also to discourage the rat from nibbling on the refreshments.

"You promised us answers," she reminded Kesh. "It is time for truth among us. You stated earlier that nothing less than eternity was at stake. What did you mean by that?"

"Immortality," he said. "For longer than you can imagine, since before your United Federation of Planets was born, I've been searching for eternal life. It's been a long and often frustrating quest, pursuing many promising leads that ultimately proved to be dead ends or at least sorely limited. Progress in life extension, yes; regrowing lost limbs and organs, yes; isolated, unreproducible instances of extreme longevity, such as on Omega IV or Juram Five; but nothing close to actual immortality. So imagine my excitement when the opportunity arose to actually obtain a living specimen of an Osori to study. It was a once-in-a-lifetime chance in what has been a *very* long lifetime, extended even further by occasional periods of suspended animation."

His gaze drifted to the holo-image of San Francisco before returning to the present.

"But there is no elusive secret to be extracted from us," Cyloo insisted. "Our entire history proves that. Many such questors visited us many ages ago, some more relentless than others, but all were disappointed in the end, no matter what dire lengths they went to. They are long gone now, and their civilizations, too."

"So I've heard," he said, "but you'll forgive me if I'm not convinced by myths and legends from eons past."

"Far more than myths. Those sad events took place in living memory of our eldest."

"Even so, who is to say where those ancient investigators may have gone astray? What techniques or lines of inquiry they may have neglected to explore?" Kesh petted Enkidu as he shook his head solemnly. "What true visionary abandons his dream because of the failures of their predecessors? Where would science be if, say, Zefram Cochrane hadn't tried to break the warp barrier simply because others had failed to crack the problem before him?"

A peculiarly Terran allusion for a Klingon, Saavik noted. Suspicion edged into hypothesis.

"The bottom line, my Osori friend? I need to see for myself—thoroughly test and examine you myself—before I accept that you do not, perhaps unknowingly, hold the key to the puzzle that has consumed me for so very, very long."

"Wonderful," Taleb said, sarcastically as usual. "In other words, we are in the clutches of a lunatic."

Kesh frowned at him. "You might want to modify your attitude, Subcommander, considering that, of the three of you, you are the *least* essential to my ambitions. Cyloo is my primary interest. Saavik's hybrid nature makes her a welcome bonus; I was not dissembling when I expressed a keen interest in studying her genome and its effects on her biology, but you, my dear Taleb, are of minimal value . . . and may prove more trouble than you're worth."

"You will regret speaking to me thus. You disrespect me at your own peril."

Saavik was less interested in the Romulan's affronted ego than in probing their captor's motives. "Why did you not leave Taleb behind? You said earlier that you had your reasons."

"In large part because you were both in the wrong place at the wrong time, but beyond that, his departure, along with the rest of us, will confuse matters by making him a possible suspect in the theft of the pod. The more the various factions are pointing fingers at each other, the less likely they are to stumble onto the truth." Kesh shrugged. "In addition, Lieutenant, I needed someone to threaten to force your compliance, someone who couldn't render themselves untouchable, that is. I assumed that, despite your differences, you would not permit Taleb to be harmed . . . although, frankly, I doubt he would return the favor."

The Romulan looked momentarily abashed by that assessment, perhaps remembering Saavik's previous heroics on his behalf, before his customary hauteur reasserted itself.

"I say again, you will not escape Romulan justice. My family is a noble one, high in the praetor's favor. You cannot abduct me with impunity."

"And I have confidence in Captain Kirk," Saavik said, looking to reassure Cyloo. "He will come to our rescue if at all able."

"I would not be so certain of that," Kesh replied. "Don't forget, we all supposedly perished when the pod self-destructed. As far as the rest of the galaxy is concerned, you are not missing, you are dead." His gaze shifted again, to the holo-painting of the fortress. "Kirk will not spoil everything this time around."

His words, and evident enmity toward the captain, implied a past encounter. Connections crystalized in Saavik's mind as she collated her brewing suspicions regarding Kesh's true origins with her extensive study of the *Enterprise*'s previous missions under Kirk and Spock. Various data points came together. A stolen escape pod. A many-towered fortress overlooking a walled city. An obsessive quest for immortality. A cunning and resourceful foe, long unaccounted for.

"The Atrazian affair," she recalled. "Some twenty-four years ago."

Kesh's bushy gray eyebrows lifted in surprise. "Very good, Lieutenant, considering that was somewhat before your time."

She scrutinized his face, looking past the prominent Klingon ridges. Starfleet's database held no actual photographic images of a certain so-called alchemist, although a computer-generated likeness based on Kirk's and McCoy's verbal descriptions of the man had been produced in the immediate wake of that episode. Saavik had not had cause to closely study that sketch, but from what she remembered, there was a definite resemblance to Kesh.

"You are not Klingon," she asserted with confidence.

"Not always, no." He looked again at the portrait of his former residence on Atraz. "Needless to say, I was amused to hear that Kirk and the *Enterprise* had been assigned to the Osori mission, given that we've been crossing paths, one way or another, since he absconded with those humpback whales way back when." He chuckled. "I spent lifetimes wondering what that was all about, until that business with the alien probe not too long ago. Finally, it all made sense."

"What in the praetor's name are you babbling about?" Taleb asked impatiently. "Have you both taken leave of your senses?"

Saavik could not blame him for not comprehending. "A long story, Subcommander. Perhaps even longer than previously understood. Briefly, Captain Kirk encountered this same individual decades ago, when he pursued similar goals under another name . . . and before he was surgically transformed into a Klingon?"

That such a procedure was possible was indisputable. Klingon spies had long been known to disguise themselves as humans on occasion. Saavik assumed the reverse was also true, even if seldom acknowledged.

"Precisely, Lieutenant," Kesh confirmed. "Practicing Klingon medicine, as a Klingon, seemed the best means of studying their physiology up close and personal, while also staying off Starfleet's sensors after my operation on Atraz attracted unwelcome attention. Give me credit, however, for learning from my mistakes. My error twenty-plus years ago was not faking the destruction of Doctor Hamparian's escape pod, which led to those very inconvenient rescue and recovery missions on the part of Starfleet and the Klingons. This time around, there will be no searches. No one will be looking for us."

Cyloo stared at him, aghast. "What do you mean to do to us? To me?"

"A full range of tests and scans, down to the subatomic level if necessary. We'll start with the most noninvasive methods first, naturally, and proceed from there depending on what we discover. Who knows? I may well find that you're yet another dead end when it comes to bestowing immortality on ordinary humanoids, but we'll never know until we investigate, will we?"

Cyloo shuddered. A rosy glow began to emanate from her gloves. "You mustn't do this. I won't let you."

"Saavik and Taleb will pay the price for any defiance on your part," he reminded her. "And let's get this out of the way so I never have to spell it out for you again. Even if you *do* choose to sacrifice these two innocents to protect yourself or your people's secrets, understand that your phasing trick can only delay me. You have nowhere to flee except the lifeless surface of this glorified iceberg, so I merely have to wait for the time limit on your phasing to expire, at which point you will have to choose whether to become solid again or risk fading away permanently." He smiled smugly. "I'm guessing that, when push comes to shove, you won't throw away your infinitely long future just to foil me."

"Monster." Tears streamed down Cyloo's face, wetting her scales. Her protective aura retreated back into the gloves. "How can you be so heartless?"

"And utterly manipulative." Taleb regarded Kesh skeptically. "So there is no way off this rock? I find that hard to believe. Surely you must have some means of escape in the event of an emergency?"

Saavik also found it difficult to accept that Kesh would not have an exit strategy. That would be significantly out of character, given his meticulous planning to date.

"Quite right," Kesh confessed. "There is in fact a shuttlecraft in a hangar two levels above us, but I have taken the precaution of removing a vital component from its engine and hiding that component in a secure location elsewhere in this complex. Not even Wight knows where it is or how to access it." He looked directly at Cyloo. "So even if you were to phase your way to the hangar, you could not fly away from here. The craft is inoperative without that crucial part."

Saavik calculated that he was telling the truth, since it would indeed be a logical precaution. "You appear to have thought of everything."

"I certainly like to think so." He adjusted the settings on his pistol, then went back to stroking his pet. "Don't you think so, Enkidu?"

As though emboldened by his owner's confidence, the rat scurried down Kesh's leg onto the carpet and began inching toward the new arrivals on the sofa. Beady pink eyes contemplated the strangers curiously. Cyloo's iridescent scales in particular seemed to draw the rat's gaze—or was it merely attracted by the treats on the coffee table in front of her?

Kesh seemed to think the former. "Interesting. Enkidu appears to find you just as intriguing as I do, Osori."

Growing braver, the rat crept nearer to the captives.

"Keep that vile rodent away from me," Taleb said, sounding both offended and revolted by the approaching animal. "Is there no end to the indignities we must be subjected to?"

Saavik recalled his impetuous attack on the Klingon in the medbay. She feared his Romulan pride and emotionalism would be his undoing.

"Calm yourself, Subcommander. It is only a harmless pet."

"It is a filthy pest . . . and I will not tolerate any more of this!"

Lashing out angrily, he kicked over the coffee table with the soles of both feet, spilling the refreshments onto the carpet—and barely missing Enkidu, who scampered away in fright, squeaking loudly.

"You arrogant pup! You could have crushed him!" Kesh leaped to his feet. Fury transfigured his face, suiting his counterfeit Klingon features. "I'll have you know his bloodline is likely older and more venerable than yours. I've been cloning him for generations!"

"How pathetic," Taleb sneered at him. "Breeding vermin for company."

"Enough!"

Kesh fired his disruptor at the Romulan, who crumpled limply against Cyloo. She shrieked and grabbed hold of Saavik, who allowed the embrace for the terrified Osori's sake. For a moment, Saavik thought that perhaps Taleb had been killed, but closer inspection detected signs of respiration. Stunned then, not murdered.

"I warned him not to test my patience." Kesh lowered his weapon. "But clearly he was going to be a persistent headache going forward." He glanced at the looming Rhaandarite. "Wight, please put the subcommander on ice for duration."

"Yes, Doctor. Right away."

"On ice?" Saavik queried.

"I have a fully equipped cryogenics unit in a lower level of this base. Among their other uses, I've occasionally found cryotubes to be a nonlethal way of storing inconvenient individuals who may still have some value to me. And yes, the irony of practicing cryogenics deep inside what amounts to an interstellar snowball is not lost on me."

"You're going to freeze him?" Cyloo asked, appalled. "Won't that damage him permanently?"

"It's perfectly safe, I assure you. I speak from experience, having periodically placed myself in suspended animation in order to leapfrog over generations of history whenever I found myself at an impasse. I have at times bypassed wars and economic collapses to reach new eras where I can reinvent myself and renew my work, taking advantage of whatever scientific progress had been made while I was sleeping. Properly applied, cryogenics is a form of time travel, albeit only in one direction."

Saavik could not help recalling Khan and his followers.

"However, if the prospect of occupying a cryotube alarms either of you, more comfortable quarters *are* available, with only certain restrictions regarding your movements." Kesh's voice hardened. "Just know that I am not above putting one or both of you in frozen storage if necessary. The choice is yours."

Wight lifted Taleb's unconscious form from the sofa and carried him out of the study toward the turbolift. Trembling, Cyloo still clung to Saavik, who felt duty bound to look after the kidnapped envoy to the best of her abilities.

"Such measures will not be necessary," she said. "Logic dictates that we have no choice but to accept the reality of our situation as you have laid it out for us. In human parlance, it appears you are holding all the cards."

This was deliberate misdirection, if not an outright lie. Saavik refused to accept that all hope was lost, but she *did* recall how Captain Kirk had outwitted Khan by feigning helplessness until the opportunity arose to turn the tables on an overconfident adversary, which raised a highly relevant question:

What would the captain do?

Chapter Twenty-Five

2024

"That was my grandma Milly, all right. Used to call herself 'Miracle Milly' and always claimed that an actual angel appeared to her, in the form of a kindly doctor in scrubs, and cured her by giving her a blessed pill straight from Heaven." Todd Coates shrugged. "Not sure I buy that he was literally an angel, but you know what? I don't have a better explanation."

No surprise, Mildred Coates was now deceased, having apparently lived a long and happy life after regrowing her kidney back in 1986, but her family still lived in the Bay Area. Her grandson, Todd, sat across from Melinda and Dennis on the back deck of his house in Oakland. A screen door, along with an obliging husband, kept his kids and the dog from raising too much of a ruckus in the background.

"Neither do I," Melinda admitted. "Yet."

"An angel, though?" Dennis scoffed. "No offense to your grandma, but I think we can safely rule that possibility out."

Never mind that he had his own theories involving extraterrestrials, alternate universes, top-secret bioweapons labs, "Big Dialysis," or some combination thereof. Personally, Melinda found those notions only slightly less plausible than the idea that Gillian had joined forces with a genuine angel to rescue an alleged Russian spy. And if so, did that mean that the injured Chekov was really a heavenly operative as well? And the man in the white robe, whom, come to think of it, Sister Mary Michelle had described as somewhat otherworldly? And what about his companion, the one Gillian had dinner with? Did angels like pizza?

And how completely flummoxed am I that I'm actually asking myself these questions?

Meanwhile, where did the whales fit in? Could humpback biology hold a clue to regrowing organs in humans? Some species of reptiles could regenerate lost body parts, Melinda knew, but whales? According to Bob Briggs, George and Gracie *had* fallen off the radar the same day Gillian did, but was that just a coincidence? At this point, she didn't know what to think.

"But you do remember this one guy coming around soon afterwards," she asked, "wanting to know all about Milly's new kidney?"

"You bet," Todd said, confirming what he'd told her over the phone earlier. Blond, blue-eyed, and in his early fifties, Milly's grandson would have been around twelve back then. "I mean, that alone wasn't too surprising. For a while there, we were constantly hearing from doctors and clinics and foundations wanting to examine Grandma one more time, but she wasn't having any of it. She had her beliefs, which satisfied her, and she didn't want to be poked or prodded anymore. Can't say I blame her, especially after the initial rounds of testing didn't turn up anything useful. I like to think that she would've gone along with more studies if she'd actually believed they might lead to other people getting cured, but . . . who knows? Maybe she was just fed up with doctors, hospitals, and procedures at that point. She stopped co-operating and they got the message, eventually."

"Or maybe," Dennis said, lowering his voice, "*somebody* made them back off. To bury the story and keep anyone from looking too deeply into where that cure *really* came from."

"You think?" Todd asked, intrigued. "Like who?"

"Just brainstorming, that's all," Melinda said, jumping in to keep the interview from being sidetracked by her partner's more out-there conspiracy theories. "Anyway, as you were saying, most everybody gave up trying to put Milly under a microscope, except for this one guy? Young, bald, deep voice, very persistent?"

Todd had not recognized Gillian from her photos or the Pizza Date from the artist's sketch. Not that Melinda had really expected him to, since Todd hadn't been anywhere near the hospital on that day, but she had hoped that maybe, just maybe, Gillian or one of her supposed partners in crime might have checked in on Mildred after gifting her with that miraculous kidney pill. No such luck, alas, but Todd *had* reacted when she told him about the unidentified young dude who had pressed Jane Temple for info on the incident. That had rung a decades-old bell in his memory.

"He was determined, I'll give him that, and intense. I was just a kid then, but I still remember him showing up uninvited at our house one afternoon, after Grandma had ignored all his calls and letters. He wasn't about to take no for an answer, even offering serious money to let him study Grandma for as long as it took to find out how exactly that pill had worked. I think my mom was tempted to work out some sort of deal, but not Grandma. By then, she bristled at any suggestion that science could explain her miracle, considered the very idea down-right sacrilegious, so she basically told him to take his heathen dollars and shove it."

"And how did he take that?"

"That's the part that really stuck in my mind. Instead of retreating, he doubled down by offering to purchase Grandma's body after she eventually passed away in the fullness of time, with a substantial bonus if her kidney was still in good shape by then. He even slipped my mom a business card when Grandma wasn't looking." He shuddered. "Creeped me out at the time."

Melinda could see that. "I have to ask: Did your mom take him up on his offer when the sad occasion came around?"

"Never had the nerve to ask her, to tell the truth, but our finances *did* take an upswing after Grandma passed away in 1997. We paid off the house, my college loans went away, Mom got a new car and stopped fretting about bills. She spoke vaguely about coming into some money from Milly's estate, but she never wanted to talk about it." He looked down, embarrassed. "And I didn't really want to know."

Melinda murmured sympathetic noises and gave Todd a few moments before getting to the question she was aching to ask.

"About that business card. Did you find it?"

Shaking off his somber recollections, he nodded. "Took some digging, but fortunately Mom was a bit of a pack rat. Kept all the correspondence and paperwork regarding Grandma's miracle, including . . ."

He took out his wallet and, with a flourish, produced a somewhat well-worn business card, a bit crumpled around the edges. Inspecting it, Melinda could all too easily imagine Todd's mom turning it over and over in her hands, worrying it as she pondered her options. A name was printed above a solitary phone number:

WILMER OFFUTT

No email or web address, she noted. *Not in 1986.*

"Thanks! This is great. More than I expected, actually."

"Glad to be of help. Would you like to borrow the rest of my mom's files from back then?"

"I was about to ask."

She wanted to call the number on the card right away, as soon as they got back to their rental car, but Dennis insisted on looking up "Wilmer Offutt" first before they went further. It was a reasonable, if frustrating, precaution, but no way was she going to wait until they drove all the way home, so they compromised by pulling into a roadside diner with free Wi-Fi and setting up shop in a corner booth surrounded by retro 1950s décor. Melinda treated herself to a milkshake and fries while Dennis searched the internet via his laptop. Jukebox oldies played in the background as she waited impatiently for the results.

"Anything?"

"What's the rush?" he replied. "That card is almost forty years old. Chances are, that number hasn't been good since before we were born."

"Probably, but I still want to know who this Wilmer Offutt character is. Might be somebody we want to track down, if possible. What have you found on him so far?"

"Next to nothing, which is more than a little suspicious. Not a lot of dudes with that name cited online, and most of them don't seem like a match for the guy the nurse and Todd remember. Wrong ages, appearances, backgrounds, et cetera." Dennis squinted at the laptop's screen, multitasking as he spoke. "Granted, I'd need to put in a lot more hours before I could reach any definite conclusions, but I'm going to go out on a limb and surmise that 'Wilmer Offutt' was not this guy's real name."

Okay, that has potential to make for a good ep, she thought. "You think he was using an alias when he was sniffing around for that kidney pill back in the eighties?"

"Maybe, probably." A worried expression conveyed that this didn't exactly put Dennis's already anxious mind at ease. "Why would he want to conceal his identity? What was he hiding?"

"That's just what I want to know." She wiped her greasy fingers off with a napkin before picking up her phone and the borrowed business card. "I don't know about you, but knowing that 'Offutt' was going under an assumed name makes me all the more eager to try this number, just in case."

Dennis gulped. He'd hardly touched his own order, which was going cold beside his laptop. "You sure that's a good idea?"

"Like you said, the number's probably long-dead anyway, so where's the harm?" She saw him start to open his mouth. "Never mind. Don't answer that."

Before he could spin any worst-case scenarios, she entered the number and held the phone to her ear. To her surprise, the call was picked up on the first ring and a recorded voice responded:

"Please leave a message at the tone."

The voice was James Earl Jones deep, the prompt as bare-bones as possible. Caught off-guard, she needed a moment to compose her thoughts before answering.

"This is Melinda Silver in San Francisco. I produce a popular podcast titled *Cetacean.* I'm seeking information about the . . . unusual . . . events that took place at Mercy General Hospital back in 1986. You can reach me at the following number."

She managed to get out most of her contact info, including the show's email address, before another beep cut her off. Putting down the phone, she looked across the booth at Dennis, who stared back at her in amazement laced with visible apprehension.

"You got their voice mail? For real?"

"Loud and clear." The more she thought about it, the more remarkable that seemed, given how many decades had passed since the enigmatic Wilmer Offutt had given the card to Todd's mom. "Go figure."

Her partner picked fitfully at some onion rings. "So now what?"

"Now we wait to see who has been waiting, all this time, for a call."

Chapter Twenty-Six

2268

"Mister Spock, the *BortaS* is creeping closer to Atraz . . . again."

"Acknowledged, Mister Chekov."

Spock's hands were steepled beneath his chin as he studied a strategic display of the two ships' positions relative to each other and the planet. The graphic currently occupied approximately 85.23 percent of the bridge's main viewscreen, with the remainder of the screen devoted to real-time observation of the actual battle cruiser, appearing as an inset window in the upper-right-hand corner of the viewer. A switch on the armrest of the captain's chair gave him the ability to toggle between the two displays, although his Vulcan discipline kept him from overusing the function as a human might under similarly tense circumstances.

"Match their movements, Lieutenant Rahda," he instructed the helmsman. "No more, no less."

"Aye, sir. Just like before."

For 28.9 hours, a duration long enough to span an entire cycle of duty shifts, the rival ships had been engaged in a slow, cautious dance, with the *BortaS* edging closer to Atraz in punctuated increments and the *Enterprise* countering to a precisely equivalent degree.

"What in thunder is he playing at?" Scott said in exasperation. He nursed a cup of black coffee as he manned the engineering station. "If he's aiming for Atraz, why not just head straight into orbit instead of creeping up on it like this? It's not like the Klingons to tiptoe around when they've got a target in their sights."

"Do not underestimate their cunning," Spock replied. He preferred tea and short periods of concentrated meditation to sustain him during this prolonged vigil. Although he had ordered the bridge crew relieved at suitable intervals, he had not surrendered the conn. "They can be subtle when they need to be. Recall their covert machinations on Neural and Deep Space Station K-7, as well as during the matter of the Dohlman of Elas, when we previously encountered Captain Khod. They understand the value of stealth, particularly when it comes to pushing the limits of the treaty."

"Aye, Mister Spock, but they're not exactly lurking in the bushes this time around. They're flying their colors in plain sight for all to see, so why all this infernal pussyfooting?"

"Perhaps they are testing our nerve," Spock speculated. "Or seek to provoke us into making an untoward first move so they can cast us as the aggressors in this affair."

"Or maybe," Uhura chimed in, "Khod can't resist trying to get a slight edge on us, just to assert his dominance or whatever, like an impatient shuttle pilot who is always jockeying for a better position compared to other flyers, regardless of whether it serves any real purpose or not."

"That is not logical," Spock stated.

"Ego and testosterone seldom are, Mister Spock. And I suspect that applies to Klingons as much as humans. Maybe even more so."

"A fascinating theory, Lieutenant, which had not occurred to me. Nevertheless—"

"Excuse me. Mister Spock, I'm receiving an urgent message from *Galileo*." She adjusted her earpiece as she manipulated the communication controls to decrypt the transmission. "Acknowledged, *Galileo*. We're reading you."

"Put the message through, Lieutenant."

"Aye, sir."

Spock was understandably eager to hear word from the planet, but did not rush Uhura. He knew she would carry out the order as expeditiously as possible. Within moments, the voice of Ensign Akbari issued from the bridge's speakers:

"*Galileo to Enterprise. I've just received an update from the rescue party. Lieutenant Sulu, to be exact. They've found Doctor Hamparian . . . but lost the captain and Doctor McCoy.*"

Spock instantly suppressed a spike of alarm. "Elucidate, Ensign."

Along with the rest of the bridge crew, he listened intently as Akbari reported that Captain Kirk and Doctor McCoy had been taken into custody by Atrazian city guards after a violent altercation with a Klingon landing party, who had also been intent on claiming Hamparian. According to Sulu, as relayed by Akbari, the rest of the landing party remained at liberty in the city, but had been unable to contact Kirk or McCoy, suggesting that the prisoners' communicators had been taken from them. In addition, the leader of the Klingon landing party, a Colonel Yorba, had been apprehended along with the two Starfleet officers. Her men were believed to be still at large—a worrisome variable that complicated Spock's calculations.

"And Hamparian?" he asked.

"Last seen consorting with the local authorities, unlike Fortier, who has come to a bad end." She related the barbaric circumstances of the spacejacker's demise; Spock mentally removed Fortier from the equation, while Akbari sounded grateful to have missed the grisly spectacle. *"What should we do now, Mister Spock? About the captain and Doctor McCoy?"*

"Remain at your post and keep us apprised of any and all new developments while awaiting further instructions. *Enterprise* out."

Uhura ended the communication, leaving Spock to ponder the evolving situation on the planet and consider what actions might be required.

He was not the only one.

"We have to do something, Mister Spock!" Scott left his post to join Spock in the command well. Coffee slopped over the edge of his cup. "Things have gone from bad to worse, for the captain *and* Doctor McCoy."

Spock knew the engineer's agitation was surely shared by everyone on the bridge. He raised his voice so he could be easily heard.

"I quite agree, Mister Scott, but we must not act precipitously. Reaction without deliberation runs the risk of exacerbating an already volatile situation. Dispatching reinforcements by shuttle or even moving the *Enterprise* into transporter range could easily provoke a hostile response from the Klingons, whether that be firing on the shuttle or sending more of their troops down to clash with our people. An escalating conflict between rival forces on a neutral world is to no one's benefit, and could conceivably endanger the fragile peace between the

Federation and the Klingon Empire. Captain Kirk is well aware of the larger issues at stake here, so we need to weigh the potential consequences."

"But we can't just sit on our hands while the captain and Doctor McCoy are locked up in some bloody dungeon, facing heaven only knows what sort of brutality. You heard what the Atrazians did to Fortier."

"Affirmative," Spock said. "Yet I remind you that we already have significant assets in play on Atraz, including a shuttlecraft, the rescue party, and Captain Kirk's own demonstrated tenacity and resourcefulness. He has escaped captivity, and survived all manner of jeopardy, on more worlds than I have time to enumerate. Furthermore, Mister Sulu and the rest of the landing party are also capable, experienced officers who can be counted on to make every effort to liberate the captain and Doctor McCoy, while dealing with the Klingons as well."

"Aye," Scott conceded. "The captain has pulled his haggis out of the fire many a time, that's for sure, as have the doctor and Sulu and the others. But we also need to have their backs, or what are we even doing here?"

"Taking the necessary steps in a logical sequence," Spock said. "Lieutenant Uhura, hail the *BortaS* once more."

"I can try, sir." She did not sound hopeful. "As you know, they stopped answering our hails some time ago."

Spock was well aware of this. *Enterprise* had diligently hailed the *BortaS* each time the battle cruiser had moved nearer to Atraz, but Captain Khod had consistently declined to reply following his initial barrage of threats and accusations.

"Correct, Lieutenant, but the situation on the ground has changed substantially with the capture of one of their senior officers. Odds are Captain Khod is currently facing the same decisions and dilemmas we are. No doubt he has strong opinions on the subject and is highly curious regarding our next moves."

"Understood, sir. Hailing the *BortaS*."

Spock addressed Scott. "Before determining our course of action, let us first assess the Klingons' present attitude and intentions. This knowledge can only aid us when it comes to anticipating their responses."

"No argument, there, Mister Spock. Always better to examine a tricky situation before hammering away at it. Measure twice, phaser once, as they say."

"My thoughts exactly, Mister Scott."

Mere moments elapsed before Uhura announced, "The *BortaS* is responding to our hail."

Scott chuckled. "You had his number, Mister Spock."

"So it appears." Spock doubted that Khod would be any less belligerent than he was the last time they spoke, but that did not preclude extracting valuable information from the encounter. "On-screen, Lieutenant."

Khod's surly countenance reclaimed the viewscreen, although the *BortaS* remained in view in the inset window in the corner. The irate Klingon eschewed any formal salutations before launching into invective.

"Vulcan! You have the audacity to show your face after your captain's bungling disrupted our intelligence operation on Atraz, resulting in the capture of a decorated officer of the Empire?!"

Spock rose calmly to his feet. In truth, he appreciated that Khod readily admitted that his Colonel Yorba had been detained along with Kirk and McCoy, as opposed to wasting time dissembling; perhaps the Klingon captain saw no point in denying that which had been witnessed by both landing parties. Or had his temper simply overcome his discretion? Both explanations were plausible enough. Spock was grateful for the results, regardless.

"Your perspective on recent events is debatable. My understanding is that it was *your* operatives who accosted our rescue party, and that Captain Kirk and his associates acted purely in self-defense."

"Bah! You had no business being on Atraz in the first place. We were only responding to your shameless incursion on the planet."

"I have already informed you of the extenuating circumstances necessitating our mission to Atraz, so there is nothing to be gained by relitigating the matter. Our time would be better spent focusing on our mutual need to rescue our respective comrades."

Khod sneered from the screen. *"What do you propose, Vulcan?"*

"A truce to begin with. Beyond that, I suggest we share whatever intelligence we may possess or acquire regarding the captives' where-abouts and situation. I also recommend that we bring both our vessels within transporter range of Atraz so that we are in position to beam our respective crew members to safety should the opportunity or necessity arise. This would, naturally, involve both ships being able to lower their shields without fear of attack from the other party."

"Fear? You dare suggest that we should fear the Enterprise! *Was that a threat . . . or are you calling us cowards, you Vulcan* petaQ!"

"That was not my intent. Perhaps I misspoke and should have said 'risk' instead of 'fear.'" Spock wondered if his father, a consummate dip-lomat, would have made that linguistic error. "I meant only that we can better achieve our common goal if we are not simultaneously on guard against each other."

"Do you think me a fool as well as a coward, Vulcan?" Khod's face was growing more flushed by the nanosecond. *"A Klingon never lowers his guard, and certainly not in the presence of his foes. You defame my honor with your every breath. Keep your* truce"—he spat the word as though it was an obscenity—*"and stay out of our way. We require no as-sistance to clean up your stinking mess!"*

Khod vanished from the screen, leaving only a view of his battle cruiser.

"The transmission has been cut," Uhura reported, shaking her head. "What did I say about ego and testosterone?"

"Duly noted." Spock did not bother asking her to hail the *BortaS* again. That would almost certainly be futile.

"So much for trying to talk sense to a Klingon." Scott scowled at the screen as though Khod's image still lingered there. "That went no-where fast."

"To the contrary, Mister Scott." Spock itemized what they had gleaned from the brief, contentious dialogue. "We have verified that Colonel Yorba remains in the hands of the Atrazians, that Khod is agi-tated over this turn of events, and that we can expect no cooperation from the *BortaS* when it comes to rescuing the captain and McCoy."

Or recovering Doctor Hamparian for that matter.

"No offense, Mister Spock, but I could have predicted that last bit, about the Klingons not playing well with others, that is."

"Indeed, but it did us no harm to at least explore the possibility of a truce, no matter how improbable. Communication before conflict is almost always the logical choice, even when dealing with Klingons."

"Amen," Uhura agreed. "But what now, Mister Spock? The captain and Doctor McCoy are still in trouble."

Spock returned to the captain's chair, his mind made up. "Lieutenant Rahda, take us into standard orbit around Atraz."

"Aye, sir!"

Scott's expression brightened. "And if that ill-mannered Klingon objects, Mister Spock?"

"We will, as he advised, keep our guard up." He pressed a button on his left armrest to alert the entire ship of his decision:

"Red alert. Shields on full."

Chapter Twenty-Seven

2024

Their apartment had been trashed.

Days had passed since Melinda had left her message on that ancient answering machine, with no response from Wilmer Offutt or any possible replacement. Frustration gnawed at her. She still had enough material banked for the next couple episodes of *Cetacean*, maybe more if she broke the aircraft carrier incident and the raid on the hospital into two separate eps, but her gut told her that the memorably "intense" Mister Offutt was a lead worth pursuing. If nothing else, maybe his probing into the Strange Case of the Regrown Kidney had turned up something about Gillian that had eluded her so far. Dennis had yet to find any solid info about Offutt, despite long hours scouring the internet, which only heightened her curiosity.

C'mon, call me back already, she'd been thinking as they returned from a grocery run, lugging reusable shopping bags laden with their usual staples, only to discover the apartment door unlocked and their place ransacked. Whoever had tossed the apartment had not been subtle about it; every closet, cupboard, and drawer had been opened, the contents rifled through and often dumped on the nearest counter, bed, or available surface. Papers were strewn across the floor, boxes dragged out from beneath beds, and prescription bottles heaped in the bathroom sink. Even the grates over the heating vents had been pried off, the better to search behind them, she guessed. Personal memorabilia, of sentimental value, had been tossed onto her bed: an *Erin Brockovich* movie poster signed by its namesake; a framed copy of the front-page exposé that got Melinda kicked off her high school newspaper and made her *very* unpopular with some of her teachers and classmates; a vacation photo of her and her older brother, Eric, a screengrab of the time *Cascade* topped 250,000 subscribers . . . all manhandled and discarded like so much junk.

"Holy crap," Dennis whispered as they numbly toured the premises, taking it all in. Their shopping bags, dropped to the floor at the first sight of the chaos left behind by the intruders, lay forgotten by the breached doorway. Putting away the perishables was the last thing on their minds right now. "They tore our place apart."

"Tell me about it." She wasn't sure if she was angry or relieved that they hadn't been home when their formerly secure nest had been pillaged. "Somebody really went to town here."

And yet, at first glance, nothing was obviously missing. Their large-screen TV was still intact. Their assorted laptops and pads had not been stolen, although she worried that they might have been violated along with their apartment. Panic surged through her at the thought of losing all their work and research.

"Please tell me that everything for *Cetacean* is backed up on the cloud."

"Of course." Dennis looked and sounded understandably stunned by the break-in. "That goes without saying."

"Thank God." She was shaken as well, but that eased her mind some. "For a moment there, I was afraid we'd lost everything: the interviews, my edits, all of it."

"Don't be ridiculous," he snapped. "I'm not an idiot."

The fury in his voice startled her. "I never said you were."

"But you didn't listen to me!" He went from stunned to raging in seconds, angrily kicking a dislodged seat cushion across the living room. "I saw this coming! I knew it, but you didn't want to hear it!"

She was taken aback by his outburst. "What are you talking about?"

"Look around! This wasn't a burglary. This is because of *Cetacean*. All the poking around we've been doing, digging into some long-buried conspiracy? Well, congratulations! Somebody noticed . . . and then some!"

She started to protest, to insist that he was letting his paranoia get the better of him again, but hesitated. Could he be right? As much as she wanted to write this off as a random break-in, she found she couldn't just dismiss Dennis's theory out of hand. They *had* been delving into deep and murky waters: cover-ups, national security, even an alleged cure for missing kidneys. It wasn't beyond reason that interested parties, possibly high up in the military and/or medical establishments, might want to search their apartment to find out just how much they did or didn't know. Wouldn't be the first time the Powers That Be raided a journalist's home or office to keep tabs on their investigation, maybe uncover their sources.

"You know, you may be on to something."

"You think?" He waded through the scattered papers littering the floor, then paused and looked over at her in surprise. "Wait. Did you just agree with me?"

"Possibly. I certainly can't rule out that this is related to *Cetacean*, which is alarming, yes, but also kinda flattering when you think about it. Means we're being taken seriously, possibly by the very people responsible for Gillian's disappearance." Her initial dismay over the break-in started to give way to a growing sense of excitement. "Don't you see what this means? We're on the right track, enough so that we've got your dreaded conspiracy worried about how far we've gotten already. This isn't just a vintage true-crime investigation anymore. We're Woodward and Bernstein, on the trail of a major news story that stretches all the way to . . . well, I have no idea at this point, but it's got to be big to provoke this kind of reaction. And this is happening now, not forty years ago!"

"Jesus Christ!" Dennis gaped at her. "Do you hear yourself? Our home is invaded, unknown entities are targeting us where we live, and you're *still* obsessed with that frigging podcast? What about our personal safety? You ever think about that? Or is having a hit series all that matters to you?"

Ouch, she thought, stung by the accusation. "It's not *all* that matters, but . . . it's what we do. It's our calling."

"Your calling, maybe. I thought it was a cool side hustle that turned into a fairly profitable full-time gig, at least in the short term. But maybe I underestimated just how crazily ambitious you are."

"And what's wrong with that?" she said defensively. "It's worked out pretty well for us so far. I didn't hear you complaining about quitting our crummy day jobs."

She wasn't about to back down just yet, but was it possible he had a point, to some degree? Was she the one who had actually gotten carried away here, lost her perspective on what really mattered? Or were there bigger issues at stake?

"And what about Gillian? Don't you want to find out what happened to her? Maybe even find some justice for her if she was the victim of foul play?"

"That was forever ago. Whatever became of Gillian, it's ancient history at this point. And it's not as though you actually knew her; she disappeared before we were even born. Anyway, has it ever occurred to you that maybe, if she *is* still alive, Gillian doesn't want to be found?"

"Of course I've thought about that. I've wrestled with that question all the way back to *Cascade* and Eleanor. But what's the alternative? Just let missing persons—missing women—be forgotten? Never try to find out what happened to them?"

"I'm not saying that," Dennis said, now on the defensive himself. "But doesn't this look like somebody's sending us a message? Telling us we've gone too far on this particular case?"

"Could be, but think about that. Do you really want *them* to get away with this?" She threw his own preoccupations back at him. "What's the point of obsessing over conspiracies if you're afraid to confront them? To uncover and expose them? Or are you just talk?"

His gaze dropped to the floor, shame bleeding away his earlier indignation. "But it's dangerous, and you don't seem to realize that. This isn't just about racking up more subscriptions to *Cetacean*. There are serious risks and consequences to consider."

"Point taken," she said, offering him an olive branch. She glanced around their ravaged domicile. "I get that now."

"So ask yourself: Do you still think it's worth it?"

She did him the courtesy of giving the question serious thought before answering. She examined her motives, finding a tangle of emotions fueling her: anger over the break-in, insatiable curiosity about where this was all leading and how it connected to Gillian, and yes, ambition and stubbornness. She had never liked being told to be a good girl, keep quiet, and not ask the "wrong" questions. Growing up in a conservative small town in Shasta County, raised by strict conservative parents, she had never quite fit in: always reading the wrong books, listening to the wrong music, and not keeping her mouth shut to avoid upsetting people. Exposing that high-school sports hazing scandal certainly hadn't made her any friends back in her old hometown, but she had stuck to her guns—and moved to the city the first chance she got. Her whole life had been about speaking truth, no matter what. Could she really buckle under now? She'd already invested too much of herself into solving this mystery to just walk away now. She remembered Javy Valdez wishing he'd stuck around to find out who actually came through that glowing doorway in the park, and Briggs and Fulton and Halley and everyone else still haunted by unanswered questions from decades ago. If she backed off now, playing it safe, would she always regret it?

"Yes. Positively," she told Dennis. "I'm not letting this go, no matter what."

He nodded. "Okay then." He seemed calmer now that they'd had it out and she'd actually listened to him. "But we're going to be more careful from now on?"

"Absolutely. Within reason."

He scowled. "What does that mean?"

Before she could answer, figures appeared at the door, which, in the shock of coming home to a crime scene, they had yet to close behind them. She recognized them as the neighbors from across the hall. Paul and Miley Something. Drawn by her and Dennis's heated voices or just the obvious signs of disarray?

"Yikes, what happened here?" Miley peered from the doorway at the mess. "Is everything okay?"

"Just a break-in," Melinda lied. "We're fine."

Maybe.

Chapter Twenty-Eight

"Keep moving."

The guards and their crossbows herded Kirk and McCoy through the lower levels of the fortress, which were lit by lamps employing either flames or luminescent fungus. An underground tunnel, large enough to accommodate wagons and carriages, had led from the coliseum to the fortress, where the prisoners had been unloaded from a cart and marched through a maze of carved stone corridors and catacombs beneath the citadel. Still out cold, Colonel Yorba snarled in her sleep as Kirk and McCoy were forced to carry her between them once more, her arms slung over their increasingly weary shoulders. Kirk found himself hoping that she would regain consciousness soon, if only so she could walk under her own power.

"Just how heavily did you tranquilize our friend here?" he asked McCoy.

"More than enough," the doctor answered, grunting from exertion. "She had the business end of a disruptor pointed at your chest, remember? I wasn't about to take any chances where her sturdy Klingon constitution was concerned."

"I defer to your professional expertise."

A guard prodded them from behind. "Less talking, more walking."

Kirk clammed up, knowing better than to push their luck. Previous efforts to speak to the guards, to discover what he and the others had been accused of and what might be in store for them, had proved futile; his demands and queries might as well have disappeared down a black hole for all the useful information they'd yielded. How and why Siroth had ordered them taken into custody remained a mystery.

At least Sulu and the rest got away, Kirk thought. *Have they already been able to alert* Enterprise *to our capture?*

In short order, they arrived at an arched stone doorway leading to what appeared to be a large subterranean vault or crypt. Kirk had tried to chart their route beneath the fortress, keeping track of every twist and turn, and although he couldn't be one hundred percent positive, it certainly seemed that they had been heading in the direction of Siroth's tower at the rear right corner of the stronghold. Given that the court alchemist was apparently responsible for their arrest, Kirk figured it was a safe bet that the archway led to a subbasement of that very tower.

We're making progress . . . in a manner of speaking.

A man waited by the archway as though expecting them. He was a stocky, dour-faced individual sporting close-cropped blond hair, a handlebar mustache, and a well-worn leather apron marked by chemical stains and acid burns. Narrowed eyes studied the prisoners warily.

"Halt!" the lead guard ordered the procession, then walked up to the aproned man. "Here they are, Gyar, as instructed by your master."

Kirk deduced that this man, Gyar, worked for Siroth, possibly as a servant or assistant.

"You have their possessions?" Gyar asked gruffly.

"Aye. Just as Siroth commanded." The guard beckoned to a subordinate, who came forward with a canvas sack. "And peculiar items they are. Never have I seen their like."

I would hope not, Kirk thought. The sack contained all the gear the guards had confiscated from him, McCoy, and Yorba back at the coliseum: their sidearms, communicators, a tricorder, and even McCoy's medkit, all of which they'd been forced to surrender while surrounded by loaded crossbows. That Siroth had instructed the guards to relieve them of their equipment was yet more evidence that the alchemist knew more about modern technology than he ought to if he was a native of this world.

Thanks to Doctor Hamparian?

Gyar took the sack and inspected its contents by the light of a fungal lamp. "This is all they carried?"

"Well . . ." The guard hesitated before divulging, "They were also in possession of a quantity of precious gems and currency."

"Which you doubtless also confiscated?"

The guard stiffened. "As was only proper."

"Quite so." Gyar smirked. "Please divide the proceeds among you and your men, in recognition of your diligence."

"That is most generous." The guard's attitude underwent a noticeable improvement. He was practically beaming. "Where shall we deliver the prisoners for you?"

"You may leave them with me. I'll take them from here."

Confusion showed on the guard's face. He looked from Gyar to the prisoners, who clearly outnumbered the solitary assistant, and back again. "I don't understand. Surely you will require protection from the prisoners?"

"Leave that to me." Gyar extracted Yorba's disruptor pistol from the sack. "I can manage these three on my own." He handled the weapon with confidence as he looked Kirk in the eyes. "You're not going to give me any trouble, are you?"

"No," Kirk said. "It appears not."

Gyar put down the sack while brandishing the disruptor. "I thought as much."

The guards' eagerness to depart with the jewels meant that only a few more minutes of persuasion were required before they departed, marching back the way they'd come.

"There goes our petty cash," McCoy observed.

Kirk shrugged, recalling how easily Scotty had fabricated the gems aboard the *Enterprise*. "Easy come, easy go."

"Don't even think of trying anything." Gyar aimed the disruptor at Kirk, who found himself facing the Romulan weapon for the second time in barely as many hours. "I know how to use this."

"I'll take your word for it," Kirk said.

"You'd better." Gyar reached beneath his apron and produced a garden-variety communicator, of the sort commonly used by civilians throughout the Federation. He flipped it open to speak to someone. "They're here, sir." He kept his eyes on prisoners. "Yes, there's three of them, including an unconscious woman. No idea who she is."

Kirk held his tongue, declining to identify Yorba until he had a better understanding of the situation. He assumed Gyar was reporting to Siroth, but what connection did either of them have to the Klingons? Gyar sure didn't seem to recognize Yorba.

"Very well," Gyar said after pausing to listen to the person on the other end of the transmission. "I'll keep them on ice until you and the doctor get here."

He closed the communicator and placed it back under his apron.

"Who was that?" Kirk asked. "Siroth?"

"Who else?"

"And Doctor Hamparian?"

"Save your questions for them." Gyar picked up the sack and slung it over his shoulder. He gestured impatiently at the archway. "That way."

"All right."

Kirk chose to cooperate for now. It was possible that, even encumbered by Yorba, he and McCoy might be able to turn the tables on Gyar, disarming him before he could fire his weapon, but if Gyar was taking them to wait for Siroth and Hamparian, why not let him? Finding Hamparian was their objective after all. Granted, this wasn't exactly how he'd hoped to make contact with the missing scientist, but it would have to do. As for their current status as captives . . . well, they'd cross that bridge when they came to it. Chances were, Sulu and the rest of the landing party were already hatching a rescue plan.

"Come along, Bones. Seems we have an audience with the blue lady coming up."

McCoy eyed Gyar's disruptor. "Lucky us."

Lugging the Yorba between them, they entered a large subterranean chamber. Sturdy stone pillars and thick timber beams supported a high ceiling. A hefty wooden door, reinforced with metal strips, secured a doorway at the opposite end of the basement. A faint electronic hum, like that produced by advanced technology, emanated from the sealed vault.

"What's in there?" Kirk asked, intrigued.

"Nothing that concerns you." Gyar put down the sack long enough to pull a lever. A metal grille descended to seal off the underground entrance to the tower, where Kirk was almost certain they were now. "Be grateful that you're not being put to rest there . . . yet."

"Some sort of morgue?" McCoy asked.

"That's one way to put it." Gyar snickered as he reclaimed the sack. "But like I said, save your questions for later. I'm not here to give you a guided tour."

A winding stone staircase awaited them. McCoy groaned at the prospect of carting Yorba up all those stairs. "Just so you know, Captain, my knees will be filing a formal protest at the first opportunity."

"Duly noted." Kirk wasn't looking forward to the climb either. He glanced over at Gyar. "How many floors are we talking?"

"Don't worry," Gyar said. "There's an easier way."

He directed them into a glow-lit alcove, large enough to accommodate all four of them. The cramped conditions forced Gyar to get closer to his captives. Perhaps in response, he placed the muzzle of the disruptor against McCoy's temple.

"In case you're tempted to some bold heroics."

"That's not necessary," Kirk said. "Trust me, I'm eager to make your superiors' acquaintance."

"I'm sure, but I imagine you'd prefer to have the upper hand when you meet, and to have your phasers and communicators back." He kept the weapon pressed against McCoy's head. "That's not going to happen on my watch."

A drop of sweat trickled down McCoy's face, but otherwise he maintained his composure. For better or for worse, this was hardly the first time he'd been threatened with death.

"That's all very well and good, but can we move matters along? What in blazes are we doing crammed into this glorified oubliette?"

"Going up."

Fumbling with the sack, Gyar reached to slide open a panel concealing an illuminated control panel. He pressed a button with his elbow, and the seemingly solid floor lurched beneath them. The floor rose, lifting the group with them.

A turbolift?

No, Kirk realized. *An old-fashioned elevator.*

Still fairly advanced technology for Atraz, though, judging from Starfleet's records and his own observations since arriving on the planet.

"I'm impressed. Installed by Siroth, I assume, along with the solar panels and sensor arrays on the roof of the tower. That *is* where we are, isn't it? Siroth's tower?"

"And laboratory. The finest in the sector, fully equipped with the latest state-of-the-art equipment," Gyar bragged before catching himself. "As he can tell you himself if he chooses. What did I say about questions?"

"Just admiring the amenities," Kirk replied. "All the comforts of modern living, to a degree."

He considered their captor. Was Gyar a native Atrazian who was oddly familiar with the Federation and its technology, or had he and Siroth come from another world, preceding Hamparian? The Prime Directive notwithstanding, visitors from beyond had obviously brought their advanced scientific know-how to this corner of Atraz long before *Chinook*'s hijacked escape pod had landed here less than a week ago.

"No comment," Gyar said.

The elevator ascended at least three floors before coming to rest. "Out," he ordered, hanging back to put more distance between him and the prisoners. As this meant that the disruptor would no longer be in such close proximity to McCoy's skull, he and Kirk were more than happy to comply. Exiting the lift, they passed through a short vestibule to reach some comfortably appointed living quarters, which Kirk judged to be preferable to a dungeon or torture chamber. Glancing about, he was surprised to spot a framed painting of the Golden Gate Bridge adorning a wall. The portrait of the sunlit bridge and harbor betrayed no indication of when it had been painted, which could have been anytime in the last three centuries.

The artwork caught McCoy's eye as well. "I don't know about you, Jim, but I'm starting to get the distinct impression that this Siroth character isn't from around these parts."

"You think?" Kirk said.

"Enough chatter." Gyar directed them to a low bench next to a stained-glass window, then sat down in in an upholstered easy chair across from them. "Get comfortable. Siroth will see you when he's able."

"And Hamparian?"

"Her too." Gyar held on to the disruptor. "Now sit tight and leave me be."

His hospitality suffered in comparison to Pujal's caravan, but it seemed this was the most they were going to get. The bench wasn't long enough to let Kirk and McCoy lie Yorba down on it, so they started to awkwardly prop her up between them, only to have the drugged Klingon stir at last. An unhappy growl escaped her lips, along with a trickle of drool, as she groggily lifted her head. Her eyelids flickered, then snapped open as she abruptly became aware of her new surroundings.

"*Fek'lhr!*" she swore, the Klingon equivalent of adrenaline kicking in. She jumped to her feet, only to reel unsteadily, overcome by dizziness. "What insulting perfidy is this?"

"Easy, Colonel." Kirk rose to assist her, but she slapped his hand away with stinging force. He backed off diplomatically. "We're in the same boat at the moment, and your weapon is in the hands of that scowling gentleman over there, so I wouldn't advise any rash actions."

Gyar brandished the stolen disruptor. "I'd listen to him if I were you."

As before, fury warred with cunning on Yorba's face, with the latter winning out. Calculating eyes surveyed the chamber, missing nothing.

"Where is this place? How did we get here?"

"Sit back down and I'll tell you," Kirk said, "while we wait for our hosts to arrive."

"Hosts?"

"A high-ranking member of the suzerain's court . . . and Doctor Hamparian."

That piqued her interest. She grudgingly sat down on the bench. McCoy shifted position to place Kirk between them. Probably a smart move, Kirk reflected, considering who had dosed her back at the coliseum. The captain briskly brought her up to speed on events since then. She shot McCoy a murderous glare when Kirk was obliged to explain how exactly she'd been rendered unconscious, but to his relief, she refrained from returning the favor in a less pharmaceutical fashion, at least for the moment. Kirk recalled that some Klingons considered revenge a dish best served cold.

Watch your back, Bones.

"And my agents?" she asked.

"They eluded arrest, as far as I know. Your only offense, from what

I can tell, was being in my company when the guards closed in." He couldn't resist pointing out, "You would have been better off if you'd let us go our separate ways, instead of pulling a disruptor on me."

"So I brought this on myself?"

Kirk shrugged. "Something to think about, perhaps."

"Maybe after my head stops pulsing like an overheating warp core." She subjected McCoy to another withering look as she massaged her temple. "I'm not impressed by your medical skills, Doctor."

"Sorry to hear it." He looked somewhat less than repentant. "Most of my patients are not armed and dangerous."

"You have yet to see me at my most dangerous, Doctor."

McCoy gulped.

"Perhaps I can do something to relieve your headache," a feminine voice volunteered. "If you're amenable."

Taya Hamparian and Siroth entered via the vestibule beyond the elevator. The purported abductee removed her Atrazian headdress; small, rudimentary antennae betrayed the Andorian branches in her family tree. Kirk wondered how much of the prior discussion she'd overheard. She turned to Gyar, who rose to attention at Siroth's arrival. "You have a medkit belonging to our guests?"

Gyar produced the item from the sack of confiscated gear. Hamparian helped herself to a hypospray and, with practiced efficiency, selected a medication and dosage. "Forgive us for keeping you waiting, by the way. Siroth had his hands full explaining to the suzerain why he'd had you taken into custody, blaming you for the disturbance in the stadium. That took some time."

She approached Yorba, who hissed at the hypospray as though it were a tribble.

"Keep that noxious device away from me! I've had quite enough of Starfleet medicine for the day."

"It's only a basic analgesic and stimulant," Hamparian said, "to relieve any discomfort and grogginess."

"Klingons do not fear pain, unlike lesser species."

"Klingon?" This revelation seemed to catch Hamparian by surprise, although she didn't let it rattle her. "Nevertheless, you surely don't enjoy it."

"That depends. Are we talking receiving . . . or inflicting?"

"The former," Hamparian said coolly, unflustered by any implied threat. "Under the circumstances, wouldn't you rather be clearheaded and undistracted by any aches or pains?"

"Rest assured that I can and have excelled under far more harrowing conditions than this." She mustered a fierce smile. "My decision is final, Doctor."

"If you say so." Hamparian lowered the hypospray. "Don't say I didn't offer to make you more comfortable, whoever you are."

"It seems introductions are in order," Siroth said, his voice as deep as a cavern. As though in response to those sonorous tones, a small white rat came scurrying from an adjoining chamber, heading straight toward Siroth, who casually scooped up the rat and cradled it against his chest. "Hello, Enkidu. I missed you too." He petted the rat as he contemplated Yorba. Dark eyes, peering out from beneath bristling black eyebrows, scrutinized her. "You say you're a Klingon?"

"Colonel Yorba." She turned her own eyes toward his companion. "I've come a long way to find you, Doctor Hamparian."

"You'll forgive me if I find that rather alarming," Hamparian said, driving a stake through Spock's defection theory. "Considering your people's . . . aggressive . . . reputation, no offense."

"None taken," Yorba replied. "We wear that reputation with pride. Indeed, we would find it insulting *not* to be feared."

"We've come a long way to find you too." Kirk was not about to cede control of the discussion to Yorba. "I'm Captain James T. Kirk of the *Starship*—"

"Oh, I'm quite aware of your identity, Captain," Siroth interrupted. "Funny finally meeting you at last. I've known of you since before you were born, although you looked somewhat older the first time I saw your face."

"What the devil do you mean by that?" McCoy asked.

"That's my secret to keep." Siroth smiled slyly, as though enjoying a private joke. "Let's just say that, nowadays, I could hardly fail to recognize the illustrious captain of the *U.S.S. Enterprise*, given you and your ship's involvement in such newsworthy, even historic, events as the onset of the Organian Peace Treaty, the planetary disaster on Deneva, the assassination of a Tellarite ambassador, first contact with the Hortas and the Kelvans and other exotic new life-forms and civilizations, not to mention—"

"We get it." Kirk cut short the recitation. "You're more than familiar with my résumé." He put the pieces together. "Am I to gather that it was you who spotted me at the coliseum, not Doctor Hamparian?"

"Guilty as charged, Captain."

"And sicced the guards on us?"

"Correct." Siroth regarded McCoy. "And this would be your chief medical officer, Doctor Leonard McCoy?"

"Pleased to meet you," McCoy said. "I think."

"Which brings us to Colonel Yorba. I confess, Captain, that when I ordered you and your associates arrested, I did not anticipate you being accompanied by a Klingon."

"'Accompanied' is not the word I would use," Yorba said haughtily. "I am hardly keeping company with Starfleet officers of my own free will."

Her tone turned "Starfleet" into a slur. Kirk let that pass. He needed answers more than an argument.

"Speaking of free will," he segued, "perhaps you can enlighten me, Doctor Hamparian. How is it you went from being the hostage of a spacejacker to a guest at a palace? If you were indeed ever actually a hostage at all."

Hamparian's antennae twitched. A sharp intake of breath indicated that his remark had struck home.

"It appears my ingenious ruse was not as convincing as I'd hoped." She settled into the vacated easy chair and took a moment to gather her thoughts. "I suppose I owe you an explanation, Captain."

Spock had already speculated about her motives, but Kirk wanted to hear what Hamparian had to say for herself. "I'm all ears."

"Careful, Taya," Siroth cautioned her. "These intruders are not our allies. We need not share our secrets with them."

"Who are you calling intruders?" McCoy objected. "You had us brought here . . . by armed guards no less!"

"Only after you intruded on this planet, where you are unwelcome."

The alchemist's saturnine features conveyed his displeasure. "And brought Klingons down on us as well."

"The Federation does not dictate our actions," Yorba said. "We came of our own volition, to serve our own ends."

As always, Kirk thought. The Klingon Empire was not known for its humanitarian endeavors. They cared only about their own interests.

"This was a rescue mission," Kirk reminded Siroth, "or so we had reason to believe."

"But clearly you had your doubts," Siroth scoffed. "Don't pretend that you were simply playing Good Samaritan. Starfleet wants Taya back for its own purposes, just as the Klingons do. Because of her genius."

"And what about you?" Kirk asked. "What's your stake in this?"

"My motives are none of your concern."

"Maybe, but Hamparian's definitely are." Kirk directed his gaze at her. "You mentioned a ruse just now. One designed to escape the Federation's stringent supervision of your work?"

He was going to have egg on his face if Spock had miscalculated her motives, but he was willing to risk that just to settle the issue once and for all. He could always apologize later if necessary.

"Don't take the bait, Taya," the alchemist said. "Watch what you say."

"Why not let the lady speak for herself?" McCoy countered.

"Please, Siroth." She waved off his warnings. "It's obvious Captain Kirk has already surmised the truth." Her antennae gave him a tiny bow. "Excellent detective work, sir."

"Credit my first officer." He frowned at her confession. "You'll forgive me if I think that staging a phony spacejacking was an extreme reaction to . . . regulatory oversight?"

"Oversight? You have no idea what it's like to be on the brink of revolutionary new breakthroughs in medical science, only to have your hands constantly tied by archaic taboos from a bygone era, based on prejudices left over from a conflict that ended centuries ago." She turned her head toward Yorba. "And the Klingons are no better. Still shunning genetic engineering because of what happened with the Augment virus way back when."

"A disfiguring plague stemming from *human* science," Yorba stressed, "which marks us to this day." Her smooth brow testified to the enduring legacy of a failed attempt to create genetically enhanced Klingons back in Jonathan Archer's time. "Can you blame us for not desiring to repeat that disastrous experiment?"

"So what *is* your agenda here?" Kirk asked, since it was clear that defecting to the Klingons had never been Hamparian's intention. "And how did you find out about Hamparian's alleged abduction anyway?"

"We in Imperial Intelligence are perhaps more pragmatic about such matters than other factions. If nothing else, security demands we keep apprised of whatever dangerous technologies our foes may be developing, regardless of their vaunted principles. The opportunity to deprive the Federation of Doctor Hamparian's brilliance—and its potential military applications—was too valuable to ignore. We cannot afford to fall behind in a genetic arms race."

"Dear Lord!" McCoy exclaimed. "Weaponizing our DNA, the fundamental codes that make us each uniquely human—or Klingon? The very notion is obscene!"

"You may find it so, Doctor, but do you deny that your leaders or mine would not be tempted by such science, should the need arise? 'All's fair in love and war' is a human saying, is it not?"

"That's the kind of thinking that almost wiped out the human race back in the day. I like to think we've learned something since then."

Yorba snorted. "I didn't take you for an idealist, Doctor, or a fool."

"That still doesn't explain," Kirk said, "how, if you weren't party to Doctor Hamparian's ruse, you came looking for her here on Atraz."

"You underestimate our intelligence capabilities," Yorba said. "Your classified secrets are nowhere near as secure as you think. And a matter of such concern to your leaders can hardly evade our detection." She smirked at Hamparian. "It may flatter you to know, Doctor, that your 'abduction' provoked much agitation at the highest levels of Starfleet and the Federation, which invariably attracted our attention."

Hamparian shook her head. "I was afraid of that, but I had hoped that Starfleet would write me off as lost rather than venture into this sector. Apparently I was deluding myself in that respect." Her expression darkened. "None of this would have been necessary if I'd just been allowed to carry on my work without so many restrictions."

"The rules regarding human genetic engineering exist for a reason," Kirk said. "No one wants another Khan Noonien Singh. Trust me on that."

That Khan was still alive and exiled on Ceti Alpha V, after being revived from suspended animation not long ago, remained a closely guarded secret that he was not about to divulge, but Kirk knew firsthand just how dangerous a "superior" human being could be. The *Enterprise* had barely survived Khan's grandiose ambitions.

"Nonsense!" Siroth said heatedly. "Why should the crimes of one strain of Augments hold science hostage for centuries? And damn an entire field of study due to guilt by association?"

"You seem to have strong opinions on the subject, Mister Siroth," Kirk observed, "not to mention being well versed in Earth's history and technology." He gazed pointedly at the painting of the Golden Gate Bridge. "You're not remotely Atrazian, are you?"

"Of course not," Siroth scoffed. "There's no point in denying it, I suppose, since you already know more than you should. Like my esteemed colleague here, I came to Atraz seeking a refuge where we could pursue our research free of the Federation's timidity. Gyar and I arrived first, years ago, to lay the groundwork for our long-term objectives. Much time and effort were required to establish myself here, winning Varkat's patronage and protection, before I could finally send word to Taya to join me on Atraz so we could continue our work without interference." He shrugged. "Fortunately, I've made a habit of keeping a low profile, so I was able to quietly disappear from Federation space without making much of a ripple. Arranging Taya's departure was somewhat more complicated."

"Hence the fake spacejacking," Kirk said. "What about Fortier. Where did he fit in?"

"A convenient accomplice, nothing more," Hamparian said. "He came to me as a patient, seeking treatment for acute xenopolycythemia. While taking part in a clinical trial, he grew intrigued by my theories regarding the possibility of regrowing human limbs and organs." Her antennae drooped sheepishly. "I may have suggested that I was more likely to achieve a breakthrough, and restore his missing hand, outside the boundaries of the Federation, which led to me soliciting his assistance when the time came to stage my 'abduction.'"

"You must have been very persuasive," Kirk said.

"Well, my understanding is that Louis also had an additional motive for dropping out of sight. He was prone to ending up on the bad side of unsavory customers. Starting a new life on Atraz appealed to him for more reasons than one."

That certainly fit with Captain Yamada's impression of Fortier. "So how did he end up in the arena?"

"He brought that on himself," Siroth said. "It was not our doing."

"Unfortunately," Hamparian elaborated, "changing worlds did not change Louis's vices or behavior patterns. He cheated one of the su-zerain's lesser sons while gambling, then tried to get out of trouble by claiming to be under Siroth's protection. This did not go over well with Varkat, although Siroth *did* appeal for mercy on Louis's behalf."

"As much as was prudent," Siroth hedged, "until he threatened to re-veal my true origins to save himself. Then he became an extortionist . . . and a liability."

"So you had him thrown to those bloodthirsty birds?" McCoy's voice rang with righteous indignation. "To be torn apart before a cheering crowd?"

Hamparian flinched, but Siroth would not be shamed.

"Would it surprise you, Doctor, to know that I once valued human life no less passionately than you do? The very thought of being re-sponsible for another person's death would have been unbearable to me. Alas, that was a *long* time ago."

"What changed?" Kirk asked.

"Time brings perspective, Captain. Don't misunderstand me; I still prize life more than most, and regret its loss, but I've also increasingly come to understand that, in the long term, the importance of our work far outweighs any present sacrifices. A few ephemeral lives are a small price to pay to achieve our ultimate goal."

"Which is?"

"Immortality, Captain. Nothing less than the secret of eternal life, which humanity has sought since the dawn of civilization." He stroked his pet rat. "Isn't that right, Enkidu?"

Kirk recognized the pet's name from *The Epic of Gilgamesh*. Enkidu had been Gilgamesh's beloved companion-in-arms, whose untimely death had spurred Gilgamesh to embark on a quest for literal immortality, to escape the maw of death forever.

"You can't be serious!" McCoy blurted. "That's not medicine, that's madness."

"And cowardly to the extreme." Yorba's face curdled in disgust. "Klingons do not fear death. What good is long life without an honorable death to give it meaning?"

Siroth took her contempt in stride. "I prefer to think of it as doing battle against the ultimate foe. I intend to achieve victory over death, rather than surrendering to its icy grasp. You'd think a Klingon would respect that."

"We also know that not even the bravest warrior can bend reality to his will. 'The wind does not respect a fool,' as the saying goes. Nature will have its way with us in the end."

"Exactly. Everything dies . . . eventually," Kirk said. "True immortality is a fantasy."

"Must it be?" Hamparian asked. "Science has already expanded the average human life-span over the course of history, while space exploration long ago revealed that some humanoids are blessed with greater longevity than others. Just compare humans to Vulcans, for instance, or even humans to Andorians. Statistically speaking, I would probably live longer if I were fully Andorian; as is, my human DNA is likely to have a negative effect on my longevity."

"Something you take personally?" Kirk asked.

"Perhaps a little," she admitted. "If nothing else, my personal biology, and its implications, may have been a factor in steering my work in the direction of regeneration and renewal via applied genetic manipulation." She wiggled her antennae. "No surprise, I suppose, that mixing genes has always been a source of fascination to me. Who knows what effects can be achieved by combining them in new, varied ways?"

She sounded perfectly sane and reasonable, Kirk had to admit. "But still . . . . immortality?"

"Maybe not in our lifetimes, such as they are. Siroth and I don't always see to eye to eye on that; he's somewhat more optimistic on that front than I am," she said. "But even if we don't achieve literal immortality anytime soon, we can still hope to extend humanoid life-spans by decades, centuries, maybe even millennia someday. Not to mention developing ways to regrow lost limbs and organs, to the betterment of all carbon-based life-forms. Doesn't that seem like a worthwhile endeavor to you, Captain? Even worth faking a kidnapping for?"

Kirk wondered if the crew and passengers of the *Chinook* would feel the same way. "And you think that you can accomplish that here on Atraz?"

"Very possibly. Siroth has managed to assemble all the equipment we need, here in this tower, far from the Federation's suffocating regulations. And as for the populace, the Atrazians are baseline humanoid enough to make them the perfect test subjects for future trials. Indeed, they are so genetically similar to *Homo sapiens* that there's good reason to believe that they're descended from ancient humans transplanted to this world by unknown aliens sometime in the distant past. A phenomenon that is rapidly gaining acceptance in xenoanthropological circles."

Like Miramanee's people, Kirk thought. A familiar pang stabbed his heart.

"I can't believe we're even discussing this insanity!" McCoy said, visibly offended by Hamparian's sales pitch. "Playing god with DNA? Humanoid guinea pigs? Do you even hear what you're saying? This whole operation flies in the face of responsible medical ethics. It's the sort of reckless experimentation that gives science a bad name. Doctor Frankenstein would be proud!"

"Don't be so melodramatic, Doctor," Hamparian replied. "Think of the greater good. And if it will ease your conscience, understand that our test subjects will all be condemned prisoners who would otherwise face death in the arena. By taking part in our experiments, they will at least have a chance at life, maybe even a prolonged one."

"You're wasting your breath, Taya." Siroth glowered at his unwanted visitors. "They'll never understand."

"At least let me try to convince them to leave us alone," she said. "Please, Captain, you've ascertained that I'm safe and not being held against my will. I've explained what we're attempting here and all the good that could come from it. Can't you see fit to leave us in peace? Maybe even have me officially declared missing or deceased? Just to spare us all any unnecessary grief or conflict."

Yorba chuckled scornfully. "Oh, I think we're well past that point, Doctor. Then again, a little grief and conflict never hurt anyone."

"I'm sorry, Doctor Hamparian," Kirk said, ignoring Yorba's gibes for the moment, "but I have to agree with Doctor McCoy. This entire operation is violating the Prime Directive, the Organian Peace Treaty, and pretty much every other law on the books. Duty requires me to do everything in my power to shut it down and complete my mission by returning both you and Mister Siroth to the Federation to stand trial."

While also keeping Hamparian from falling into the hands of the Klingons, he thought. *And hopefully making it back to the* Enterprise *in one piece.*

Hamparian's face fell. Her antennae drooped.

"You're quite certain we can't change your mind, Captain? For your own good, and that of your companions?"

"I'm afraid not," he said firmly. "Sorry."

Siroth nodded grimly. He appeared unsurprised by Kirk's decision. The captain suspected that Siroth had only been humoring Hamparian by letting her plead her case to Kirk and the others. He'd never expected Kirk and others to come around.

"I regret you feel that way, Captain. I truly do."

He nodded at Gyar, who was still standing by with Yorba's disruptor.

"Take them away!"

Chapter Twenty-Nine

"Anyway, we were jogging that afternoon, on a clear spring day, when this sudden blast of wind came out of nowhere, blowing dust and grit in our faces and nearly knocking us over. Just like those garbage men you talked about on your series."

Melinda was back in Golden Gate Park, at a site that was starting to feel very familiar to her. It was lunchtime, the sun high in the sky, and that same grassy field and adjacent roadway had attracted a variety of visitors. Two young women were playing Frisbee not far away. A geriatric dogwalker was cleaning up after a corgi on a leash, which had just done its business on the lawn. A college student, wearing a USF sweater, sat with his back against a tree trunk on the edge of the field, perusing a paperback copy of *Ethan Frome*. A mom or nanny pushed a baby carriage along the side of the road. A Parks Department maintenance truck trundled by. Still feeling paranoid after the break-in at her apartment, Melinda was uncomfortable with so many anonymous eyes and ears nearby. She fought an urge to keep an eye on the assorted parkgoers, maybe catch someone looking at her *too* attentively, and forced herself to focus instead on today's interviewees.

Ken and Regan Dows had been in their twenties on May thirteenth in 1986, the day Gillian had vanished. The couple, who now qualified for AARP, still looked trim and athletic, although Regan appeared to have had a little work done. They wore matching his-and-hers track suits as they sat across the picnic table from Melinda, who had needed to set up the mics and recorder herself since Dennis was absent for . . . reasons.

"Did you see anything that might have caused this freak gust of wind?"

"Like what?" Ken asked.

"A helicopter maybe?"

"Nope. Didn't see anything like that." He turned to his wife for confirmation. "Did we, honey?"

"Not at all. We were jogging along, getting our daily miles in, when . . . whoosh! Felt like a jet taking off or something, and then it just went away." She snapped her fingers. "Like that."

Shades of Valdez and his work buddy, Melinda thought. It was possible, of course, that the Dowses were just parroting what Valdez had supposedly experienced the day before, as reported on *Cetacean*, but she couldn't imagine why they'd want to do so. They struck her as too healthy, well-adjusted, and altogether ordinary to collaborate on a hoax just for kicks. And at least they could back up each other's stories, unlike Valdez, whose coworker was not around to corroborate his tale. So, two identical experiences in the same location, one day apart?

She slotted the Dowses' experience into her timeline. By her reckoning, this would have been less than an hour after Gillian and company liberated Chekov from Mercy General. And then what? Gillian had hightailed it over to the park to catch a ride on a stealth aircraft or flying saucer? And where did Valdez's glowing "door from nowhere" fit in? Dennis might argue that Gillian, her partners in crime, and Chekov had all escaped through a hole in the spacetime continuum, but that didn't explain the indentation in the ground or the flattened trash can. *Something* had sat down hard in the field.

"By any chance, did you see a blue Chevy pickup in the vicinity?" She gestured at the spot where the abandoned vehicle had been found. "Possibly over there?"

The couple gave each other quizzical looks. "I'm not remembering that," Regan said. "You?"

Ken shook his head, then turned his head back toward Melinda. "Sorry. That was a *long* time ago. If there was a blue truck around, it didn't stick in our memories." He shrugged. "Doesn't mean it wasn't there."

Did that mean that second freak wind happened before Gillian arrived in her truck, or simply that the distracted joggers hadn't noticed the empty pickup at the time? Both scenarios fit the facts as Melinda knew them.

She asked them a few more questions, showed them her images of Gillian and the Pizza Date (whom they didn't remember seeing), and inquired about the deep dent in the field (which they had jogged past without noting), before thanking them for their time and wrapping up the interview. They took off at a jog, heading deeper into the park, while she packed up her gear, stowed it in her backpack, and vacated the picnic bench. Despite herself, she couldn't resist scoping out the other parkgoers again. The dogwalker and carriage pusher had moved on, but the Frisbee players and the English Lit reader were still on the scene and not paying any attention to her.

That she could tell.

On my way, she texted Dennis, getting a thumbs-up emoticon in response. She set out on foot, leaving the field behind. She kept her gaze fixed on the path ahead, as planned, and her body language as relaxed as possible.

Here goes nothing, she thought. *Don't look up.*

As soon as she rounded a curve and was safely out of eyeshot, the Frisbee players halted their game and, with practiced efficiency, altered their appearance. Wigs went into a waiting gym bag. Jackets and sweaters were turned inside out to display very different colors and designs. Sweatpants from the bag were pulled over the shorts they were wearing before. New hats and sunglasses completed the disguise. One of the women took out her phone.

"She's on the move," she reported. "Continuing surveillance."

Only moments later, walking along Lincoln Way, Melinda sent another text to Dennis. Per their plan, it was carefully crafted to fool anyone who might be monitoring their communications.

You need me?

He replied promptly: *No rush. Take the scenic route.*

"Omigosh," she whispered under her breath. His response caused her heart to skip a beat, almost throwing her off her stride. She knew what that coded answer really meant.

It was happening. She was being followed.

Ever since the break-in, three days ago, they had both occasionally felt as though they were being watched or followed when they were out and about. It was nothing they could put their finger on, and it could be that they were just on edge after having their home invaded, but it wasn't beyond the bounds of possibility either, given that spies and cover-ups were now part of their investigation. Best, perhaps, to trust their instincts, just to be safe?

They'd reported the break-in to the police, naturally, but refrained from sharing their more dire suspicions to avoid sounding crazy. The cops had done their due diligence, checking out the crime scene, but hadn't seemed all that optimistic or motivated about catching the perp. Whoever had picked the lock on the door had done a slick job of it, leaving no prints or other evidence behind. Meanwhile, the fact that nothing appeared to have been stolen had left the police scratching their heads. "Anybody have a personal grudge against you two?"

"Nobody we know of," she'd answered, which was true, more or less.

It was only later, after the cops had departed, that Dennis had confirmed that their computers had been searched and their files downloaded, including the encrypted ones. What's more, he'd found indications that the hardware had been tapped as well, allowing a third party to monitor them remotely—and maybe even use them as listening devices. Which possibly explained why the intruder(s) hadn't taken the computers with them to make the break-in look more like a burglary. They didn't want to halt the investigation; they just wanted to stay on top of it.

Because they were looking for Gillian too?

For better or for worse, Dennis's paranoid attitude didn't seem so overboard anymore. So, in light of her promise to be more wary from then on, they'd hatched a plan to find out whether they were actually being followed or not, using a compromised laptop to set up the meeting with the Dowses—while Dennis watched from above via a high-flying drone equipped with telescopic lenses and a camera.

Don't look up, she thought. *Act natural.*

The drone had cost a pretty penny, covertly purchased by a friend they'd reimbursed in cash, but apparently it had been worth the price. Keeping her eyes aimed straight ahead as she ever-so-casually strolled past the Botanical Garden, she managed to avoid looking back over her shoulder to try to spot who was tailing her. Tracking her shadow or shadows was Dennis's job now. She simply had to lead them on long

enough for him to get a good look at them and hopefully figure out
who they were.

You want to spy on us? Okay, two can play at that game.

The scenic route was designed to keep any possible shadow interested. Leaving the park, she caught a bus to Pacific Heights to check
out the former address of the pizza place Gillian and her dinner companion had visited that one time, which was now occupied by a newer
restaurant offering Laos-Colombian fusion cuisine. Melinda didn't
really anticipate picking up any valuable leads or insights at this location; she just hoped the Gillian connection would not be lost on her
shadow, intriguing them enough to keep them tailing her.

As she treated herself to some stir-fry with peanut sauce, she
couldn't help trying to visualize the site's former life as a pizza joint.
Even with more immediate things to worry about, up to and including the fact that she was indeed under surveillance, she still got goose
bumps thinking about how Gillian had dined here the night before she
vanished. What had she been thinking that night? What had she and
her date talked about? What urgent business had called them away so
abruptly? Something involving Chekov's infiltration of the *U.S.S. Enterprise*? And most importantly, had she known that less than twenty-four
hours later she would disappear forever?

Melinda glanced around the repurposed eatery, wondering where
exactly Gillian had been sitting that night in 1986. *If only I had a time
machine, so I could walk right over to her table and ask her everything
I'm dying to know. Maybe even warn her of . . . what?*

But time travel wasn't real, at least as far as she knew. The way this
investigation was going, she was starting to think anything was possible.

Finishing off her snack, she made her way to Mercy General, taking
care to stay aboveground, where the drone could see both her and her
shadow; no subterranean Metro lines or stations for her today. Taking
her time, she leisurely circled the hospital, studying every entrance and
exit. Which route, if any, had Gillian and friends used to spirit Chekov
away, right beneath the noses of the FBI and navy security guards?
Had a certain hypothetical stealth aircraft been involved? Somewhere
between the times Valdez and the Dowses had their respective experiences in the park?

Casing the hospital, however, brought her no closer to solving Jane Temple's locked-elevator mystery, not that Melinda had truly expected any "eureka" moments. The actual point of the excursion was to keep her shadow engaged while Dennis watched them from above.

Hope you're enjoying this historical walking tour, dude or dudes.

Tired and ready to go home, she texted Dennis: *How's it going?*

Getting it done, he answered. *Come home so I can tell all.*

"Okay then," she murmured. Seems he didn't need her to lead her shadow on anymore, which meant he'd already gotten something useful from the exercise. Excitement washed away her fatigue. She couldn't wait to find out what he'd discovered via the drone.

brt, she texted back. Be right there.

She scurried away from the hospital, making a beeline for home without being too obvious about it. In theory, she was still being watched. She had to keep cool.

Don't look up. Don't look back.

Pausing only to drop off her gear in their apartment, she found Dennis on the roof of the building, operating the drone from the comfort of one of the folding chairs they'd lugged up there earlier. She didn't waste time saying hello.

"Okay, spill. What have you got for me?"

She was breathing hard, having taken the steps two at a time on top of having traipsed all over the city today. A half-empty water bottle was sitting on the floor of the roof next to Dennis; she finished it off without asking.

"It was the Frisbee girls," he reported, his gaze fixed on the screen of a brand-new, uncompromised laptop, which was still displaying an aerial view of the city streets courtesy of their expensive new drone; this sting was taking its toll on their bank accounts. "Plus, a third operative waiting to pick up your tail once you headed away from the field. It was a pretty well-coordinated operation, actually; they took turns tailing you, trading the point position back and forth among them so there was less chance of you noticing any one of them sticking to you the whole time. It was very professional. They knew what they were doing."

His face fell as the implications of that sank in. "Oh, crap."

232

"I didn't spot them," she admitted, "although, in my defense, I was trying hard not to look for them." She peered over his shoulder at the screen. "What about the other way around? Any chance they spotted our drone?"

"I doubt it. It was way up high, camouflaged to blend in with the sky, and just to play it safe, I tried to keep it between the sun and the shadows so that they would have needed to stare into the sun to see it."

"Good job," she encouraged him. On the screen, what looked like a Vespa motor scooter was heading down a street. "What are we looking at now?"

"One of the Frisbee girls is staying put across the street, keeping watch over our front door. But I'm hoping the pair on the scooter are heading somewhere interesting, maybe back to their HQ." He shrugged apologetically. "I couldn't follow all of them at once now that they've split up, so I chose to stick with the scooter."

"Makes sense to me." She assumed they'd used the scooter to keep up with her whenever she'd resorted to mass transit. "Hey, any chance you can zoom in on the license plate?"

"Way ahead of you. Got some clear screen grabs earlier. Haven't had a chance to run the number yet. Been too busy operating the drone and tracking your shadows." He used the laptop's keyboard to control the drone's flight. "I'm not *that* good at multitasking."

"Understood." She was eager to find out who the scooter belonged to, but curbed her impatience. She pulled the other folding chair over and settled in as they watched the scooter weave in and out of traffic on its way to somewhere. The aerial view made it tricky to orient herself since she was used to traversing the city at street level, but she got the impression that the scooter was heading toward downtown. She assumed that Dennis would be able to work out the exact route and coordinates from the drone's feed if he hadn't already done so. "We know where this is?"

"Northeast on Bryant."

She smirked. "Knew you'd know that."

Minutes passed. Now that her part in the sting was done, the wait gave her time to reflect on what exactly they'd discovered and what it meant. While part of her was positively smug that they'd pulled this operation off without a hitch, they *had* confirmed that the break-in was just the beginning; unknown parties were going to great lengths to keep them under observation.

So . . . yay?

"You know, I keep thinking that it seems like this all started—the surveillance, I mean—when I called that number on the business card and left a message for 'Wilmer Offutt.' Find it hard to believe that's just a coincidence." She fished another water bottle from a cooler. "Then again, we'd already gotten Halley's attention by then. So maybe he's behind this, or his past or present superiors?"

"Could be, I suppose," Dennis said, preoccupied with tracking the scooter. "Hang on. I think they've reached their destination."

The scooter veered into a back alley where an automated garage door rolled up to admit them. The vehicle and its riders darted into the murky opening, disappearing from view. The garage door descended behind them.

Their home base?

"Where'd it go?" she asked urgently. "What is that place?"

"Give me a minute." Dennis's eyes gleamed; for the moment, the thrill of the hunt seemed to have trumped his nerves and anxiety. Under his control, the drone swooped around to check out the front of building, descending to get a better look at the establishment. Letters stenciled on a tinted first-floor window advertised:

DISCREET DETECTIONS, INC.
Confidentiality Guaranteed

"A private detective agency?" Melinda said. "For real?"

"I said they were professional." Dennis paled a little, the implications of that sinking in again. "Shit's getting real."

"You're not kidding." She peered at the screen, already thinking ahead. Their crazy scheme had worked and then some. This wasn't just proof they were being watched; it was an honest-to-goodness lead, crying out for further investigation. "Which begs the question: Who hired these ace detectives . . . and why?"

Chapter Thirty

"This is unconscionable, Siroth. It's not too late to save them."

The top two floors of the tower had been converted into a fully equipped bioscience laboratory, comparable to anything found in a modern Federation facility. A diagnostic biobed, computer terminals and servers, advanced metabolic scanners, quantum microscopes, molecular synthesizers, and other sophisticated hardware had been smuggled piecemeal to Atraz over the years and painstakingly assembled by Siroth and his assistant all on their own, with access to the labs stringently restricted. Doctor Taya Hamparian, late of the Yegorov Institute on Ninevah II, could not fault their efforts; the facilities were just as first-rate as Siroth had promised her years ago, when he'd first proposed relocating to Atraz to pursue her work more freely. Ordinarily, she'd be in her element right now, busily reviewing the results of her most recent tests and simulations, without any interfering UFP bureaucrats looking over her shoulder, but how could she concentrate on her work when Kirk, McCoy, and even that odious Klingon witch had already been taken from the tower and turned over to Varkat's guards to face the tender mercies of Atrazian "justice"? Unable to sit still, she crossed the lab to confront Siroth. The gruesome death of Louis Fortier, torn apart in the arena before her eyes, remained horribly fresh in her memory. She couldn't stop seeing it.

The blood, the screams, the baying crowd, hungry for more carnage.

"What's done is done." Siroth looked up from examining a tissue sample under a quantum microscope. Like her, she had traded the elegant finery they'd worn to the coliseum for more practical lab attire. A classic ditty from late-twentieth-century America played softly in the background; Siroth insisted the antique tunes helped him focus. "I sympathize with your distress, but we had no choice. You offered them a chance to leave us be, but they forced our hand. What happens next is on them, not us."

"But they were just doing their duty," she protested.

"Even the Klingon?"

She hesitated. To be honest, she had mixed feelings about Colonel Yorba being sent to her doom. Being captured by hostile Klingons was not high on Hamparian's bucket list; she preferred fake abductions to real ones. And yet, despite the genuine threat posed by Yorba and her mission, did even she deserve to meet the same ghastly end as Louis?

Did anyone?

"Maybe even the Klingon." She tried and failed to stop thinking about the arena. "If I'd known what it would be like, watching Louis be savaged by those creatures . . ."

"It would have made no difference in the outcome." Siroth turned away from his scope to reassure her. "In the short term, yes, what's befallen Kirk and McCoy is tragic, but we need to take the long view. Centuries, even millennia, from now, when humanoids have literally conquered death thanks to our efforts and sacrifices, the loss of three short, ephemeral lives will be infinitesimal compared to all the eternally long lives we've made possible. Kirk and McCoy would have lived only the tiniest sliver of eternity regardless."

She recognized the conviction in his voice, as well as the steady intensity of his gaze. It was the same unshakable confidence she'd noted when he'd first approached her at the institute years ago, after seeing the vast potential in her work in tissue rejuvenation and regeneration. She'd found that utter confidence inspiring at first, enough to make her seriously consider his more radical proposals, but now it was starting to worry her. How determined was too determined? When did single-minded purpose cross over into obsession—and ruthlessness?

Not for the first time, she questioned just how much she truly knew about her colleague, aside from the fact that he'd had the cunning, wherewithal, and scientific acumen to successfully pull off this Atrazian transplant. After winning her confidence, he had eventually divulged that he was an Augment, genetically engineered before his birth centuries ago, who had used cryogenics to "leapfrog" through time to the present day, but beyond that he was habitually tight-lipped about the particulars of his past and previous identities. The future was what mattered, he always insisted, not whatever lives he lived before.

Yet she couldn't help wondering.

"You remarked earlier that you'd first met Kirk before he was born? What was that all about?"

"The first time I saw his face," he corrected her, "but never mind. I should've kept that observation to myself; it was self-indulgent of me to say it aloud."

"But you did say it, so now I'm asking."

"I'd rather not discuss it. Truth to tell, it's a long, complicated, rather painful memory that I'd just as soon not revisit if you don't mind. It was lifetimes ago and bears no relevance to our present endeavors. Let it rest."

"Whatever. So we're just going to let them get savaged by beasts before a cheering mob? Maybe you can accept that as collateral damage, given your 'expanded' perspective, but what about me? How am I supposed to live with it?"

"By doing what you've always done: making your work your foremost priority and letting nothing stand in your way. That focus, that dedication, is what's brought you this far, and it's what will carry you through to the completion of your life's work, to the ultimate benefit of sentient humanoids throughout the galaxy and beyond. Think of the lengths you've already gone to to find a haven where you can pursue your experiments wherever they may lead, without restriction. Where you can explore new ground and new horizons, your innovative genius uncurbed by red tape and regulations." His tone softened. "You will get over this in time, I promise. Trust me on this."

"I don't know," she said. "I hear what you're saying. It makes sense, intellectually, in the abstract, but we're talking about actual, flesh-and-blood human beings . . ."

"Who are doomed to die in due time anyway. And who face death regularly just by serving in Starfleet. They knew the risks when they entered this sector, leaving Federation space."

"But—" she began.

An electronic chime, coming from a nearby intercom terminal, interrupted them.

"Excuse me." Siroth responded to the chime. "Yes?"

Gyar's voice issued from the wall unit: "Pardon me, sir, but Varkat requests your presence. I gather he's feeling his age and wants a restorative. A page is waiting to escort you to the royal quarters."

"Understood." Siroth turned away from the intercom. "I'm sorry, Taya, but the suzerain cannot be refused. Our operations here depend on his favor and patronage." He gave her a concerned look. "Will you be all right?"

"I'm fine," she lied. "Go attend to Varkat. Honestly, I can probably use some time alone." She returned to a workstation and sat down in front of a computer display running a comparative analysis of Atrazian DNA samples, taken from a range of subjects of varied ethnicities, to establish a baseline for future surveys and experimentation. "Perhaps you're right, and I just need to bury myself in my work for the time being."

Siroth nodded in approval. "I can think of nothing better to ease your mind." He shed his lab jacket and hung it on a peg before heading for the elevator. "I will return shortly."

"Take your time. I'm not going anywhere."

She waited, watching the minutes tick by on the computer's chronometer, until she was sure he was gone and would not wander back to offer one last piece of advice. And then she stalled for a few more minutes, working up her nerve.

Do I really want to do this?

Siroth wasn't wrong. She had uprooted her own life, turned herself into an outlaw, and taken extreme measures to pursue her goals. And both Kirk and Yorba had made clear their intentions to shut her down and, if necessary, forcibly remove her from Atraz. Getting rid of them was the smart, sensible thing to do. Anything else risked destroying everything Siroth had built here and all they hoped to achieve.

But . . . the blood, the screams . . .

She shook her head. Maybe Siroth could live with it as long as somebody else got their hands dirty, maybe she'd thought she could, before the arena, but not anymore.

Blood. Screams. Slaughter.

Moving quickly, before she could change her mind, she went to a

cabinet and retrieved the gear taken from Kirk and the others. She had
brought them upstairs earlier, ostensibly to add McCoy's medkit to her
own supplies, but perhaps another idea had already been forming at
the back of her mind all along. Fortunately, Siroth hadn't objected to
storing the high-tech equipment in the lab, away from Atrazian eyes
and hands. She glanced about nervously, even though Gyar was nowhere around.

Please don't let me regret this.

She claimed a Starfleet communicator that had belonged to either
Kirk or McCoy. Her gaze fell on its Klingon counterpart, its burnished
gold-and-silver shell taunting her like an unwelcome reminder. Her
conscience pricked her.

Maybe later?

First, however, she flipped open the Starfleet device and lifted it to
her lips, taking pains not to alter whatever channel and operating frequency it was already set on.

"Hello? This is Doctor Taya Hamparian. Can you read me?"

She sweated through what felt like an endless pause before a male
voice answered:

"Lieutenant Hikaru Sulu here." His tone was wary. *"This is a surprise.
A good one, I hope."*

His voice was too loud for her peace of mind. She fiddled with the
volume control to lower it before replying.

"You need to trust me, Lieutenant, if we want to save your captain
and Doctor McCoy. Listen closely . . ."

Chapter Thirty-One

"Hate to break it to you, Discreet Detections, but you didn't live up to your name. I absolutely know it's you who have been tailing me lately, sticking to me like glue whenever I'm trying to go about my business, not to mention refusing to answer my emails and phone calls and playing dumb when I showed up at your downtown digs the other day. Fine, play it that way. I'm looking into my legal options, so I'd think twice about invading my privacy again. And while I can't say for certain that you're also responsible for breaking into my home and searching through all my personal stuff, I have to wonder: Who else could be so interested in poking their nose into my affairs—and this investigation?

"All of which raises the burning questions: Who hired you and why? What about looking into Gillian's disappearance has stirred up such a hornet's nest? Who out there has the answers, and what do they know that we don't . . . yet. Rest assured, Cetacean will be exploring these mysteries—and keeping an eye out for you, my not-so-subtle shadows, from now on."

Replaying the podcast, Melinda smirked as she imagined the professional snoops at Discreet sweating big-time now that the latest episode had dropped, airing their "confidential" doings to all her subscribers; that those same snoops surely listened to *Cetacean* every week stood to reason. She'd stretched the truth a bit by threatening legal action; she and Dennis hadn't actually spoken to any lawyers yet and weren't entirely sure how strong a case they might have. For now, she just hoped that the threat alone, along with the unwelcome light shone on their covert activities, would be enough to get Discreet to back off. If nothing else, she had to assume that their unknown employer wasn't going to be happy about this kind of publicity, let alone all their other clients. Who wants to employ a discreet, confidential detective agency that's getting dragged all over a hit podcast—and can't even keep from being caught in the act?

Hope you're squirming, detective dudes. Serves you right for horning in on my case.

She and Dennis had debated the pros and cons of publicly shaming their shadows. They might be sacrificing a strategic advantage by letting Discreet know they were on to them. Likewise for unbugging their personal hardware and replacing any hopelessly compromised devices with virgin gear. It had been worth it, though; not being able to talk freely in their own home was no way to live. They couldn't constantly be mindful of unseen ears and lurking shadows every waking moment—and autumn in the Bay Area was way too chilly to spend all their time on the roof.

That airing Discreet's dirty laundry *also* made great content was a bonus.

"What do you think?" she asked Dennis, who was working his new laptop at the other end of the couch. She put down her phone, which she'd been listening to the new episode on, and stretched. Their handy-dandy drone—a matte blue-gray for camouflage purposes—was recharging on top of a file cabinet. "Wanna bet our shadows are already feeling the heat?"

"Please, God, I hope so," Dennis said. "I don't know about you, but I can't cope with looking over my shoulder twenty-four seven. Keeps me up at night."

He wasn't exaggerating, she knew. Purple shadows under his eyes testified to sleepless nights. He also seemed more jittery than usual, probably because of all the caffeinated energy drinks he was consuming to compensate for the lack of shut-eye. She felt a twinge of guilt for dragging him into this pressure cooker and refusing to let it go, but wanted to think it would all pay off if and when they stuck the landing. She'd just have to make it up to him afterward.

"Think how good it will feel to get to the bottom of this mystery once and for all."

"Here's hoping."

He kept slaving over his laptop, scouring the internet for info. The irony was that deep dives into conspiracy theories were his comfort zone, but also heightened his anxiety, which drove him back to his computer, keeping him up nights. Was that a paradox or a vicious circle or both?

"How's it going? Dig up anything juicy on Discreet, like maybe who exactly paid them to spy on us?"

She'd deliberately used the first-person singular on the show for the sake of Dennis's nerves, but could refer to "us" when it was just the two of them talking.

"Possibly," he hedged. "No luck getting a peek at their client list or financial ledgers. Turns out that private detective agencies take pains to keep their private records private. Their firewalls are nothing to sneeze at."

She frowned. "Can't you just hack into the bank accounts? Follow the money back to their client?"

"Just like that?" He snorted at the suggestion. "I'm not some teenage computer genius from a TV show who can hack into the Pentagon with a few keystrokes. I'm more a research guy, remember? That being said, rooting through public records did turn up something . . . interesting."

"Do tell."

"If you dig deep enough and wade through a maze of shell companies and all-but-impenetrable corporate misdirection—you're welcome, by the way—you can, with considerable effort, discover that Discreet Detections is a fully owned subsidiary of . . . Amaranth, Incorporated."

The name meant nothing to her. "Which is?"

"A cutting-edge biotech firm, based over in San Jose."

"Never heard of it," she admitted. "Enlighten me."

"As Big Pharma goes, it's not one of the big names like Pfizer or Soong, but more of a streamlined boutique operation specializing in radical new techniques for extending health and longevity. Immunotherapy, nanosurgery, gene splicing, cryogenics, and so on. Groundbreaking stuff, apparently, pushing the envelope of medical science."

A lightbulb went off over her head. "Just the kind of operation that would be *very* interested in learning all about a pill that can regrow human kidneys."

"Bingo. Figured that would get your spider-sense tingling."

"And then some." She scooted closer to him, feeling a heady rush of excitement. "Tell me more about this Amaranth outfit."

"Okay, here goes." He took a swig of caffeinated sugar water to power his info dump. "Amaranth was founded in 2007, so it's only been in business for about seventeen years. In other words, long after Wilmer Offutt was chasing after the kidney pill back in the late eighties, right after Gillian disappeared. So maybe Discreet spying on us has nothing do with that old phone number you called?"

"Maybe." Her gut told her otherwise. "Any connection between Offutt and Amaranth?"

"Not that I can find. Records indicate that Offutt died 'after a short illness' back in 2002. If that was his real name, of course."

She recalled Dennis's theory that "Wilmer Offutt" was just an alias, existing mostly on paper.

"Speaking of names," he continued, "I googled 'Amaranth.' Turns out it's a plant, but get this: the ancient Greeks believed it had unique healing properties and regarded it as a symbol of immortality. You can find it on plenty of old tombs and temples. Pretty on the nose, right?"

"Kudos to their branding." She mulled over what she had just learned. "So why does a hot-shot biotech firm need to own a private detective agency? Can't imagine it's a super-lucrative financial investment, so maybe . . . industrial espionage?"

"Preventing or committing?"

"Either/or, possibly. Big money involved either way, I'm guessing."

"But why buy the agency?" Dennis asked. "Why not just hire some private snoops as needed?"

"Maybe to keep any shady stuff in-house, while still keeping Discreet at arm's length so that nobody asks the same questions we're asking now, about why a biotech company even needs private eyes on the payroll?"

Dennis nodded, getting it. "Hence the shell companies and all."

Now we're getting somewhere, she thought, *but where exactly?*

There were still plenty of fuzzy spots, but the picture was coming clearer in places. Amaranth wanted or knew something about the kidney pill, and the pill related to Gillian's participation in the hospital raid right before she disappeared, so *Cetacean* got Amaranth's attention, either because they were out to uncover the secret of the pill—or because they already knew something about the case they didn't want exposed?

"I don't suppose Amaranth has patented a miracle cure for regrowing kidneys?"

Dennis shook his head. "Pretty sure that would be big news if they'd announced something like that. No way I could've missed it."

Which suggested that they were still after the formula for the pill, like so many other doctors and laboratories back in the day, and hadn't already cracked the puzzle. No wonder they hadn't tried to halt her investigation, only keep tabs on it.

"Wanna bet they're hoping we find out for them where that kidney pill came from?"

"I'd settle for a revolutionary new antacid," Dennis said, wincing. "I feel like I'm down to my last layer of stomach lining."

Maybe ease up on the energy drinks, she thought to herself. "So who's in charge of Amaranth?" Personalizing a conflict with a nameless corporation would be challenge for *Cetacean,* narratively. "Do we have a face and name?"

"You bet." Dennis turned on the TV screen remotely, then uploaded an image from his laptop. "Meet Orlando Wilder, founder and CEO of Amaranth, Inc."

The photo, which was transparently a professional head shot, depicted a man in his late twenties at most, his youthful features unlined by age. A sober expression conveyed a serious attitude befitting his work. Avid brown eyes peered out beneath bristling black eyebrows. Slicked-back hair, a bronzed complexion, and a lantern jaw were among his distinguishing characteristics. An entrepreneurial boy wonder, Melinda gathered, presenting a mature and responsible face to stockholders and potential investors. She wondered how much of that was staged and what he was actually like in real life.

"Not a lot of images of him online, actually," Dennis said. "For a CEO, he keeps a low profile. Generally avoids publicity and personal appearances, preferring to let his PR people handle the press, with a marked emphasis on the company, its discoveries, and their potential rather than him personally. He seems to want his work out there, not him." He shrugged. "I can relate."

"A tech tycoon who shuns the spotlight?" she marveled. "Will wonders never cease."

"Eh. Not everyone wants to be a household name, you know." He gave her a pointed look. "Although I realize that may be a difficult concept for you to grasp."

"*Touché.*" She contemplated the oh-so-serious visage on the screen. From the sound of it, she and Orlando Wilder were overdue for a serious discussion. "But if he won't come to the spotlight, we'll have to bring the spotlight to him.

"Where exactly in San Jose is he based?"

Chapter Thirty-Two

"The *BortaS* has followed us into standard orbit around the planet," Chekov reported from the science station. "They are directly ahead or behind us, depending on how you look at it."

"As anticipated, Ensign," Spock said evenly, committed to his chosen course of action. Second-guessing himself at this juncture would be illogical. "The question now is whether they will content themselves to match our position or initiate an armed response."

The *Enterprise* remained at red alert. Annunciator lights shone crimson about the bridge, but the warning klaxons had been muted once the entire ship had been alerted to its current status. An orbital view of Atraz rotated slowly on the viewscreen, augmented by inset windows monitoring the *BortaS* and a tactical display, respectively. Deflector shields were on high in anticipation of a possible attack. Phaser banks were fully charged. *Enterprise* was braced for battle should it come to that.

"I wouldn't bet against them opening fire," Scott said. "They're Klingons after all." He glanced at the turbolift doors. "I should get myself to engineering, to be on hand in case matters go sideways."

"A prudent suggestion, Mister Scott, but your experience and counsel may be required on the bridge as well. Let us see how Captain Khod reacts to our incursion before taking combat for granted."

"Aye, sir." Scott exited the command well to reoccupy the bridge's engineering station, where he could better watch over the engines as well as the ship's other vital systems. "At least we're ready for whatever those Klingon rascals throw at us."

Spock wanted to think so.

"Tactical analysis, Mister Chekov?" he asked. "Has the *BortaS* come within firing range of the *Enterprise*?"

"Not quite, sir, but close enough as to make little difference. One burst of acceleration and they can close the gap within moments. As could we."

"That is my assessment as well." Spock was gratified but unsurprised that the science station's specialized sensors and instrumentation confirmed his own estimation. Despite the pressing issues facing them, including the distinct possibility of armed conflict with the enemy battle cruiser, he took note of Chekov's able performance in his stead; the young human was making positive progress in his training as a Starfleet officer. "Continue monitoring the *BortaS*'s position and weapons systems."

"Aye, sir. I'll call out if one of their torpedo tubes so much as burps!"

"Your zeal is commendable, Ensign. Your colorful commentary less so."

Chekov looked appropriately abashed. "Aye, sir. Monitoring, sir."

"Lieutenant Uhura," Spock said, "any further communications from the *BortaS*?"

"Negative, sir. No hails, threats, ultimatums, or calls for surrender." She looked over at Spock. "It seems as though Captain Khod has nothing further to say to us."

"But he has yet to resort to weapons instead of words," Spock observed. "An encouraging, if inconclusive, indicator."

"I dinnae understand it." Scott's brow furrowed. "Why hasn't he laid into us already, after we provoked him by taking *Enterprise* into orbit? Not that I fault you for doing so, mind you, not with the captain and the others in jeopardy, but you'd think the Klingons would have taken the gloves off by now."

"I surmise that Khod is still averse to starting a war over one errant scientist, no matter how valuable she might be. *BortaS* is here for Doctor Hamparian, not to vaporize the Organian Peace Treaty. As I anticipated, based on his earlier pattern of restraint."

"A lucky roll of the dice, Mister Spock."

"Vulcans do not gamble, but we do take probability into account. Consider it a calculated risk."

"If you say so, sir, but to what end?" Frustration tinged Scott's voice. "What's the use of being within transporter range of the planet if we can't lower our shields long enough to beam any of our people to safety? The instant we drop our shields, we'll be inviting a photon torpedo spread or whatever else the Klingons choose to fire at us."

"True, Mister Scott, but the Klingons are similarly inhibited. They cannot beam out their soldiers, let alone Doctor Hamparian, the captain, or any other captives while their own shields are in place. What's good for the goose is good for the gander, as your human expression goes."

As Captain Khod is well aware, Spock thought. He saw nothing to be gained in hailing the *BortaS* again. He could not risk trusting the Klingons while Khod was not about to lower his own shields on the world of a Vulcan. Further discussion would not alter those parameters.

"Aye, it's a standoff all right," Scott said. "What next, Mister Spock? How does this stalemate help us get Captain Kirk and Doctor McCoy back?"

"We have improved our position on the board, providing us with more options should the situation on the planet change." Spock elaborated on his reasoning for the sake of the bridge crew's morale. "Only an incremental improvement, perhaps, but not without value. A working truce with the *BortaS* would have been preferable, if unlikely, but a stalemate is still better than actual combat, which would not just jeopardize the ship but also our ability to assist the landing party if and when the opportunity arises."

"Aye," Scott conceded. "Now we just need to hope that our people can get themselves out of hot water before the Klingons' patience wears out." He gazed soberly at the planet on the viewer. "I'd rest easier if I knew what the captain and Doctor McCoy were up to right now."

"As would I, Mister Scott." Spock swiveled the command chair toward Uhura. With the *Enterprise* now in orbit around Atraz, it was no longer necessary to relay messages via *Galileo*'s long-distance communications array. "Have you managed to make contact with the captain or the doctor via their communicators?"

"I'm afraid not, sir, but I am receiving a reply from Mister Sulu." Her eyes widened. "It seems he's been in touch with Doctor Hamparian."

"Indeed?" Spock lifted an eyebrow. "Patch him through, Lieutenant."

The situation on Atraz appeared to be reconfiguring faster than he'd anticipated. More data was required, however, before he could confidently predict how this would affect the present stalemate in space. Was Khod also now conferring with his agents on the ground, and what of the Klingon colonel reported to have been captured along with Kirk and McCoy? Vulcans did not indulge in wishful thinking, but Spock would have preferred fewer variables in this increasingly complex problem. Much was at stake—including the captain's and the doctor's life and liberty.

Do what you always do, Jim. Find a way to turn the odds in your favor.

Chapter Thirty-Three

2024

"Mister Wilder! Orlando Wilder!"

San Jose's Innovation District, smack-dab in Silicon Valley, was only slightly more than an hour away from San Francisco by BART. Melinda had been staked out here all afternoon, waiting for the camera-shy CEO to emerge from Amaranth's headquarters in a modern glass-and-steel complex. It was past seven, and most of the district's office workers had already cleared out, so all she'd learned so far was that Wilder worked late. She'd started to wonder just how long she was willing to camp out on the sidewalk, and whether she had possibly missed him somehow, when a limo pulled up to the curb. Moments later, the man himself emerged, wearing a Burberry coat and toting a briefcase. He was shorter than she expected. About her size, actually.

Adrenaline surging, she darted forward to intercept him. "Excuse me, Mister Wilder! We need to talk!"

He turned toward her, scowling. His eyes widened beneath those bushy brows. Recognition flashed briefly across his face, quick but unmistakable.

He knows who I am, she thought. *Good.*

Dennis was back at their apartment, monitoring the scene via drone while maintaining a lookout for any Discreet shadows. On the bright side, he had yet to spot any sign of her being tailed, leading her to think that possibly Discreet had backed off after being called out on *Cetacean.* Certainly, nobody seemed to have alerted Wilder that she was lying in wait outside his headquarters.

All the better to ambush him.

"No comment," he said brusquely. His deep, basso-profundo voice was likely to record well, even over the phone she held out to capture it. Stakeout conditions precluded a more elaborate setup.

"C'mon, don't be like that." She inserted herself between him and the waiting limo, grateful and relieved that he was not such a public figure that he required bodyguards to escort him to the car. He glared at her, their eyes level with each other. It was a pleasant change to face off against somebody who didn't have a height advantage on her. "I've been waiting out here for hours."

"Your mistake. I don't do interviews."

"So your publicity department keeps telling me." She didn't bother introducing herself, since that would obviously be superfluous. "I've already gone through channels and gotten nowhere."

"Which should have told you something." He tried to scoot past her, but she was quicker on her feet, blocking his path to the limo. His expression darkened further. "No comment."

"Not even about Milly Coates? And her magic kidney pill?"

He faltered, thrown off-balance for a moment, but quickly recovered. "I have no idea what you're talking about."

She snickered. "We both know that's not true, so maybe we should skip the playacting and cut to the part where we compare notes on what we each do and don't know about Miracle Milly . . . and whatever happened to Gillian Taylor? Seems to me that might be more productive, for both of us, than having my apartment broken into and bugging my devices."

His fierce gaze bored into hers like he was lasering into her skull. "Listen to me, Ms. Silver—"

He caught himself too late.

"Gotcha!" she crowed, sticking the phone in his face. "You *do* know exactly who I am and what—"

"That will be enough, miss." Strong hands, wearing leather gloves, seized her shoulders from behind and physically moved her out of Wilder's way. "Whenever you're ready, sir."

Rats, she thought. *The limo driver.*

Who could apparently moonlight as a bouncer if so inclined. She squirmed in his grip, unable to pull free.

"Goodbye, Melinda." Wilder slipped past her into the back seat of the limo, closing the door behind him. He lowered the tinted window long enough to offer a parting piece of advice. "Please don't attempt this again."

Apparently he didn't really know her at all.

"So what's Wilder like, anyway?"

Dennis had outdone himself with some delicious lemon-glazed salmon, which Melinda dug into since she'd been surviving on food-truck fare and granola bars during her stakeout. They were having dinner at the kitchen table, reasonably confident that they were not being spied on. Or at least working on the assumption for their own peace of mind.

"You heard the recording," she said between mouthfuls. "Such as it is."

"Yeah, but it's hard to get much of an impression from a sky-high view."

"I suppose." She tried to paint a picture of the uncooperative tycoon. "Short, brusque, our age. Clearly used to getting his way and not shy about staring you down if you get in his way. Real laser eyes, if you know what I mean. The deep voice probably helps intimidate people too. Gives him a certain gravitas that makes up for how short and young he is."

Dennis listened, nodding. "Sounds kinda . . . intense."

"That's one way to put it," she agreed, then froze in mid-bite. "Hang on. Listen to ourselves. This description sound familiar to you? Short, intense, deep voice, not inclined to take no for an answer? Deep interest in miracle cures like Milly's kidney pill?"

He got where she was going. "Wilmer Offutt?"

Dropping her fork, she pulled out her phone and studied Wilder's official portrait again.

Bushy eyebrows, check. Intense gaze, check. All about biotech, check. The photo failed to convey his short stature and abysmally deep voice, which is why she hadn't made the connection immediately, but now that it hit her, she felt like slapping her forehead. She turned the photo toward Dennis. "Tell me this doesn't match the description of that guy who was so dead set on finding out about the kidney pill back in '87.

The guy whose number I left a message on not long before we were burgled?"

Dennis squinted at the image. "I guess. Although wasn't Offutt supposed to be bald?"

"True," she admitted. "Still, now that I think about it, even the initials are the same, just reversed. Wilmer Offutt. Orlando Wilder."

Oh God, she thought. *I sound just like one of the crazy YouTube nuts I usually roll my eyes at, seeing hidden patterns and connections everywhere, building conspiracies on random connections. Who's losing perspective now?*

"Offutt died in 2002 supposedly," Dennis reminded her, "but even if he faked it, he'd be, what, in his sixties now?" He stroked his scruffy whiskers. "You think he's Offutt's grandson or great-nephew or something, carrying on a family tradition? Right down to monitoring that old answering machine?"

"Only one way to find out."

The salmon forgotten, she called up her phone contacts. The eight-hour time difference between California and Scotland made it way too late to reach out to Jane Temple, at least until morning, but thankfully, Todd Coates was in the same time zone. Calling immediately, she caught him just as he was putting his kids to bed. A few minutes later, they were FaceTiming.

"Sorry to bother you, but would you mind looking at a photo for me? I want to know if a certain individual looks at all familiar to you?"

Todd looked intrigued, not annoyed. "What individual?"

"Let me keep mum on that for now. I don't want to prejudice the results by putting ideas in your head."

"Understood. Hit me."

Dennis had put Wilder's portrait on their big screen while Todd was coming to the phone. She aimed her phone at it and flipped its camera lens so that Todd could see the photo.

His reaction was instantaneous. "Holy shit! That's him. The guy who bought Grandma Milly's body!"

She and Dennis exchanged looks. "You mean, you see a resemblance, right?"

"No, that's the guy. Sure, he was bald as an egg the last time I saw him, umpteen years ago, but I guess he got a wig or stopped shaving his scalp for some reason. I'd know that face, that expression, those intense eyes and bushy eyebrows anywhere. That's him, the guy whose business card I gave you. Wilmer Offutt."

"And you're absolutely certain about this?" she asked.

"I just said so, didn't I? What's up? What did you find out about him?"

"That's . . . a developing situation. To be honest, I don't think I was really expecting quite this definitive a response. We were playing a hunch," she said, not wanting to go too far out on a limb until they figured out exactly what this meant. "And now we've got a lot more digging to do, but thanks so much! This is *huge*. You have no idea."

"Really?" he protested. "You're just going to leave me hanging here?"

Understandably full of questions, Todd required some effort to get off the phone, but she finally succeeded in ending the call after promising him the full scoop farther down the road, even before it hit *Cetacean*. "You'll be the first to know."

She put down the phone, still processing this latest bombshell. She and Dennis stared at each other for a few moments before diving into it.

"So, we have to be talking about a family resemblance, right?" she said. "Heredity at work."

"Maybe, but . . . Amaranth symbolizes immortality, remember? And the company is all about finding radical new ways to stimulate health and longevity."

She balked at where this was going. "What are you suggesting? That Wilmer Offutt and Orlando Wilder are one and the same?" She pointed at the portrait on the screen. "You tell me. Does that guy look like he was pestering Mildred Coates and her family back in the eighties? He looks like he's only a few years out of college."

"Hey, you're the one who twigged onto the resemblance in the first place. And Todd seemed pretty sure."

"I know, I know, but we can't completely ignore common sense. This has to be one of those freak things you see on social media sometimes, like when some old Civil War soldier is a dead ringer for Nicholas Cage or whoever. I've seen family photos of older relatives that look a lot like folks from our generation. My uncle Rich, for instance, looks uncannily like my cousin Zack in his old wedding photos. Doesn't that seem less insane than jumping to the conclusion that Orlando Wilder is a vampire or something?"

"Not a vampire," Dennis said, missing the point, "but maybe . . . not of this Earth? Remember what Valdez saw in the park? The door from nowhere? Maybe Wilder is from another time or plane of existence?"

"So we're just tossing Occam's razor out completely now?" she asked, as much to herself as to Dennis. "*Anything* is possible?"

"Maybe. You gotta admit: that razor hasn't been cutting it for a while now."

Could he be right this time? Was she refusing to follow the leads wherever they led, even if they were pointing somewhere impossible to believe? She picked up her phone again, sorely tempted to call Jane Temple right away, never mind the time difference, and see if she recognized Wilder's portrait too. Despite everything, though, she still couldn't bring herself to wake up the retired nurse in the middle of the night.

First thing in the morning, she promised herself, and in the meantime . . .

She turned to Dennis, feeling just as obsessed with solving this puzzle as Wilmer Offutt, whoever he was, had been about finding that kidney pill.

"Listen up. I need you to find out everything there is to know about Orlando Wilder. And I mean *everything*!"

Chapter Thirty-Four

2268

"Get out there, fresh meat! Crowd's waiting."

At the guards' ungentle urging, Kirk, McCoy, and Yorba entered the arena. Hundreds of Atrazians once more filled the coliseum for a special nighttime exhibition. The sun having gone down in the east, polished mirrors reflected the light from several large, elevated torches onto the sandy floor of the arena. The blazing torches perched atop tall poles, overlooking the killing ground, while smaller, more subdued glow lamps were lodged about the seating area to help spectators make their way in the dark. A metal gate slammed shut behind Kirk and his cohorts, leaving the three of them trapped in the spotlight. No one else, he noted, appeared to be on the menu tonight.

"Showtime," McCoy said wryly. "I think I preferred being in the audience."

"You and me both," Kirk agreed. "Not looking forward to being the star attraction this time around."

"Who says you're the star?"

Less than an hour had passed since they'd been taken from Siroth's tower by armed guards. Varkat had wasted no time condemning them to the arena; he must have wanted to make an example of them after the disturbance at his previous spectacle, or had Siroth personally urged the suzerain to have them eliminated with all deliberate speed? At least they hadn't been gagged as Fortier had been. Kirk assumed Siroth was counting on the Prime Directive to keep them from revealing their non-Atrazian origins.

"Ready yourselves," Yorba said. "If we must die for the amusement of these backwards primitives, let us make a good accounting of ourselves." She sneered at the masses gazing down at them from the stands. "Let them enjoy themselves while they can. My agents will surely avenge me if I perish here today."

Another good reason to stay alive, Kirk thought. He didn't want Klingon death squads terrorizing Atrazian civilians or, worse yet, using Yorba's execution as an excuse to overthrow the local government and establish some sort of puppet ruler. Granted, the Klingons were here for Hamparian, not the planet's resources, but it was never a good idea to give the Empire a pretext for an invasion, treaty or no treaty. *Klingons don't belong here—and neither do we.*

Squinting against the glare of the flickering spotlights, he glanced about to get his bearings. The royal box was already fully occupied, with both Siroth and Hamparian in attendance, along with Varkat himself, but what about the rest of the coliseum? Were Sulu and the others among the spectators? He scanned the audience, but couldn't immediately spot any members of the landing party among the sea of faces filling the amphitheater. Yorba's eyes searched the audience as well.

"Any sign of your men?" he asked.

She shook her head. "Not yet, but that means nothing. Klingons are seen only when we want to be seen, and by then it is too late for our enemies."

"There's a comforting thought," McCoy muttered. "Klingons in camouflage."

A fanfare of trumpets and drums kicked off the proceedings as a mixed assortment of simple, low-tech weapons were thrown into the arena. Kirk and the others scrambled to arm themselves. No surprise, Yorba immediately lunged for the most lethal weapon: a studded metal mace. Kirk let her have her pick as a gesture of good faith. He claimed a coiled leather whip, while McCoy selected a sturdy wooden staff worthy of Robin Hood or Friar Tuck. A mesh net lay in reserve upon the sandy floor. Kirk was tempted to grab it as well, but worried about encumbering himself. Perhaps they could use the net later, if they lasted that long.

He locked eyes with Yorba. "We fight together, as agreed?"

While imprisoned in a cell awaiting their turn in the arena, the prisoners had concluded that they stood a better chance of surviving the spectacle if they worked as a unit rather than every man or Klingon for themselves. Kirk remembered the audience cheering for the prisoner who had brought down a bloodbeak the day before. If they were lucky, maybe they could survive long enough to win over the crowd, or at least until Sulu or the other Klingons could stage a rescue attempt. Kirk hadn't given up on finding his own way out of this predicament either. They just needed to stay alive until the right opportunity arose.

"You may rely on me." Yorba grimaced as though the promise left a bad taste in her mouth. "If I can rely on you."

"Not as though we have much choice." McCoy nodded at the other end of the arena. "Look sharp."

The roar of the crowd all but drowned out the creaking of another metal gate, which rose to unleash a flock of ferocious bloodbeaks on them. Squawking and flapping wildly, the man-eating ratites charged flightlessly at the unwilling gladiators, who formed a defensive triangle, back to back to back. Yorba let loose with a blood-curdling war cry as she swung the mace at any razor-sharp beak or claw that came too close. Beside her, Kirk cracked his whip repeatedly, like an animal trainer from Earth's less humane past, while McCoy jabbed and parried with the staff, more than holding up his end of the fight. Kirk was not surprised by McCoy's showing; although a healer by temperament and training, this was hardly the first time Bones had been forced to fight for his life against hostile life-forms. United in a common cause, the trio held the bloodbeaks at bay, but for how much longer? Was putting up a strong defense going to be enough in the long run, or did they need to go on the offensive if they wanted to survive? Kirk wished he had a better sense of the rules governing these blood sports. Did they win their lives if they defeated the beasts? Nobody had bothered to explain the rules to them, probably because no one wanted or expected them to come out of the contest alive.

And his whip arm was already getting tired.

Then, without warning, an incandescent scarlet beam lit up the night, eliciting gasps all across the coliseum as it blazed straight up into the sky from the royal box. Driving off a hungry bloodbeak with a lash across its beak, Kirk risked a glance at the stands, where he saw Doctor Hamparian standing at a rail, firing a phaser up into the air above her head.

Like a beacon—or a signal?

"Jim!" McCoy blurted. "Do you see that? What's she up to?"

Trying to get our attention? Kirk thought.

Their eyes met across the distance, and the scientist clicked off the phaser. Before anyone could stop her, she drew her arm back and hurled the compact type-1 phaser toward Kirk and the others. Hope flared inside him as the device arced through the air, then sputtered as it began descending too quickly. Her throw fell short and the phaser bounced off a bloodbeak's wing and hit the ground several meters away from the three humanoids. The offended avian scratched at the fallen weapon with its talons before determining that it was neither alive nor edible, then returned its predatory attentions back toward Kirk and his outnumbered partners in peril.

"Fek'lhr!" Yorba swore. She broke from formation to bolt for the phaser.

"Yorba!" Kirk honestly wasn't sure if he wanted her to get hold of the phaser or not. How long would their forced alliance last once she was in possession of a fully charged phaser?

Before he could even try to outrace her, he spotted another gleaming object flying from Hamparian's hand. Practice improved her aim, so it came soaring toward him. Cracking his whip and keeping one eye on the nearest bloodbeaks, he reached out and caught the device one-handed. He identified it instantly from touch alone.

A Starfleet communicator!

Yorba saw an opportunity and took it. Leaving Kirk and McCoy to fend for themselves, she raced for the phaser. She howled like a demon to put the fear of Kahless into the hearts of her foes and swung her mace at the feathered carnivore foolish enough to get between her and the Starfleet sidearm. A *bat'leth* would have made short work of the bird, but a true Klingon warrior could make use of most any weapon, including their own hands and teeth if necessary. The mace would do for now.

At least until she got her hands on that phaser.

The bloodbeak lunged and snapped at her. Putting her back and shoulders into the blow, she met the beast's attack by smashing the mace into the beak with strength enough to crack it. Shrieking, the injured bird slashed at her with a vicious talon, but she ducked and rolled beneath the strike, bringing her past the bloodbeak and closer to the phaser, which lay half-buried in the sand less than a meter way. A wolfish grin lifted her lips as she anticipated turning the tables on the presumptuous Atrazians, not to mention Kirk and McCoy. She had neither forgotten nor forgiven how the Earthers had cravenly drugged her before; she would not be in jeopardy now if not for their underhanded methods. Scrambling across the sand, she reached for the weapon that would put her in control of the situation once more.

Pity it's not a proper Klingon disruptor pistol instead, but . . .

A crossbow bolt struck the ground before her, barely missing her outstretched fingers.

Who dares?

Yanking back her hand, she glared up at the royal box, where a scowling Atrazian guard stood ready to fire again if she went for the phaser. He may not have known exactly what a phaser was, but he clearly wasn't about to allow her use of any unauthorized implements, let alone one that had just fired a radiant beam of light into the sky.

"*QI'yaH!*" she snarled under her breath. She froze, torn between abandoning the phaser and making a desperate dive for the weapon in hopes of securing it before she could be skewered. Would the guard risk another warning shot before shooting to kill, to avoid spoiling the night's entertainment? It might be worth finding out.

"Heads-up, you Klingon lunatic!"

Wood smacked loudly against flesh and bone and feathers, provoking an angry squawk. She spun around to see McCoy defending her from the plumed monster she'd evaded moments ago. Blood dripped from an ugly gash on his forearm, where a claw or beak had obviously grazed him. He jabbed the blunt end of his staff at the bloodbeak's chest.

"You're welcome," he cracked.

She shot a covetous glance at the phaser, which remained tantalizingly within reach.

"Not a chance," McCoy said, reading her mind. He blocked a slashing claw with the staff, then thrust it at the creature's skull to buy them more time. "They'll never let you touch it." He stumbled backward, recoiling from a jagged beak, which remained deadly despite the hairline crack she'd put in it. "But I *could* use an assist here if you're not too busy."

She silently cursed his ancestors back through three generations. Mace in hand, she rushed to join him in battle against the loathsome animal. She refused to give him the satisfaction of facing the bloodbeak alone.

"Are all human physicians so insufferable, or are you singularly aggravating?"

"It's one of my specialties."

"Good God, Taya!" Siroth stared at Hamparian in shock and outrage. "Have you completely lost your mind?"

"You gave me no other choice!"

She plucked another phaser from her purse, hoping to be able to throw it to Kirk or McCoy, but he grabbed her wrist, twisting it roughly, and wrested the phaser from her grasp. Royal guards closed in on her, seizing her by the shoulders, as he also confiscated her purse, which contained two more communicators. She had left Yorba's disruptor pistol back at the tower, being in no hurry to arm the Klingon as well. In hindsight, perhaps she should have taken that weapon to defend herself, although she had never actually fired a weapon at anyone in her life. She was a scientist, not a soldier after all. How in the cosmos had she gotten herself into this fix?

"I'm sorry, Taya." Siroth shook his head mournfully. "You should have listened to me."

"Listening to you was my first mistake." She peered down at the arena, where three more lives were at risk because of her folly. She could only hope it wasn't too late for them to save themselves.

I've done my part, she thought. *It's out of my hands now.*

The communicator chirped in Kirk's grip. Flipping it open while also cracking the whip at any bloodbeak that got too near, he held it to his lips.

"Kirk here."

"Standby, Captain," Sulu's voice answered. *"The cavalry has arrived."*

Rapid phaser bursts, almost subliminal in duration, flashed briefly in the night, like lightning leaping upward from the stands to strike the mirrors focusing the torchlight onto the arena. The mirrors shimmered brightly before dissolving into atoms, throwing the floor of the arena into murky shadows. Kirk winced at the infringement of the Prime Directive, but couldn't blame Sulu for bending the rules under the circumstances. A few bright flashes in the night were a relatively re-strained use of phasers, considering; with any luck, they'd be remembered as only a puzzling freak event in the city's history.

Assuming we all make it off Atraz alive, Kirk thought. *Hamparian included.*

The dazzling beams, and ensuing darkness, yielded immediate confusion and tumult throughout the coliseum. Startled Atrazians, unsure what was happening, jumped to their feet, shouting and calling out to each other as they began rushing for the exits, pushing and shoving in their haste to flee the amphitheater. Even the bloodbeaks were taken aback by the sudden loss of light. They milled about uncertainly, squawking in confusion, distracted from the hunt if only for the moment. Assuming the chaos was all part of Sulu's plan, Kirk got ready for whatever the next phase of the operation was.

"Bones! Yorba! Get over here, pronto!"

So far, so good, Sulu thought. *More or less.*

Overseeing the rescue attempt from the stands, he was disappointed that Hamparian's first toss had fallen short, failing to return Kirk's phaser to him, but relieved that everything else was going as planned. He and Landon and Levine had commandeered front-row seats on the southwest side of the coliseum, just below the wall surrounding the arena, putting them in fine position to disintegrate the spotlight mirrors with short, contained phaser blasts. Loose, voluminous clothing concealed a rope wrapped around Sulu's torso. A picnic basket, resting at Landon's feet, held more supplies, smuggled past the guards at the gate.

Now it was time for their unlikely allies to play their part.

Klingon agents, positioned throughout the seating areas, moved quickly to take out the distracted security guards posted in the stands, employing brute force and handheld agonizers to incapacitate the startled guards before they even realized they were under attack. Befitting their name, the agonizers delivered an excruciating shock to

a victim's nervous system, rendering them helpless and even unconscious if necessary, without inflicting any lasting physical damage.
Convincing the Klingons to avoid lethal force had been almost as
challenging as persuading them to collaborate in the rescue attempt,
once Hamparian put both landing parties in touch with each other,
but the agonizers had been a compromise, albeit an ugly one. Sulu
feared that the Klingons would almost surely end up spilling some
Atrazian blood anyway, but that was bound to happen regardless.
Better to work with the Klingons to minimize any casualties, he'd
judged, than give them free rein. It also served to keep both sides
from getting in each other's way while trying to liberate their respective commanders.

That's the idea at least, Sulu thought. *Hope I didn't make the wrong
call.*

The communicator chirped again. *"Ready to get out of here, Captain?"*

"And then some, Mister Sulu."

*"We're in the stands, roughly 270 degrees from your location. Head
for the light."*

As promised, a Starfleet-issue light lit up like a beacon on the southwest side of the coliseum, several meters away. Kirk applauded Sulu's
resourcefulness. Just like a helmsman to show them the way.

"That way!" he shouted at McCoy and Yorba as they fought their
way through the bloodbeaks to rejoin him. The sudden darkness had
briefly thrown the frenzied ratites, but only for a few moments; all too
quickly they'd remembered their appetites and prey. Both McCoy and
Yorba were already looking ragged and beaten-up. Torn clothes and
nasty lacerations testified to the ferocity of the bloodbeaks, as well as to
the pair's failure to get hold of the thrown phaser. Kirk pointed hopefully toward the incandescent glow of the light. "That's Sulu's signal.
He's our way out."

"About time," McCoy said.

Yorba shrugged. "Any port in an ion storm."

Now that he knew where to look, Kirk could dimly make out Sulu,
Landon, and Levine calling to them from the stands. Levine tossed
one end of a sturdy rope or cable over the railing, offering Kirk and

the others a lifeline—if they could reach it before being torn apart by hungry bloodbeaks.

"Stop them!" Varkat bellowed, red-faced with rage. The suzerain lurched to his feet and shook his fist at the shadowy figures in the darkened arena. "They're trying to get away, making a mockery of my justice!"

Bingo, Hamparian thought.

Emotions were running high in the royal box. Agitated courtiers offered conflicting advice to the suzerain, while assorted hangers-on held back, trying to keep a low profile lest they get blamed for tonight's spectacle spiraling out of control. The royal guards were overtaxed, torn between protecting Varkat, halting the ongoing escape attempt, and not incidentally, keeping a close eye and tight grip on Hamparian, who found herself the target of abundant fear, suspicion, and anger. Her headdress had been yanked from her head, exposing the antennae that, along with her bluish skin, marked her as an outsider or worse. Parents clutched their offspring to themselves while casting baleful glares and whispers in her direction. Nobles, attendants, and other members of Varkat's court made superstitious gestures to ward off evil. Did Atrazians burn witches at the stake? Hamparian feared she was going to find out.

"I wish you hadn't done that, Taya," Siroth said in a low voice. "I had such high hopes for our collaboration."

"So did I," she replied. "I just didn't take into account the cost."

He tucked her purse, containing the contraband tech, under the folds of his robe as he purposely distanced himself from her. Ever the survivor, it seemed.

"Do you hear me?" Varkat gesticulated wildly at the arena. "Don't let them escape!"

"Yes, sire!" The same guardsman whose crossbow bolt had discouraged Yorba from claiming the tossed phaser raised his weapon anew. He squinted at the arena, attempting to target the uncooperative gladiators despite the gloom and commotion below. "Just let me get a clean shot—"

A bolt from across the stadium struck him in the shoulder, causing him to cry out and drop his weapon. Guards and guests alike ducked and dove for cover. Loyal subjects threw themselves in front of Varkat in order to shield the monarch. More bolts arced over the arena, some falling short, but others thudding into the royal box, forcing the guards to defend themselves and Varkat's entourage instead of firing upon Kirk and company.

Thanks to the Klingons, Hamparian knew. As planned, they'd taken the crossbows from the guards they'd subdued in the stands, arming themselves in Atrazian fashion in order to provide cover for Yorba and the two Starfleet officers, in that order no doubt. Hamparian still had reservations about using Yorba's communicator to bring her fellow Klingons into the loop regarding the rescue plan, but it seemed to be paying off so far. Varkat's own guards were on the defensive for the moment. *Long enough for Kirk and the others to make their escape?*

"Sire!" An anxious minister tugged on Varkat's arm. "It's not safe here. We must away to the fortress!"

Varkat shook him off. Furious eyes fixed on Hamparian.

"You! This is your doing!" He swept his arm toward the arena. "Throw that horned she-devil to the birds! She wants to aid those foreign troublemakers? Let her share their doom!"

"What?" Siroth, to his credit, tried to intervene. "Sire, I urge you—"

"Silence, alchemist! Lest you join her in the beasts' bellies."

Rough hands seized Hamparian and flung her bodily out of the royal box.

Watching each other's backs, Kirk and the others reached the wall, despite the bloodbeaks coming at them every centimeter of the way. Yorba's mace was spattered with avian blood and brains, while McCoy's staff was chipped and scored from fending off too many claws and beaks. A pouncing ratite almost got Yorba, going for her throat while she was occupied by another bird, but a well-placed crossbow bolt through its skull saved her just in time. More shots from the stands helped to thin the relentless flock assailing them.

Works for me, Kirk thought, not about to question any backup from above. *Good marksmanship too.*

Tipping his head back, he spotted the rest of the landing party just above them, leaning over a rail. Yeoman Landon had signal-light duty, while Sulu and Levine were holding on to the other end of the rope, ready to pull them up if needed. Kirk smiled, proud of his crew. Oddly, though, none of them seemed to be brandishing a crossbow.

"Any time you're ready, sir!" Sulu called.

Kirk nodded. "You first, Bones. That's an order."

"You're the captain." For once, McCoy didn't argue the point. Panting, he handed over the battered staff and took hold of the rope. "Just make it snappy, okay? I think we've overstayed our welcome here."

That's putting mildly, Kirk thought. Tucking the communicator beneath his belt, he used both his whip and the staff to hold the remaining bloodbeaks back as McCoy half climbed and was half pulled up the wall and over the railing into the front row of a seating area. Sulu threw the other end of the rope back down to them. Kirk swung it toward Yorba.

"After you."

She snorted derisively. "Your ridiculous human chivalry will be the death of you."

"Not if I can help it."

Holding on to the mace's handle with her teeth, she scrambled up the wall with ease, suggesting that Klingons also had simian ancestors in their evolutionary family tree. Kirk strenuously guarded her ascent with whip and staff until she reached the top. Following her was going to be a challenge, since it would mean turning his back on the birds.

"Cover me!" he shouted to his allies above. "I'm coming up!"

"Aye, sir!" Sulu threw the rope back down to Kirk, who counted on them having a crossbow at hand, if not a phaser in a pinch. "We have your back."

A scream came from across the arena. Kirk turned in time to see Hamparian crashing onto the sandy floor of the arena, just below the royal box. Dazed, defenseless, she searched frantically for the lost phaser, but couldn't find it anywhere near her.

"Kirk! McCoy! Somebody! Help me!"

He didn't hesitate. Abandoning the rope, he started toward her.

"Leave her, Kirk!" Yorba yelled from the stands. "Let her pernicious science be lost to both our peoples! Neither will gain an advantage!"

Kirk ignored her. He had a mission to complete and a life to save.

But Hamparian's desperate cries had already attracted the attention of the bloodbeaks. Turning away from Kirk in search of easier prey, they charged toward her instead. Kirk experienced a surge of alarm. Could he make it to her in time and then back again across the arena, against all the birds? He didn't like their odds, but he had to try. Chances were, her sudden arrival in the arena had something to do with her throwing him the communicator.

The communicator . . . of course!

Memories of Capella IV came back to him, giving him an idea. He threw the staff like a javelin at the closest bloodbeak and reached for the communicator. Flipping it open, he hastily fiddled with the controls to produce the desired subsonic vibration. The trick was more effective with two communicators working in tandem, but he wasn't trying to start an avalanche, just repel some man-eating ratites.

Here goes nothing.

A persistent bloodbeak, still intent on making a meal of Kirk, charged at the captain, who turned the communicator to face the oncoming bird and switched it on. A low thrum emanated from the speaker, much to the distress of the animal, which responded by flapping its wings and ruffling its feathers before rushing away from Kirk.

Success!

Wielding the vibrating communicator like a talisman, Kirk drove off the bloodbeaks as he raced to Hamparian's side and helped her to her feet. Her antennae trembled, along with the rest of her.

"Can you run?" he asked.

"I'll have to."

Crossbow bolts arced over their heads as they dashed across the arena.

"Seal the gates!" Varkat raged as his guards practically dragged him out of the royal box. "All of them! Let no one escape!"

Mixed emotions churned inside Siroth as he watched Kirk and Hamparian make a break for it, with Kirk somehow using a Starfleet communicator to repel the bloodbeaks. Part of him wanted Taya to survive, yet he also dreaded the consequences of Kirk and his Starfleet compatriots escaping back to the *Enterprise*. And what about the Klingons? They were also bound to keep interfering with his activities on Atraz.

Why can't they just leave me alone? Don't they realize how important my work is?

He hated the idea of leaving Atraz after all the time and trouble and expense he'd gone to set up shop here, up to and including importing Hamparian from the Federation. Was there any way to salvage this operation, or was it time to move on to another world, another identity, maybe even another era?

"The gates!" Varkat demanded, refusing to leave before he was satisfied that the prisoners could not escape. Ire and affronted pride vitalized the aging monarch as much as Siroth's twenty-third-century treatments and pharmaceuticals. "Someone tell me the cursed gates are shut!"

To Kirk's relief, the sonic vibrations kept the bloodbeaks at a distance as he and Hamparian raced back to the wall, where Sulu and company hauled the endangered scientist to safety before Kirk hastily scaled the wall himself, reuniting with the rest of the landing party even as panicked Atrazians continued to flee the stands in droves. He switched off the communicator, glad to see to that McCoy was already looking over Hamparian, even without his medkit. Sulu greeted Kirk warmly.

"Good to see you again, Captain."

"That goes double for me, Mister Sulu." Kirk nodded at Levine and Landon. "I appreciate the timely assist."

"I just wish we could have found a way to get to you and Doctor McCoy sooner," Sulu said.

"No complaints here," Kirk said. "Not that we're out of the woods yet."

They would have to compare notes later. Assessing the situation, Kirk saw that the fleeing spectators were running headlong into armed reinforcements rushing to deal with the disturbance and apprehend the escapees. Newly arrived guards had to shove their way upstream against yet another frantic exodus. Kirk had a flash of déjà vu as he recalled the last time he attempted to exit the coliseum via the gates downstairs.

That hadn't turned out well.

"I don't suppose an emergency beam-out is an option?" he asked Sulu. As far as he knew, the *Enterprise* was still maintaining a diplomatically discreet distance from Atraz.

Sulu shook his head. "The ship's in orbit, but they can't lower their shields with that D7 stalking them."

"Understood," Kirk said. "Do we have an exit strategy, Sulu?"

"Aye, sir." Sulu gestured toward the rapidly emptying rows of seats above them. "Up, not down."

Kirk trusted Sulu knew what he was doing. "Lead on, mister."

"Landon!" Sulu called out to the yeoman. "Break out the smoke!"

"Aye, Lieutenant!" She reached into a picnic basket resting at her feet, which she had apparently brought to the festivities, and retrieved a tinted glass bottle. A refreshing beverage was not on her mind, however, as she smashed the bottle against the railing, releasing a billowing cloud of thick mustard-colored smoke. A pungent odor, sour but not acrid, assailed Kirk's nostrils.

A smokescreen, he realized, *to aid our escape.*

"Curious provisions, Yeoman. Not exactly Starfleet rations."

"Credit Mister Sulu," she said. "Using materials found in a local market."

Sulu shrugged. "Just putting my botanical know-how to good use."

With no time to lose, they got a move on. Eschewing the aisles, they hurriedly climbed the rows from bench to bench. Starfleet lights helped to pierce the gloom and smoke. Kirk would've liked a breathing mask, as used by landing parties on less hospitable worlds, but those weren't regularly issued when visiting Class-M planets; the nearest such masks were stored on *Galileo* many kilometers away.

"What the devil was in that bottle, Sulu?" McCoy made a face, his nose wrinkling in disgust. "Or do I not want to know?"

"Nothing toxic, Doctor, I promise!"

Despite the smokescreen, Varkat's guards chased after them. "Halt! In the name of the suzerain!"

Kirk braced himself for a fight, but was caught by surprise when the guards met resistance from—Klingons in Atrazian garb? Glancing back through the swirling fumes, he spied an Atrazian soldier tumbling down an aisle with a crossbow bolt in his side. Another guard, the one who had ordered them to halt, spasmed and collapsed after being ambushed by a disguised Klingon lurking among the fleeing civilians. Kirk recognized the brutal effect of a Klingon agonizer.

"Yorba's men?" he asked, coughing because of the smoke.

"I would hope so," she answered from a few paces away. "Perhaps we stand a chance after all."

Yet another guard was flipped over a railing into the arena. Excited squawks greeted the offering, followed by frantic screams. Kirk flinched at the cries.

Sulu winced as well. "The devil you know," he said apologetically. "An alliance seemed like a good idea."

Kirk nodded grimly. He wasn't inclined to second-guess Sulu's command decisions during a crisis. Hard choices were part of the job.

The party hustled up the steps, which were increasingly free of Atrazian bystanders. Landon lobbed another bottle from her basket into the rows behind them, masking their escape behind a fresh cloud of smoke. McCoy stuck close to Hamparian, helping her keep up with the others; as near as Kirk could tell, the scientist was more bruised than broken from her fall into the arena. Levine followed closely behind Kirk, ready to take a crossbow bolt for the captain. Kirk hoped it wouldn't come to that.

"Pick up the pace, Kirk!" Yorba hurried ahead of him. "My men are paying the price for our freedom!"

The Klingons' fierce defense of their commander's escape was indeed coming at a cost. Guttural cries and defiant death howls told Kirk that the outnumbered soldiers were taking casualties. Peering back through the smoke, he glimpsed an unknown Klingon receiving a crossbow bolt to the skull. The undercover soldier fell backward in the mob behind him.

"Yorba!" he shouted. "Call back your men. Order a retreat!"

She kept climbing the rows, not looking back. "They are doing their duty. I would not dishonor them by endangering our mission for their safety's sake. I will see them in Sto-Vo-Kor, sooner or later."

Kirk was vaguely aware that Sto-Vo-Kor was some sort of Klingon Valhalla, at least according to Starfleet's current understanding of their culture. "But their lives—!"

"Are none of your concern." Yorba took a moment to give him a warning look. "And make no mistake: they would sooner die in glorious combat than heed the words of a Starfleet captain!"

Kirk believed her, unfortunately, even as he was appalled by Yorba's callous attitude, which struck him as ruthless even for a Klingon. He'd reluctantly ordered personnel into mortal danger before, but he liked to think that he valued the lives of his crew far more than Yorba did. He would never willingly leave anyone behind. Yet climbing the coliseum alongside the others, he belatedly realized someone was missing.

"Hang on. Where's Jaheed?"

A grin lightened Sulu's expression. "Not too far away . . . in theory."

Before he could elaborate, they reached the top of the seating area, below the top of the wall surrounding the city. Another rope, secured by a grappling hook, was already in place to allow them to climb up onto the wall. A surly-looking Klingon waited by the rope. Levine drew his phaser to discourage any last-minute betrayals. Sulu and Landon did the same.

"Colonel." The Klingon saluted Yorba, smacking his right arm against his chest. "For the Empire!"

"Wrultz," she acknowledged him curtly. "Your communicator . . . now."

Kirk eyed the wall before them, deducing what Sulu had in mind. "Up and over . . . and out of the city?"

"Rappelling down the outer wall," Sulu confirmed. "With alacrity, as Mister Spock might say."

Not a bad plan, Kirk judged, although someone was going to have to defend the wall to make sure no Atrazian guards unhitched the rope before the rest all reached the ground. *And that someone is going to be me.*

He approached Hamparian. "You up to this?"

She glanced back at the arena, only faintly visible through the swirling fumes. "Given a choice between this and those ghastly birds? What choice do I have?"

"None, I suppose." Kirk contemplated Yorba and her warrior. Should he let them descend the wall first or last or somewhere in between? He made a point of keeping between the Klingons and Hamparian in case Yorba would still rather see the scientist dead than returned to the Federation. At the moment, she appeared to be using a borrowed communicator to check in with the *BortaS*, which was presumably in the same fix the *Enterprise* was in when it came to not being able to lower its shields. She couldn't just beam back up to her ship either.

"Yorba to *BortaS*. Imperial authorization code *Qam-Chee Xol* 7979V." She stared across the coliseum at the fortress looming over the city. "Target previously noted anomalous structure, designated JX118. Full disruptors!"

"What?" Kirk started toward her, only to be blocked by Wrultz. "You can't do this!"

"I beg to differ, Kirk." She lowered the communicator. "Behold."

A devastating viridian beam shot down from the sky, striking Siroth's tower. Fired from orbit, the disruptor beam lit up the night, drawing shocked gasps and screams from awe-stricken Atrazians throughout the coliseum and the city beyond. The tower shimmered and glowed before collapsing into rubble. The crash of falling stone and timbers could be heard all the way down to the stadium, even as the sizzling beam blinked out abruptly, letting darkness rush back in to fill its absence. A huge plume of dust rose from the ruins of the tower.

"Merciful heavens," McCoy said in a hushed tone. He glared at Yorba. "Have you lost your bloodthirsty Klingon mind?"

"So much for an egregious violation of your precious Prime Directive." She smirked at Kirk and McCoy, unrepentant. "You're welcome."

Chapter Thirty-Five

"I was a whaler in those days. Don't judge me. I was young, I needed work, and I didn't know any better. One did what one had to do."

Dmitri Katkov, former citizen of a Soviet Socialist Republic, spoke to them remotely from his current residence in Cape May, New Jersey. He was an older gentleman, with craggy features weathered by sun and sea, a thick gray beard, and a Russian accent. He'd reached out to *Cetacean*, claiming to have had his own remarkable experience, involving a pair of humpback whales no less, on the day Gillian vanished.

"Understood." Melinda sat on the couch, facing her laptop at the approved Room Rater height. As ever, Dennis stood off to the side, staying off-camera. "Trust me, we're not here to question your choices back then. We just want to hear your story . . . about a huge invisible UFO?"

There'd been a time, not too many weeks ago, when she wouldn't have bothered responding to such a "lead," consigning it to the kook folder instead, but that was before their investigation (and lives) came to entail Miracle Milly, unearthly happenings in the park, ray guns, Russian spies, and, possibly, an obsessed biotech tycoon who hadn't seemed to have aged over the last thirty-plus years. Beneath the professional poise she'd assumed to interview Katkov, Melinda was still reeling from the fact that Jane Temple, once Melinda had managed to get hold of her, had also positively ID'd Orlando Wilder as Wilmer Offutt, which defied all logic and biology. At this point, a retired Russian whaler reporting yet another UFO encounter was pretty much par for the course.

"*Da*," he said. "I remember it well, even after all these years. I was serving aboard the *Moryana*, out of Vladivostok, hunting for whales in the Bering Sea, when we sighted two young humpback whales breaching the surface. In hindsight, perhaps the 'George and Gracie' you mention on your series. This was indeed the thirteenth of May in 1986, the same day your Doctor Gillian Taylor was last seen."

And when the whales' radio transmitters abruptly went silent, Melinda recalled, somewhere in the Bering Sea.

"We closed in on the whales, expecting easy kills. Indeed, the whales did not seem alarmed by our approach at all, as though perhaps they had been raised by humans in an aquarium? We fired the harpoon, which shot toward the nearest whale. It was just about to make a direct hit when . . . *klang!* The harpoon struck an unseen barrier and fell into the sea, leaving the whales untouched."

Thank goodness, Melinda thought. "So you couldn't see what the harpoon hit?"

"Not at first. From where we stood, on the deck of the boat, it looked as though the harpoon had somehow been blocked by empty air, but then the sky above the waves shimmered like a mirage and this . . . vessel . . . materialized out of nowhere, many times larger than poor *Moryana*, hovering before us like some great metallic bird-of-prey." Awe filled his voice at the memory. "It was like nothing any of us had ever seen, before or since."

Off to the right, Dennis's eyes were wide. He was hanging on the old whaler's every word, barely monitoring the sound levels. Melinda braced herself for his reaction, after the interview was over, even as she tried to hang on to her skepticism. Despite herself, she immediately recalled the deep indentation at the park, the flattened trash can, the sudden blasts of air out of clear days, and the way Gillian and her accomplices had somehow escaped Mercy General unseen. Almost as though spirited away by an invisible aircraft?

"Can you describe what it looked like?"

"I can do better than that, young lady. I've been drawing and painting it for the better part of my life now. From memory, yes, but such a memory!" He leaned forward to fiddle with a mouse or keyboard at his end of the transmission. "Feast your eyes on this."

An oil painting took over most of the screen. The striking image depicted an exotic, thoroughly unidentifiable aircraft hanging in midair, dwarfing the much smaller whaling ship caught in its immense shadow. The ship was dark green in color, with twin wings flanking a long central hull. A glowing red ring stood out upon its bulbous prow, like a cyclopean eye. Stylized renderings of feathered pinions, vermillion in hue, adorned the undersides of the wings, conveying indeed the impression of some mammoth avian predator, like the mythical roc that menaced Sinbad in the *Arabian Nights*. Melinda could only imagine what it would be like to suddenly see such an apparition looming before you, way out on the open sea.

"You say it . . . materialized? As in it abruptly descended from the clouds, or perhaps rose up from beneath the waves?"

Katkov's image now occupied a small window in the upper right-hand corner of the screen. He shook his head vigorously.

"*Nyet.* The air wavered and blurred, as above hot pavement, then there it was: as big and solid as anything I've ever seen, putting the fear of God—or the Devil—into every one of us." He crossed himself instinctively. "From out of nowhere!"

Just like the doorway Javy Valdez saw hovering above the park one day earlier. Maybe not a portal through time or space then, but . . . an open hatch on an invisible stealth aircraft? If such a thing was even possible, that was.

"Then what?" she asked.

"What do you think, in the face of such a fearsome sight? Our pilot spun the wheel and slewed the boat around so sharply he nearly swamped us. We raced back to port at full speed, not letting up even after that monstrous vessel was well behind us."

"So you didn't see what it did next . . . or where it went?"

He shook his head. "Wasn't worth my life to find out. For all I know, it faded from sight as swiftly as it appeared. But that brief sighting? I'll take that with me until the day I die."

I'll bet, she thought, *if that painting is to be believed.*

Katkov didn't have much more to tell her. Unfortunately, he no longer knew, if he ever had, the precise coordinates for where his UFO had materialized, so she couldn't compare them against whatever records the Cetacean Institute might still have of George and Gracie's last known location. Despite this, Melinda felt certain that Katkov had encountered Gillian's whales, rescued in the nick of time by a stealth aircraft of unknown origin, presumably the same one that had landed in Golden Gate Park the day before, leaving its impression in the field, and taken off the next day, just as the Dowses had been jogging past. Insanely, all the pieces fit—if you bought into some pretty unbelievable premises.

Invisible aircraft? Spaceships?

Just how quickly had the "roc" traveled from San Francisco to the Bering Sea? If her timeline was right, and the jet blast that had staggered the joggers was indeed the UFO departing from the park, that great green bird would've had to have made the trip in no time at all? She was no aeronautics expert, but that seemed like a stretch even for advanced military aircraft.

How fast was too fast to be possible?

Her mind was spinning. After making sure Dennis clipped a frame of the oil painting, she thanked Katkov for his time and story, closed out the interview, and took a deep breath before turning toward Dennis, who was pacing all around the living room, barely able to contain himself. He ran both hands through his hair, like he was trying to hold his over-excited brain in place.

"Holy crap! It's all true! Gillian didn't just disappear, she—"

She cut him off, not ready for what was surely coming. "Don't say it."

"What? That she left the planet altogether?" He pointed at his laptop where the great green UFO still cast its shadow on the sea. "Open your eyes. Does that resemble any aircraft ever built on Earth? It's obviously extraterrestrial!"

"Let's not get carried away," she said, with less conviction than she would have liked. "Maybe something experimental? Like those ultra-top-secret projects at Area 51 you used to go on about?"

"Reverse engineered from the ship that crashed at Roswell," he reminded her, taking for granted this was established fact and not just the stuff of rumor and conspiracy theories. "But wouldn't Halley and his fellow spooks already know all about that? And why would an experimental new design still be unknown today, forty years later? Shouldn't that technology have filtered out into more mainstream usage by now? And even back then, why would the Feds be parking their top-secret invisible aircraft in a public park . . . and using it to rescue whales and an injured Russian spy?"

"Why would aliens?" she countered.

"I don't know," he admitted. "Mars needs whales?"

She struggled to bring them back down to Earth. "That UFO decorated its wings with feathers, symbolically. Would aliens do that? Do they even have birds where they come from?"

He shrugged. "Parallel evolution?"

"Seriously?"

"You got a better explanation?"

"No, damnit," she cursed, breaking her self-imposed embargo on profanity. Everything about this investigation kept steering them into what felt more and more like science fiction, so that she increasingly felt like she was the one being unreasonable for refusing to think outside the box. When had Dennis started sounding like the voice of reason?

She stared at the futuristic roc on the screen. It was just a painting, not a photograph, but she had to admit it didn't look like any kind of aircraft, experimental or otherwise, she had ever seen or read about. Its exotic design, and seemingly impossible capabilities, certainly seemed like something from (*say it,* she dared herself) another world.

Literally?

She couldn't duck the question any longer. Had Gillian been abducted by aliens?

Or even gone with them willingly?

"Screw this." She needed to get to the bottom of this, one way or another, not just for *Cetacean,* but for the sake of her own sanity. She had to know what was real in this world and what was mere fantasy. Before Dennis could protest or try to change her mind, she grabbed her phone and called the number from the ancient business card.

"Wait! What are you doing?"

He tried to snatch the phone from her, but she darted away from him, keeping it out of reach as the answering machine played its recorded greeting. Now that she heard it again, she recognized the distinctive bass tones of Orlando Wilder, which only spurred her to take the bull by the horns, despite Dennis's frantic attempts to forestall her.

"Hello? Willard Offutt? Orlando Wilder? Whoever this is and whatever you're calling yourself, I know where that precious kidney pill came from," she lied, "and where it can be found today. Let's talk, ASAP. You won't regret it."

She put down the phone, feeling a rush of anticipation. Dennis stared at her, aghast.

"Crap, Melinda. What have you done?"

Chapter Thirty-Six

2268

"Mister Spock, the Klingons just fired on the planet!"

The *Enterprise*'s viewscreen verified Chekov's emotive announcement. Disruptor beams, blazing green against the darkness of orbital space, burst from the *BortaS*'s nacelle-mounted disruptor cannons, targeting the world below. The twin beams converged as they burned through Atraz's atmosphere toward a continent in the planet's southern hemisphere, where, Spock noted with controlled concern, Captain Kirk and the rest of the landing party were currently situated. The attack was over in an instant, the merged beams vanishing in a flash, but had doubtless inflicted significant damage on the planet's surface.

"Those blackhearted devils!" Scott exclaimed from the engineering station. "Firing on a planet that hasn't even invented lasers yet!"

Let alone orbital defenses, Spock thought. "Can you identify the precise coordinates of the targeted area, Mister Chekov?"

"I'm working on it, sir!" The young ensign looked up from the sensor viewer with an abashed expression on his face. "I'm sorry I didn't see that coming, Mister Spock. I was focused on watching out for any sign that the Klingons were locking their weapons on the *Enterprise.* I never expected them to fire on the planet instead!"

Spock wanted information, not explanations. "The coordinates, Ensign, with all due speed."

"Aye, sir! Got it, sir!" Chekov peered into the viewer. "The disruptors struck a location somewhere in the city, Reliux, but that's as precise as I can get right away."

"But not the entire city?"

"No, sir. It appears to have been more of a surgical strike than an obliterating assault."

"Acknowledged." Spock greeted the report with a degree of relief. He remained concerned regarding the landing party's safety, but saw no reason to assume the worst in the absence of any conclusive evidence. "Lieutenant Uhura, can you establish contact with the landing party?"

"Already on it, sir." She expertly manipulated her control panel. "Their communicators are still receiving our signals, but the party members are not immediately responding . . . wait, hold on, I'm getting through to them."

A subjectively lengthy interval transpired as she listened to a transmission via her earpiece. "Well, come on, lassie," Scott said anxiously. "Don't keep us hanging."

"Understood," Uhura replied to whomever she was addressing, then bestowed a reassuring smile upon the bridge. "I reached Yeoman Landon briefly. They've got their hands full at the moment, rescuing the captain and Doctor McCoy, so she couldn't talk long, but . . . those disruptors didn't get them. The beams struck a fortress some distance away from where the landing party is now."

"Thank you, Lieutenant," Spock said. "Continue monitoring all frequencies."

"Definitely, sir." Relief was supplanted by worry on her face. "It sounds as though they're encountering serious hostilities down there. I could hear shouts and fighting in the background."

"They're in thick of it, I'm sure." Scott's frustration was evident. "If only we could beam them out of whatever tight spot they're in!"

"Not without lowering our shields," Spock said, restating their dilemma as a reminder to the bridge crew, "which would be injudicious at present, considering our proximity to the *BortaS*."

"Aye," Scott conceded. "That's putting it mildly, Mister Spock."

Logic dictated that the landing party was on its own for the present, but the Klingons' unprovoked attack on Atraz required an immediate response. Spock did not hesitate before activating the intercom on his armrest.

"Battle stations. Load photon torpedoes. Phaser crews, prepare to fire on command."

Back when he and his father were still on speaking terms, Sarek had once shared with Spock the unspoken secret to negotiating with Klingons: for better or for worse, a show of force was often necessary to get the Klingons to even acknowledge any dissenting views. A pained expression had betrayed Sarek's discomfort with this unpleasant reality, but the *BortaS* firing on Atraz not only gave the *Enterprise* grounds to return fire in the planet's defense, it made such a response imperative; to permit the Klingons to assault Atraz with impunity would invite further attacks on the planet and its people.

"Phasers locked on the Klingon vessel." Rahda employed the pop-up targeting scanner at the helm. The two ships were still essentially chasing each other around the planet. "*BortaS* within firing range."

"Full phaser power, approximately two point five seconds in duration," Spock said, calculating what intensity of attack would be sufficient to register their displeasure—and perhaps draw the Klingons' fire away from the planet. "Fire at will, Lieutenant Rahda."

She nodded grimly. "Aye, sir."

Incandescent red beams cut across the vacuum of space to strike the *BortaS*'s deflector screens. Bright blue discharges of Cherenkov radiation flared where the phasers impacted the battle cruiser's invisible shields.

"Evasive maneuvers," Spock ordered in anticipation of a retaliatory blast, which was not long in coming. The D7 deployed its rear cannons to fiery effect. Despite swiftly altering its direction and heading, the *Enterprise* was still seared along its port side by the Klingons' disruptors. A shudder vibrated the bridge, but the lights did not flicker and no consoles sparked. "Damage report."

"All shields holding," Chekov said. "Portside shields are down six point three percent along the engineering hull and pylon support."

"Rerouting power from reserve subsystems," Scott reported. "Repair crews dispatched to affected areas." Scott turned toward the main viewer, where the *BortaS* remained on display. "Seems you rattled their cage, Mister Spock."

"As intended," Spock said coolly. "If nothing else, they are no longer attacking the planet."

On-screen, the *BortaS* banked away from the *Enterprise*, presenting a moving target while apparently circling around for a strafing run at the Federation ship. Spock recalled that Khod had employed similar tactics during his previous skirmish with the *Enterprise*: darting in to unleash a blast of disruptor fire at close range before speeding away to come around for another attack. On that occasion, Khod had already conspired to sabotage the *Enterprise*'s matter/antimatter integrator, rendering both the warp drive and weapons systems inoperative until some fortuitous last-minute repairs. Thankfully, that was not the case in this instance. The *Enterprise* and the *BortaS* were evenly matched.

"Transfer weapons control to navigation," Spock instructed Rahda, to allow her to focus entirely on piloting the ship. "Maintain tactical maneuvers." He turned toward the nav station. "Lieutenant Farrell, return fire."

"Aye, sir!" Farrell subjected the battle cruiser to a well-aimed phaser blast barrage, resulting in telltale flashes along the battle cruiser's starboard side. "Winged her . . . . literally!"

"Klingon shields still holding," Chekov reported, scanning the other vessel, "but we put a dent in them."

Spock nodded, his stoic expression betraying nothing. "Maintain offensive and evasive actions."

"Mister Spock," Uhura said. "The *BortaS* is hailing us. It appears Captain Khod wants to give you a piece of his mind."

"I imagine so. On-screen, Lieutenant, but only as an inset window."

Spock did not wish to deprive Rahda and Farrell of a full view of the battle cruiser and its movements, which, along with their sensor readings, was of significant tactical value. He could not expect the battle cruiser to pause its attack while Khod railed at his foes.

"Aye, sir. On-screen."

Khod's furious visage took over the lower-right-hand corner of the main viewer, leaving the *BortaS* occupying the *sehlat*'s share of the screen. The smaller window was more than sufficient to convey Khod's predictably livid countenance. His tone of voice was equally belligerent; he snarled from the screen.

"*Vulcan! How dare you fire upon an imperial battle cruiser! This unwarranted attack cannot be tolerated. You have proven yourself without honor or sense!*"

"Hardly unwarranted," Spock replied. "Your attack on Atraz violated treaty, forcing our hand. We could not sit by while you took hostile action against a defenseless world that, by mutual agreement, was to be left alone by both our fleets."

"*We have our reasons and will not be lectured to by the likes of you, Vulcan. You have foolishly invited our wrath. Surrender or be destroyed!*"

"That is hardly a forgone conclusion. I remind you that, unlike the last time our ships engaged in combat, the *Enterprise* is not recovering from sabotage. Our weapons, defenses, and propulsion systems are fully operational. You will not find us easy prey."

Khod snorted. "*And they say Vulcans have no sense of humor! Your pathetic starship, with all its decadent creature comforts, is no match for my battle cruiser.*"

"Klingon propaganda notwithstanding, we both know that is not true. Indeed, the mathematics of the equation favor us. Our capacities being more or less equivalent, any conflict between our two ships will likely become a war of attrition as we exhaust our arms and defenses at comparable rates. This puts the *Enterprise* at an advantage since you have already expended a measurable portion of your firepower in attacking Atraz, an action that did not weaken our shields in the slightest. In short, you wasted your first move on another target, allowing us to begin compromising your shields before you inflicted a single blow on us. Probability therefore suggests that we will ultimately outlast you, albeit after what could be a very costly exchange."

A momentary pause ensued, as though Khod was weighing Spock's cautionary words despite himself. The delay was scarcely detectable but did not escape Spock's notice.

"*Do not speak to me of probabilities, Vulcan. This is war, not a math problem. I'll put my hot blood against your cold logic anytime!*"

"Perhaps, but bluster and bravado only go so far. I'll do you the courtesy of assuming that you are too well-versed in matters of combat to be outmaneuvered by any strategic ploy on our part, and I would strongly advise you to credit us with the same tactical expertise and training." Spock spoke with firm assurance, unruffled by Khod's militant posturing. "Which brings us back to the mathematics of attrition. I would think twice before discounting a Vulcan's calculations."

Alas, his cogent argument failed to convince Khod.

"*And you should know better than to underestimate the fury of a Klingon's heart. Let us test our might against your calculations, Vulcan, if you have the stomach for it!*"

Spock resisted the all-too-human temptation to remind Khod that the *Enterprise* had sent the *BortaS* fleeing once before. He could not risk Khod choosing to go down fighting rather than retreat from the same foe again. The challenge then was to devise a means by which Khod could withdraw from battle without losing face.

A matter rendered academic when Khod suddenly disappeared from the screen.

"Lieutenant Uhura?" Spock queried.

"Transmission terminated at their end," she confirmed.

"Typical," Scott said. "Bloody Klingon manners!"

Swooping around, the D7 launched another attack. Disruptors strafed the underside of the saucer section even as the *Enterprise* replied in kind, blasting the battle cruiser's forward command bulb from above. Spock absorbed the resulting damage reports while simultaneously reviewing their previous encounter with Khod and his vessel, when Kirk had routed the *BortaS* by feigning helplessness, concealing the fact that the *Enterprise* had regained its weapons capacity, in order to lure the battle cruiser into a trap. The *BortaS* was thereby caught off-guard by a full spread of photon torpedoes, forcing the damaged battle cruiser to limp back to Klingon space. Spock could not expect Khod to fall for the same ruse twice.

But what if we attempt a similar ploy—in reverse?

"Lieutenant Uhura," Spock said; there was no need to mute the audio since Khod could no longer listen in. "Prepare to launch a recorder marker conveying our current status and logs to the nearest Starfleet relay station—with modifications."

She gave him a knowing look, her eyes narrowing.

"What kind of modifications, sir?"

Chapter Thirty-Seven

2024

"I still don't think this is a good idea," Dennis said.

"You got a better one?" Melinda asked. "We need answers—okay, I need answers—and this may be our only shot at finding out just what the heck we've stumbled onto here. We have to take it."

And not just for *Cetacean*, but for her own peace of mind. Everything she thought she knew about what was fact and what was fantasy had been thrown into question. The shape of the world depended on her replacing some of those question marks with periods, which meant getting solid, indisputable answers, no matter what.

A private limo, dispatched by Orlando Wilder, carried them toward Hiberna House, the elusive millionaire's personal residence in San Francisco, only a helicopter ride away from Amaranth's corporate HQ in San Jose. The space-age, modernist-style mansion was perched on a rocky cliff overlooking the Bay. Melinda could only imagine how much Wilder must have paid, and what strings he might have pulled, to secure such prime real estate.

"So it doesn't bother you that we may be walking right into a trap? Whatever happened to being more careful from now on?"

Wilder had taken the bait she'd left for him on Wilmer Offutt's answering machine. His terms had been nonnegotiable: a face-to-face meeting, off the record, on his home turf, where he could guarantee his privacy and security. Her counteroffer of meeting on neutral ground, as they had with Halley, was a nonstarter. And honestly, she'd been in no mood or position to haggle; no way was she passing up this opportunity.

"Don't be so melodramatic," she teased him, adopting a light tone to allay his anxiety. "He's a camera-shy tycoon with a murky past, not a Bond villain. Probably has more lawyers than assassins on retainer."

"Or he's an alien or a time traveler, who already had our home bugged and burgled. And we're strolling right into his lair?"

It's that or never know what's real again, she thought. "You didn't have to come along," she said gently. "You could've let me do this by myself."

"No, I really couldn't. Watching over you remotely isn't an option this time, and I couldn't live with myself if something happened to you while I stayed safe at home." He wolfed down a couple of Tums. "*Somebody* has to have your back when you get like this and let your curiosity get the better of caution."

"And don't think I don't appreciate it." She looked him over, concerned by his drawn features and the bags under his eyes. "You get any sleep at all last night?"

"Not really."

"Me either," she admitted, although in her case she was more wired than apprehensive. *Manage your expectations,* she told herself. There was no guarantee that Wilder could or would provide solutions to every mystery surrounding Gillian's disappearance.

In the meantime, she couldn't fault the efficiency of Wilder's arrangements—and security precautions. A formidable-looking steel gate opened automatically at the limo's approach, admitting them to a long private drive that eventually dropped them in front of the mansion before turning around and leaving them behind. A short flight of steps led up to the open front door, where Wilder was on hand to greet them.

"Right on time. I'd compliment you on your punctuality, but of course, that was all my doing." His voice was as sonorous as ever. "I trust the ride went smoothly."

Compared to his brusque demeanor when she'd ambushed him before, he seemed to be making an effort to be a bit more cordial this time around. His attire consisted of a neatly pressed blazer, turtleneck sweater, slacks, and loafers.

"Like clockwork." She'd put on a jacket, jeans, boots, and a plain black T-shirt for the occasion, and redyed her hair magenta. "I'm sure I don't need to introduce my partner, Dennis Berry. You probably already have full files on both of us, along with samples of our DNA."

"I plead the Fifth," he said dryly. "Still, in the interest of good manners, I'm pleased to finally meet you, Mister Berry."

He held out his hand to Dennis, who, after a moment's trepidation, accepted. She noticed it was shaking a bit; she hoped his palm wasn't too sweaty. *He's braving this for my sake, despite his fears. Don't forget that.*

Wilder turned toward her. "For that matter, I don't believe we've ever been formally introduced, Ms. Silver."

"Call me Melinda." She gave him a firm handshake and a steady gaze, noting again that he and she were roughly the same height. "But I'm unclear. Should I address you as Orlando Wilder . . . or Wilmer Offutt?"

His smile grew strained. "Orlando will do, but let's table that . . . misunderstanding . . . until after we've settled in and made ourselves comfortable." He glanced at the sky, which was cloudy and threatening rain, and gestured toward the door. "If you please."

"All right," she said. *As long as I don't have to wait too long for some real talk.*

She had no intention of being strung along by Wilder's attempts at hospitality. She was here for answers, not evasions. They followed him through the doorway into a tiled vestibule with a long vertical mirror on one wall and an abstract painting on the other. No sooner had he exited the foyer than a high-pitched klaxon went off, startling Melinda and nearly causing Dennis to jump out of his skin. A transparent glass or plastic barrier shot up from beneath the floor in front of them, cutting them off from Wilder and the rest of the house. The front door closed automatically behind them, shutting with an ominous click. Glancing back, she noticed the absence of any obvious door handle or control panel.

"Oh, crap!" Dennis tried the door anyway, which naturally refused to open. "I knew it! I knew this was a trap!"

"No need to be alarmed." Wilder addressed them from the other side of the barrier, which had perforations to permit sound to pass through it. "Simply a routine security measure, which I neglected to mention."

Sure you did, Melinda thought. "Not exactly making a good first impression here, Orlando. Paranoid much?"

She rapped the barrier with her knuckles, producing an oddly metallic ring. Not glass or plastic then, but some kind of transparent steel alloy?

"A man in my position can't afford to take chances. Nothing personal." He raised his voice to be heard over the klaxon. "Iduna, mute weapons alarm."

The shrill keening fell silent.

"Done," a bodiless female voice confirmed.

"Voice operated." She guessed the handleless door was programmed to respond to Wilder's spoken commands as well. "Very slick."

"State-of-the-art smart-house technology, Melinda. This is the twenty-first century after all." He gestured at the mirrored vestibule, which was starting to feel more like an interrogation chamber—complete with one-way mirrors? "A discreet scanner detected possible weapons on your persons."

A panel beneath the mirror slid aside, revealing a concealed compartment about the size of a standard microwave oven.

"Please deposit any problematic items in the niche," Wilder instructed.

"Didn't realize I'd be going through airport security today," she said. "Do I need to take off my shoes, too?"

"That won't be necessary, provided you're not hiding a shiv in one of your boots." He glanced to one side as if to get confirmation of that assumption from someone monitoring the scanner results. He nodded at the waiting compartment. "The sooner we get this rigamarole over, the sooner we can get down to the business at hand."

Can't argue with that, she thought. Figuring the scanner had flagged her Mace, which she'd pretty much forgotten she had on her, she placed the cannister in the compartment. "There you go. Brought it with me out of force of habit, honestly."

"I'm sure," Wilder said affably. "Mister Berry?"

Dennis went pale. He glanced around anxiously, looking trapped. His hand fumbled in one of the many overstuffed pockets of his rumpled coat. He was sweaty and twitchy and generally a bundle of nerves. "This was a bad idea. We should go."

Melinda was confused. Sure, Wilder was going a bit overboard with the security theater, but that was hardly reason enough to turn around and go back home now that they'd literally gotten past his front door. And what was the holdup anyway? As far as she knew, Dennis never carried anything more lethal than a Swiss Army knife.

"Dennis?"

"We're waiting, Mister Berry." He looked again to the side. "Kindly surrender the firearm."

Firearm?

"What's he talking about, Dennis?"

"I . . . I'm sorry, Melinda," he stammered, "but . . . I needed to be ready for anything. You keep taking these crazy chances, despite every warning. It's like I said before: somebody has to protect us—protect *you*—from whatever danger we're in."

He sheepishly drew a handgun from his pocket. No gun nut, she couldn't name the make or caliber, but she knew a real gun when she saw one. Her eyes bugged out.

"What the freak, Dennis? Since when do you even own a gun?"

"Since this stopped being just another retro cold case. I kept telling you we were taking this too far, but you didn't want to hear it." His voice quavered. "I had to do something. We weren't safe!"

"And you thought *this* was a good idea?"

She took the gun from him, despite his plaintive protests. Handling it gingerly, keeping her fingers well away from the trigger and making sure it wasn't pointed at anyone in the vicinity, she placed it carefully in the compartment before turning back to Wilder, afraid that the meeting had gone down the tubes before it had even truly begun.

"I'm so sorry," she said, mortified. "I swear, I had no idea."

"That much is obvious."

The compartment closed, vanishing back into concealment. The gun and pepper spray went with it, like library books dropped off after-hours. Dennis gazed forlornly at the now-pristine wall, as though already regretting giving up the weapon.

"I hope you know what you're doing."

"We'll talk about this later." She had to try to salvage this meeting, if possible. "But under the circumstances, maybe it would be better for everyone if you did head home now. Let me handle this on my own."

"No! I'm not going to leave you here! There's no telling what could happen to you!"

"Ahem," Wilder said. "If I may intervene here, I think it best that you both stay until we can get various matters sorted out."

He nodded at an unseen presence, and the transparent barrier receded back beneath the floor, opening up the interior end of the vestibule.

"Please come in, now that we needn't concern ourselves with security issues."

"*Your* security," Dennis muttered.

Wilder took the remark in stride. "You're in no danger, Mister Berry. I've devoted my existence to prolonging and preserving life, not ending it. Death is my enemy."

"Amaranth," she said, nodding. "Miracle cures."

"Precisely. I'm no mafioso or arms dealer. I'm a medical innovator."

"Who occasionally employs private detectives?" she observed.

"Only for the greater good. Health and healing, not harm." Wilder beckoned them in. "But let us make our way to my study, unless you care to linger in the foyer all afternoon?"

"Lead the way." She tugged on Dennis's arm, torn between being seriously pissed off at him for buying a gun behind her back and feeling guilty for pushing him to the point where he felt that was necessary. "Chill, dude. It's going to be okay."

"Wanna bet Gillian felt the same way?"

Exiting the vestibule, and none too soon, she glanced to the left. Just as she'd suspected, another individual was stationed in front of a security monitor. Big and beefy, with a stony expression, the guy's intimidating proportions and body language practically screamed hired muscle. He made that muscular chauffeur back in San Jose seem like a scarecrow in comparison. Turning away from the monitor and one-way window, he glowered at her and Dennis. A tight black T-shirt strained to contain his steroid-sized chest.

Melinda declined to cower. "More security?" she asked Wilder.

"As noted, one can't be too careful—for obvious reasons." He looked pointedly at Dennis, who all too clearly wanted to be anywhere else. "In any event, we can speak freely in front of Vasily. He doesn't understand a word of English."

"I'll take your word for it." She had no way of verifying Wilder's claim, but after the business with Dennis and his gun, she was in no position to object to the bodyguard's presence. "Anyone else lurking around we should know about?"

"Only the house itself." Wilder lifted his eyes and voice to address a built-in presence. "Iduna, prepare the study for our guests. Fireplace, music, the usual amenities."

"Done."

Wilder smirked, clearly proud of his smart house. "Iduna helps me keep staffing down to a minimum, as I prefer. Fewer people underfoot, more privacy."

The better to protect his secrets?

Accompanied by Vasily, he led them to the study, which was probably bigger than their entire apartment, in height as well as floor space. High ceilings looked down on elegant contemporary furnishings. Towering picture windows offered a panoramic view of the Bay. A cozy gas blaze crackled in the fireplace, thanks to Iduna. A fully equipped bar was surely well stocked with first-class spirits. An oldie from the eighties played softly in the background, issuing from hidden speakers. It took Melinda a moment to place the tune:

"Forever Young."

Cute, she thought, *if deliberate. Or maybe just a personal favorite?*

"Very posh. Biotech clearly pays better than podcasting."

"That may be something we can discuss later," Wilder said, "if this conversation goes as I hope."

Was Wilder planning to throw money at her to make her go away? Melinda couldn't say she was surprised.

They settled in to talk. Wilder occupied a throne-like wingback chair, while she and Dennis shared a settee across from him. More minutes were eaten up by pleasantries as they were offered drinks and refreshments. Dennis refused to touch anything, no doubt terrified of being drugged or infected with some sort of insidious biotech, but Melinda accepted a glass of wine as a show of good faith and, honestly, to soothe her nerves after all the drama with the gun. Vasily, playing bartender as well as bodyguard, left the open bottle on a low coffee table between them and Wilder. Growing impatient, Melinda was about to insist they move things along when, unexpectedly, something small and white and furry scurried out from beneath the settee, right past her feet.

"Ohmigosh!"

Beady pink eyes looked back at her. Whiskers twitched. A long pink tail could be seen at the rear of the creature. Melinda yanked her feet off the floor and gaped at Wilder in confusion.

"A rat? This deluxe domicile has rats?"

"A lab rat, actually, albeit retired at this point." He made a clicking sound with his mouth, and the rat came toward him. He gently scooped it up off the floor and set it on his knee, where the rat nestled down, looking quite at home. "Meet Enkidu."

Melinda wasn't familiar with that name; she made a mental note to Google it later just in case it offered some insight into Wilder's background. "So what's the deal with the rodent? He your emotional-support rat?"

"Something like that." He stroked the rat, which noisily ground its teeth. Pink eyes boggled happily. "I'm quite fond of Enkidu. We go back a long ways."

"How long?" she asked, seeing an opening. Another classic eighties tune started playing. "I see you like the oldies. Just how old are you, Orlando? Really?"

"First things first. In your message on . . . Wilmer Offutt's . . . answering machine, you claimed to have found the source of the pill that regrew Mildred Coates's kidney. Do tell."

Melinda had debated when to come clean about that little white lie. Perhaps she could still work it a while longer? "How about some *quid pro quo*? You answer my questions, then we get to Miracle Milly?"

"Let us save us some time. You don't actually know where the pill can be found, do you? That was just a ruse to get this meeting?"

"What makes you say that?"

"I wasn't born yesterday, Melinda. Far from it."

"If you think that," she asked, not admitting anything, "what are we doing here?"

"It should be obvious by now that I value my privacy. As it happens, you've been digging into matters of family history that I would rather not be shared with your many subscribers, and since you are clearly nothing if not persistent, it's become increasingly apparent that we did need to have this talk." He leaned back in the chair. "As you said when you confronted me outside my offices, there may be something to be gained by comparing notes . . . and perhaps coming to a mutually beneficial arrangement."

"Quite a change of heart," she said. "I remember you telling me to *never* bother you again. Not that I'm complaining."

"You had me at a disadvantage before, a situation I neither relish nor take well. You'll forgive me if I was overly curt, but I could hardly be expected to welcome being interrogated without warning or invitation." He indicated their plush surroundings. "These circumstances are much more conducive to a productive discussion."

"On your turf, where you're in control?"

"Just so. I'm in the longevity business after all, and part of achieving a long life is minimizing risk and avoiding hazardous situations."

"I don't know," she replied. "The way I see it: no risk, no reward."

"The motto of many who go out in a blaze of glory, long before their time. Not a threat," he added quickly, perhaps to avoid alarming Dennis. "Merely an observation."

She shrugged. "We all have to go sometime."

"Do we? I refuse to accept that. Why should any life, no matter how long or accomplished, have to come to some inevitable termination, regardless of what we do? At Amaranth, we work to preserve and prolong life, yes, but that's just the beginning. Our ultimate goal—*my* ultimate goal—has always been to someday conquer death entirely." His deep voice rang with conviction. "I have, to quote the Bard, 'immortal longings.'"

Melinda gazed at him in disbelief. "You really think you can find a cure for death?"

"Why not? It won't be easy, of course, but if there's a way to regrow human organs, swiftly and painlessly, as with Mildred Coates's kidney, what else might we achieve through science and technology? History proves, time and again, that science can accomplish wonders once deemed impossible. Splitting the atom. Breaking the sound barrier. Putting a man on the moon. Maybe even someday finding a way to travel faster than the speed of light?"

"Or building an invisible aircraft?" she suggested.

"I'm afraid I don't know anything about that." He raised his right hand as though taking an oath on the stand. "I swear on my life-span, which I hold sacred, I was unaware of any alleged UFOs connected to the Mildred Coates affair until *Cetacean* came along. I knew about Gillian Taylor going AWOL, of course, due to her illicit activities at Mercy General when Milly was cured, but the garbage man's story, the mysterious depression at the park, and that Russian whaler's story about witnessing a UFO appear out of nowhere over the Bering Sea? All of that flew beneath my radar until your series brought it to light. Probably because I was looking to solve an earthbound medical mystery, not searching the skies. UFOs were not something that ever crossed my mind."

"Back when you were calling yourself Wilmer Offutt?"

"And we're back to that again." Irritation edged his voice. "Very well. Let's address that confusion, since you're clearly not going to rest until it's resolved to your satisfaction."

"You've got that right. You ready to come clean there?"

"I hate to disappoint you, but the awkward truth is simply that Wilmer Offutt was my father. Like me, he was dedicated to the cause of extending human life-spans by unconventional means. Alas, he took some, shall we say, ethical shortcuts, as well as making some dubious alliances that would not hold up well to scrutiny these days. As a result, I would prefer not to have my own more legitimate efforts, including Amaranth, sullied by association with my father's potentially controversial legacy." His eyes sought out Melinda's. "As a media personality, you must surely understand that. Perhaps even sympathize?"

Could he be telling the truth? Was this simply a case of Wilder wanting to bury an embarrassing skeleton in his family tree? After so much suspense and speculation, that was frankly a bit of a letdown, but she had to admit it made more sense than any more fantastic explanations . . .

"Bullshit!" Dennis blurted. "I researched both you and Offutt up and down the internet, staying up all night until my eyes bled, and 'Orlando Wilder' is as much a hoax as 'Wilmer Offutt.' They're both just well-crafted fictions, good enough to stand up to pretty close inspection, but you can't fool me. Who are you really? *What* are you?"

Vasily responded instantly to Dennis's outburst, coming up behind Dennis and placing two heavy hands on Dennis's shoulder, pressing him down into the seat cushions, just in case Dennis had any intention of acting out against Wilder, who signaled the hulking bodyguard to stand down. Scowling, Vasily unhanded Dennis but remained close at hand, looming menacingly behind the seated guests. Melinda hoped Dennis got the message, for everyone's sake.

"*What* am I?" Wilder echoed incredulously. "How am I supposed to take that?"

"You tell me." Dennis was literally shaking. "Are you an alien? A mutant? A time traveler?"

Wilder laughed out loud. "Is that what's worrying you?" He turned toward her. "What about you, Melinda? Are you entertaining the same absurd notions?"

"I don't know." She felt obliged to stick up for Dennis to some degree. "Dennis has taken me through his very in-depth background checks on both you and Offutt, and I trust his research. You're certainly not who you say you are . . . and the evidence *does* point strongly to you and Offutt being one and the same. I can't explain it, given how young you appear, but you do seem to be pretty much the same person. Same looks, same voice, same personality, same agenda, the same answering machine." She waved a hand at the oldies wafting through study. "Maybe even the same taste in music."

"No crime in liking vintage tunes," he said, "and I've already explained why I've taken pains to dissociate myself from my roots, right down to rewriting my biography."

"Not good enough." Her doubts receded as she recalled just how readily both Todd Coates and Jane Temple had recognized Offutt when shown Wilder's portrait. "Give me one reason to think you *aren't* Wilmer Offutt."

"Besides the fact that I'm obviously not in my fifties?"

"Yes, besides that. Heck, you just gave us a whole spiel about how science—and Amaranth—is capable of extending human lives in ways that seem impossible. Are we supposed to not connect the dots there?"

"I was speaking theoretically."

"Uh-huh. And we're supposed to believe that because . . . ?"

"I note you haven't shared this particular theory on *Cetacean* yet. Perhaps because you know just how ridiculous it sounds?"

That's one reason, yes, she thought. "Or maybe I was holding on to it as leverage to get you to talk to me. Unless you'd rather I share it with all my listeners?"

He frowned. "That would be less than ideal."

"I thought as much, so . . . spill. Tell me something worth keeping quiet about, *then* maybe we can come to that mutually beneficial arrangement you alluded to before."

She wasn't actually looking for hush money, but if Wilder wanted to think so . . . well, she could work with that.

"I see." His eyes narrowed. "If this is about money . . ."

"Not *just* about money." She deployed sincerity as a lure, speaking from the heart. "If you must know, Orlando, this case is driving me nuts. UFOs, a magic kidney pill, Russian spies, and now a guy, in search of immortality, who may or may not have aged in forty years. I honestly don't know what's impossible anymore, or how I'm supposed to distinguish common sense from craziness. But I do know this: If I don't get some answers soon, just for the sake of my own sanity, I don't know what I'm going to do. Have a nervous breakdown, probably."

And Dennis was already halfway there, it seemed.

"So give me a break, okay?" she said. "Be straight with me for once, put my mind at rest, or I'm never going to be able to let this go. Then, afterwards, we can talk about just how much my discretion is worth."

Wilder fell silent, mulling over her heartfelt appeal. Melinda chose to take this as a good sign, that he was weighing precisely how much he needed to tell her to get her to back off. He stared into the flames dancing within the fireplace while absently stroking Enkidu. She kept quiet, giving him time to think about it. She held her breath, mentally crossed her fingers, and placed a hand on Dennis's knee to steady him, hoping against hope he wouldn't say or do anything to mess things up. *Give Wilder a chance to open up.*

"Eugenics," he said finally. "That's the answer."

Dennis started at the word. Melinda rushed to reply first. "Go on. I'm listening."

"Back in the day, a couple generations ago, there was a concerted effort to improve the human species through applied scientific techniques: selective breeding, genetic manipulation, and so on, with the aim of accelerating evolution by increasing human intelligence, strength, endurance—"

"The Chrysalis Project!" Dennis exclaimed.

She gave him a puzzled look. This sounded vaguely familiar, like something Dennis had expounded upon at some point, but most of his fringier conspiracy theories blurred together in her head, if they lodged there at all. A lot of them went in one ear and out the other.

"I told you all about this," he insisted, no doubt accurately. "Chrysalis was an early, top-secret attempt to create a new breed of superhumans back in the seventies. The Powers That Be suppressed the truth about whether they succeeded or not, but the untold story can't stay buried forever . . . and it all began with Chrysalis."

At least according to the internet, Melinda thought.

"Be that as it may," Wilder said, "Chrysalis—or projects like it— spawned various splinter programs, including one focused more on longevity than superhuman strength or intelligence. So when it comes to me looking somewhat younger than my years . . . let's just say I have very good genes."

"By design?" Melinda asked. "Thanks to . . . eugenics?"

If nothing else, that struck her as somewhat more plausible than space aliens, even if she still wasn't sure where the stealth UFO fit in.

Wilder nodded. "Unfortunately, that word has acquired very ugly connotations, in large part because of its unfortunate associations with Nazism and other vile racial-purity agendas, but also because, as Mister Berry just demonstrated, of various wild rumors and conspiracy theories involving human genetic engineering." He stopped petting Enkidu, who squeaked in protest. "Can you blame me for not wanting my life's work, and personal history, tarred with that brush? I can assure you the word 'eugenics' appears nowhere on Amaranth's website, let alone in my bio."

"Probably a good call," she conceded.

"I knew I could count on your media savvy." He poured himself some more wine and lifted his glass to her. "Not to mention your instincts and initiative. Tell me, would you be interested in taking over as

Amaranth's new social media director? I'm certain we can offer you a highly attractive salary and benefits."

And there it was: flattery and a bribe wrapped up in one sweet package. Too bad she wasn't for sale.

"Of course, you would have to sign an NDA," he added. "And Mister Berry as well."

Naturally, she thought. "Thanks for the glowing endorsement and tempting offer, but I'm an investigative journalist, not a PR flack."

Wilder scowled. "I had no idea podcasters had such elevated professional standards, but perhaps I'm showing my age, figuratively. Are you sure you won't reconsider? I'm quite amenable to sweetening the deal to make it more than worth your while."

It was tempting. A cushy, well-paying position at Amaranth certainly beat returning to the mind-numbing drudgery of corporate videos, but that once-urgent concern felt distinctly trivial at this point. As Dennis kept reminding her, they were playing in the big leagues now. And the bigger the story, the bigger her duty to the truth. Dropping the investigation now would mean becoming part of a cover-up. In a very real sense, she'd feel like she was letting Gillian down.

Plus, who was to say that Wilder wouldn't throw her under the bus later on, once he got her signature on that NDA?

"No thanks. Nothing personal, but it wouldn't feel right. Think of it as a conflict of interest."

Wilder turned his attention to Dennis. "What about you, Mister Berry? Do you feel the same way? I'd rather have you working for me than against me. Perhaps you'd feel more comfortable that way too?"

Was that a veiled threat? Or was Wilder just trying to exploit Dennis's paranoia to his own ends?

Dennis swallowed hard before answering.

"I'm with Melinda." Unable to sit still any longer, he rose and looked longingly at the exit from the study. His foot tapped nervously against the floor. "Are we done here? Can we go now?"

Melinda stayed where she was. "Soon, I promise, but I still have questions." She took a sip of wine before engaging Wilder again. "Just because I passed on your generous job offer doesn't mean we don't still have matters to discuss. I might be persuaded to present your story in a more favorable light, maybe even soft-pedal the eugenics angle, in exchange for more of your time and whatever else you may have learned about Gillian's disappearance over the years. Perhaps even an actual interview at some point, on the record?"

"I'm not sure that would be in my best interests," he said dourly.

"Then you'll just have to trust us to report what we already know as we see fit, along with whatever else we may dig up on the connection between Wilmer Offutt and Orlando Wilder."

How was that for playing hardball?

"C'mon, Melinda," Dennis pleaded. "It's no use. He's not going to tell us anything he doesn't want us to know. Let's get out of here, please!"

She didn't budge.

I walk away now and Wilder will think I'm just bluffing. I have to play this out without blinking.

"Wait for me outside," she told Dennis. "Orlando and I aren't finished yet."

"No," Wilder said. "I think not."

His coolly emphatic tone spooked Dennis enough that he started edging toward the door, very obviously torn between staying with her and bolting for safety. He couldn't take much more of this, she realized; he was on the verge of running out on her, which might just make things easier in the short term. She couldn't handle him *and* get tough with Wilder right now.

I really *need to make it up to him when all of this is over.*

"Iduna, seal study."

A door slammed shut automatically, locking them in. *"Done,"* the house answered.

Apparently Wilder wanted Dennis to stay put for the time being.

"Crap, crap, crap!"

Dennis clutched his head, running both hands through his hair. He looked even more trapped and panicked than he had in the vestibule earlier. Frantic eyes searched desperately for a way out, zeroing in on the tall picture windows.

"Don't even think about it, Mister Berry. Those windows are transparent aluminum, all but unbreakable. And even if you could breach them, they lead only to a long, fatal drop to rocks below."

Not surprisingly, Wilder's words did little to calm Dennis. He reeled about the study, practically tearing his hair out while venting to himself. Vasily watched Dennis like a hawk, taking care to always stay between him and Wilder.

"How is this happening? How did I let this happen? What are we going to do . . . ?"

Melinda didn't blame him for losing it.

"What the freak, Orlando? You're taking us hostage now?"

"Hardly. As I stated before, I mean you no harm, but I can't have either of you storming off, even just as a negotiating tactic, before I make my position absolutely clear."

"Which is?" she asked warily.

"I've proffered the carrot, now here's the stick. You two do *not* want to go to war with me, and, no, I'm not threatening any crude gangster methods. I'm talking lawyers and money and influence. Trust me when I say that I'm not without friends in high places. You embarrass me in any way, and I'll drag your reputations through the mud, discredit everything you say, bury you in lawsuits, and generally make you laughingstocks, which, truthfully, won't be difficult given the bizarre, far-fetched nature of your claims. You want to be taken seriously as an 'investigative journalist' or whatever?" He chortled. "By the time I'm done with you, you'll be lucky to find work writing X-rated fortune cookies."

Melinda's blood pressure rose. "Are you serious?"

"Use your brain, Melinda. Think about your future. Which would you prefer: a lucrative career with plenty of perks and opportunities for advancement, or an excruciating trial by media that's bound to cost you dearly? Not to mention your loved ones?"

She didn't have to think about it. She wasn't about to be bribed *or* bullied.

"Listen to me, you smug, vermin-loving son of a boomer!" She leaped to her feet, alarming Enkidu, who sprang from Wilder's lap and scurried for safety as she got in Wilder's face in a big way. "If you think for one minute that—"

Vasily seized her from behind, grunting something in what sounded like Romanian. She experienced a moment of déjà vu, recalling the muscular limo driver pulling her away from Wilder on the sidewalk outside Amaranth. *Must be nice,* she thought, *to always have hired help on hand to keep people from invading your space.*

"Get your paws off me, King Kong. This is between me and your boss!"

Glass shattered loudly against Vasily's skull, splattering her with wine. His grip loosened as his hefty body slumped heavily against her, almost knocking her over as he collapsed to the floor. Spinning around, she spotted Dennis standing behind the fallen bodyguard, gripping a broken wine bottle by its neck.

After smacking Vasily over the head with it.

"He was distracted. It was our only chance!"

Ohmigosh, she thought, horrified. This was all her fault. She should have realized how close Dennis was to snapping, especially after she saw that gun. *But I never thought he'd actually resort to violence. That's not who he is!*

Until now.

"Are you totally insane?" Wilder lurched to his feet, his face flushed with anger. "I'll have you charged with assault!" He stared at the sprawled form of Vasily, who thankfully still appeared to be breathing. "Iduna, call the—"

"Shut up! Don't say another word!" Dennis brandished the jagged end of the broken wine bottle. "You're going to let us out of here . . . now!"

Wilder went pale, anger giving way to alarm. He held his palms out defensively. "Stay back, you maniac! Don't come any closer!"

"I said shut up!"

"Put that down, Dennis, please." Melinda tried to talk him down before anyone else got hurt. "Don't make things worse than they already are. You're not thinking straight. You don't know what you're doing."

"I'm trying to save us both . . . before we vanish like Gillian!"

Melinda didn't know what to do or say. Things were happening too fast, spiraling out of control. On the floor between them, Vasily moaned, stirring slightly; Melinda thanked goodness he was still alive, but wasn't sure she wanted him to wake up too soon. That could just escalate an already precarious situation.

"Please, Dennis, this isn't you. You don't want to do this. You're not saving us; you're scaring me. Put the bottle down."

"Listen to her!" Wilder was trying to put up a brave front, but failing badly. "You want to go? Fine. Iduna, unseal the study! Open all doors to the outside!"

The door to the study swung open. *"Done."*

Melinda felt a twinge of hope. Maybe Dennis would choose flight over fight, leaving Wilder unharmed. She could calm him down once they were free of the mansion, maybe convince him to turn himself in and plead temporary insanity. They were going to need a good lawyer, that was for sure.

But instead of taking the offered escape route, Dennis kept his sights on Wilder, menacing him with the jagged end of the bottle. He licked his lips nervously.

"Go!" Wilder urged him. "You wanted to leave, do it!"

"And then what?" Dennis stepped over Vasily, waving his makeshift weapon. "I can't let you keep after us. Haunting us, hounding us, never giving us a moment's peace, never letting me sleep . . ."

"I'm warning you! Stay back!"

An ashen Wilder reached beneath his blazer—for a weapon?

"I knew it!"

Dennis lunged at Wilder with the broken bottle. Melinda's mind flash-forwarded to a vivid image of him plunging the jagged glass into Wilder's face or throat, destroying both men's lives forever. Desperate, she tackled Dennis, slamming into him while frantically groping for the arm holding the bottle. Knocked off-balance, he stumbled over Vasily's prone form, causing both him and Melinda to tumble to the floor. She landed on top of him, his rangy body cushioning her own. Glass broke against the floor, much to her relief. Dennis gasped out loud.

I did it, she thought. *I stopped him from killing Wilder. Kept him from becoming a murderer.*

The fall knocked the wind out of her, but adrenaline and necessity gave her barely a moment to catch her breath. Scrambling clumsily off Dennis, she looked urgently for the bottle, hoping that that the crash had shattered it completely, but she couldn't immediately locate it. Still dazed from the impact, it took her a second to grasp that the arm that had been holding the bottle was beneath him, that he must have landed on it . . . hard.

A wet, agonized gurgle escaped him.

Her heart plummeted. "Oh, fuck, no."

Praying she was wrong, she rolled him over to discover it was even worse than she feared. The neck of the bottle was jabbed deep into his abdomen, right below his rib cage. Bright arterial froth bubbled from the edge of the wound and spurted from the hollow glass shard like water from a tap. He coughed up crimson, bleeding internally.

He was dying, right before her eyes.

Because of her. Because of *Cetacean*.

"No, don't die on me! Hang on! You always have my back, remember? This isn't how it's supposed to go . . ."

She crouched over him, freaking out and not knowing what to do. Should she remove the glass from his gut or would that do more harm than good? Blood and wine soaked through her clothes. Sobbing, in shock, she dimly registered Wilder coming up behind her.

"We're losing him! We have to do something!"

"It's too late, Melinda. I'm sorry, I truly am."

He pressed something cold and metallic against her jugular vein. Air hissed and she felt a sudden sting.

Then the world mercifully went away.

Chapter Thirty-Eight

2268

Sky-high plumes of smoke, ash, and dust rose from the blasted remains of the tower as Kirk and his fellow escapees clambered up onto the top of the high stone wall surrounding the city. The devastating disruptor strike, blazing down from the night sky without warning to the unsuspecting populace, threw the coliseum into an even greater uproar. Guards and any remaining spectators gaped in shock and dismay, understandably distracted from the tumult in the stands by what must have seemed like an unnatural green thunderbolt hurled down by the gods. More than a few guards abandoned their pursuit of Kirk and the other fugitives to rush for their homes, their families, or perhaps to the suzerain's fortress to render aid and force of arms. Gazing over at the suddenly missing tower, Kirk could only wonder what impact the Klingons' brazen attack would have on the Atrazians' culture, politics, and future development. Would the fall of the tower pass into history as merely a freak natural disaster or would it inflict a lasting trauma on generations to come?

What had Yorba been thinking? Did she truly think halting Siroth's illicit experiments was worth this extreme a response? Kirk intended to have words with her, eventually, but first they had to make good their escape from the city, taking advantage of the confusion.

"Quickly!" he urged the landing party, Doctor Hamparian, Yorba, and her last surviving lieutenant, Wrultz. "On the double!"

A steel piton, driven into the top of the wall by Wrultz, secured the rope the fugitives used to rappel down the city's outer wall to the ground at least fifty meters below. Temporary camps and tent cities, established by travelers who could or would not pay for accommodation within the city proper, cluttered the terrain. Another rope, the one they'd used to climb onto the wall, had already been pulled up to delay their pursuers. Sulu and Landon went first, to test the rope and establish a defensive posture at the base of the wall. McCoy accompanied Hamparian next, carrying out the landing party's original mission to reclaim the missing scientist. Kirk kept a close eye on the two Klingons as Hamparian descended; he hadn't forgotten Yorba's willingness to sacrifice Hamparian to the bloodbeaks rather than risk losing the scientist to the Federation. She would need watching.

"See you below, Kirk." Yorba accepted a disruptor pistol from Wrultz before descending to the ground with both speed and agility. Kirk counted on Sulu, Landon, and McCoy to keep Hamparian safe from Yorba, on top of their shared need to get away from the city as soon as humanly (or Klingonly) possible. For the moment, they were all still united in a common cause: escape.

Yorba's departure left only Kirk, Levine, and Wrultz atop the wall.

"I go next," the Klingon declared, his tone daring the other two men to challenge him. "After the colonel."

"Be my guest," Kirk said.

He didn't know whether Wrultz had a double cross in mind or if the man simply wanted to stick close to his superior's side, but Kirk preferred to have both Klingons before him instead of behind him. Wrultz grunted, as though he'd expected an argument, but wasted no time following after Yorba. Kirk turned to Levine.

"You next."

"But, Captain—" the security officer started to protest. He glanced with concern at a handful of Atrazian guards making their way toward them through the lingering smoke and chaos. Although reduced in numbers thanks to the fallen Klingons and the game-changing catastrophe at the fortress, they were almost to the top of the stands. Kirk crouched low atop the wall to present a smaller target for any guard still wielding a crossbow. He intended to guard the landing party's escape route until everyone else was safely on the ground.

"That's an order, mister. I need you providing security for Hamparian and the rest. Got that?"

To his credit, Levine didn't question him. "Aye, Captain. Don't keep us waiting."

Moving briskly, even before Wrultz reached the ground, the athletic young crewman was over the edge and sliding down the rope.

And none too soon. A strident voice, hoarse from charging through Sulu's smokescreen, hollered from just below the wall at the rear of the coliseum. A wild crossbow bolt whooshed past Kirk's skull, and he dropped flat onto the rough-hewn top of the wall to avoid a second shot.

"Seize him! Varkat will have our heads if we let that foreign devil get away!"

Kirk hoped, for the guards' sake, that was hyperbole. He bought time by shining a light in the oncoming soldiers' eyes, blinding them with the glare, then tried to capitalize on the fresh shock of the Klingons' blazing assault from orbit by crying out:

"Beware! The sky is angry again! Run for your lives!"

Already dazzled by the incandescent beam of the light, the guards paused to glance fearfully up at the heavens. Who knew if and when more viridian fire might shoot down from above? This had been a night of unimaginable surprises and upheavals, or so it must have seemed to the shaken Atrazian guards.

They froze, just long enough for Kirk to make his exit from the coliseum. He'd had enough of being the star attraction in this bloodthirsty exhibition and wasn't about to stick around for any curtain calls. Securing his light and communicator, he rolled off the edge of the wall and grabbed onto the rope with both hands. With no time to rappel down the wall, he slid down the rope instead. Friction burned his palms as he descended at what felt like only slightly less than terminal velocity.

But would even that be fast enough?

"The rope! Cut the rope! Let him fall!"

Glancing up, Kirk saw that a guard had already managed to climb atop the wall. The man started hacking away at the rope with a knife while Kirk still had a long way to go before reaching the ground. A fall from this height would put a rapid end to his flight. Atraz's gravity was far too earthlike in that respect.

I could use a good pair of levitation boots right now . . .

A scarlet phaser beam lit up the night, stunning the knife-wielding guard, who tumbled backward into the stands, dropping out of sight. Kirk gasped in relief as he swiftly made it to the bottom of the wall. He touched down hard on the ground, the impact jarring him through the soles of his boots. He glanced over at Sulu, whose phaser was still aimed upward. Another short red pulse severed the rope from its moorings, causing it to plummet to the ground, cutting off their escape route behind them. The eagle-eyed helmsman shrugged apologetically at Kirk.

"Sorry, Captain. I know we're supposed to avoid using our phasers in front of the locals, but—"

"Under the circumstances, I'm inclined to overlook this instance. Nice shooting, Lieutenant."

Overall, Kirk judged, the rescue party had demonstrated considerable restraint when it came to displaying their phasers, confining their use to brief, discreet flashes of phaser fire as opposed to tearing through the opposition with weapons blazing.

Unlike the Klingons' egregious attack from space.

Kirk surveyed their new surroundings. Tents, wagons, and campfires spread out from the base of the wall, fringing the city. The fugitives scrambled away from the wall to get clear of any attacks from above, but were still too close to Reliux for comfort. Despite the commotion at the fortress, which was presumably of more urgent concern to the suzerain and his troops, Kirk still anticipated a number of city guards being dispatched to recapture the escapees. He and the others needed to put Reliux well behind them.

"What now, Sulu?" Kirk figured the helmsman's rescue plan extended beyond simply escaping the arena, but he also assumed that Sulu wouldn't be so reckless as to have *Galileo* waiting in plain view of the city; that would be bending the Prime Directive out of recognition. "Are we running anywhere in particular?"

"Not running, Captain. Riding."

Sulu whistled sharply. Moments later, an answering whistle came from the shadows between a row of tents, followed by the clamor of pounding hooves as a half dozen horned *vuseco*s arrived on the scene, led by a mounted Jaheed, who had five other ungulates on a string. Dark coats of fur, draped with black blankets, helped the animals blend into the night's shadows.

"O Captain!" Jaheed hailed Kirk the old-fashioned way. "It heartens me to see you both free and unharmed!"

"You're a welcome sight as well." Kirk took charge, calling out to the others, "Saddle up, everyone! Pair off as needed."

Yorba balked at approaching a waiting *vuseco*, which didn't appear too keen on her either. The beast snorted and pawed the ground, lowering its shaggy head to warn the Klingon of its horns. She backed away uncertainly.

"Is there a problem, Colonel?" Kirk asked.

"I'm a decorated intelligence officer from a highly advanced civilization, not one of your Earthborn cowboys." She masked her unease behind a look of withering disdain. "I do not *ride* livestock."

Kirk made only a halfhearted attempt to conceal his amusement. He picked out a mount and released it from the lead line. "All right then. You're with me."

Just as well, he thought. *Keep your enemies close and all that.*

"Make haste!" Jaheed called out over the rumble of massive metal gears grumbling. "The city gates are opening! The suzerain's troops will soon be upon us!"

That dire reality overcame whatever objections Yorba might have had otherwise.

"Hu'tegh!"

Cursing, she let Kirk help her onto the restive *vuseco* before he deftly mounted behind her and took hold of the reins, even as the rest of their party saddled up as well. McCoy shared a steed with Hamparian, while Wrultz reluctantly joined Landon on an ungulate, looking no more pleased or comfortable astride a *vuseco* than Yorba was; Klingon schooling was clearly deficient when it came to riding lessons. Jaheed, Sulu, and Levine each ended up with mounts on their own, with Jaheed leading the way as they bounded away from Reliux at a rapid pace. Kirk hoped the doubly burdened *vuseco*s would be able to keep up.

"Follow me, O Captain and comrades!"

The mounted fugitives raced through the night. After more than a day in captivity, Kirk felt an undeniable sense of exhilaration as the ungulate thundered beneath him, a warm summer wind blowing in his face. His enjoyment was not shared by Yorba, judging from her tense posture and unhappy utterances. Kirk found himself getting a crash course in Klingon profanity.

"*QI'yaH!*"

Slowing down or dismounting was not an option. Sooner than he would have liked, Kirk heard angry shouts and speeding hooves behind them. Glancing back over his shoulder, his eyes adjusting to the dark, he spied blazing torches held aloft by over a dozen mounted soldiers, churning up a cloud of dust as they rode after Kirk and company. Toppled tower or not, it seemed the city guards were not about to let the escaped prisoners elude the arena without a chase.

Jaheed had better know where he's taking us, Kirk thought.

Ideally, they would not be trusting their fate to a guide whom they had first found strung up by his enemies, but events hadn't left them much choice. Jaheed was bound to know the local terrain and territory better than any of them.

In theory.

To shake their pursuers, they veered away from anything resembling a main thoroughfare, speeding instead down narrow dirt roads and paths, most of which barely qualified as trails, and through fields of leafy stalks, vines, grasses, and other crops. They splashed down the middle of a shallow creek, then up onto a slippery, overgrown riverbank when the rushing current grew too deep to navigate. Startled villagers and farmers, roused perhaps by the uncanny green thunderbolt that had split the sky earlier, yelped and ran for shelter as the mounted strangers barreled past. Farther on, in a relatively undeveloped stretch of countryside, a brick-and-mortar footbridge spanned frothing whitewater rapids. Levine, riding at the rear of the party, waited until they were all across the bridge before twisting at the waist to fire his phaser back at the bridge, which flared brightly as it was reduced to atoms. Glowing particles swarmed like red-hot fireflies, then evaporated into the night.

Smart move, Kirk thought, nodding in approval.

With any luck, disintegrating the bridge would slow down their pursuers to some degree, perhaps long enough for the landing party to find someplace safe to call *Galileo* for a pickup? They still wouldn't be able to return to the *Enterprise*, what with that battle cruiser lurking in orbit, but the shuttlecraft could readily transport them beyond the reach of the suzerain and his soldiers, even to another continent if they felt so inclined.

At the moment, though, Kirk's *vuseco* was already laboring beneath the weight of its two humanoid passengers. It was panting hard and slowing despite his best attempts to spur it on. Glancing back again, Kirk saw torches milling about on the other side of the rapids. How long would it take Varkat's soldiers to find another way or place to ford the river? And how much longer could the escapees' own mounts keep up this headlong pace?

"They're still after us!" Kirk called to Jaheed over the hoofbeats. "How do we lose them?"

"Do not lose heart, O Captain!" the guide shouted. "Sanctuary, of a sort, awaits!"

Of a sort?

A murky grove of withered, skeletal trees came into view. Formerly orderly rows, now clotted with underbrush and fallen tree trunks and branches, hinted that this had once been an orchard of some kind, but the blighted limbs looked dead and barren, as though it was the depths of winter and not early summer. Rotted logs suggested years of neglect. This was a ghost orchard.

Jaheed led them through the lifeless grove, weaving through dead and dying trees, until they arrived at what was evidently the ruins of an abandoned estate. They rode past the crumbling stone foundations of a mansion or villa that had apparently burned to the ground long ago to reach a barn-sized outbuilding whose weathered stone walls were still standing, even if its roof was long gone. Thorny briar bushes obscured the structure's gaping entrance. Kirk slowed his exhausted mount as the party took refuge within the building. Dilapidated stalls revealed that it had once been used as a stable. Buckets of water and fresh bales of hay waited to refresh the weary ungulates. An earthen ramp appeared to lead to a lower level. An underground storage area, storm cellar, or emergency escape tunnel?

"You see, O Captain!" Jaheed brought his mount to a halt. "Rest and respite for man and beast, at least for a time."

"And just in time."

Kirk dismounted and helped Yorba do the same. She did not thank him but looked relieved to be back on her own two legs. The rest of the party did the same. Kirk inspected the premises, keeping the beam of his light low so that the light wouldn't escape through numerous gaps in the masonry where the chinks and mortar had crumbled away.

"What is this place?" he asked.

"A very sad story, O Captain. Once this was a prosperous farm, but a blight caused it to fall into ruin, and it became shunned as a place of ill fortune." He led his mount to water. "Some say it's now a frequent haunt of smugglers, but I would not know anything about that."

"Of course not," Kirk said dryly.

Not that he could complain about Jaheed's choice of hideaway. They were badly in need of a place to catch their breaths and regroup, although they probably shouldn't linger too long; Kirk suspected it was only a matter of time before their pursuers tracked them to this site, whose reputation as a smugglers' lair might well be known by Varkat's men. The sooner *Galileo* came to get them, the better.

He rescued his communicator from his belt and flipped it open. "Kirk to *Galileo*—"

"Belay that order, Kirk." Yorba leveled her disruptor pistol at him, as did Wrultz. Her free hand reached for her own communicator. "We'll be calling for *our* shuttlecraft now . . . and taking Hamparian with us."

"I don't think so," Sulu said.

His own phaser was aimed at the Klingons, as were Landon's and Levine's. They spread out to surround Yorba and her lieutenant. Kirk positioned himself between the Klingons and Hamparian while McCoy also shielded the scientist with his own body. Swallowing hard, Jaheed slipped back among the recuperating *vuseco*s, doing his best not to be noticed.

"Oh joy," McCoy drawled. "An old-fashioned standoff. Just what we need to make the night complete."

"Get your patient somewhere private, Doctor." Kirk gestured at the ramp to the lower level. He wanted Hamparian out of the line of fire if and when the shooting started; a disruptor blast at full power could possibly burn through a body or two to strike its target. "The colonel and I need to renegotiate our alliance, it seems."

"Don't test me, Kirk." Yorba's finger rested on the trigger of the disruptor; only a slight movement would send a disruptor beam straight at Kirk. "Our weapons are not set on stun."

"I don't doubt it." Kirk didn't budge. "But the moment you fire, my people will stun you and your associate, so there's no scenario here in which you walk away with Hamparian. That's not happening. Period."

"Unless you choose your own life over a turncoat scientist who deserted your precious Federation of her own free will, in order to violate your laws with impunity. Hardly worthy of such an extreme sacrifice, I would think."

Kirk didn't bother pointing out that Hamparian had risked everything to save them from the arena. Yorba didn't seem like the grateful type.

"I have my orders. Hamparian stays with us, no matter what."

"A pity."

Her pistol was aimed directly at Kirk's heart, suggesting that while she may not have ever learned to ride, she had definitely studied human anatomy.

"I have my orders too."

Chapter Thirty-Nine

2024

Melinda awoke to the sound of someone humming a familiar melody. Groggy and disoriented, it took her a moment to place the tune.

"Forever Young."

Wilder! she realized with a start. She tried to sit up, only to find herself strapped inside what appeared to be a translucent, torpedo-shaped capsule resting perhaps a yard above the floor of a well-lit laboratory equipped with plenty of sophisticated-looking medical technology. The sleek, curved lid of the capsule was only partly closed, covering most of her body but leaving her head and shoulders open to the air. Unknown machinery buzzed and chirped beneath her, in whatever apparatus was supporting the capsule. Foam padding within the capsule further restricted her movement as she struggled fruitlessly to free herself. That her prison was roughly the size of a coffin did not escape her.

"What the—? Get me out of here!"

"Ah, you're awake. Right on schedule."

She could just rotate her head enough to see Wilder turn away from a sterile black epoxy workbench a few paces away. A smooth, hairless scalp suggested that he had indeed been wearing a wig before, perhaps to distinguish himself from Wilmer Offutt. He had traded his blazer for a clean white lab coat. Enkidu perched on his shoulder as he calmly approached her.

"Please refrain from testing your restraints; I assure you they're quite secure. We can't have you dislodging any of the IV connections, which are already in place."

IVs, as in hooked up to her bloodstream? A jolt of terror dispelled any last trace of fogginess from her brain. What had Wilder done to her, and what else was he planning to do? Some kind of ghastly science experiment?

"Let me out of this casket-sized test tube! Unhook me right now!"

"My apologies if you suffer from claustrophobia. I took the liberty of dosing you with a mild tranquilizer just in case, as well as to help you cope in general." He gazed down at her like a physician checking on a patient, applying his most comforting bedside manner to soothe any anxieties she might be experiencing. "It seemed best in light of recent events."

Abruptly, cruelly, it all came back to her: Dennis freaking out and clobbering Vasily with the wine bottle, then going at Wilder with the broken bottle, her frantic attempt to stop him from hurting anyone else, and . . .

"Dennis?"

"Gone, I'm afraid, although I'm happy to say that Vasily received only a minor concussion. He's recuperating upstairs as we speak, after helping me transport you down here to my private lab and workspace."

Not Amaranth then, she registered. A private basement lab—for secret projects best conducted away from his corporate facilities? Like disposing of nosy podcasters who wouldn't leave him alone?

"For what it's worth," he continued, "I'm genuinely sorry about the loss of your partner, even if he brought about his own demise through his unreasoning paranoia. Believe me when I say that I value life above all things. Death is abhorrent to me."

That Dennis was truly gone hit Melinda like a whaler's harpoon, piercing her heart. It didn't feel real, like this was just another of his far-out conspiracy theories and alternate realities. She felt numb, as though she was the one who had died instead. Her throat tightened. Tears blurred her vision. Guilt made her grief even more agonizing. It was her obsession, and stubbornness, that had driven Dennis over the edge. How had she not seen just how great a toll it had been taking on him?

I'm sorry, dude. I swear, I was going to make it up to you.

Now she'd never get the chance.

"If it's any consolation, you saved my life, Melinda. Don't forget that. I certainly won't."

Wilder's words brought her back to her own dire situation. For all she knew, she would be joining Dennis soon enough.

"You've got a funny way of showing it," she said bitterly. "What kind of mad-scientist shit is this?"

"A drastic measure, I admit, but you and the late Mister Berry have forced my hand. You've already learned too much about me and shown no inclination to keep it to yourself. Nor can I tolerate the increased scrutiny of a criminal investigation into the circumstances of your partner's death." He shook his head forlornly. "You should have accepted my job offer."

"I'm guessing that's off the table now?"

A pained smile answered her. "I think we're well beyond that."

He placed a finger against her throat, checking her pulse. She would have slapped or bitten it if she could.

"So what now? You're just going to make me—make all of this—disappear?"

"In a manner of speaking." He withdrew his hand. "As far as the rest of the world will be concerned, you and Mister Berry never arrived here today. At this very moment, Iduna is using cleaning bots to remove every last drop of blood, every stray fingerprint or trace of DNA, from the premises. Vasily is sworn to silence, the limo driver already paid off. My best private operatives are carefully culling any incriminating evidence from your home and devices. Trust me, we're being *very* thorough."

Melinda could just imagine.

"It's not going to work. We told friends and family we were coming here today," she lied. "People will come looking for us. We can't just disappear without anyone noticing!"

"True, but even if you did inform people of your plans, I'll simply claim you never showed up . . . and there will be no evidence to the contrary. Meanwhile, *Cetacean* has already conveniently laid the groundwork for your ever-so-puzzling disappearances, with its compelling insinuations of government conspiracies, international espionage, and even extraterrestrial encounters. You've provided no shortage of likely culprits who might want to silence you. Ultimately, you'll be just another unsolved missing-persons case, vanishing into thin air like Gillian Taylor. Who knows? Maybe someone will produce a podcast about you."

She glared at him. "You'll forgive me if I don't find that funny."

"Perhaps in time. A very long time, probably."

She guessed she was missing a private joke. "What's that supposed to mean?" She glanced around as much as she was able, taking in the impressive array of high-tech gear, which implied something more elaborate than simply dumping her body in the Bay. "What exactly are you up to?"

Wilder lifted Enkidu from his shoulder and cradled the rat against his chest.

"You present me with a problem, Melinda, ethically as well as practically. You saved my life . . . at great personal cost. I owe you for that, more than you may realize, for far more than an ordinary lifetime was nearly lost there."

"Wait." Her reporter's instincts kicked in despite her desperate circumstances. "Are you saying what I think you're saying?"

He nodded.

"After what you've sacrificed for my sake, the least I can do is provide you with some of the answers you crave. Your Mister Berry was quite right. The Chrysalis Project, and like endeavors, are no mere urban legends. I'm indeed the genetically engineered progeny of an equally covert splinter program devoted to extending human life-spans. Conceived in a test tube, I was born in 1967, nearly sixty years ago. My original birth name is not your concern, but yes, I was Wilmer Offutt before I became Orlando Wilder, and will doubtless acquire many other names and identities over what promises to be a very long existence, albeit still a finite one . . . for now."

He glanced down at the rat resting in the crook of his arm. "Would you believe Enkidu is pushing ten years old? That's several times longer than the average lab rat. Credit his distinguished heritage. He's cloned from one of the first successful test subjects of the experiment that led to my own conception." He stroked the supposedly long-lived rodent. "As I told you before, we go way back, genetically speaking, that is. This is Enkidu number six, to be precise."

"So he's not literally immortal?" she asked, fascinated; as ever, her curiosity demanded answers, regardless of any other pressing concerns. "And neither are you?"

"Not yet. I *am* aging, although far more slowly than the average human specimen." His expression darkened, deeper, more intense emotions burning through his genial bedside manner. "But here's the paradox, Melinda. Knowing that, barring accidents and broken bottles wielded by insecure people, I can expect to live an almost impossibly long time only makes it all the more galling that even my extraordinary life-span has an expiration date, that I'm ultimately doomed to gutter out like any other mortal. What is the point, I ask you, of acquiring all that knowledge and experience, all those memories, just to lose them in the end?"

His deep voice thrummed with emotion, betraying the depth of his obsession.

"None! None at all. But I refuse to accept that death is inevitable. You saved my life, granting me countless decades to come, but even that bounty will all go to waste unless I use those many added years to find a way to become truly immortal." He peered down at her, driven eyes blazing beneath bushy brows. "And you, Melinda, may have finally pointed me in the right direction."

He pointed upward.

"My mistake, it seems, was looking for the secret here on Earth when I should have been aiming at the stars. If Milly's miracle pill indeed came to Earth via a UFO, then perhaps the answer lies on an alien world far beyond ours?"

Was he serious? He sounded insane, but if he was really almost sixty years old, thanks to some long-ago genetic engineering, Melinda wasn't sure what the difference between sanity and insanity was anymore. Hadn't she just spent the last several weeks documenting allegedly true accounts of a medical miracle, invisible aircraft, and now a man who never seemed to age? Who was to say what crazy really meant these days? Dennis would absolutely be on the same page as Wilder here, and it turned out he'd been right about a lot of things.

But still . . . was Wilder actually planning a trip to outer space?

"Good luck getting there," she said skeptically.

"Easier said than done, I agree. After all, I can hardly count on a friendly UFO to swing by to offer me a ride. No, I'm simply going to have to stay alive long enough for humanity to make its own way out into the cosmos."

"Assuming we last that long," she said. "You looked at the headlines lately?"

"Call me an optimist. I'd have to be, wouldn't I, to aspire to living forever?"

Or deranged, she thought. "You may have to wait a very long time, even for a potential Methuselah like you. I'm no space buff, but even I know that we haven't even set foot on Mars yet, let alone figured out any sort of faster-than-light drive that would allow us to travel beyond our own little solar system. In fact, according to Einstein, isn't that supposed to be completely impossible outside of science fiction?"

Her cogent argument failed to discourage him.

"You forget that I'm living proof that science can achieve the impossible. Unlike you, I have faith that human ingenuity will crack the FTL problem eventually. Just wait and see."

She considered her own rapidly shrinking life expectancy. "Somehow I doubt I'll be around to find out, one way or another."

"I wouldn't be so sure of that." Putting down Enkidu, he patted the sci-fi sarcophagus holding her prisoner. "Did Mister Berry ever mention that Amaranth has made great strides in cryogenics?"

As a matter of fact, he had.

"Hang on!" she objected, alarmed by the obvious implication. "You're not planning to freeze me alive, are you?" Her blood went cold, maybe only slightly ahead of schedule. "What about all that noble talk before about meaning us no harm? Now you're going to use me as a guinea pig to test out some sort of refrigerated coffin, turn me into a human Popsicle? This is premeditated murder and you know it, you hypocritical phony!"

"Murder?" He looked positively wounded by the accusation. "I wasn't lying, Melinda. Your life is safe in my hands." He smiled down at her. "Indeed, you're going to live longer than you ever dreamed of."

He reached out and flicked a switch on the apparatus beneath the capsule. An icy sensation began flowing through her veins, along with a sudden lassitude. Her trapped body felt unbearably heavy all of a sudden. Her eyelids drooped, even as the lid of the capsule slid upward toward her head and shoulders, moving automatically to seal her in completely. A flash of panic at the prospect was swiftly muted by whatever drugs were already coursing through her system. She couldn't keep her eyes open any longer.

"Sweet dreams, Melinda. I'll see you in the future, somewhere in the universe."

Chapter Forty

The battle above Atraz was taking its toll on both vessels.

"Shields down to forty percent," Chekov reported. "Plasma and radiation leaks reported on decks nine, twelve, and twenty-one. Turbolifts out of commission below deck seventeen. Life-support compromised on the hangar deck, botanical gardens, brig, and science labs."

"Sickbay receiving multiple casualties," Uhura informed Spock. "No fatalities so far."

"Emergency bulkheads sealed," Scott said. "Repair crews at work or en route to affected areas. All Jefferies tubes still accessible. Diverting discretionary power to primary systems."

The acrid odor of fried circuitry, along with scattered wisps of smoke, contaminated the once-pristine atmosphere of the bridge. Tense personnel labored to restore broken and malfunctioning consoles to full working order, while other crew members made do at auxiliary stations. Energy surges and shock waves had tested the sturdy construction and built-in redundancies of the ships' hardware and systems, even as the *Enterprise* and the *BortaS* continued to exchange heavy fire, speeding past, above, and below each other as they circled the planet at impulse speed.

"Brace yourself!" Rahda called out from the helm. "Here she comes again!"

On the viewscreen, the battle cruiser swooped toward them, growing larger in perspective by the millisecond. Caustic green energy lit up the screen, momentarily overwhelming the brightness filters. Spock's inner eyelids blinked against the glare as yet another disruptor blast rocked the *Enterprise*, striking with increasing force as the ship's deflector shields steadily weakened over the course of the conflict. The impact challenged the inertial dampers, resulting in a gravitational tilt across the bridge. An overworked yeoman, dashing from one station to another, was thrown off his feet and slammed into the turbolift doors.

Other members of the bridge crew grabbed onto consoles, railings, and seatbacks to keep from falling. Crackling and sizzling noises emanated from within the environmental subsystems station; its monitors and displays went dead.

But the *BortaS* was in similar straits. Its latest attack brought it within easy range of the *Enterprise*, which fired its phasers at the same time that the battle cruiser's disruptor cannons flared green once more. Working in tandem, Rahda and Farrell scored a direct hit on the Klingons' forward torpedo launcher. The resulting energy discharge was of sufficient magnitude to suggest that the phaser beam had inflicted considerable damage on the launcher, despite whatever protection was afforded by the *BortaS*'s progressively threadbare shields. Scorch marks on the battle cruiser's hull, along with trails of leaked vapor and plasma, attested to the wounds sustained by the ship. Spock had no doubt that the *Enterprise* had also been visibly scarred.

The mathematics of attrition indeed, he thought.

"Shields down to thirty-seven point three percent," Chekov updated him. "Phaser banks at half capacity."

Scotty scowled at his engineering displays. "We can't take this much punishment indefinitely."

"Nor can the *BortaS*," Spock said, "as Captain Khod is surely aware, even if he is loath to admit it."

Uhura glanced at Spock from her station, where she monitored, sifted, and collated status reports from throughout the ship with practiced efficiency. "Isn't it almost time, Mister Spock?"

Spock checked his own mental countdown against the ship's chronometer, finding them in agreement down to two decimal places. "Almost, Lieutenant. Just a few moments more."

"I hope so," she murmured under her breath. "And none too soon."

In fact, the anticipated signal arrived precisely 2.864 minutes behind schedule. Spock blamed gravimetric fluctuations, ionic turbulence, quantum filaments, interstellar obstacles, spacial anomalies, or some other random variable for the delay, which had caused him to briefly entertain the dire possibility that an unforeseen factor had derailed his plan completely. He allowed himself a modicum of relief at the signal's tardy receipt.

"Mister Spock!" Uhura winked at him. "I'm receiving an encrypted subspace transmission from the *Yorktown* and the *Argosy*."

"On speaker, Lieutenant."

"Aye, sir. Decrypting now. Code Two-Zeta."

"*Attention* Enterprise," said a voice that bore a distinct resemblance to Lieutenant Charlene Masters in engineering. *"Your situation has been relayed to us on a priority channel. By order of Starfleet Command, we are en route at top speed to provide reinforcements and are authorized to take whatever measures are necessary to protect the planet and the* Enterprise *from Klingon aggression. Hold the fort until we get there. We won't be long. Yorktown, over and out."*

The message was, of course, a hoax.

The recorder marker they had launched earlier, supposedly to convey their logs to the nearest subspace relay buoy, had also been programmed to transmit a recorded signal back to the *Enterprise* once the marker had traveled sufficiently far enough to mask its origins. The counterfeit signal had been carefully crafted by Uhura to resemble a genuine Starfleet communication in all particulars, employing a code known to have been cracked by the Klingons' Romulan allies, with the full expectation that the *BortaS* would be monitoring all transmissions to and from the *Enterprise*.

But would Khod see through the deception?

In a very real sense, this was the *opposite* of the ruse Captain Kirk had employed in the Tellun system. Kirk had tricked Khod into thinking the *Enterprise* was far more helpless than it actually was. By contrast, Spock wanted Khod to believe that the *Enterprise* was about to achieve a decisive advantage, with the battered battle cruiser soon to be outnumbered three to one.

"You think they bought it?" Uhura said in a low voice.

"That remains to be seen, Lieutenant."

Their gambit relied on Khod being so determined not to fall for the same trick again that he would fail to discern its reverse image. Spock was also counting on the Klingon's pragmatism to win out over his combative nature and temper now that Spock had provided him with a legitimate and indisputable reason to abandon the battle. Khod was warlike, not suicidal, as proven by the fact that he'd chosen retreat over certain defeat the last time he'd fought the *Enterprise*. In theory, his pride and honor would survive not throwing away the *BortaS* in a quixotic clash against three Starfleet vessels, two of which were fresh to the fray.

Or so Spock estimated.

"The *BortaS* is hailing us again," Uhura said. "Funny coincidence, that."

"Indeed, Lieutenant. Put him through."

Khod's hirsute features reclaimed a corner of the viewscreen.

"*So, Vulcan, it seems you lack confidence in your vaunted calculations, nor do you possess the heart to face me in combat, your ship against mine. Instead you cravenly call for others to save you from our righteous fury!*" He sneered at Spock and the bridge crew. "*Do not deny it! We know full well that even now your precious Starfleet is sending more ships to fight your battles for you. Coward!*"

Spock replied carefully, not wanting to provoke Khod into prolonging the armed conflict. He needed to allow the Klingon the opportunity to salvage his pride and dignity before retreating in the face of overwhelming odds. The sooner the *BortaS* withdrew, the less likely Khod was to discover that no actual Starfleet reinforcements were imminent.

"If you say so," he said evenly. "As a Vulcan, my pride cannot be wounded by accepting aid from my allies, which is only logical. All that matters is the result of the equation, where the variables are now indisputably in our favor. What you choose to do with that information is naturally up to you, but I surmise that the Klingon Empire did not become a galactic superpower without choosing which battles to fight to the end . . . and which are not worth the expense."

Khod nodded on-screen. "*Never underestimate our cunning, Vulcan. We are warriors, yes, but we are seldom fools.*"

"I never thought otherwise," Spock said.

"*See that you don't!*" Khod snarled, perhaps as much for his own troops as for Spock. "*To die for victory is glorious, but to risk total destruction for . . . a misplaced scientist?*" He spat out the last word with audible contempt. "*Very well. Have your renegade professor if you can take her, but never cross me again, Vulcan. I will not be so merciful the next time we meet!*"

Khod vanished abruptly from the viewer, claiming the last word.

Now occupying the whole of the screen, the *BortaS* executed a loop that sent it soaring away from the battle, but not before its rear-firing cannons took a parting shot at the *Enterprise*. A final barrage of disruptor beams punctuated the battle cruiser's exit, blazing through space toward the starship's saucer section.

"Hold on tight!" Rahda shouted, taking evasive action. "We're taking the plunge!"

The bridge tilted forward precipitously as the *Enterprise* dived beneath the vicious viridian beams, the prow of the ship all but skimming the upper edges of Atraz's exosphere before leveling out. The steep, rapid descent reminded Spock of a classical human diversion known as a roller coaster, whose appeal had always eluded him. A jarring vibration ran through the ship, agitating display screens and indicator lights all around the bridge. Evidence of disruptor contact despite Rahda's swift reflexes?

"Damage?" Spock asked.

"Only a glancing blow," Chekov said. "Scraped the shields over our stern, but only minimal damage to the hull." He cast an aggrieved look at the departing D7 cruiser. "That Cossack just had to get a last lick in, I guess."

"Just as long as we've seen the last of him," Uhura said. "And that ridiculous forked beard of his."

"You said it, lassie." Scott grinned at Spock. "Well done, Mister Spock. Remind me to never play poker with you."

"A highly unlikely scenario." Spock was gratified by the apparent success of his ploy and made a mental note to see to it that Uhura's invaluable contribution to the hoax was duly noted in the logs, but he resisted the temptation to pronounce the crisis over prematurely. "Course and heading of the battle cruiser, Mister Chekov?"

The ensign consulted the long-range sensors.

"They've left orbit and are heading out of the system, sir. Toward the Klingon border."

"Good riddance," Scott said. "But now then, what about the captain and the others?"

"My thoughts exactly, Mister Scott."

Chapter Forty-One

2292

"Forever young . . ."

A vintage melody from Earth's past played softly in the background as Doctor Kesh, once known as Siroth, strapped Cyloo onto a customized biobed boasting extensive modifications unfamiliar to Saavik. An oversized monitor was mounted on the wall overlooking the bed while an elaborate sensor array occupied the ceiling directly overhead. The restraints were merely to hold Cyloo still during the scanning process, Kesh had assured them; nevertheless, the nervous Osori had insisted on retaining her phase gloves for this first procedure, which was intended to analyze her anatomy, metabolism, and assorted other life functions down to the atomic level. In his haste to begin examining the Osori, Kesh had chosen not to argue that point, for the present at least.

"You're certain this isn't going to hurt?" she asked again.

"Perfectly painless and noninvasive." Kesh adjusted her positioning on the bed; Cyloo had traded her mesh poncho for a formfitting white bodysuit embedded with sensor nodes for the procedure. "Just a bit time-consuming, which is why I want to get started promptly. These scans will provide me with a full, comprehensive survey of your unique physiology that will help narrow down the focus of any subsequent tests and experiments. We're just mapping the terrain for now."

"I'm not sure I like being treated as a piece of geography." Cyloo turned her head toward Saavik, who stood beside the bed providing moral support. "You'll be here the whole time, won't you? You won't leave me alone with them?"

"I am not going anywhere," Saavik promised.

Kesh and his accomplice had wasted no time escorting the two women from the living quarters upstairs to the lower-level laboratory facilities. Saavik was impressed by how state-of-the-art the labs were; the various components appeared to be modular in nature, perhaps accounting for how Kesh managed to establish this hidden base in time to intercept the *Lukara*'s voyage from Osor to Nimbus III. Wight was on hand to operate the equipment, after placing Taleb in cold storage, although it seemed Kesh's pet rat was not allowed in the labs. Saavik approved of that restriction since it gave her one less variable to plan around as she plotted their escape. She had no intention of letting Kesh use either her or Cyloo as guinea pigs any longer than absolutely necessary.

"Is everything set on your end?" Kesh asked Wight, who was manning a rather complex control panel a few meters away from the biobed. The Rhaandarite's yellow eyes were fixed on a battery of illuminated indicators and displays.

"Yes, Doctor. Systems green across the board."

"Excellent." Kesh placed a protective visor over Cyloo's three eyes. "Lieutenant Saavik, please step away from the bed."

She did as told, still feigning compliance. "I am not going far," she assured Cyloo.

Kesh backed away from the bed as well. "Proceed."

An intense white spotlight shone from the sensors above Cyloo. Multiple streams of data, orders of magnitude beyond that reported by a standard biobed, began scrolling across the monitors. While Kesh treated himself to a fresh mug of *raktajino* from a convenient food synthesizer, Saavik covertly inspected her surroundings, planning her next move.

What would Kirk do under these circumstances?

He would not wait for an opportunity to act. He would create one, by guile if necessary.

"How long is this procedure estimated to take, Doctor?"

"Three hours at least. Do you have someplace you need to be, Lieutenant?"

"I am merely considering how best to occupy my time for the duration," she said mildly. "A thought: I was admiring your library earlier. Might I fetch a book to pass the hours? Perhaps *The Photonic Eternity* by Lilyan Colbert?"

She had in fact noted that, in addition to a wide variety of nonfiction tomes on matters scientific, medical, historical, and philosophical,

Kesh had an entire bookshelf devoted to Terran literature involving immortality: *The Epic of Gilgamesh*, "The Mortal Immortal," *Orlando*, *The Picture of Dorian Gray*, *She: A History of Adventure*, "Rip Van Winkle," *Tuck Everlasting*, *Methuselah's Children*, *The Endless Andorian*, *Bid Space-Time Return*, and others. Kesh's enduring obsession, it seemed, extended even to his recreational reading material.

"And you just now thought of that?" Kesh frowned. "Can't you simply meditate like a proper Vulcan?"

"As you are fond of pointing out, I am half Romulan. This results in a certain innate . . . restlessness." She started toward the turbolift outside the lab. "You need not trouble yourself. I will return promptly with the desired volume."

"No!" Cyloo called out from the bed. "Don't leave me."

"I will be only a few minutes. Just up to the study and back."

"Not so fast." Kesh put down his coffee mug. "You're being a tad presumptuous, Lieutenant, assuming you can come and go as you please."

"You have hostages to compel my cooperation," she reminded him, "and took pains to explain that there is nowhere to flee to." She turned back and settled onto a stool next to a work counter. "Yet if this poses too great a difficulty . . ."

"Fine. I'll get you the book myself." Kesh sighed irritably and turned toward Wight, who was conscientiously monitoring the readouts from the sensors. "Watch yourself, Wight. Don't let yourself get nerve-pinched while I'm raiding my library for a certain bored spectator."

"That is not my intention," Saavik stated. "Perhaps I will meditate in your absence, like a proper Vulcan."

"See that you do."

She waited patiently as Kesh departed, appearing distinctly exasperated. In theory, her plan would work just as well if he'd dispatched Wight to retrieve the book instead; she merely needed to get one of their captors out of the way long enough to carry out her strategy. Despite this, she was not displeased to see the back of Kesh, if only temporarily.

"Cyloo! Phase through your bonds . . . immediately!"

Unfortunately, she'd had no opportunity to share her plan with Cyloo in advance. She had to trust that the captive Osori would follow her lead without hesitation.

"Wait! What are you doing?" Wight spun away from the control panel in alarm, reaching for the phaser at her hip. Her anxious gaze swung back and forth between Saavik and Cyloo. "What's happening?"

"Saavik?" Cyloo asked.

"With alacrity, please, Cyloo. Time is short."

"All right."

Saavik's trust in Cyloo was vindicated as a rosy glow enveloped the Osori, causing the readouts on the screens to fluctuate erratically or else zero out completely, much to Wight's distress. "Stop it! You're spoiling everything!"

Cyloo sat up, passing effortlessly through her restraints, and swung her legs over the edge of the bed. Wight impotently waved her phaser at her.

"Get back on the bed!" the flustered Rhaandarite ordered while lifting the wrist communicator to her lips. "Doctor, we have a prob—"

A quantum microscope rested on the countertop next to Saavik. Moving swiftly, she hurled the heavy instrument at Wight, whose large domed cranium made an easy target. Saavik had once been the star pitcher on her class's baseball team back at Starfleet Academy, and her accuracy had not diminished since. The impact knocked the Rhaandarite to the floor, and Saavik pounced like the feral hunter she'd been as a child, administering a nerve pinch to the stunned technician in what struck Saavik as an effective combination of Hellguard instincts and Vulcan technique.

"By the Endless Tapestry!" Cyloo gaped at Saavik through her protective visor. "You took her down in mere instants! That was terrifying . . . and amazing!"

"Merely necessary." Saavik relieved Wight of her phaser and headed for a computer console. "We must act quickly to bar Kesh from these compartments." She scanned the control panel. "Presumably there is a lockdown protocol in place for emergencies."

"Allow me."

Phasing back into solidity, Cyloo took off the visor and flung it away. She eased past Saavik to lay her gloved hands on the panel. The liquid metal flowed from her fingertips to interface with the circuitry beneath the panel. Warning lights flashed on throughout the lab.

"There! I've tricked Hiberna's computer systems into thinking that its lower levels are experiencing a biohazard outbreak *and* a radiation leak. Force fields and safety doors are in place at all entry points, including the turbolift. The transporter is also disengaged." Cyloo grinned at Saavik. "Doctor Kesh is not the only one who can fake a catastrophe."

"Poetic . . . and impressive." Saavik admired the capacities of the Osori's gloves, and the formidable scientific prowess they implied. "I did not realize your attire was quite so versatile."

"Multipurpose smart fabric, neuro-controlled. Our civilization is much older and more advanced than yours, remember. We've had ages to develop and refine our technology. It's not as though we've spent all those millennia frolicking in fields of flowers . . . or at least not all the time."

"Duly noted."

"What the devil do you think you're doing?" Kesh's outraged features appeared on the screen above the vacated biobed, as well as on a number of smaller monitors around the lab. *"You don't truly expect me to believe this nonsense about an emergency lockdown?"*

Cyloo gulped. "Shall I disable internal comms as well?"

"Not yet."

Saavik reasoned that there might be an advantage to knowing how Kesh was reacting to their insurrection. She addressed the main screen while simultaneously binding Wight to the now-empty biobed, using the same restraints previously employed on Cyloo.

"I would not insult your intelligence thusly, Doctor. The fact remains, however, that we no longer desire your hospitality and are taking measures to remedy our situation."

"Damn it, I should have known better than to trust you or any of Kirk's people, but I foolishly expected even a half Vulcan to be more logical. This entire exercise is pointless. I've already explained how and why. You're not going to be able to lock me out forever. I'll blast my way in if I have to."

"You are free to try. In the interim, we will pursue options other than surrender."

She did not wish to spend too much time sparring verbally with Kesh while there were more urgent tasks before them. She signaled

Cyloo to cut off the transmission at their end. The myriad screens went dark.

"Now what?" Cyloo asked. "He's not wrong. We can't get away."

"Not on our own. Therefore, we must endeavor to make contact with the *Enterprise* or any other nearby vessel, provided they are still within communications range."

It seemed not improbable that the *Enterprise*, or possibly the *Lukara* or the *Harrier*, was still in the vicinity, investigating the theft and destruction of the escape pod. There was also a substantial probability that some or all of the ships had already engaged in battle—or were doing so at this very moment. Whether such a conflict would help or hinder her and Cyloo's odds of being rescued from Hiberna was difficult to estimate.

"Right! I should've thought of that." Hope lit up Cyloo's scaly face. "And I may have some ideas about how to accomplish that."

Withdrawing her smart-fabric finger extensions from the control panel, she scampered over to the biobed and commandeered Wight's wrist communicator. She slid it onto her own wrist, where her glove began to interface with it.

"It won't be easy, but I should be able to link into Hiberna's long-range communications array. Or, in a pinch, maybe just boost the signal from this wrist device. I simply need to figure out the best way to make that happen."

"Acknowledged. How may I assist you?"

"In truth? After all that's happened, I have qualms about letting our advanced science fall into the hands of outsiders like Kesh, the Klingons, the Romulans, or even your own Federation. You must promise that if anything . . . happens . . . to me, you will destroy my gloves and any equipment I may have tampered with."

The Prime Directive, Saavik recognized, *applied to us primitive, younger races.*

She cast an envious look at the smart gloves, reluctant to deprive the Federation of such innovative technology, but she appreciated Cyloo's concerns and had no time to debate them. Fortune willing, there would be time enough in the future for the diplomats to haggle over any exchanges of scientific knowledge.

"Agreed. Anything else?"

"Taleb. We can't just leave him frozen somewhere. We have to free him too."

Must we? Saavik thought. *Right away, that is.*

Naturally, they would want to liberate Taleb eventually, if and when they had matters well in hand, but defrosting him at this critical juncture had not been Saavik's top priority. She had enough unpredictable variables to factor in at present without adding a temperamental Romulan to the equation.

"Perhaps we should concentrate on summoning assistance first?"

"And leave Taleb trapped in a tube? I can manage the comms, Saavik. You need to free him. You have to!"

She was clearly adamant on this point. And it *was* possible that they could benefit from Taleb's assistance. Maybe.

"Very well. Continue with your efforts to contact the *Enterprise* while I attempt to locate our missing companion."

"Thank you, Saavik! I'll feel ever so much better once we're all together again."

Saavik was rather less enthused by the prospect, but embarked on the task anyway. With the turbolift disabled, she descended a spiral stairwell to the level directly below the labs, where efficient scouting soon led her to the cryogenics vault Kesh had mentioned earlier. She entered via an unlocked doorway to discover eight horizontal cryotubes installed within the notably refrigerated chamber. The tubes resembled sleek, futuristic sarcophagi, giving the compartment the impression of a burial chamber. Concealed machinery hummed in the background. The ambient temperature was such that she could see her own breath.

Six of the tubes were unoccupied, but two clearly held sleeping subjects, visible through a transparent aluminum viewport in the lid of the tube. She immediately spotted Taleb and hastened toward him, sparing only a curious glance at the other tube, its window frosted over so that only a blurry outline of a humanoid figure could be glimpsed inside the sarcophagus. Saavik recalled Kesh alluding cryptically to other "inconvenient" guests he'd been obliged to freeze for safekeeping.

Who was this individual—and how long had they been sleeping?

Such questions would have to wait until she revived Taleb. Deciphering the tube's miniature control panel, she initiated the warm-up sequence. A toasty red radiance suffused the sarcophagus while an embedded monitor charted Taleb's vital signs as they climbed back toward standard Romulan norms. She was grateful for her Vulcan self-discipline as she impatiently endured the several minutes that passed before the viewing pane retracted, exposing Taleb to the air, and a locking mechanism audibly disengaged, allowing her to lift open the lid of the cryotube. Gasping, he awoke with a start and glanced about in confusion.

"What is this? Where am I?" He shivered even as a healthy green tint returned to his cheeks and lips. "And why is it so absurdly cold?"

Despite their differences, she was relieved that he appeared to have come through his ordeal unscathed, his aggrieved disposition included.

"You have just been awakened from cryogenic suspension. Do not overtax yourself; you may require some time to recover fully."

She helped him out of the tube and onto his feet, then concisely briefed him on their situation. To her slight surprise, he did not refuse her assistance or question the actions she had taken on their behalf.

"It seems I am in your debt, Lieutenant." Condensation provided a damp sheen to his hair and features. "Perhaps I underestimated the quality of your Romulan blood."

She elected to take that as the compliment he intended. "You're welcome."

With Taleb revived and brought back up to speed, Saavik's attention was once more drawn to that other tube and its nameless occupant. Who else had Kesh relegated to suspended animation? Prudence dictated that she and Taleb rejoin Cyloo with all deliberate speed, but both curiosity and ethics lured her over to the mystery tube. Peering through the frosted viewport, she discerned that the figure appeared to be female.

"Who might this be?" Taleb asked.

"That is what I wish to determine."

Awaking this stranger posed a risk, as Kirk had discovered when he'd brought Khan out of his long slumber years ago, but what if this was another innocent victim frozen against their will, as Taleb was? There might not be an opportunity to liberate them later, depending on how events unfolded over the next few hours.

"I mean to revive this individual," she told Taleb. "Do you object?"

He hugged himself in an attempt to dispel the icy chill of the tube. "I would not wish such a fate on a Klingon. Do not let me stop you."

She repeated the procedure she'd employed to thaw out Taleb. The same warm radiance melted away the frost veiling the viewing window, revealing what appeared to be a young humanoid woman with bobbed magenta hair. The pane retracted and she stirred within the tube. Groggy brown eyes snapped open as she spied Saavik and Taleb gazing down at her.

"What the freak? Are you . . . aliens?" asked Melinda Silver.

Chapter Forty-Two

Kirk's communicator chimed, intruding on the standoff in the abandoned stables.

"Mind if I take this?" Kirk stared down the barrel of Yorba's disruptor as he consulted his communicator. The patterned frequency display indicated that the transmission was from the *Enterprise*. "Kirk here. What is it?"

Spock's voice emanated from the receiver:

"*Excuse me, Captain, if this contact is ill timed, but you should know that the* BortaS *has retreated from the system after an exchange of weapons fire with the* Enterprise."

The startling report, delivered with Spock's characteristic equanimity, was almost enough to make Kirk forget his own precarious situation. "And the ship?"

"*Damaged, but operational. Repairs are underway.*"

Kirk took as granted that Scotty had matters well in hand. "Very interesting, Mister Spock. Would you mind repeating that news for our Klingon friends? I think they need to hear this as well."

He held out his communicator, its speaker facing Yorba and Wrultz. Her eyes narrowed suspiciously.

"*Very well, Captain. Be aware that we engaged the battle cruiser after it fired on the planet and have successfully repelled it from this system. The* Enterprise *remains in orbit at your disposal.*"

"Thank you, Mister Spock. I'm in the middle of a rather crucial negotiation here, but I'll be in touch at my first opportunity. Kirk out."

Yorba shook her head. "A trick. A transparent deception."

"Prove me wrong," Kirk said. "Contact your battle cruiser . . . if you can."

She gestured at Wrultz with her free hand. "Do it."

"Yes, Colonel." He kept his own weapon aimed at Kirk as he fumbled with his communicator. "Hailing *BortaS*. Respond!"

Only static greeted his command.

"Repeat. Respond at once! By order of Colonel Yorba!"

Invoking Yorba's authority failed to yield any better results. Worry showed on the Klingon's bewhiskered features as he glanced away from Kirk to study the readouts on his device. An unhappy grunt betrayed his displeasure.

"It's no use, Colonel. The ship is gone, out of range." He hastily tried something else. "Our shuttle pilot confirms the *BortaS* has left orbit."

Thank you, Spock, Kirk thought. *You may have just dealt me a winning hand.*

"Satisfied?" he asked Yorba. "Seems like the *Enterprise* is now the only way off the planet for all of us, which means this standoff just became academic. Even if you do capture Hamparian, you can't get her back to Klingon space."

"We still have our own shuttlecraft!" Wrultz blustered.

"And how far will you get in that, with the *Enterprise* in orbit, fully equipped with phasers, photon torpedoes, and tractor beams?" Kirk imagined that Yorba was already running possible scenarios in her head and finding her options severely limited now that the *BortaS* had left her high and dry. "Well, Colonel, what now? Can I offer you a ride off the planet? Provided you lay down your weapons, naturally."

If looks could truly kill, her fierce glare would have vaporized Kirk on the spot. He braced himself for some blistering Klingon invective, but before she could reply, furious shouts and hoofbeats came from outside the building, surrounding them.

"Hark, you in there! The hunt is over! We have run you to ground at last! Surrender to the suzerain's justice or suffer the consequences!"

So much for catching our breaths, Kirk thought. Despite Jaheed's evasive maneuvers, Varkat's troops had caught up with them. Kirk kicked himself for not posting a lookout, not that the Klingons had given him any opportunity to do so. He'd been too busy trying to save Hamparian from their fellow escapees to set a watch for their mutual enemies.

"Time's up," he told Yorba. "Ready to leave Atraz on my terms? Or would you rather be carted back to the arena . . . or worse."

"You think I fear these primitives?" she scoffed. "Cavalry and crossbows against Klingons armed with disruptors?"

"And then what? You'll still be stranded on Atraz, chased and hounded until your disruptors' cells run out."

She nodded pensively, a calculating look on her face. "Perhaps you have a point, Kirk, after I've disposed of a certain loose end." She peered past him at Hamparian, whom McCoy was already hustling toward the storm cellar. "Time enough to ensure that neither of us gets what we want."

"Don't move a muscle," Sulu warned, his phaser ready. "Unless what you want is a phaser at point-bank range."

"What he said," Landon added, targeting Wrultz.

"Copy that." Levine kept Yorba in his sights. "We have you outnumbered."

"But only a twitch of my finger is required," she reminded them all, "to erase your captain from existence."

Kirk weighed his odds. Could Sulu and the others stun the Klingons before they fired on him or Hamparian? A split second could make the difference between life and death, even before the soldiers outside could try to flush them out of the stables.

"Think about it, Yorba," he said. "Is it worth risking war, by assassinating a Starfleet captain, just to keep Hamparian out of our hands?

"You mean when you're tragically killed by the Atrazians, don't you?" She nodded at the entrance and the briars defending it. "Those barbarians will make excellent scapegoats if it comes to it. My word against . . . well, whoever survives."

Just then, Jaheed broke the stalemate. Cupping his palms around his mouth, he mimicked the ear-piercing squawk of an enraged bloodbeak, alarming the grazing *vusecos*, who reacted wildly, trumpeting loudly as they stampeded for the door. The commotion startled Yorba, who recoiled anxiously from the agitated beasts, looking away from Kirk for a vital instant. Seizing the moment, Kirk dived beneath where her disruptor was aimed, hitting the ground with his shoulder and rolling toward her legs. Her weapon went off, a lethal green beam

sizzling above him to pass through the empty air he had just been occupying. The ray crossed the stable to strike the prickly shrubs outside
the entrance, setting them ablaze, just as his rolling body collided with
her legs, knocking her off her feet. Twin phaser beams stunned her,
ensuring she wouldn't be getting back up as readily as Kirk did. Wrultz,
flummoxed by Yorba's sudden reversal of fortune, took a second too
long to retaliate. A third phaser beam, fired by Landon, dropped the
Klingon onto the packed dirt floor.

"Find your own ride next time," she said to the unconscious lieutenant, whom she'd shared her ungulate with before. She moved swiftly
to relieve both Klingons of their weapons. "Should have left you in the
dust when we had the chance."

Between the panicked *vusecos* bolting from the stable and the flam-
ing briars at the door, Varkat's men sounded momentarily distracted as
well, at least for a few more minutes. McCoy and Hamparian rejoined
Kirk now that the Klingons were no longer an immediate threat. The
doctor helped support Hamparian, who was limping slightly and
looked more than ready to return to the Federation. He rolled his eyes
at the hornet's nest Atraz had become.

"I don't know about you, Jim, but a transporter beam actually
sounds pretty good right now. Even if Spock is at the other end of it."

Kirk smiled. "I couldn't agree with you more, Doctor." He reacti-
vated his communicator and did a quick head count, including Jaheed
and the stunned Klingons. "Kirk to *Enterprise*. Adjust the transporter
to widespread. Nine to beam up."

Varkat's troops would find only an empty barn—and a mystery.

Chapter Forty-Three

2292

"Are you aliens?"

Melinda's voice was hoarse from disuse. The last thing she remembered, aside from vague, unsettling dreams of a building collapsing on her, was Orlando Wilder sealing her up inside an experimental cryogenics tube in his private lab at Hiberna House. It felt as though she'd been sleeping only for a short time, so where had these pointy-eared strangers come from? Sitting up, her head spinning, she didn't recognize her surroundings at all. Chilled air made her shiver.

"Where the freak am I?" A shocking possibility hit her. "Are we aboard a UFO?"

"UFO?" The male alien scowled. "What is a UFO?"

"An archaic human term for an alleged extraterrestrial vessel." The alien woman regarded Melinda with curiosity as she helped her out of the tube. She removed a maroon jacket and placed it over Melinda's trembling shoulders, on top of an unfamiliar white bodysuit incorporating an intricate lattice of wires and tubing. "You are from Earth, I gather?"

"*From* Earth?" That phrasing did not escape Melinda. "Does that mean I'm . . . not in San Francisco anymore?"

"Far from it," the woman said gently. Melinda got a more considerate vibe from her than from the male. "I am called Saavik, and my companion is Taleb. You are . . . ?"

"Melinda. Melinda Silver."

She struggled to process what was happening. Aliens from another world? Had Dennis been right all along?

Dennis . . .

Dennis was dead. That awful reality came back to her suddenly, wrenching an agonized moan from deep inside her. Tears flooded her eyes as she remembered how he'd accidentally been killed when she'd tackled him to save Wilder, right before that ruthless son of a bitch drugged her and put her into the tube for . . . how long?

"How long has it been?" Worst-case scenarios flashed through her brain. Had she been on ice for months? Years? "When are we? What's the date?"

"By your reckoning, it is the year 2292."

Melinda's jaw dropped. She wasn't sure what answer she'd been bracing herself for, but . . . 2292? She had been frozen alive for nearly three hundred years? Dennis had been dead for close to three centuries?

"No, no, this can't be real. It was 2024 just a few hours ago. For me, I mean. It can't be 2292 for Pete's sake. That's impossible."

"I understand this must be disturbing to you," Saavik said. "It may comfort you to know that San Francisco still exists, albeit many light-years from our present location. I attended the Academy there, in fact."

"Really?" As always, shock and grief were not enough to entirely curb Melinda's boundless curiosity and journalistic instincts. "Space aliens go to school in California these days? So we didn't blow ourselves to atoms eventually?"

"Negative. Earth abides. Humanity thrives, and not only on the planet of your birth."

"Yes, yes, this is all very moving," Taleb huffed, his arms across his chest. "But with all due respect to this poor, befuddled human's plight, need I remind you that we are still being menaced by a homicidal madman?"

Melinda was jolted by his words. "Wilder? He's still around too?"

"Who is this Wilder you speak of?" Saavik asked.

"Orlando Wilder? The tech millionaire? The nutcase who stuck me in a tube, *way* back in the day?" The two aliens gave her puzzled looks. "Hang on, if Wilder's name means nothing to you, just who *are* you worried about?"

"We don't have time for this," Taleb objected. "Cyloo is waiting for us. Bring this stray along if you must, but we need to concentrate on liberating ourselves."

"Liberate?" Panic edged Melinda's voice. "Liberate from where? Who? What the freak is going on?"

"There are many questions and little time." Saavik looked at Melinda thoughtfully. She nodded to herself, as though reaching a decision. "Leave us, Taleb. We will rejoin you once I have dispelled Melinda's confusion . . . and my own."

"But—" he started to protest.

"It may be that her memories hold secrets we would do well to uncover."

"If you insist." He threw up his hands in frustration. "But be quick about it. We can be sure Kesh is not sitting on his hands waiting for us to surrender. Even now he is certainly plotting to recapture us . . . and I, for one, have no intention of going back into a tube!"

He stormed out of the vault, leaving them alone.

"Friend of yours?" Melinda asked.

"Not precisely." Saavik guided her out of the vault into a sterile, futuristic corridor, which was notably warmer than the sci-fi icebox Melinda had wakened to. The female alien's voice and expression grew more serious. "I must ask much of you, Melinda. As you have surely deduced, our situation is precarious and your presence here a mystery."

"Tell me about it. I have *so* many questions."

"As do I," Saavik said. "It is within my abilities, however, to temporarily join our minds so that we can share our memories in a matter of moments. This requires considerable trust on your part, and I do not ask it lightly, but it may serve to unravel the mysteries confounding us."

Melinda swallowed hard. "Are you talking about . . . telepathy?"

"Exactly. My people call it a mind-meld, and we have practiced it for centuries. It is a deeply personal experience, though, so I must have your consent before we proceed. Are you willing to share your memories with me?"

"I'm not sure. This is a lot to take in all at once. I'm in outer space somewhere, I'm far in the future, and now an alien, no offense, wants to probe my mind? I kinda need a moment here."

"Acknowledged, but Taleb was not wrong that time is scarce."

Melinda knew what Dennis would advise. He'd run screaming into the night before he'd let some unearthly being slide their telepathic tendrils into his brain. For all Melinda knew, she'd be setting herself up for some sort of insidious alien mind control. And yet she got a good vibe from Saavik, and since when did she ever let fear get in the way of solving a mystery?

"And I'd be able to read your mind as well?"

"That is correct."

"All right then. I need answers, more than ever, so let's do this."

"Thank you, Melinda. I will not abuse your trust." Saavik took a deep breath, as though centering herself for what lay ahead, and softly placed warm fingertips against Melinda's newly defrosted temples. "My mind to your mind. My thoughts to your thoughts . . ."

Melinda stiffened, girding herself for . . . what? She was about to ask what exactly to expect when, all at once, she found out in the most profound way possible. Understanding flowed into her as she gazed into Saavik's bottomless brown eyes and saw herself gazing back at her.

She was Melinda. *She was Saavik.* She was human. *She was Vulcan* and *Romulan.* She had searched for Gillian. *She'd sought Spock.* She grieved for Dennis. *She mourned David.* Wilder had double-crossed her. *Kesh was not who or what he seemed.* I am her. *She is me.* We are one. *We are ourselves . . .*

And then it was over.

A peculiar sense of loss afflicted Melinda as she found herself back in her own head again, all by herself, but that lonely pang was almost immediately swept away by the treasure trove of new information and concepts downloaded into her brain. It was overwhelming and awesome at the same time.

"Whoa! Talk about a rush!"

"Affirmative." Saavik withdrew her hands. A solitary tear rolled down her cheek, and she wiped it away. "I grieve for your loss."

Dennis, Melinda realized. "Are you okay?"

"I require a moment to compose myself. His loss is very fresh, subjectively."

No kidding, Melinda thought, although melding with Saavik seemed to have granted her some degree of distance from that trauma, which was centuries in the past from the Vulcan's perspective. Meanwhile, any doubts or fears Melinda might have had regarding Saavik and her intentions were also history now. *I'd trust her with my life.*

And might just have to.

"That was . . . illuminating," Saavik said, her eyes dry once more. "Much that was obscure has become clear. Doctor Kesh is indeed none other than—"

"—Orlando Wilder." Melinda finished Saavik's sentence. "Who is a Klingon now? And whoa, I know what a Klingon is. But yeah, that's positively him. I'd recognize that face anywhere, even with some weird new ridges on his skull. He's aged some since I last saw him, two hundred and sixty–plus years ago, but he hasn't changed that much: the pet rat, the cryotubes, the same crazy obsession with immortality. And he's carted me around with him, across time and space, as . . . what? A trophy? A souvenir? A good-luck charm?"

"You did save his life long ago," Saavik said, now privy to her memories. "It would appear he takes that debt seriously, even after all this time."

Wilder's cavernous voice echoed in Melinda's memory: *"Your life is safe in my hands. Indeed, you're going to live longer than you ever dreamed of."*

"Lucky me."

Melinda sorted through Saavik's recent memories, resisting the temptation to dive down nearly three centuries' worth of rabbit holes concerning this strange new future she found herself in. She could all too easily lose herself for hours, days, weeks, getting a crash course on the ins and outs of the twenty-third century. (Transporters? Warp drives? A United Federation of Planets?) But Taleb, that Romulan jerk, was right. Now that she and Saavik had compared notes telepathically, they had to focus on getting away from Wilder, aka Doctor Kesh, aka . . .

"Siroth? Wilder was also a bogus wizard on a planet called . . . Atraz . . . decades ago? Who was foiled by your captain—" Kirk's face surfaced from the memories Saavik had imparted to Melinda, bringing a shock of recognition. "Kirk! Captain James T. Kirk of the *Starship Enterprise* was Gillian's pizza date? How is that even—?"

Rapid footsteps on a spiral stairwell heralded Taleb's return.

"If you two are quite finished getting to know each other, we could use your attendance in the control room. Cyloo is attempting to contact the *Enterprise*!"

Chapter Forty-Four

"*We have crossed the border, Captain,*" Spock reported from the ship's bridge via the intercom. "*We are now unquestionably in Federation space.*"

"Thank you, Mister Spock. Good to know."

Kirk turned away from the wall unit to address their soon-to-be-departed guests. Colonel Yorba, accompanied by two subordinates, occupied the transporter platform, ready to be beamed over to their captured Klingon shuttlecraft, the *Skral*, which was presently tethered to the *Enterprise* by a tractor beam. McCoy was also on hand to see the Klingons off, along with a full complement of armed security guards to ensure that Yorba and her men left quietly.

"Well, Colonel," Kirk said, "it seems this is where we part company."

The *Enterprise* had made good time back to Federation space after the landing party had beamed aboard with Doctor Hamparian and a few other guests, followed closely by Akbari in the *Galileo*. Unwilling to leave a party of unsupervised Klingons behind on Atraz, Kirk had prevailed on Yorba to order the *Skral*'s pilot, a surly individual named Koxar, to take the Klingon shuttle into orbit where the *Enterprise* had latched onto it, with the promise that the Klingons would be set loose to make their way back to their own territory once the *Enterprise* was safely clear of the unaligned sector. In truth, Kirk hadn't given Yorba much choice; the alternative was the *Enterprise* firing on the *Skral* from orbit, then delivering the captive Klingons to the Federation authorities, where they were likely to be held until the diplomats arranged their return to the Empire—in due time.

No surprise, Yorba had elected to leave under her own power.

"Indeed. Rest assured, Kirk, I will not forget your hospitality."

In deference to her rank, she'd been confined to suitable guest quarters while her men languished in the brig. Her icy tone cast doubt on whether she was being sarcastic or not.

"Is that a promise or a threat?" McCoy asked.

"Think of it as a statement of fact," she said with a smirk. "Yet you may take some comfort in knowing that I have other, more pressing scores to settle first." Her expression curdled. "General Khod will pay for abandoning me, the cowardly *petaQ!*"

Kirk briefly feared she might vent her animus by spitting onto the transporter platform, but she refrained from contaminating the pristine apparatus. He didn't envy Khod; the *BortaS*'s commander would do well to watch his back once Yorba returned to the Empire.

"That's between you and him," Kirk said diplomatically. "Your internal disputes are none of our concern."

"See that they remain so." She swept her gaze over the crowded transporter room. "I gather Doctor Hamparian did not care to bid me farewell?"

"Can you blame her?" McCoy asked. "After you tried to kidnap or kill her how many times?"

"For the good of the Empire," Yorba said, unapologetic as ever. "Which reminds me, Captain, Doctor: you never did thank me."

McCoy snorted. "For what?"

"Eliminating Siroth's secret biotech research laboratory, thereby sparing you that unpleasantness."

"By firing upon an independent, pre-warp planet?" Kirk shook his head. "I can't say I approve of your methods. There had to be less extreme measures."

"A swift and decisive blow was called for. My only regret is that I failed to eliminate Hamparian as expeditiously. You can't deny that her work threatens to destabilize the balance of power between our two civilizations, as well as perhaps the very nature of our respective species."

She indicated her smooth brow, which testified to the risks posed by reckless genetic engineering on humanoid subjects. Kirk tried to reassure her.

"For what it's worth, Starfleet has no intention of weaponizing Hamparian's work, which would be in serious violation of our own standards and principles. Whatever research she may or may not pursue in the future will be conducted under close scrutiny to ensure that it stays well within the appropriate Federation guidelines."

"So you say," she said skeptically. "We will be watching, with or without your knowledge."

Kirk didn't doubt it. Seeing no further point in prolonging the Klingons' departure, he turned toward the officer at the transporter controls.

"Beam our guests over to their shuttlecraft, Mister Kyle."

"Aye, sir."

"So they're gone . . . for good?"

Taya Hamparian looked understandably relieved to hear that the Klingons were no longer aboard the *Enterprise*. Like Yorba had been, she was confined to guest quarters with a security officer stationed outside the door to make certain she stayed put. Kirk had seen to it that she and Yorba never crossed paths during their shared stay on the ship.

"Taking the slow boat back to Kronos," he assured her. Chances were, of course, that the *Skral* would eventually manage to send a subspace distress call to a larger, faster Klingon vessel, which might come to retrieve them, but Hamparian didn't need to hear that. It was enough for her to know that Yorba wasn't busily plotting her death a few decks away. "We won't be seeing them again anytime soon, if ever."

"That's something at least." Hamparian, now wearing a standard-issue red jumpsuit, sat at a desk in front of a computer terminal, where she appeared to be reviewing a scientific journal that, at a glance, was far too abstruse to be readily understood by Kirk. McCoy, who was also present to check on the scientist's mental and emotional well-being, had discharged her from sickbay after treating whatever minor injuries she'd sustained after being thrown into the arena. To date, she had been a model prisoner, posing no security issues. She looked at Kirk, her face still somewhat drawn and apprehensive. "What's going to happen to me, Captain, now that we're back in Federation space?"

Kirk didn't sugarcoat his answer.

"That's up to the authorities once we've delivered you into their custody at Starbase 17, but you're going to have to answer for that staged spacejacking and the lives you put at risk there, along with whatever other charges the Federation prosecutors see fit to file against you."

She nodded in resignation, seeming genuinely contrite.

"I suppose I have that coming. I only hope I'll be allowed to continue my work, under supervision. Perhaps I can still atone for my lapses in judgment by advancing the cause of medical science."

"I would certainly hope so," McCoy chimed in. "I've had an opportunity now to review your work, classified and otherwise, and its potential truly is staggering. It would be a crime if you weren't allowed to pursue your research wherever you end up . . . and I'm willing to testify to that effect, to whatever court needs to hear it."

Kirk took McCoy's word for it. He recalled that Spock had also been impressed by Hamparian's work to date. "It's that promising, Bones?"

"No question, Jim. We could be talking a major breakthrough down the road, allowing for maybe a decade or so of further research and testing. Who knows? Someday soon, patients may be able to grow a new kidney just by taking a pill, eliminating the need for lab-grown transplants or artificial organs."

It sounded fantastic, but Kirk had learned never to underestimate what science could accomplish, both on Earth and beyond. There'd been a time, not too many centuries ago, when the notion of starships exploring the cosmos had been merely the stuff of speculative fiction. Certainly, he wanted to think that their perilous mission to Atraz might ultimately benefit the Federation, its allies, and life-forms throughout the galaxy.

If nothing else, Jaheed had profited from their visit to his world. After the wily guide had been beamed to safety with the rest of the landing party, Kirk had kept Jaheed isolated in the transporter room before having him beamed back down to Atraz, with a quantity of freshly synthesized gemstones for his troubles. Kirk had also impressed on him the need to keep quiet about what he had seen in the landing party's company, for his sake as well as the Prime Directive's.

"*Worry not, O Captain!*" the grateful Atrazian had declared. "*My lips are sealed, for who would believe such an astounding tale anyway!*"

Which left just one loose end unresolved.

"If only we knew what became of Siroth after his tower came down," McCoy said, speaking for all of them. "I don't like the idea of him picking up where he left off, experimenting on captive Atrazians in his lunatic pursuit of immortality."

Kirk knew how McCoy felt, but saw reason for hope as well.

"I can't imagine it will be that easy, Bones. He knows we're on to him now, and the Klingons will be watching for him too." Kirk had already recommended that Starfleet conduct regular long-range sensor sweeps of Atraz, by unmanned probes and spy satellites if necessary. "He'll want to keep a low profile from now on. Maybe even find a way off Atraz as soon as possible."

"He did have an emergency exit strategy planned," Hamparian volunteered, "just in case things went south in a big way. He was typically cagey about the details, insisting that there was no immediate need for me to be privy to them, but I gathered that he had a safe house or two prepared should he fall out of Varkat's favor, and a compact spacecraft of some variety tucked away in a shielded location off the beaten path." She sighed ruefully. "Trust me, gentlemen, I would not have relocated to Atraz without assurances that we could leave the planet in a pinch."

Makes sense, Kirk thought. "Any idea where he might head next?"

She shook her head. "I'm sorry, Captain. I wish I knew, but . . . Siroth had his secrets, not all of which he shared with me."

"A man of mystery, you say?" McCoy said.

"You have no idea, Doctor."

Kirk frowned, wondering what Siroth was up to now.

And whether they had seen the last of him.

"Vandals," the expatriate Earthman muttered, scowling. "Small-minded, self-righteous idiots."

Siroth gazed bleakly at the ruins of his tower-slash-laboratory. Years of planning, politicking, and preparation had been reduced to rubble by the Klingons' disruptor cannons. He silently cursed both the Empire and Starfleet for their maddening interference, while directing some bitterness against Hamparian as well. He had no way of knowing if his faithless former colleague had been party to the Klingons' ruthless attack on the tower, wiping out his meticulously acquired home and workplace in one devastating blast, but she'd undeniably thrown her lot in with Kirk, Yorba, and that entire band of blinkered, twenty-third-century witch hunters, too wedded to their archaic fears and prejudices to embrace the radical, transformative future he was determined to bring about.

No matter how long it took.

Rumors, spreading like a contagion throughout the fortress and the city, had it that Kirk and the others had mysteriously vanished without a trace, eluding Varkat's men. In other words, they had beamed to safety, taking Taya with them.

Good riddance, he thought ungraciously. In the end, her resolve had not matched her brilliance, proving her a tragic disappointment. *And Atraz is no longer safe for me—and my quest.*

Standing in a courtyard, beneath an overcast sky, he contemplated the heap of charred and pulverized debris that had once housed his labs. Superstitious Atrazians eyed him warily, keeping their distance. Already, he knew, whispers were afoot that his arcane doings had somehow drawn down the vengeful green thunderbolt that had targeted his tower alone, while his ill-fated association with the treacherous "blue lady" had further damaged his reputation at court. Varkat had yet to publicly denounce Siroth, being loath to abandon the benefits of certain rejuvenating tonics, but there was a definite chill in the air whenever Siroth was summoned to attend to the suzerain; he doubted he could count on Varkat's generous patronage much longer.

Nothing remained of the tower itself, and Gyar had doubtless perished in the catastrophe, but possibly some of the equipment and materials in the underground vaults had survived and were still salvageable, albeit buried beneath tons of rubble? Including, perhaps, a certain cryotube just waiting to be unearthed?

Determination saved Siroth from despair. He wasn't finished, not by a long shot. Unlike Hamparian's faltering convictions, his ageless resolve could not be shaken. No power in the galaxy, not the Federation, the Klingons, the Romulans, or any other shortsighted authority, could keep him from achieving his goal eventually. He would rebuild, restart, reinvent himself anew, somewhere and sometime else. Eternity still awaited him.

No matter what.

Chapter Forty-Five

2292

"Red Alert!"

The deep-space standoff was escalating by the moment. With Captain B'Eleste demanding the return of the Klingon observers, Commander Plavius refusing to surrender his hostages in light of the unexplained tragedy that had claimed the lives of everyone aboard the doomed escape pod, and Kirk not about to let Plavius depart with Spock in custody, the *Enterprise*, the *Lukara*, and the *Harrier* had all come within firing range of each other. The only question, it seemed, was who would start shooting first—and at whom?

"Phaser batteries fully charged," Chekov reported. "Photon torpedoes armed and ready." He grimaced. "If only I knew where to aim them."

"That makes two of us, Mister Chekov."

Kirk stared grimly at the main viewer. A split screen monitored both the Klingon bird-of-prey and the Romulan warbird. The captain's chair was flanked by Gledii on one side and McCoy on the other. Motox was cooling his heels in the brig, *sans* ceremonial dagger, while Varis had been confined to her guest quarters for the time being. Chronometers mercilessly ticked down each tense moment. B'Eleste's deadline for the return of her officers was fast approaching.

"The *Lukara* is hailing both us and the *Harrier*," Uhura announced.

"Oh boy," McCoy said. "Want to bet her mood hasn't improved any?"

Kirk figured that was a safe assumption. "On-screen, Uhura, and Plavius, too, if he's responding."

"Aye, sir."

Both the Klingon and Romulan commanders appeared on the viewer. B'Eleste looked characteristically fierce; Plavius, world-weary but resolute.

"Well?" she challenged them. "Your time grows short. Will you return my men or must we do battle?"

"My position has not changed," Plavius said. "I am willing to deliver our Osori guests to Nimbus III or back to their homeworld, depending on what they prefer, but Spock and Chorn must remain in my custody until the circumstances surrounding Subcommander Taleb's death have been thoroughly investigated . . . and the guilty parties brought to justice."

"What about Varis?" Kirk asked. "You don't want to trade Spock for her?"

"That is for our respective governments to decide in due course. For now, duty requires that Romulan justice come first, even at the cost of Varis's liberty. She knew the risks when she undertook this assignment."

So much for a nice, peaceful prisoner exchange.

"And you need to appreciate the risks you and your ship are facing," Kirk said. "Don't even think about trying to warp away with Spock aboard."

"Or my officer!" B'Eleste snarled. "And that goes for you as well, Kirk." She smiled wolfishly. "Although perhaps you should both beam your Osori guests over to my ship before the fighting starts, for their own safety's sake . . . since I cannot guarantee that either of your vessels will survive my wrath."

"You'd like that, wouldn't you?" Plavius accused her. "Getting your hands on our Osori envoys after losing your own."

"Captain Kirk!" Gledii looked not at all enthused about being relocated to the bird-of-prey where Cyloo had seemingly fallen victim to foul play. "You cannot allow Nawee or me to be taken anywhere but back to our homeworld. We are not bargaining chips in your juvenile conflicts with each other."

Heated voices overlapped. Kirk stood and raised his own voice to be heard over the threats and accusations flying back and forth.

"Gentlemen, Captain B'Eleste! None of this rancor is benefiting anyone. Has it occurred to you that possibly we are all being played, perhaps by a fourth party who has a vested interest in preventing any of us from establishing fruitful relations with the Osori?"

Kirk pondered the possibilities. The Orions? The Gorn? Maybe even some unknown entity like that vampiric energy being on Beta XII-A?

He was reluctant to point a finger at anyone in particular without more to go on. It was enough that *someone* might be trying to derail the diplomatic conclave on Nimbus III.

"*What are you implying, Kirk?*" B'Eleste bared sharply filed teeth. "*That I unknowingly nursed a viper in my midst? If there was treachery afoot, look to the 'observers' who attacked my crew, one of whom has testified that Taleb and Saavik conspired together to ambush him, with the Romulan disarming him and your half-blood lieutenant administering a nerve pinch while Kulton's back was turned.*" She sneered in contempt. "*A coward's attack.*"

"Coward?" McCoy responded indignantly. "If Saavik put the pinch on your man, she must have had good reason. Self-defense, I reckon."

"*She was my guest, under my protection! How dare you suggest that she would need to defend herself against any member of my crew!*" B'Eleste shook her painstik at the screen. "*Muzzle your doctor, Kirk, while you still have one. Unlike my ship, which, need I remind you, has lost its medical officer to perfidy most foul!*"

"Muzzle me? Like hell you will where Saavik's reputation is concerned. If you think—"

"Stand down, Bones." Kirk tried to reason with B'Eleste. "We all want to find out what happened to your doctor and the others, Saavik included, but we need to consider every possibility before we jump to conclusions."

Plavius removed his monocle and coolly wiped it with a cloth. "*And do you have any evidence, Captain Kirk, to support your theory that we are being manipulated?*"

"Not as such," Kirk admitted. Scans of the subatomic residue left behind by the pod's self-destruction had yielded only confirmation that an antimatter charge had detonated, leaving no survivors. "More like a hunch."

"*Sadly,*" Plavius replied, "*Romulan law and policy do not recognize the validity of . . . hunches.*"

McCoy rolled his eyes. "And they say Vulcans and Romulans have nothing in common anymore."

"What about you, B'Eleste?" Kirk asked. "Has your internal investigation turned up anything about how the pod was released in the first place?"

"*Only that the perpetrators tampered with our medbay's computer* and communications systems to fake a catastrophic warp-core emergency, no doubt in an attempt to trick Doctor Kesh into evacuating the Lukara *via an escape pod. A ruse that positively reeks of both Romulan duplicity and Vulcan scientific prowess.*"

Kirk shook his head. "You keep pushing that conspiracy theory, but I swear to you that Lieutenant Saavik would never collaborate with Subcommander Taleb to sabotage our mission, let alone abduct your doctor or Cyloo. I never met Taleb, but I *know* Saavik. She's no schemer."

"*Your word is not enough for me, Kirk. In fact, my investigation has turned up one thing more. A closer look at Saavik's history reveals that there is no love lost between her and the Empire. She nearly died at our hands once, and lost a friend to a Klingon blade, during the notorious Genesis affair. A blood debt seems motive enough to conspire against my people.*"

You do not *want to go there,* Kirk thought, biting his tongue. "Saavik is a Starfleet officer and a Vulcan. She wouldn't let any personal grudges compromise her integrity."

"*So you say,*" B'Eleste said, unimpressed. A harsh clang rang out on the bridge of the bird-of-prey. "*Time's up, Captain, Commander. Who wishes to return my officer while they can?*"

"Not without concessions on your part," Kirk bargained. "Perhaps to refrain from attacking the *Harrier* until we can sort this mess out?"

And while Spock was still a captive aboard the warbird.

"*Speak for yourself, Captain.*" Plavius placed his monocle back over an eye. "*We don't need you to advocate on our behalf . . . although I am open to a temporary alliance against this bloodthirsty Klingon animal. If we combine forces, two ships against one, we should be able to make short work of the* Lukara *so that we can then deliver the surviving Osori wherever they wish to go.*"

"While leaving Spock and Chorn your prisoners?" Kirk rejected that scenario in a heartbeat. "You'll have to do better than that, Commander."

"*Here's another idea, Kirk,*" B'Eleste said. "*We unite against the Romulans to get back our respective officers . . . and take that Osori off their hands.*"

"And possibly get Spock, Nawee, and Chorn killed while we're blasting away at the *Harrier*? There has to be another way."

"None that includes entrusting another Osori to the Klingons!" Gledii insisted. "Not after what became of Cyloo!"

"*Don't reject my offer too quickly, Kirk.*" B'Eleste leaned back in her chair, betraying no trace of apprehension about the brewing conflict. "*Or perhaps Plavius and I will join forces against you.*"

"*Is that a feeble attempt at a joke?*" Plavius asked. "*As if we would ever ally ourselves with Klingons again.*"

"*Not even against the* Enterprise?" B'Eleste asked. "*If only just to wipe Kirk's ship from the board before we engage each other in battle? Leaving us each one less enemy to contend with?*"

"And then what?" Kirk asked. "What would you gain from it?"

"*Victory, Kirk. What else?*"

McCoy groaned. "Anybody else getting a headache from all this strategizing? Never did like war games. Give me a relaxing hand of gin rummy any day."

Could be worse, Kirk thought. At the moment, this tactical one-upmanship was probably all that was delaying a full-on space battle, which wasn't going to commence until someone decided whom to ally with and until when. But how long could this preliminary jockeying last? Odds were, this was going to turn into a general free-for-all anytime now.

And then heaven help them all.

"*Last chance, Kirk, choose an ally or find yourself outnumbered.*" B'Eleste shrugged. "*Frankly, I'd rather fight beside a human than a Romulan, but the one is only slightly less preferable than the other. I will do what I must to avenge the wrongs done to me and mine.*"

"*Heed my words, Captain,*" Plavius said. "*A vengeful Klingon can't be reasoned with. We can vanquish her, and perhaps find some justice for those who perished under her alleged protection.*"

"Children!" Gledii exclaimed. "You're all bickering children. It was folly to ever think we could find common cause with any of you!"

Then why do I feel like the only grown-up in the room, Kirk thought. "You both need to listen to me! We don't need this fight. Attacking each other is not going to bring our lost comrades back, but we can try to make their deaths count for—"

"Captain!" Uhura interrupted. "We're being hailed!"

The urgency—and excitement—in her voice compelled Kirk's attention, even on the brink of all-out combat.

"From who? Starfleet? The Federation?"

"No, sir!" Her voice quavered with emotion. "It's Lieutenant Saavik!"

Chapter Forty-Six

2292

"Saavik, you're alive!"

"Obviously, Captain."

Her image flickered and wavered on the viewscreen, the signal choppy. Static and feedback distorted the audio, which faded in and out of audibility. Nonetheless, Kirk's heart soared to see the young Vulcan alive and in one piece, as opposed to blown to atoms. Joy and relief showed on faces across the bridge.

"As are Cyloo and Taleb," she reported through frustrating crackles and a blizzard of visual snow. *"We live, but—zzz—dire straits—zzz—require immedi—zzz—assistance—"*

Kirk glanced at Uhura. "Can we clean this up?"

"I'm trying, sir, but the signal is weak and inconstant." She massaged the subspace frequency controls. "Shall I share this transmission with the *Harrier* and/or the *Lukara*, assuming they haven't intercepted it already?"

"Not just yet." He wanted to hear what Saavik had to say before letting B'Eleste or Plavius into the exchange. "Stall them, Uhura, for as long as it takes. Inform them that we've received new information that changes everything, but we need a few minutes to confirm it."

"Aye, Captain. I'll keep them on hold as best I can."

"My apologies—zzz—poor quality—zzz—transmission—improvising under—zzz—circumstances—" Saavik's distinctive features rippled like a reflection in a funhouse mirror. *"—be brief—zzz—beamed off pod—zzz—Doctor Kesh—zzz—captives—zzz—interior of frozen—zzz—Oort—"*

"Oort . . . Oort cloud?" Kirk recalled that the stolen pod had been heading into the outermost reaches of a nearby solar system when it self-destructed. Was Saavik saying she and the others had been beamed onto one of the innumerable chunks of icy space debris surrounding that system? And what had she been trying to say about Kesh? B'Eleste was going to want to know about her lost medical officer.

"What's that, Saavik?" he asked. "We're losing you. What about Doctor Kesh?"

"—*party responsible*—zzz—*not a Klingon*—zzz—*Captain, Kesh is actually*—"

A ragged burst of static cut off whatever she said next. Her image fragmented, dissolved, then blinked out altogether.

"Damn it," Kirk said. "Uhura?"

"I'm sorry, sir. We've lost her." She stared forlornly at the viewer. "And sir, our friends out there are demanding answers."

Kirk made a snap decision. "Send them Saavik's message, what there is of it. Then trace that signal back to its source."

"Gladly, sir!"

"Saavik . . . alive?"

Just for a moment, Spock's face betrayed an emotional reaction, but he immediately regained his composure. Both he and Chorn had been brought to the bridge of the *Harrier*, under armed escort, to provide their thoughts on the startling transmission the *Enterprise* had just shared with the other two vessels.

"Finally you let us loose!" Chorn appeared more sober than before, although no less boisterous. "Confined to quarters, without even a steady supply of ale, let alone any congenial company"—his meaty hands mimed an exaggerated hourglass figure—"to relieve my solitude!"

"Never mind that!" Nawee said, impatiently dismissing the Klingon's petty grievances. The Osori envoy nervously phased in and out of solidity, a rosy aura strobing like a pulsar. "Cyloo is in jeopardy. We must come to her aid at once!"

"Forgive me, Envoy." Hepna peered scornfully at the viewscreen, where a distorted image of Saavik was paused. "But this is almost surely a ploy on Kirk's part. He is infamous for his trickery and deceit. This so-called 'transmission' has obviously been manufactured, and crudely at that, to make us think Taleb and Cyloo still live, no doubt to gull us into returning our hostages."

Nawee's face fell. "But couldn't Cyloo and the others have been beamed off the pod in time, as this message states?"

"Did we see Cyloo in that transmission? Or Taleb? Have we been offered any actual proof of life?" The subcommander attempted a sympathetic expression, which sat incongruously on her severe features. "It gives me no pleasure to say this, but we cannot possibly take this dubious message at face value."

"But might it not be true?" Nawee looked anxiously to Plavius and Spock for support. "What do you think, Commander, Mister Spock?"

Plavius studied Spock. "I also wish to know your assessment of this unexpected communication."

"*Alleged* communication," Hepna stressed.

Spock ignored her aggressive skepticism, directing his words to Plavius instead. It was the commander who needed to be convinced, not his hostile subordinate.

"I will not insult your intelligence by asserting that neither Captain Kirk nor I have ever resorted to subterfuge to achieve a greater good." Spock did not know if Plavius was personally acquainted with the incident decades ago when he and Kirk had committed espionage against another Romulan starship commander in order to steal an advanced cloaking device, but it would be foolish to pretend that Starfleet never engaged in such tactics. Honesty was required if he hoped to sway Plavius by building on the tentative rapport they had already established. "But I do not believe that to be the case here. Saavik lives, as do Cyloo and Taleb, and they are in urgent need of rescue."

"And what convinces you of this?" Plavius asked.

"Saavik and I share a special bond, going back many years. Our minds have met, in the Vulcan sense."

"I'll wager they have!" Chorn grinned lewdly. "What sort of bond, exactly?"

"Curb yourself, Lieutenant!" Nawee scolded him. "Let Spock speak!"

Spock appreciated the Osori's intervention. "Trust me when I say that I would know if Saavik had truly ceased to be, and was puzzled that I had *not* in fact sensed her passing."

"Sensed? Believe?" Plavius said. "Hardly the most logical of arguments, Spock."

"Acknowledged, but I have lived long enough to know that some things transcend logic. You asked me my opinion, and I tell you this message is genuine."

Plavius nodded. "I too have learned to trust my instincts, particularly when it comes to matters of life and death."

"Which means Cyloo could still be alive?" Nawee asked hopefully.

"That is my conviction," Spock said.

Plavius turned toward Chorn. "And what do you think, Lieutenant? That communication seems to implicate your Doctor Kesh, suggesting that he was not truly Klingon at all. You alone have knowledge of this individual. Do you find these accusations credible?"

Chorn shrugged his mammoth shoulders. "Do I look in need of a physician's services? I had few dealings with Kesh. Never gave him much thought, if you must know." He stroked his fulsome beard. "But if he is responsible, then he cannot be a Klingon . . . because no true Klingon could ever be so dishonorable." He crowed at his own brilliance and slapped Spock soundly on the back. "Flawless logic, correct?"

"Impeccable," Spock said dryly.

"Commander!" Hepna appealed to Plavius. "Tell me you are not falling for this transparent ruse? What would the praetor think of relying on suspect intel from our foes?"

Plavius wheeled about to confront her.

"And if there is even a chance that Subcommander Taleb is alive and in desperate need of succor, and we fail to act accordingly? Do you wish to answer to his family for that? Or to the praetor?"

Her face paled. "No, sir!"

"I didn't think so," Plavius said.

B'Eleste was proving a tough sell.

"Kesh? You dare accuse my ship's doctor of this heinous crime? It is your Saavik who obviously faked her death, in tandem with her Romulan partner, to steal the Osori from us, and who now seeks to shift the blame to Doctor Kesh."

Kirk addressed her via the viewscreen, which she shared with Plavius, Nawee, and Spock. He couldn't blame her for not wanting to believe her chief medical officer was responsible, despite what Saavik had managed to tell them.

"But even your own investigation discovered that various systems in your medbay had been tampered with. That was Kesh's domain. Who else would have such ready access to and familiarity with those systems?"

"Have you forgotten? The medbay is where Saavik and Taleb assaulted the crewman assigned to watch over them. I have the sworn testimony of Sergeant Kulton himself."

"I don't know what happened there," Kirk admitted. "It's possible there *was* an altercation of some sort. It's no secret that Klingons can be quick to defend their honor if they feel they have just cause and are not afraid to settle their differences with force. Is it that hard to imagine that a tense moment or argument came to blows? With a Klingon, a Romulan, and a Starfleet officer in the same room? Interview your sergeant again. Find out what if anything might have provoked a physical confrontation."

Plavius spoke up. *"As reluctant as I am to criticize my esteemed sub-commander, it must be said that Taleb can be somewhat . . . proud . . . in bearing. It is not beyond the bounds of possibility that some might take issue with his tone or manner."*

"Full of himself, is he?" McCoy said.

"A Klingon might find him so," Plavius conceded.

"Sounds like a potentially explosive mixture to me," Kirk said, "of the sort that could lead to people losing their tempers." With Saavik perhaps intervening to shut down the fracas before it got out of hand? "And by Kulton's own account of the incident, he was out cold when the pod was stolen and ultimately destroyed. We have only Saavik's distress call, fragmentary as it is, to tell us what happened after Kulton was rendered unconscious."

"And of course you rush to blame a Klingon to hide your own culpa-bility." B'Eleste glowered at Kirk. *"No matter how absurd the scenario. Kesh kidnaps our guests, kills a fellow crewman, flees his own vessel? No Klingon would behave so dishonorably."*

"Indeed," Spock said from the warbird. *"Which, as your Lieutenant Chorn so sagely reasoned, supports Saavik's assertion that Kesh is*

not actually a Klingon. And if Kesh is not a Klingon, then no dishonor attaches to the Empire in this affair . . . unless you fail to deal with the imposter who deceived you."

"Do not school me on matters of honor, Vulcan," B'Eleste said, although somewhat less forcefully than was typical of her. Furrows deepened on her impressively ridged forehead, suggesting that she was giving the situation serious thought. That Kesh might not be a Klingon *would* help the Empire save face. "A barely coherent message from a half-Romulan Starfleet officer is flimsy evidence, Kirk. You ask much if you expect me to accept it as proof that Kesh was a viper in disguise."

"Never mind Kesh!" Gledii's booming voice rang out. "What about Cyloo? You claimed, Captain B'Eleste, that she was under your protection. Does not your vaunted honor demand that you now help us recover her?"

"And Saavik and Taleb," Kirk was quick to point out, "whose safety was also your responsibility. Surely fulfilling that obligation takes priority over a senseless battle that could cost the lives of the other two Osori, not to mention your observers aboard the *Harrier* and the *Enterprise*?"

B'Eleste growled unhappily. She snapped her painstik in half.

"If this is a hoax, Kirk . . ."

"Then you can have the glorious battle you're itching for. Photon torpedoes, disruptor cannons, phasers, the whole nine yards. Fire away at us with everything you've got, no holds barred . . . *if* you discover you've been tricked. But waging war can wait. Our lost people can't."

Chapter Forty-Seven

"Captain? Captain Kirk? Can you read me?"

A spike of high-pitched feedback hurt Saavik's ears, but the *Enterprise* did not respond. The screen above the biobed, where the unconscious Rhaandarite remained bound, went dark.

"My apologies, Saavik." Cyloo's smart glove flowed over, under, and around the wrist communicator she had commandeered from Wight. She flexed and wiggled her fingers as though operating an invisible control panel. "Kesh is blocking me. He's accessed Hiberna's systems through an upstairs terminal and is fighting me to regain control of the base's systems."

"Can't your advanced Osori tech defeat him?" Taleb paced restlessly back and forth across the besieged laboratory, perhaps in an effort to further warm himself after escaping the cryotube. "Aren't you supposed to be thousands of years ahead of us?"

"Yes, but it's his tech we're contending over. I have my glove, true, but he knows all the passwords, codes, and hidden back doors." Strain showed on Cyloo's iridescent countenance. "Could you operate an ancient Romulan chariot or blacksmith's shop better than your ancestors? It's all I can do to keep these lower levels locked down and inaccessible to him, physically *and* virtually."

"Your efforts are appreciated," Saavik said, "as are the challenges."

"So that's it? We managed only one paltry distress call?" Taleb stopped pacing long enough to scowl at Melinda. "Meanwhile, your stray keeps looking at me. Can I help you, human?"

"Sorry, I've never seen a Romulan before . . . except in Saavik's memories, I mean." Melinda had fully donned Saavik's maroon jacket, which fit her reasonably well. She glanced around, as wide-eyed as Cyloo had been not long ago. "Just like I'm still trying to wrap my head around the fact that I'm actually inside an asteroid, zillions of miles from Earth."

"Zillions is an imprecise measurement," Saavik noted, "but that is essentially correct. The question before us is how and when we can escape this location."

"Just my luck. I snooze for nearly three hundred years and wake up in the middle of an outer-space hostage crisis!"

"But the *Enterprise* will come for us?" Cyloo asked plaintively. "Now that they've received our message?"

"I have every confidence in Captain Kirk's ability to track our signal to these coordinates. He is almost certainly en route as we speak."

"And the *Harrier*," Taleb added. "Maybe even the *real* Klingons as well."

"But how will they find us?" Cyloo asked. "Amidst the countless icy bodies surrounding us?"

"Now that they know what to look for, they will be able to scan for anomalous energy signatures, deflector shields, and the like," Saavik said. "Certainly, that is what I would do."

"I hope you're right," Cyloo said. "I've never been so scared in my life!"

"Tell me about it," Melinda said.

"I know this must seem very new and frightening," Saavik said to the other women; Spock had spoken to her of the importance of maintaining morale when in charge of more emotional species. "It may reassure you to know that I have personally been in far more hazardous situations than this and survived to see better days, thanks in large part to the crew of the *Starship Enterprise*."

Cyloo gaped at her. "I don't know whether to find that comforting or horrifying. Are such perils normal beyond the safety of Osor?"

"For some more than others. Exploring unknown space carries risks, increasing the probability of encountering personal jeopardy. The experiences of Starfleet personnel are thus not entirely representative of 'normal.'"

Melinda chuckled. "Oh, I think we left normal long ago. I sure have."

"So what are we to do now?" Taleb asked impatiently. "Simply sit back and wait to be rescued, preferably before Kesh regains access to this level?" He armed himself with a laser scalpel he salvaged from a tray of medical equipment. "We should spend less time talking and more time preparing to defend ourselves should—"

A chime sounded from the food-synthesizer slot on a nearby wall, signaling that a meal or beverage was ready. Taleb shot it an annoyed glance.

"Which of you requested food at a time like this?"

Saavik's eyes widened with alarm. "Cyloo! Did we disable—?"

A loud bang went off inside the slot, blowing open its sliding door. Thick green fumes billowed from the slot, expanding rapidly across the lab. The acrid vapor obscured Saavik's vision and stung her eyes, producing an extreme lachrymal response despite her protective inner eyelids. Tears streaming down her face, she clapped a hand over her mouth and nose, but the vapor still invaded her throat and lungs. Nausea racked her abdomen, and sour bile rose in her throat. An unseemly quantity of mucus issued from her nostrils. Squinting through tears and fog, she saw that her companions were similarly afflicted. A coughing fit woke Wight, who found herself in restraints.

"What the—?" Melinda exclaimed, gasping and coughing. She doubled over, clutching her stomach. "Freaking tear gas?"

Too late Saavik realized what Kesh had done. While Cyloo had focused on keeping the turbolifts, transporter, and safety doors out of his control, he had covertly gained access to the lab's overlooked food synthesizer, disabled its safety protocols, and programmed it to produce a volatile, toxic compound out of basic elements and ingredients.

"Vent this infernal gas!" Taleb slashed futilely at the fumes with the scalpel. "Clear the air!"

"But . . . these levels are sealed off!" Cyloo glowed amidst the swirling gas, phasing to remain untouched by the poison in the air; the wrist communicator fell through her intangible arm to crash onto the floor. Her eyes alone were dry, although the lack of visibility presumably hampered her as well. "I can't clear the atmosphere without compromising the seals."

Taleb vented his disgust instead. "Lovely!"

"By the Tapestry," Cyloo cried out, "are you all going to die?"

Unlikely, Saavik thought. Kesh would not want to lose his test subjects without resorting to nonlethal options first. *On the other hand, he deems only Cyloo essential, rendering the rest of us expendable?*

"Breathing masks!" Taleb, his eyes and nose gushing, ransacked drawers and cabinets, throwing their contents onto the floor. "We must find breathing masks!"

Her stomach cramping painfully, Saavik joined him in his search, regretting that there had not been time to conduct a thorough inventory of the lab earlier, even as she wondered what Kesh ultimately hoped to gain from this attack. To force them to abandon the lab—or simply to create a distraction?

Her keen hearing detected a telltale whine coming from the adjacent transporter room. Deducing instantly that Kesh had taken advantage of the confusion to wrest back control of the transporter, she whirled about, stolen phaser in hand, to see, through the fumes, Kesh entering the lab, wearing a breathing mask and goggles and brandishing a type-3 phaser rifle.

"Stay where you are, Doctor."

He advanced through the vapor, and she did not hesitate. She fired the phaser—or rather she attempted to. No beam was emitted.

"Note the biometric grip," Kesh gloated through his mask. "An early innovation of mine. Only Wight or I can operate it."

"I'm sorry, Doctor," the Rhaandarite called out from the bed. "She threw something at me!"

Taking Kesh at his word, Saavik employed a similar strategy, hurling the inert phaser at Kesh in hopes of duplicating her earlier success, but the *faux* Klingon was not so easily taken unawares. He easily ducked the missile and menaced her and her companions with the rifle. Unarmed and impaired by the gas, they found themselves at a severe disadvantage. A stun beam targeted Taleb, dropping him before he could even attempt to employ his purloined scalpel.

"That's enough, all of you. This pathetic uprising ends now."

"Forget it, Orlando! You're the one who needs to stop once and for all," a ragged voice objected. A figure in a red Starfleet jacket staggered past Saavik, placing herself between Kesh and his captives. "This insanity has gone on *way* too long!"

Kesh's eyes bulged behind protective lenses. Bristling gray eyebrows shot upward.

"Melinda?"

Chapter Forty-Eight

2292

"Melinda?"

She recognized him all right, despite his alien makeover, the tears streaming from her burning eyes, and the translucent respirator mask covering the lower half of his face. She could hardly forget that same face leaning over her as he sealed her up in a coffin-sized tube back in San Francisco, what felt like only hours ago. A few weird ridges on his forehead couldn't disguise Orlando Wilder from her, even if he was apparently calling himself "Kesh" these days.

"Surprise." She wiped her running nose on the sleeve of Saavik's jacket. "Long time no see . . . for you at least. Can't say I'm crazy about your new look. Not that I've got anything against body modification, but we're way beyond some tattoos and piercings here."

He glared past her at Saavik and Cyloo.

"You did this! You woke her prematurely. How dare you—?"

"Rescue me from that tube?" she challenged him. "As opposed to keeping me on ice for . . . what, another three hundred years?" Anger poured out of her, along with tears and snot. "I mean, what the freak, Orlando?"

He recoiled, taken aback by her fury and their unexpected reunion. "You don't understand. I was going to revive you when I finally succeeded in my quest so that you, along with the rest of humanity, could share the fruits of my triumph. Eternal life, Melinda. I was keeping you alive for that."

"By turning me into a human Popsicle . . . and carting me halfway across the galaxy? Oh yeah, thanks for that, Orlando."

"You will someday." His expression hardened, and he tightened his grip on the phaser rifle keeping her and the others at bay. "But that's a conversation for another time, after I've put down this troublesome insurrection."

She shook her head. "Over my freshly defrosted body."

"Please, Melinda, stay out of this. You don't know the lengths I've gone to in order to keep you preserved for centuries, even after the Klingons dropped an entire tower on you, on a primitive world light-years from here. I dug your battered tube from the rubble and up-graded it time after time, brought you with me on my travels . . ."

"To be what? A souvenir? An ice sculpture? A nostalgic relic of the good old days back on Mother Earth?"

"As a talisman, to remind me where I came from, and of the sacrifices we've both made to get this far."

"Speak for yourself, Orlando. I never asked for this, and neither did Dennis."

"Don't listen to her, Doctor!" Wight strained against the restraints binding her to the biobed. "Let me loose, please!"

"Quite right." He forced his way past Melinda, shoving her aside, and turned the rifle toward Taleb's stunned body lying sprawled on the floor. "Free Wight, Saavik, or I'll dispose of this insufferable Romulan once and for all."

"Stop it, Orlando! You can't do this!"

Melinda wanted to stop him, to tackle him like she had Dennis hours/centuries ago, but the twenty-third-century tear gas had her on the ropes. She was in no shape to tussle with a tribble (which, insanely, she actually knew about now), let alone a gun-toting obsessive in a gas mask.

"It is all right, Melinda." Saavik moved to liberate the bizarre, big-headed alien from the high-tech hospital bed. "This concession is not worth endangering Taleb over."

The alien—a Rhaandarite?—gave Saavik a dirty look as she sprang off the bed as soon as the restraints were loosened. An ugly bruise on Wight's uber-sized cranium testified to the strength of Saavik's pitching arm. Her yellow eyes weeping from the gas, the alien retrieved her wrist gadget from the floor and her biometric phaser pistol as well.

"Cleanse the air on this level," Wilder instructed. "Activate the vents and filters."

Wight hastened to comply, taking a seat at a control console. Within moments, concealed pumps, humming behind the walls and ceiling, went to work. Fresh air rushed in to drive out the offensive fumes, much to Melinda's relief. She still wanted to wash her eyes and throat with enough water to fill the Grand Canyon, but at least she could breathe freely again, and her eyes and lungs weren't under constant assault.

"Very good, Wight." Wilder removed his goggles and respirator as the last of the gas dissipated. "Now increase the power to Hiberna's deflector screens. I fear we may be having company soon."

"That's right." Cyloo put up a brave front while staying safely intangible. "The *Enterprise* is on its way to rescue us. They're going to make sure you never hurt anyone again."

"It is over, Doctor Kesh," Saavik stated. "There is no point to any further violence."

Cyloo kept close to Saavik, despite being untouchable. "You heard her. You might as well give up now."

"I wouldn't be so sure of that," Wilder said. "Don't forget that I have three very valuable hostages—especially you, Cyloo—and that your phasing stunt isn't going to protect you indefinitely. Sooner or later, you have to become solid again or risk fading away for good. I don't think any of us wants that. Personally, I can't think of a more atrocious waste."

Melinda wondered how long the young Osori could safely stay untouchable. Was the clock already ticking down too quickly?

"What's happened to you, Orlando? Sure, you were always obsessed, but you never seemed quite this homicidal before. You told me once you valued life 'more than most,' but Saavik saw you kill that Klingon in cold blood back on their ship, and now this? Waving a ray gun around, threatening people?"

He flinched at her accusation, then sighed ruefully.

"I was much younger then, when you knew me on Earth centuries ago. I didn't yet realize what it would take to achieve my goal. Lifetimes of struggle and false leads and disappointments have taught me better. If I had to become harder, more ruthless to get this far . . . well, I need to think in the longest possible terms. Ultimately, the ends will justify the means."

But you kept me alive, she thought, *out of sentiment or obligation or whatever.*

Maybe she could still get through to him? Reining in her entirely justified outrage, she softened her tone, hoping to somehow talk him down before this hostage crisis turned into a bloodbath.

"Listen to yourself, Orlando. You've lost perspective. You've let your obsession eat away at your humanity, but it's not too late. You can still call this off, remember the person you once were."

Who had not exactly been all warm and fuzzy, but still . . .

He gazed at her with a guilty expression. The muzzle of the rifle drooped slightly. For a moment, she dared to think that maybe she'd hit a nerve, given him a *long*-delayed reality check, but then he shook his head and steadied his weapon.

"It *is* too late, Melinda. Very much so. I've come too far, sacrificed too much, committed too many crimes, to give up now." His voice was grave, resigned. "Plus, I'm getting older, Melinda. Even with my genetic augmentations, and buying additional years with punctuated periods of cryogenic suspension, I'm still aging slowly but surely. I'm running out of time."

"I don't know. You're still looking pretty good for three-hundred-plus years. Maybe—"

"Enough," he said, cutting her off. "This is not a debate or therapy session. Go stand over there with Saavik and Cyloo." He turned the gun toward her. "I'm not above stunning you, Melinda, if you force me to."

He means it, she realized. *Just like he doped me with that hypo back in the day.*

She backed away from him, toward the other hostages.

"You and Saavik," he ordered. "Pick Taleb up and carry him back to the cryovault. Drag him if necessary. Unfortunately, you've all proven that I can't trust you with even limited freedom of movement. I need to put everyone except Cyloo on ice for the time being. Even you, Melinda."

A chilling case of déjà vu came over her.

"Oh no, Orlando. Not again."

"I'm sorry, Melinda. You've given me no choice. If it's any consolation, cryotech has improved by leaps and bounds since 2024. No more IVs required."

Shining brightly, her scales shimmering in the glow, Cyloo started toward him. "You can't do this, Doctor! I won't let you!"

"And how are you going to stop me, Osori, as an immaterial wraith?" He gestured with the rifle toward the exit and the stairwell leading down to the cryotubes. "Come along, Wight. I'm going to need your assistance tucking our guests in for their long, cold nap."

"Yes, Doctor. I'll be right—"

A klaxon sounded, causing Melinda to jump. *Now what?*

"The proximity alarm!" Wight hurriedly consulted a display panel. "Sensors detect a vessel—no, *three* vessels—approaching at impulse speed."

"Congratulations, Doctor," Saavik said. "You have united Starfleet, the Klingons, and the Romulans in common cause. An impressive feat."

Hope surged within Melinda. Maybe she didn't have another refrigerated coma in her future, and her attempts to reason with Wilder hadn't been in vain. Had she stalled him long enough for the cavalry to arrive?

"Blast it!" Wilder raged. "Those blinkered fools. Why can't they leave me and my work alone? Why can't they ever let me be?"

A beep sounded at Wight's console. She scanned a subspace activity monitor.

"Doctor, we're being hailed. It's the *Enterprise*!"

Chapter Forty-Nine

"Destination dead ahead," Chekov announced from the nav station. "We found her."

The *Enterprise*, accompanied by the *Lukara* and the *Harrier*, had converged on the Oort cloud surrounding the supposedly lifeless star system. Working together, Uhura at the comms and Ensign Dupic at the science station had successfully tracked Saavik's short-lived signal to its point of origin: an otherwise unexceptional chunk of ice only about thirty kilometers in diameter. A magnified image on the viewscreen betrayed no signs of habitation; if Kesh did have a base there, it was well camouflaged.

"Are we sure this is the right place?" Kirk asked.

"Affirmative, sir." Dupic looked up from the specialized viewer at his station. The young Deltan spoke with confidence. "Sensors confirm that this particular object is heavily shielded. In addition, energy signatures indicate an advanced pergium generator powering a habitat beneath the frozen exterior of the object."

"Then it's true!" Gledii gasped in relief. "What your Saavik said, about Cyloo and the others being beamed to safety. You *must* recover her, Captain. She's barely more than a child!"

"That's what we're here for, Envoy." Kirk inspected the deceptively innocuous planetesimal before them. "How heavily shielded?" he asked Dupic. "Can our phasers overcome their deflectors?"

"Probably, sir, especially if the Klingons and Romulans add their firepower to ours, but with that much force, we can't guarantee the safety of the hostages. We could accidentally knock out their life-support, expose them to the vacuum, or trigger some other disasters: cave-ins, coolant leaks, plasma fires, you name it. Worst-case scenario: We inflict irreparable damage on that generator, causing it to go hypercritical. There's no way to calibrate just how hard to hit them without breaking the habitat."

"Understood," Kirk said. "And that's assuming our Klingon or Romulan cohorts even try to apply a scalpel instead of a sledgehammer."

"Fat chance of that," McCoy said. "Especially that Klingon terror."

"Hopefully, it won't come to that, Bones." Kirk hoped to avoid a full-scale military assault if necessary. "Uhura, hail that base."

Knock first, Kirk thought, *before smashing down the door.*

"They're responding, Captain, and they don't sound happy to see us."

"On-screen, Lieutenant, and let our allies listen in."

"Aye, sir."

A middle-aged Klingon appeared on the viewscreen. He looked vaguely familiar, but Kirk couldn't place him. His disposition was definitely hostile, however. He glared balefully from the screen.

"*Here we are again, Kirk,*" he rumbled. "*With you showing up uninvited at my doorstep once more.*"

The man's cavernously deep voice rang a bell as well, sounding from somewhere deep in Kirk's past. "Doctor Kesh, I presume?"

"*You don't remember me, Kirk? I certainly recall you, always self-righteously barging in where you don't belong.*"

The face, the voice, the aggrieved tone, a stolen escape pod and faked spacejacking. Kirk's memory finally coughed up the connection.

"Siroth?"

"*Ah, so you do remember me, after so many years. Thanks to you, my tower was destroyed, years of work and planning and progress wiped out in a single night. Don't think I'm going to let you do it again, Kirk. Not this time.*"

"Siroth?" McCoy echoed. "That so-called alchemist on Atraz way back when." He squinted at the screen. "Well, I'll be damned, it *is* him. Always wondered where he scurried off to."

"Saavik tried to tell us," Kirk said. "She said Kesh wasn't really Klingon."

"Captain?" Gledii asked in confusion. "Who is this man? How do you know him?"

Kirk muted the audio transmission before replying. "An old adversary, Envoy. A human scientist who we caught conducting illegal experiments on another planet decades ago. He was obsessed with finding the secret of eternal life."

Small wonder he had gone to such extreme lengths to capture an Osori.

"Of course," Gledii said bitterly. "The same old story, even after so many ages. The jealousy of you short-lived beings never abates."

"We'll do our best to get Cyloo back. I give you my word." Kirk unmuted the audio. "Listen up, Siroth or Kesh or whatever your name really is. We're here for our stolen people. Turn them over at once."

"Not a chance, Kirk. I won't let you ruin everything again. My work is too important for that."

"You should have thought of that before you kidnapped three people and tried faking their deaths. Lower your shields, surrender your captives, and maybe, just maybe, I can see to it you face Federation justice, as opposed to the tender mercies of the Romulans or Klingons."

B'Eleste and Plavius would doubtless have strong opinions on that, Kirk knew, but if he could get the hostages back safe and sound, it would be worth any wrangling down the road. Saving Saavik, Cyloo, and Taleb was Job One right now.

"Spare me the dire admonitions, Kirk. I hold all the cards here. The Osori's precious, all-but-endless life is in my hands, not to mention Lieutenant Saavik and Subcommander Taleb. You can't attack this base without endangering them, so I'd advise you and your allies to retreat before I'm forced to take more drastic measures. Believe me, Kirk, I'll let you destroy us all before I'll surrender the Osori."

Was he bluffing? Kirk racked his brain, calling up his impressions of the man from nearly a quarter of a century ago.

"I don't buy it, Siroth. You never struck me as suicidal, quite the opposite in fact. You want to live forever, not throw your life away by going out in a blaze of glory."

"Don't underestimate my determination, Kirk. I'm gambling for the highest stakes of all, and counting on the fact that you'd rather leave the hostages in my custody for the indefinite future than see them dead for real."

"Not if it means letting the Osori's advanced technology, not to mention their unique biological essence, fall into the hands of a murderous renegade. I don't *want* to sacrifice the hostages, you're right about that, but this has become a matter of galactic security for all three powers involved. If we have to, we *will* obliterate your base to protect the Osori's dangerous, destabilizing secrets." Kirk gave Gledii a pointed look, hoping the elder Osori would get the message. "Isn't that right, Envoy?"

Gledii assumed a grim, forbidding mien as he stepped forward into view of the screen.

"Tragically so, Captain. While my ageless heart aches for Cyloo's plight, we cannot tolerate any abductions of this nature lest we encourage yet more assaults on our people. History teaches us that there will be no end to such atrocities if we permit even one of our people to be probed and persecuted with impunity. Cyloo understands that as well as any Osori."

Kirk found his oration convincing, maybe a little too much so. Was Gledii just playing along or was he utterly sincere?

"*Nonsense. You're bluffing, both of you.*"

"Maybe," Kirk said. "But what about the other interested parties?"

He signaled Uhura to allow the Klingons and Romulans into the discussion. B'Eleste and Plavius instantly shared the screen with the rogue scientist.

"*Kesh! You treacherous, false-faced slime devil!*" B'Eleste raged impressively. "*You will rue the day you violated my trust . . . and undeservedly claimed the supreme honor of being Klingon!*"

Plavius was less vitriolic, but no less implacable. "*The Romulan Star Empire does not negotiate with brigands and terrorists. If any harm comes to Subcommander Taleb, or either of the other hostages, you shall pay dearly for it. Release your prisoners if you hope to survive another day.*"

Kirk hoped they were also bluffing but had his doubts.

"*Save your saber-rattling bluster,*" Kesh responded. "*Fire on this base and first Taleb dies, then Saavik. Choose your next actions wisely.*"

His face vanished from the screen.

"Guess he didn't blink," McCoy said. "So now what?"

Wilder turned away from the darkened monitor. Wight looked anxiously at him as she employed her reclaimed phaser pistol to keep the hostages under control. Melinda thought the towering alien woman appeared rather less confident about their odds than her boss.

"What are we going to do, Doctor?"

"*You* are going to follow orders, which is what you're good at," Wilder said sharply. "The ball is in Kirk's court now. Let's hope he can talk sense into B'Eleste and Plavius, convince them they need to back off for the time being. Who knows? If we're lucky, they'll end up fighting among themselves."

"I would not rely on that," Saavik said. "Captain Kirk always finds a way to prevail."

"Not this time! Not again!"

He's losing it, Melinda thought, *but is that a good thing or a bad thing?*

Taleb stirred upon the floor. Moaning, he reached groggily for the laser scalpel he'd had when he was stunned, only to discover that it had since been confiscated by their foes. Sitting up, he massaged his temple and looked about in bewilderment.

"What did I miss?"

"Much," Saavik informed him as she and Melinda helped him to his feet. "Help has arrived, but Kesh remains defiant. Our prospects are . . . uncertain."

"They'll hold their fire," Wilder insisted. "For Cyloo's sake if nothing else. Her potential life-span is far more valuable than your fleeting existence, Lieutenant."

"No," the Osori said. "Gledii is right. I can't allow you to get away with abducting me, let alone benefit from that transgression. You will never touch me, even if it means I phase out of existence entirely." She looked apologetically at Saavik, Taleb, and Melinda. "Even if it means we must all perish . . . together."

"Noble words," Wilder mocked, "but let's see how long your resolve lasts once your friends start dying before your triple eyes, just because you chose to defy me." Hefting the rifle, he targeted Taleb once more. "Get out of the way, Melinda. This isn't your fight."

"The heck it isn't."

She stepped forward into the line of fire. Her last attempt to get through to him had run into the brick wall of his obsession, but she couldn't stand by while Wilder gunned down somebody in cold blood. She and Wilder came from the same bygone era; if anybody could reach him, maybe she could.

"Are you trying to get us all killed, Orlando? I've only been up and about in this century for a few hours, but even I can tell that the jig is up. We've got three freaking *spaceships* closing in on us, ready to let loose with their biggest guns. You heard what that Romulan dude with the monocle said: You kill Taleb, and there may be no way to keep them from going full *War of the Worlds* on us, death rays and all. We need to put out this fire while we still can, before we all go up in flames."

"They've forced my hand. I need to make an example of Taleb to demonstrate that my threats are not idle ones."

"You're going to kill someone just to prove a point? Yikers, Orlando, just how badly have you gone off the rails since the days of Miracle Milly? Seems like it was just yesterday, from my perspective, since you were telling me that 'death was abhorrent' to you. What happened to that guy? Was that just bullshit all along, or has your 'quest' well and truly turned you into a monster?"

"It's the only way left to me. The only way to reach my ultimate goal. But you needn't worry, Melinda. You're not a hostage. You're in no danger."

"Really? So what *is* in store for me, Orlando? Even if by some miracle Kirk and the others don't blast this place to smithereens, even if you do somehow get them to turn around and leave you alone, what happens to me then? Back into the ice for another three hundred years? Five hundred years? Forever?"

"Not forever! Only until I crack the riddle at last. I promise you, Melinda, it will all be worthwhile in the end. When I make you immortal."

"The heck with immortality! Don't you get it? I don't want to live forever; I just want *a* life back, even in this strange new future. You took my old life from me, Orlando. Let me have this second chance, please."

She took a cautious step toward him, despite the futuristic rifle aimed at her, then another.

"Stay back," he warned her.

"No way."

Her heart was pounding like a SWAT team at the door as she faced down the barrel of the phaser rifle. How well did she truly know

Orlando Wilder, or what he was capable of these days? It could be her new twenty-third-century life was about to come to a very abrupt end. *Dennis always did say I took too many chances . . .*

"Let us live, Orlando. You owe me that."

Half expecting to be disintegrated at any instant, she reached out and took hold of the business end of the rifle (the emitter?) and gently eased it to one side, away from her. Kesh's remodeled face fell. His shoulders sagged in defeat.

"I just wanted more life," he said. "For everyone."

"Then don't let there be any more senseless deaths."

She took the gun from him.

Wight offered no resistance. If anything, Saavik judged, the Rhaandarite appeared relieved that an imminent conflagration had been averted. She surrendered her phaser to Saavik without protest.

"Your wrist communicator as well, please."

Cyloo phased back into reality, the protective radiance retreating back into her gloves, then sat down on a stool by a counter. Saavik could not be sure, but the Osori gave the impression of being somewhat depleted. Had she indeed been nearing the time limit on how long she could safely remain immaterial, or was her enervated appearance simply a result of the emotional duress she had been under? Saavik found this difficult to determine with certainty.

Taking over Wight's control panel, she swiftly and efficiently lowered *Hiberna*'s defensive shields and reestablished contact with the *Enterprise.*

"The crisis is concluded, Captain, with no further casualties." She glanced over at Melinda, who was keeping watch over Kesh. "Thanks to the efforts of an additional captive unknown to you. An Earth-woman, in fact."

"*Really?*" Kirk said. "*I look forward to hearing your full report, Lieutenant. Stand by for rescue parties.*"

"Acknowledged."

Cyloo lifted her head, which had drooped toward her chest. Her central eye met Saavik's two. "Don't forget your promise."

"I have not."

Only minutes later, three separate security teams—Starfleet, Klingon, and Romulan—beamed into the lab, the varied pitches of their respective transporter beams clashing somewhat discordantly. The landing parties regarded each other warily, but no more than that. The Starfleet contingent was led by Chekov, who beamed happily at the sight of Saavik.

"Lieutenant! Talk about a sight for sore eyes."

Given that her own eyes were still enduring the lingering effects of Kesh's lachrymatory gas, she found this a singularly inapt expression.

"Excuse me, Commander, may I borrow your phaser?"

"My phaser?" He handed it over to her. "Certainly, but why?"

"One last task to attend to."

She placed the confiscated wrist communicator atop the console Cyloo's gloves had interfaced with, set the phaser on disintegrate, and opened fire. Startled cries and gasps erupted around the laboratory as the communicator, along with much of the control panel, flared up brightly before dissolving into nothingness. Agitated Romulans and Klingons drew their weapons on her—until Taleb intervened.

"Stand down, Centurions." He nodded at Saavik. "The Vulcan has her reasons."

The helmeted soldiers muttered but lowered their weapons. The Klingons grumbled more loudly but followed suit, so the Starfleet team was not required to come to her defense.

"Thank you, Subcommander." She calmly returned the weapon to Chekov. "Your phaser, sir."

He gaped at her, not quite dumbfounded. "Er, what exactly was that about, Lieutenant?"

"Fulfilling a promise, sir."

Chapter Fifty

"I'm sorry you've decided not to proceed with the conclave," Kirk said. "Are you certain you won't reconsider?"

He appealed to the reunited Osori in the *Enterprise*'s observation lounge, which was currently the site of a post-crisis gathering. Compared to the lavish welcoming party thrown when Gledii had first arrived, tonight's reception was a rather more subdued affair; still, the fact that they had all come through the potentially tragic conflict more or less unscathed, and that no one was presently locking phasers on anyone else, was cause for celebration, if only to allow all involved to part on relatively cordial terms, minus any red or yellow alerts.

"Can you blame us, Captain," Gledii asked, "after all that has transpired? We have no choice but to return to Osor before any more calamities befall us."

"Regretfully, I must concur with my senior." Nawee had beamed over from the *Harrier* along with Commander Plavius for the occasion. "For the present. However, this is not necessarily the end of the story. We are patient. We can wait until the rest of the galaxy is ready for us." He smiled wanly. "Perhaps after you've all grown up a bit more."

"Indeed," Cyloo said, appearing fully restored from her ordeal. "I look forward to encountering your Federation again, sometime in the future."

Kirk wondered just how long that would be.

"It was a privilege to meet you." Saavik offered a Vulcan salute to Cyloo. "Live long and prosper, although that first part is possibly redundant in the extreme."

"The same to you," the young Osori said. "Despite everything, this has been the adventure of a lifetime."

"And that's saying something," McCoy quipped, "considering the source."

"A pity the Klingons chose to abstain from this little soiree," Varis said. No longer confined to her guest quarters, she had donned another elegant evening gown for the reception. As before, she merely nursed her cocktail. "Or perhaps not."

There were in fact no Klingons present. With Cyloo understandably reluctant to return to the *Lukara* and the conclave called off, the chronically antisocial Captain B'Eleste had seen no reason to stick around after getting Motox and Chorn back. The former had left the *Enterprise* in high dudgeon after being liberated from the brig and reunited with his beloved *d'k tahg*. Kirk couldn't say he was sorry to see him go.

Or the rest of the Klingons for that matter.

"They're just sulking because we wouldn't turn Siroth over to them," McCoy said, "or whatever he's calling himself these days."

There had been some heated words regarding who took custody of Doctor Kesh, considering that he'd murdered a member of B'Eleste's crew, but Kirk had argued, and the Romulans had backed him up, that "Orlando Wilder," having been born on Earth, was the Federation's problem. Truth be told, Kirk suspected that much of B'Eleste's furious protests had been for show; in the long run, she probably didn't want to call attention to the fact that a disguised human had infiltrated a Klingon bird-of-prey under her own nose. More politic for her, and even the Empire as a whole, to avoid an embarrassing scandal back on Kronos. No wonder she had wanted to put this business behind her as briskly as possible.

Good riddance, he thought. The less he had to make nice with Klingons, the better. *David's blood is still on their hands.*

"What is going to happen to Wilder, Captain?" Melinda asked.

Saavik had briefed Kirk on the fluorescently tressed young woman's story. As unfrozen refugees from Earth's turbulent past went, Melinda Silver was a far cry more personable and sympathetic than Khan and his followers had been. Modern civilian attire helped her to blend in, even as her gaze kept drifting to the starry vista outside the high panoramic viewports, as though she still couldn't truly believe where she was.

"That's up to the courts to decide," he said. "I'm not entirely sure what the statute of limitations is for crimes committed in the twenty-first century, but just his more recent activities as 'Siroth' and 'Kesh' should be enough to put him in a high-security rehabilitation facility for some time, if not for the rest of his very long life."

Kesh was presently locked up tight in the brig. That, according to Melinda, he was also an Augment of some variety complicated matters, legally. Kirk wondered if that was another reason B'Eleste had ultimately ceded the prisoner to the *Enterprise*. If anything, the Klingons were even touchier about Augments than the Federation was, due to that gene-engineered virus back in Jonathan Archer's time, making Kesh even more of a hot potato. Privately, B'Eleste probably considered herself well rid of him.

"I see," Melinda said quietly. Kirk could only imagine what it must feel like to suddenly find yourself living hundreds of years in the future, with everything and everyone you knew now consigned to the history books. "Thank you, Captain."

"No, Ms. Silver. Thank you . . . for everything."

As time went by, the assemblage broke apart into assorted small groups, comparing notes and making their farewells. Spock was partaking of a glass of distilled water when Commander Plavius approached him.

"Mister Spock, my fellow Romulans and I will be taking our leave soon. I wished to thank you for your contribution to resolving the late crisis and for your congenial company during your stay upon my ship. I hope you did not find the experience too arduous, despite your brief confinement to quarters."

"I have no complaints, Commander. I too enjoyed our discussions prior to the advent of the emergency."

"Despite the somewhat overbearing presence of Lieutenant Chorn?"

"And Subcommander Hepna," Spock added. He observed that the persistently antagonistic Romulan officer had not beamed over to the *Enterprise* and was presumably looking after the *Harrier* in Plavius's absence. Was that his choice or hers? Both scenarios struck Spock as highly plausible.

"Her too," Plavius conceded. "If nothing else, the success of our joint rescue mission, uniting to recover both a Vulcan and a Romulan, suggests that Unification might not be a completely unattainable goal, regardless of the differences between our peoples."

Spock deduced Plavius could speak more freely away from the inquisitive ears of his more ambitious subordinates. "I share your assessment."

"We are of like minds then, on that point at least." Plavius chuckled wryly. "Certainly, I can more readily see our respective peoples reuniting than, say, the Federation achieving a lasting peace with the likes of B'Eleste or Chorn."

Spock shrugged. "Who can say? As my father is prone to observe, where diplomacy is concerned, there are always possibilities."

Saavik kept Melinda company as they gazed out the viewports at the depths of interstellar space. She felt some responsibility for the temporally displaced human, since it was she who had chosen to awaken Melinda from cryogenic suspension. Their brief mind-meld had also inevitably created a certain kinship between them.

"It's still sinking in, now that the adrenaline rush is over and we're no longer in mortal peril." Melinda surveyed the new universe awaiting her. "Three centuries, space travel, a United Federation of Planets . . . it's a lot to process."

"Acknowledged, but I have touched your mind and personally experienced its remarkable tenacity. I am confident you can cope with whatever challenges await you."

"You mean, I'm just too darn nosy and stubborn to let the twenty-third century beat me."

"That is not precisely how I would phrase it, but yes, your intrinsic persistence and curiosity will serve you well in the days ahead. May I ask what you intend to do next, when we return you to Earth?"

"Well, first thing—"

Before she could complete her reply, Taleb politely intruded on them.

"We shall be departing for the *Harrier* soon. Before we go, I would be remiss if I did not acknowledge the role each of you played in securing our deliverance. I am not too proud to admit that I would not be standing here without your efforts. You both accorded yourself well."

"Despite my Vulcan blood?" Saavik asked.

"It seems that is not quite the liability I mistook it to be. I have learned better now."

"Then our shared trials yielded some positive results." She lifted her hand in salutation. "Live long and prosper, Subcommander Taleb."

"*Jolan tru*, Lieutenant Saavik, and to you as well, Melinda Silver. I will never underestimate a 'stray' again. May you find our century to your liking."

"Well, it's been full of surprises so far." She offered her hand, which he accepted a trifle stiffly. They shook briefly before she released him. "You and your elf ears included."

His hand went instinctively to the tapered point of one ear before mustering a reply. "I might say the same of your somewhat garishly hued locks."

Varis, the Romulan observer, joined them.

"Come along, Subcommander, it's time to be on our way." She smiled slyly. "We wouldn't want to wear out our welcome."

Saavik waited for them to exit before resuming her conversation with Melinda.

"You were about to inform me of your plans?"

After the Romulans departed, leaving all three Osori behind on the *Enterprise* since the envoys did not wish to be separated again, Kirk and Spock took Saavik aside.

"A moment, Lieutenant."

She experienced a measure of trepidation. "Certainly, sirs. Is there a problem?"

"Not at all," Spock said. "To the contrary, we have simply not yet had the opportunity to commend you for a difficult job well done."

This was not the response she had anticipated.

"Forgive me, I do not understand. My mission ended in near disaster. The conclave was cancelled. The Osori diplomatic initiative has failed."

"For the present," Kirk said, "but you kept Cyloo alive in an extremely hazardous and unexpected situation, and were instrumental in bringing the hostage crisis to a satisfactory and bloodless conclusion. Moreover, you may well have planted a seed that will blossom into a better relationship between the Federation and the Osori in some distant season." A smile lifted the captain's lips. "That's no small accomplishment, Lieutenant."

"Indeed," Spock concurred.

She remained puzzled. Were they simply attempting to make her *feel* better about what had transpired? That would be illogical.

"But—"

"Take the win, Saavik. That's an order."

"Very well, Captain. If you insist."

Chapter Fifty-One

2292

Melinda beamed onto the deck of a schooner somewhere in the South Pacific. Twin masts rose toward a clear blue sky. Sunlight glinted on the surface of a vast expanse of azure water. A salt breeze and spray took her back to that long-ago morning centuries past when she and Dennis had launched their investigation by the Bay in Sausalito. A wooden deck rolled gently beneath her newly fabricated sneakers. After crossing the galaxy in a starship, she wasn't used to being on an old-time sailing vessel.

"Welcome aboard the *Cetacean*," Gillian Taylor said.

Once upon a time, Melinda had dreamed of finding an elderly Gillian alive and well in her seventies, but the attractive blonde before her, wearing a shiny purple wetsuit made of some exotic future fabric, looked as though she'd barely aged a day since she vanished back in 1986. Melinda recognized her instantly from the photos and film clips she had pored over endlessly back in the day.

"Ohmigosh, it's really you. Finally."

"In the flesh." She smiled warmly. "I understand you've been looking for me."

"You have no idea."

After all Melinda had been through, in this century and a past one, after all the puzzles and intrigue, she'd been floored to discover that Captain Kirk, he of the mysterious pizza date, knew exactly where Gillian was and how to reach her. It was that easy.

"I like the name of your boat." Her throat tightened as a rush of emotion came over her. "I think I need to sit down if you don't mind."

"I'll bet."

They settled down on the edge of the deck before a low guardrail, their legs dangling over the waves lapping against the hull of the schooner. Melinda felt somewhat overdressed compared to Gillian, having donned what she'd been assured was a stylish civilian skant for this long-anticipated meeting. Gazing out over the ocean, trying to get her bearings, she spied a couple of whales frolicking in the distance. The humpbacks leaped and breached and splashed from sea to air and back again, apparently having the time of their lives.

"George and Gracie?"

"And baby Harpo. The first humpback whale born on Earth in three centuries."

"Wow," Melinda said, meaning it. "All thanks to you."

"And a certain time-traveling Klingon spaceship and its crew."

The famous invisible UFO, Melinda thought. "Them too."

They sat in silence for a few moments, whale watching. It was weird; Melinda found herself atypically at a loss for words now that she was finally sitting beside Gillian. Kirk and the rest had already briefed her on the particulars of how and why Gillian had ended up in the future. Melinda wasn't sure what to say, let alone where to begin.

"So," Gillian said, breaking the silence, "I've listened to *Cetacean*."

"Seriously?" Melinda hadn't seen that coming. "It's still available?"

"Survived World War III and everything. It took some digging, and calling in a few favors from some grateful historians for whom I'm a living, breathing Rosetta stone, but they found it buried in a bunkered digital archive from the early twenty-first century . . . which means I do have some notion of what you went through trying to figure out what became of me." A stricken look came over her face. "I'm so sorry, Melinda. I never wanted my disappearance to mess up anybody else's life. If I had known that someday the mystery would cause—"

"Stop right there," Melinda said. "None of that is your fault, so don't even think about beating yourself up about it. Nobody forced me to reopen your cold case and chase down every wild lead, no matter what. My choice, my consequences. You got that?" She took a moment to let that sink in. "Honestly, sincerely, I couldn't be happier to discover that you're alive and well and young and *gorgeous*."

Gillian laughed, her mood lightening. "Not looking too bad for 345 years old, right? And you're still rocking it, too, despite being only a few decades younger than me. Love the hair, by the way. Reminds me of a race of alien ichthyologists I've been corresponding with by sub-space. They have the most brilliantly colored crests and fins."

"How about that? Who knew?"

Another awkward pause ensued before Melinda worked up the nerve to ask what she really wanted to know.

"Do you regret it? Relocating to the future, I mean."

"Not really, no." A thoughtful look came over Gillian's tanned, sun-kissed face. "I won't lie. It hasn't always been easy, adjusting to a whole new era, accepting that the world I knew, the life I once lived, has been gone for centuries." She smiled wryly. "You have no idea how hard it is to find a decent pineapple pizza in the twenty-third century, and then there're the blank looks I get when I drop some three-hundred-year-old pop-culture reference that *nobody* remembers anymore. A word to the wise: 'New Coke' jokes are not going to fly anymore."

Melinda had no idea what that was. "Okay, boomer."

"Seriously, though," Gillian said, "there are some dazzling bright sides to leaving the past behind. Twenty-third-century Earth is so much better than the troubled world we come from. No wars, no poverty, no prejudice, no pollution, no constant sense that the whole planet is on the brink of disaster. I don't lie awake at night anymore, worrying about the environment or the nuclear arms race or the econ-omy. I'm not fighting a losing battle to save the whales from extinction, and you know what, I can live with that. I'm more relaxed and at peace than I ever was back in the eighties, even if I do feel like a dinosaur sometimes."

Melinda was encouraged by what she heard. "That sounds pretty great, actually."

"It's astounding. I mean, I spent most of my professional life trying to study and communicate with nonhuman intelligences, and now I'm on a first-name basis with actual extraterrestrials, including fish people, bird people, lizard people, silicon-based life-forms, you name it. What's more, it's not as though I'm just sitting on my laurels, bask-ing in retirement while pining for the Reagan years. Most days, I'm too busy blazing new trails to wax nostalgic."

"What kind of trails?"

"Saving the whales, repopulating the oceans, is just the beginning. Turns out linguistic science and software have made huge strides since our time, especially when it comes to deciphering and translating alien languages."

Melinda nodded. "The universal translator. I've seen that in action already."

"Bingo." Gillian radiated enthusiasm as she warmed to the topic. "But here's the thing: in theory, the UT's not just for talking to sentient beings from other worlds. We can also use it to better communicate with other intelligences right here on Earth."

"Like whales?"

"And dolphins and porpoises too. It's early days yet, and there's still plenty of work to be done to adapt the technology to aquatic, non-humanoid life-forms, but the possibilities are mind-boggling. Between you and me, I've already had some tentative discussions with folks at Starfleet, who are very intrigued by the way whales and dolphins and such are naturally adept at navigating in three dimensions."

Melinda saw where she was going. "Like space travel."

"Yep. To be clear, this is all hypothetical at this point. Nobody is installing saltwater classrooms at Starfleet Academy yet, or building starships designed to accommodate cetacean crew members, and there are still a few diehard skeptics who aren't convinced that the higher species of aquatic mammals are fully sentient, but things are happening, people are talking, progress is being made, et cetera. Just wait, within a generation Starfleet will have some sort of cetacean operations division. It's going to happen, mark my words."

"And you're right on the ground floor," Melinda said. "A pioneer of a whole new era of human-whale relations."

"You betcha." Gillian grinned. "Which is more than worth an occasional bout of temporal homesickness. But enough about me. What's next for Melinda Silver?"

She beamed back at her. "Well, first I've got a podcast to finish."

". . . and that's the story. How I started out looking for a missing woman and ended up becoming one, and how I finally found her at last, centuries after we both disappeared.

"So where does that leave us? The thing about true crime is that, sadly, the only comfort it can usually hope to offer is closure: a mystery solved, a body found, a killer exposed. Endings, yes, but not happy ones. No joy, only justice at most. The lost remain lost.

"Not this time. This, the final episode of Cetacean, ends with a new beginning. No closure, no finality, but a galaxy of unlimited wonders and possibilities . . . for Gillian, for me, for all of us. Orlando Wilder was wrong. Who needs eternity when every day is a miracle, full of infinite diversity in infinite combinations? We don't have to live forever. We just have to live our lives to the fullest.

"This is your host, Melinda Silver, signing off."

Acknowledgments

I first conceived of this book way back at the beginning of 2020. Real life, including a global pandemic, slowed things down a bit, but I couldn't be happier that it's seeing print at last.

Plenty of people deserve thanks for making that happen, including:

My editors, Margaret Clark and Ed Schlesinger, who waited patiently for this book and who were never less than encouraging and supportive; my agent, Russ Galen, and also Dayton Ward, who adjusted his own schedule to make mine easier and who gave me a much-needed pep talk at one point. And of course, all the fans and readers who have offered kind words about my books over the years, both online and in person.

And finally to Karen, who was behind this book right from the start, while we were nesting at home, listening to true-crime podcasts together.

About the Author

GREG COX is the *New York Times* bestselling author of numerous *Star Trek* novels and stories, including *A Contest of Principles, The Antares Maelstrom, Legacies, Book 1: Captain to Captain, Miasma, Child of Two Worlds, Foul Deeds Will Rise, No Time Like the Past, The Weight of Worlds, The Rings of Time, To Reign in Hell, The Eugenics Wars (Volumes One and Two), The Q Continuum, Assignment: Eternity,* and *The Black Shore.* He has also written the official movie novelizations of *War for the Planet of the Apes, Godzilla, Man of Steel, The Dark Knight Rises, Ghost Rider, Daredevil, Death Defying Acts,* and the first three *Underworld* movies, as well as books and stories based on such popular series as *Alias, Buffy the Vampire Slayer, CSI: Crime Scene Investigation, Farscape, The 4400, Leverage, The Librarians, Roswell, Terminator, Warehouse 13, The X-Files,* and *Xena: Warrior Princess.*

He has received six Scribe Awards, including one for Life Achievement, from the International Association of Media Tie-In Writers. He lives in Lancaster, Pennsylvania.

Visit him at: www.gregcox-author.com